PUP

Picking up the pieces in peacetime.

PAUL HARVEY

Published by Wilkinson Publishing Pty Ltd
ACN 006 042 173
PO Box 24135, Melbourne, VIC 3001, Australia
Ph: +61 3 9654 5446
enquiries@wilkinsonpublishing.com.au
www.wilkinsonpublishing.com.au

WilkinsonPublishing
wilkinsonpublishinghouse
WPBooks

© Copyright Paul Harvey 2024

All rights reserved. No part of this publication may be reproduced, stored in a retrieval system or transmitted in any form by any means without the prior permission of the copyright owner. Enquiries should be made to the publisher.

Every effort has been made to ensure that this book is free from error or omissions. However, the Publisher, the Authors, the Editor or their respective employees or agents, shall not accept responsibility for injury, loss or damage occasioned to any person acting or refraining from action as a result of material in this book whether or not such injury, loss or damage is in any way due to any negligent act or omission, breach of duty or default on the part of the Publisher, the Authors, the Editor, or their respective employees or agents.

Title: PUP. Picking up the pieces in peacetime.
ISBN: 9781922810571 : Printed - Paperback

Design by Michael Bannenberg.

Front cover image designed using Adobe Firefly AI.

Printed and bound in Australia by Ligare Pty Ltd.

For Woolly, Robbo & Kev.

Three mates sorely missed.

Paul would like to thank:
Dr Angelo Annunziata, Andrew Rice,
Dr Michael Rice, Chris McLeod, Michael Bannenberg
and Caroline Harvey for their help with the book.
Also the publisher Michael and Jane Wilkinson for
giving me a chance to be in print.

RTA

Everyone was a little startled. Even the guy who spat on me seemed a little surprised. He was young, maybe in his early twenties. He was probably about my age, well, the age I was before I left. Go away 21, return 42 the diggers used to say. He had neatly cropped hair and was smartly dressed. Ironed shirt, pressed slacks. He dressed like he had a date in court or was headed to the first day of a new job. He had a smatter of petulant pimples which bounced across his forehead. Long haired, greasy teens always get a forehead full of acne; so Pop Dempsey used to say. He stood in the front row of a small group of anti-war protestors, their hand-made placards held high; their flags waved. Contorted faces, young and old, accused and condemned. I don't remember what he screamed at me, but I can still feel the spit; thick, ropey, and foul. He was on my blindside, so I didn't see it coming. I caught most of it on my nose, a large and easy target.

We'd heard all about the anti-war sentiment back home. It was the talk of *Nui Dat*. I'd noted a metastasis of protest as I left for Nam and in the time I was away the mood had grown and hardened. It was black and malignant now I'd returned home.

I had bigger concerns than a little expectorant. It was a lot less lethal than everything flying around my head in Vietnam. Still, it didn't help my disposition. I was blacker than the pit.

The spitting seemed to take the wind out of the protestors though; those passionate souls who had given up their morning to 'welcome' home the troops. I suppose it is never a good look spitting on a damaged man in a wheelchair, even if he might have been a child killer.

I didn't think I needed the chair. The repatriation staff had their hands full with others and I believed I could walk. A young air hostess, who was helping to direct us across the tarmac and through the airport, thought I looked a bit grey and decided I should sit in one of a dozen wheelchairs lined up for those in need. I was feeling a bit grey to be honest. I sat. My legs were ablaze. It wasn't until I was in the chair though we both realised I wasn't going to be able to propel it, except in circles. My right arm sat uselessly in my lap. The hostess looked around earnestly for someone to assist us and a short, hard fellow with a face like a house brick told the young woman he'd be happy to push me through the building and out to the waiting ambulances. He had rolled sleeves, one of which concealed the square knoll of his smokes. He wasn't RTA, well not a recent return to Australia anyway; he wore civies, blue jeans and a red, checked shirt. He looked like a taxi driver touting the terminal.

There were about seven drab, green souls in front of us, some shuffling, some being propelled by efficient men and women in medical white. We passed together through the big sliding, glass doors of the airport and into the raucous din. I sat in the wheelchair; with my feet in the footrests, my long legs tucked up so far I felt like my knees were brushing my ears. The protestors consisted of maybe eighteen angst filled, chanting and finger pointing civilians.

"Dirty hippies and university bludgers who couldn't tell shit from chocolate," growled the 'house brick', an unlit smoke gripped firmly between gritted teeth. As he swung me along the footpath and passed the noisy throng, the yells and jeers reached a crescendo. Inspired and emboldened, the pimply bloke took two quick steps forward and spat. My chair stopped, dead. 'House brick' turned on the spitter who'd stepped back quickly to conceal himself within the mob. When it became clear he'd been found out he stood defiantly with a 'what you gonna do about it' look on his pudgy, red face, two chins proffered pugnaciously. 'House brick' dropped him with a hard, open-handed smack to the side of his mouth. Pop Dempsey submitted later that 'the pimply fella shouldn't have been surprised. If you spit in a man's eye, you should expect a whack in the face.' The bloke landed on his back with a *WHUMP* and a cough as the air left his lungs. The rest of the protestors backed away. There was a murmur of outrage, a few catcalls but nothing much else. No riot or unbridled uprising. A couple of policemen stood nearby, obviously charged with keeping an eye out. They looked much more interested in their shiny black shoes when the fellow hit the footpath. Maybe they too believed spitting on a long, sickly serviceman with bandages around his head was going a little bit far.

My champion returned and handed me a blue and white speckled handkerchief and for the 100th time that day I went to grab it with my right hand before I remembered that hand was no longer good for grabbing. He leant forward and wiped away the spit. The slapped protestor took an age to get to his feet, his hand covered a bloodied mouth, a red and swollen nose. 'House brick' returned his hanky to his pants pocket and with measured slowness plucked the pack of Benson & Hedges from beneath his sleeve. He offered me one with a practiced jerk of his wrist that slipped one slender cigarette away from its brothers.

"No mate," I croaked. He shrugged and I could feel every eye on us as he lit the chewed fag in his mouth with a Redhead and breathed in deeply. 'House brick' goaded the protestors to say something. They didn't. I just wanted to hide.

"Thanks," I croaked.

"Don't thank me cobber," he grunted, "I've been wanting to smack one of those long hairs for ever and a day – cowards are bold in a crowd!" I might have suggested that the bloke he clocked had short, cropped hair, but he was not the type to let facts sway his argument. I admired his fire. I had but a few dying embers of fight left and they would soon be extinguished by a long convalescence in the Army Repatriation hospital. I stood with Azrael. Blackened cawl, sharpened scythe, sightless eyes. I'd battled the reaper each day then fought my memories at night for almost a year. He inexorably devoured me.

My tour of Nam, like my hellish pit, had swallowed me whole.

WAR

One fateful day can change your life. That day, for me, was the day I was born. Of course, every little, bald headed baby's life changes when they leave Mum's warm cocoon and are dragged, blue and bedraggled into the world. A quick smack on the bottom and life comes for you, ready or not while you scream blue murder. Birth is a big change for everyone. Let's say, March 3rd was a particularly tumultuous day for Terry Shepherd. That was the date, written on a little wooden ball pulled from a Tattersall's Barrell, which saw me conscripted into another man's army, and another man's war. The wicked irony is that the very same barrel was used, pre-conflict, to draw the numbers of the luckiest who were holding the winning lottery ticket in charmed hands. My luck saw my birthdate drawn by our Lord Mayor, an over-inflated windbag of a man. March 3rd ensured I'd be ushered off to battle at the behest of the Prime windbag in our capital Canberra, the honourable 'Pig-Iron' Bob Menzies. Menzies had worn that particular moniker after trying to smash the Port Kembla dockers strike after they refused to ship Pig Iron to the militant Japanese in '38.

Pop Dempsey never had much time for our longest serving, double Prime Minister. He called him a 'self-serving, narcissist'. And now Prime Minister Bob was sending Pop's favourite grandson, in truth his only grandson, offshore. The enmity gnarled and twisted Pop.

Menzies could talk the talk. He had the posh, pseudo-Brit accent that was *de rigueur* for newsreaders and actors in the 60s. He blended it with an air of righteous sanctimony and a platinum comb-over. He had the ineffectual knobs in the Labor Party scared witless of him. When challenged he was a scrapper with a tongue like a bayonet and often left the floors of Parliament bloodied. A colourful mix of classy and nasty. He'd leave Arthur Calwell and the Labor brethren in strips and ribbons when of a mind. Of course, my mum thought the sun shone out of his baby-powdered arse; Bob and his DLP anti-commie mate, Bob Santamaria. She particularly liked Santamaria because he was a Catholic.

"Santamaria is a devout man Terry," she'd say with pious sincerity. "His name is Italian for Saint Mary!"

Mum liked all the Libs. The great and vanished Harold Holt who sported the year-round tan. Gorton the dill. McMahon with his good-looking wife. Pop said McMahon's gargantuan ears and spherical head made him look like a VW Beetle with its doors open. Mum was a rusted-on supporter, and she would take on all comers and dissenters on the 'lean' streets of Fitzroy where I grew up.

"Bob Menzies was going to stop the Communist hordes," she'd hector often following up with, "Those Chinese were getting too big for their boots!" Mum often held court in the bar of the Rob Roy pub, where she liked the odd beer with her girlfriends or in front of the greengrocers in Gertrude Street near the Albanian Social club.

"The countries will fall for Communism like dominos!" she'd opine to anyone silly enough to question her. "If one country goes, they all follow, click, click clack!"

"It'll be a hegemony." This was mum's new favourite word. She completely wore it out and I'd bet the family jewels that she had no idea what it meant. My Pop didn't like any politicians, any of them at all.

"God gave them two ears and one mouth, but not one bastard has ever had the sense to use them in that proportion."

When Mum was a young girl our home suburb of Fitzroy had been a left leaning Methodist and Protestant enclave. That slowly changed after the war as the Catholic Greeks and Italians swarmed in great numbers to fill the commission houses, with their funny accents and glorious food. Fitzroy was pure working class and proud of it.

Mum was all for the Vietnam war, especially if it meant safety for the Catholic Nuns being killed over there. She was mortified by the stories in the press.

"Murdered at prayer – it has to be stopped." Mum swallowed, hook and line, the whole deification of South Vietnamese President Ngo Dinh Diem, the ecumenical paragon who was paraded around Australia like Dame Nellie Melba.

"Diem was a great man, for a Vietnamese. He'll need Australia's help to push back those Commie Russians, the Chinese and those terrible Japs." I didn't have the heart to tell her the Japanese weren't invited to this one. I also never told her that President Ngo Dinh Diem was a murderous despot who banned dancing and singing, but freely allowed torture and assassinations. She would have denied it as propaganda spread by all those traitors against the war.

"Propaganda," Pop Dempsey would say, "Is a goose with three testicles. That's a proper gander!"

I never warmed to Menzies either, well before he decided to drag me away from the comforts of home. Menzies was a Carlton supporter. I believed it a reason enough be wary of him. He used to pull up to the fence at Princess Park, but a stab pass from the Parkville cemetery, on a Blues match day and watch the VFL footy through the windscreen of his EJ Holden. The only car in the whole ground! He acted as though he was at a country carnival watching the Jingellic thirds and not surrounded by the great unwashed and partially inebriated masses of roaring, city dwelling, fandom. If you can't stand in the outer and barrack with the raucous rank and file, you're not one of mine and never will be.

Mum loved those Liberal sycophantic Sinophobes with all her heart until it was decided, by a little wooden ball, that some mothers' sons would be shipped away to stand up for the West. The day St. Bob decided he was going to force conscription down our throats, Mum's staunch conviction began to waver. Mum had been 'all the way with LBJ' the US President Harold Holt fell in love with. When they started choosing young Australian like me to go forth and possibly die in a war the Aussie politicians were gagging to be a part of, cracks in her veneer started to show. Pop said Menzies and Holt had crawled so far up LBJ's Presidential bum that you could just see their feet kicking feebly in the air. They so desperately wanted to gate-crash the green-tie affair they never noticed the Yanks (the spetic tanks or seppies in the Australian verncular) laughing at our shorts and cork hats. The South Vietnamese didn't even know who we were.

When my birthdate, March 3rd, was pulled and a few weeks later I received the dreaded brown envelope telling me to get a haircut and pack some boot polish for a ten-week camp in Puckapunyal Mum's stoic facade completely crumbled.

"Sure, we'd show the bludgers how to fight!" said Pop, "We Aussies are great fighters, but to what end?" For Mum it was soul-crushing to realise her loyalties were so misdirected. The bitter taste never quite left her mouth. In a heartbeat she had donned the blue and white sash of the *Save our Sons* movement and found other likeminded souls with whom she could rail against the Government and the world.

I took little solace when Pop told me of her joining the S.O.S. in a short, vindicated and poorly written letter. Nan had corrected some of the spelling with a red pen; you could take the teacher out of the primary school. It was all too late for me of course. I read that letter many times in the far east being shot at by both the red and the yellow perils.

DAD

I don't know if Dad was a Liberal man or a Labor supporter. I don't know if Dad was even a Catholic like Mum and her parents. More importantly, I don't even know if Dad barracked for Fitzroy. I never asked and he didn't live long enough to tell me. All I really knew about dear old Dad is that he made a very long corpse, he had a very long coffin and they buried him in a very long grave. He also helped make a very long son that he would never see grow up. According to Mum, Dad came back from the second world war in body but left the best parts of himself in the mud of Kokoda. He left his laugh, his smile, his milk of human kindness and, as it turned out, his will to live. He shot himself in the garage when I was five. I remember the day well enough. Mum and I had caught the tram to the Brunswick Street oval to see the mighty Fitzroy Gorillas, as they were known then. After they tired of the opposition making simian comparisons they changed the mascot again and became the Lions in '57. We were playing Melbourne in the thick mud that constituted an oval in those days. Melbourne was just starting to find their feet and become the juggernaut that won flag after flag, but we beat them that day in 1954. We got up by 11 points and I remember Jack Gervasoni kicking 3 goals. Mum said he was a striking 'Eyetalian' man and I thought she meant he used to belt blokes. I liked him because he was

Italian like my mate Ricky who lived two doors down. The great Ron Barassi played that day. He was 18. Mum said Baron Ruthven cleaned his clock – I had no idea what that meant either – did a clock ever need to clean its face?

I remember singing the new Fitzroy song to the tune of the French national anthem *'La Marseilles'* with a group of delirious supporters on the tram ride home. Mum was twirling her maroon scarf above her head and one old bloke in a long black coat that smelled of cat piss and camphor lifted me onto his shoulders so all the passengers could hear me butcher the stirring words penned by Fitzroy champion back pocket, Bill Stephen. The tram pulled up near Napier Street and we waved goodbye to our new friends as it clattered away. We could hear the old Roy's song start up again above the clanking and rattling of the green beast. Mum and I laughed, and she squeezed my hand.

Outside the Builders Arms hotel there was a small group of middle-aged men milling.

"How'd the Lions go, mum?" enquired a grey-haired man in a grey pork pie hat. I punched a fist into the air and the men roared.

"Up the Roys!"

As we got close to home there were two policemen squashed into the front of a shiny black Studebaker police car parked in the gutter outside our neat little weatherboard. One square shouldered, centre-half-back climbed from the passenger side and approached us.

"Are you Mrs. Shepherd?" came a voice not used to asking twice.

"Yes."

"Can I have a quick word with you inside, away from the boy?"

"It's Bill, isn't it?" said Mum, her voice flat and emotionless.

"Ahh, yes missus. We'll chat inside over a cuppa. Sergeant O'Brien here will take the boy for a ride around the block."

"Is that OK with you, boyo? Jump in," the other bear of a man called from the driver's side window. Mum turned to me with a look of bewilderment or was it, relief? I remember that look, even today. I didn't like it then and all these years later, I still don't. I don't remember the ride. That is a shame. I think everyone should remember their first ride in a police car.

A lot of old blokes came back from the war changed. I must say, looking back through the prism of my own troubles, I feel sorry for the old man now, trying to deal with the demons of his service. Of course, he wasn't spat on when he got home; those Kokoda men were Australian heroes. Dad discovered the bottle, as so many did back then, and like so many more since, they discover the bottle can't answer any of their questions – it just ends up as empty as their souls.

My grandma used to say, although I think Frida Kahlo said it first, "The danger of drowning your sorrows is you just may teach the buggers to swim." Dad wasn't a nasty drunk, but he definitely wasn't a happy one: he was a sad drunk. His sorrows could swim like Dawn Fraser. They ended up drowning him.

My lasting memory of Dad's passing is the curtains being open in the lounge room and the winter sun streaming in across the kitchen table when Mum and I would have toast and marmalade for breakfast. I remember Mum seemed much taller. I remember days being much shorter. I remember old men coming to the door to take Dad's clothes. I'll never forget the Lions beating the Demons in the rain at Brunswick Street. I can still smell the wet of the mud in the chewed-up goal square where ankle high, hard leather boots leapt and landed. The aroma carried on the breeze. That smell makes me smile.

I remember the tram ride home most of all. I can barely remember Dad who died in the war and just didn't know it.

I still love trams.

BIG

I've always been tall. Mum used to say I'd grow overnight. For years she'd say she would put me to bed in long pyjamas and I'd wake up in short ones. I even told the kids at school that one. I think some of them even believed it. I grew something like 12 inches in one two-year period between the ages of 12 and 15. I had stretch marks up and down my back for ages, probably still do. Rosemary, the ex-wife, used to call them my tiger stripes when we were, 'feeling amorous'. I kept growing right through my teens and finally pulled up at 6 foot-nine inches in the old vernacular – you can work out what that is in centimetres if that's what floats your boat. I went from being a rover to a ruckman almost overnight. A batsman to a bowler just as quickly. Today that height is a little more common, but back then it was a little freaky. I was all teeth and elbows, angles, and edges. When you grow that quickly clumsiness becomes your constant, well it did with me anyway. It takes a lot of time to get all the instruments playing in tune.

    I was a shy sort of kid, which is an anathema to being tall, of course. The shy kid wants to hide away, but where does a six-foot two inch 12-year-old go to hide. School was all right I suppose. I was smart enough, and the teachers left me alone. There was one nun who used to give me the rounds a little, but when I agreed to play in the ruck for the school footy team, she was the coach, she ended up my biggest fan. Her name was Sister Michael Aloysius, something or other – I used to wonder if the nuns' surname was Christ as in Sister Michael Aloysius Christ – after all, they were all married to God, right? I never even found it weird, until Ricky pointed out to me, that she had a boy's name. Ricky said she probably was a boy, and she probably had a donga under that heavy, black habit of hers. I didn't want to think about that, or surely, I would burn in hell. Thinking about a nun's donga had to be a mortal sin – definitely a venial one. Whichever one was worse. Either way, there would be a warm place put aside for you if you had visions of nun's peckers dancing around your brain.

Sister Michael wasn't 'strap-happy' like some of the nuns at Sacred Heart PS. Some of the nuns couldn't handle classes of up to 50 and 60 students, most of whom barely spoke a word of English. It would get to them in the end. I used to see some fearsome punishments meted out. In the playground it was a badge of honour how many wooden rulers had broken on you whilst getting belted. There was one big, Polish kid who never did his homework. Poor bugger probably had to work all night in Daddy's grocery or hardware shop or something. Sister George, who was a nasty old battle axe if ever there was one, broke three rulers on him in one afternoon. Ricky grabbed his hand after class and told him it was the most amazing thing he had ever seen. The kid had no idea what the little kid with the bright red ears was talking about but ended up laughing anyway as Ricky acted out being strapped on the arse by Sister George. The pantomime of her stunned face as yet another ruler splintered was priceless. Ricky and Andrzej became firm friends.

Ricky's surname was Pepi, which I thought was wonderful. Ricky Pepi was a name that just rolled off the tongue. It was a joy hearing that name during roll call. Ricky was just a little kid, but he had this infectious personality you couldn't help but love. He was a prize nutbag, the class clown. He couldn't shut up and was always looking for a laugh. Today he would be diagnosed as having an attention deficit disorder and drugged accordingly. In those days you were just considered wilful and rambunctious, nothing a regular beating couldn't cure. Still, no-one yet had found a way to take the pep out of Ricky Pepi. He was gloriously hyperactive.

Everything was funny to Ricky. Most of us loved him – even the Maltese kids and they didn't like anyone. If the truth be told, it was probably my friendship with Ricky that kept me from getting picked on – and I was about two whole feet taller than him! Even, the nuns liked him, of sorts, although that didn't stop them from whacking him mercilessly every time he stuffed up. Sister Michael used to say she had sourced some heavy-duty wood to hit Ricky with because Ricco (his real name) meant "strong ruler" in Italian and in Australia all our rulers were pretty flimsy. She thought this little witticism the height of hilarity. Of course, we all smiled, some of the brown-nose kids would laugh aloud. Ricky would bay like a bloodhound right up until she belted him, then laugh some more. He'd have tears in his eyes from the pain and the mirth. His ears glowed the colour of baboon's bum. I once asked him how he could laugh when getting bashed and he confided that when Sister Michael said she had "heavy duty wood" for him he decided she was talking about that hidden penis beneath her habit. Soon we were both crying and spluttering with laughter. "Gee," I remember thinking, "we were both headed for hell".

I'll tell you a funny story. It was funny to Ricky anyway and he never tired of bringing it up. Sister Michael Aloysius Christ was the first girl, who wasn't my mum, my two aunties, and grandma, that I ever kissed – right on the lips! I even agonized about telling this one in the confessional but decided God would never forgive me for pashing on with his missus. I was extremely tall and ridiculously skinny. I looked as though I might snap in a light zephyr. Rangy, lanky, big nose, large overbite, you know my type, every school had one. My thighs were as thick as some other kids' biceps and some of the bullies or opposition ruckmen might have a crack at me because I looked frail, but then, of course, clumsiness does have its benefits. Noses and elbows are mortal enemies in a tussle. They hate each other almost as much as testicles hate knees. When they meet in combat there are always fireworks. I was angular and pointy. A bag of sharp-edged bones that I couldn't control and didn't intend to.

I remember one game for the school team, Sister Michael Aloysius was coaching. She used to wear her habit with an old pair of ankle high footy boots she'd bought somewhere, or maybe they were given to her. Ricky said she'd probably pinched them from the St Vincent De Paul poor box. She wore a silver whistle on a string around her neck. Sister Michael would arrive at training already wearing the boots. Ricky said "she most likely had them on all day at school, who knows what goes on under those nun dresses?" Ricky spent a lot of time thinking about what went on under nuns' clothing. Twisted little perv.

I used to wonder about the four inches of habit which used to get dragged through the puddles and mud holes every week. It would cake on so thickly she must have been carrying around 10 extra pounds by the end of training. Still, next morning her habit was always clean and black. Maybe she had two. Maybe she had the detention kids scrape the mud and scrub the habit... I digress.

We were playing the boys from Preston Primary, I think. They were a nasty bunch and Sister Michael had let us know in no uncertain terms that we were going to stand our ground and NOT let the heathen Protestants beat us.

"This was a holy war!" she bellowed. I didn't even know what a Protestant was, and I had no idea if the Preston boys did either. They were obviously quite evil though. They looked evil. Of course, the most evil looking one was my opposing ruckman who, despite being nowhere near my height, had a fair moustache going on his upper lip at 12 and that was practically unheard of and quite the talking point. Ricky, my sometimes rover and ever the motivator, whispered to me, so that everyone in the small change room could hear (Ricky never had a volume control): "Hey Tezz, did you see the bloke you're rucking against... I think he's 40!"

Out in the middle the opposition, moustachioed, ruckman kept eyeballing me and punching his fist into his hand.

"Come and get it!" he hissed with each meaty "whap" as the hand and fist came together. As Ricky liked to say: I was "crapping my dacks". Sister Michael bellowed from the boundary where she stood in front of the tin coaches' box, oblivious to the sheets of rain rolling across the ground.

"Don't let him intimidate you Terry boy!" It seemed to echo off the clouds. Ricky was sitting on the bench behind her with his arms around his skinny legs, a look of pure joy on his face. The umpire held the ball up and said in a loud and clear voice,

"Let's get to it then fellas shall we, before we drown!" and tossed the ball up. 'Moustache' came straining across the circle, with his outstretched arms in front of him like some Frankenstein monster and pushed me straight in the chest.

I snapped in two and went down on my back with a splash of mud and ooze.

"Play-on," yelled the ump, throwing his hands in the air. I was barely back on my feet before the ball was back in the middle for the next ball-up. They'd swept it clear and scored the first goal for the game – possibly the only goal if this rain keeps up, I thought.

"More where that came from," sneered Frankenstein's monster. He had such a punchable face. I thought I better get going a little more quickly this time and maybe jump over him a little, especially if he tries the push again, as he most surely would; it had worked so well after all. I had a good leap, even though I walked on stilts, my skinny legs could still launch me from the mud because I was 'all lean and no lard' as my Aunty Jenny used to say. I weighed about 8 stone, ringing wet, and just at that moment, I was soaked. As the ball went up, I was already running in, and I leapt high. I missed the ball by a mile, but I did happen to connect one pointy elbow with Moustache's nose on the way up. I will swear to the day I die it was an accident, but no-one believed it for a second. Moustache had, of course, been coming in ready to push me over again and didn't see my elbow until it was too late. To add insult to bloody injury, my right boot connected with his groin on the way up and the poor bugger went down like he'd been shot by a sniper. He lay curled up in a ball, mewling softly, his forehead in the mud, his hands knotted tightly around his scrotum.

"Too high!" yelled the ump and he held the footy out to Moustache, who was having none of it. He barely moved. He was emitting this high-pitched whine that only dogs can hear. I could clearly hear Sister Michael call to the other coach in that same raucous roar,

"You better see to your boy Mr Anderson; he doesn't look too well."

We smashed Preston Primary school that day who gave up the ghost seeing their enforcer go down and off. They just let us roll over them.

"He spewed next to their coaches' box too, all green and carroty," Ricky took great care to let everyone know, even the tram conductor, as he kicked us off the tram later that day for not having tickets… and being covered in mud. Someone told me Ricky even went and poked the vomit with a stick. He chased a couple of other kids with it outstretched before him, braying like a donkey.

Their back-up ruckman was a good foot smaller than me and had obviously decided I was not to be trifled with. He didn't even attempt to compete for the taps. He made me look like Roy Wright, Richmond's dual Brownlow goliath. I was just grabbing the ball as it went up and running down the field with it; no-one even wanted to tackle me. It was cold, wet, and miserable and I was having the game of my life. When the umpire checked his watch and called time – a good five minutes early we reckoned (even the umpie had had enough of the rain), we had won by about twelve or thirteen goals. I even kicked one off the ground and I never kicked goals. The boys were buzzing and surrounded me with hugs and back slaps. Ricky ran from the boundary and jumped on my back. The large puddle in front of the break in the wire link fence had swollen to become a small lake. Before the game we had delicately tiptoed around it, but now we stomped on through. Sister Michael Aloysius was standing in the doorway to the rooms as we went in. She was slapping backs and congratulating each boy in turn for their magnificent games.

"Well done Sandro, you were terrific on the half back flank," and "Josef, that was your best game of the year."

"It is one of life's great things to best a Protestant, boys. Mr Anderson will be choking on his supper tonight I have never been surer of anything in my life." As I entered the small, dimly lit room I was assailed by the wet boy smell; all slugs, snails and puppy dogs' tails and even smellier now dripping wet. Sister Michael bellowed, "And here he is, the hero of the day. Terry Shepherd smote the Philistines today boys, a warrior, a crusader, our *Athleta Christi nobilis*." And with that she reached up, grabbed my head between her meaty hands and kissed me on the lips.

"WHAT!" Ricky bellowed and screamed with laughter. In a heartbeat the whole stinking room was in uproar. Even Sister Michael was laughing. Our opponents on the other side of the paper-thin wall must have thought we were insane. We didn't have a school song as such; if the truth be told I can't actually remember a need for one as we never won. Sister Michael Aloysius instead started up a rousing rendition of 'Onward Christian Soldiers' and we all joined in if we knew the words and hummed along if we didn't.

Usually, we had to make our way back to school to change back into our school gear for the trip home, but Sister Michael told us we were too dirty and let us leave for home straight from the ground. We all gathered around the one sink in the room to wash the nastier lumps of mud away, but the tepid water soon turned cold and then icy, and we all decided the pelting rain outside would clean us off.

"Hurry off home now lads and clean up before you catch a cold. Don't be putting your clean school clothes over the mud. I'll see you all on the morrow."

"THE LIPS, ON THE MOUTH! SHE KISSED YOU ON THE MOUTH!" was all Ricky could say as we walked home in the pelting rain.

"DOES JESUS KNOW YOU'VE BEEN DIDDLING HIS MUM?"

"Oh, shut it Rick, you're such an idiot."

"GIRLS OF THE WORLD HEAR ME NOW – TERRY SHEPHERD HAS LOST ALL INTEREST IN YOU, HE'S TASTED PENGUIN!" Even I giggled at this one. My laugh just emboldened the bastard.

"Terry, I fear for your mottle soul – you can't go around kissing God's missus. Does that mean they are getting a divorce?"

"The word is mortal you retard!"

"I might be a retard, but at least I'm not a wife stealer. Did you stick the tongue in Tezza?"

This went on for the whole of a very wet walk home. When we got to my house Mum rushed us into a steaming hot bath, "lest we catch our deaths". Ricky told her all about our day as he was stripping off his filthy gear, utterly untroubled by his nakedness in front of my mum. I'd become the hero of Ricky's Iliad.

"…and the ruckman with the moustache threw up – and then Sister Michael Aloysius kissed Terry on the lips." His filthy face beamed from the bath as I worked the mud from my knees at the other end. Mum was standing in the doorway holding dry towels and belly-laughing along. Even mothers could not resist Ricky. He was in his element telling his tale. I'd never seen him so happy.

When, years later, Ricky discovered that Sister Michael Aloysius Christ had indeed divorced Jesus and left the church to marry an ex-Priest and the happy couple had six kids, he'd tease me unmercifully that at least one of them must be mine.

"It all starts with a kiss you know Terry." He vowed to track them down just to see if one of the kids was really tall with orange hair and a whopping nose. Then he'd know for sure.

Good God, Ricky Pepi was an idiot.

DR K

So, there's these three Nam vets laying in their repat beds in all states of shit and corruption see, and this Government fella sidles in and tells the poor bastards that they were gonna get compensation for their injuries – I know right, don't hold your breath. He told them he would measure their injuries between two points, and he would then give them $100 for every inch. The first bloke, he was a tall fucker like you, he says – "Righto. I lost me right leg. I want you to measure my left leg, from me arsehole to the floor." The assessor says. "Fine," and he takes a long tape measure out of his dacks and measures the bloke's leg. That's 26 inches brother, and he writes out a cheque for $2,600, signs it, and hands it to him.

"Beauty!" says the first bloke.

The second bloke thinks about this, and he goes –

"Mate, from bullets and bayonets, mossie bites to leeches, jock rash and one serious dose of the clap, I think Vietnam has left it's mark on my whole body." He stands up tall and reaches his arm above his head.

"I want you to measure from the tips of my fingers to the tips of my toes." The Government bloke knows he's messing with him, but he says OK and he measures the second fella.

"Right, your seven foot nine inches, that's 84 plus nine, we owe you $9,300." And he writes him a check, signs it and tears it off!

Here comes the last poor bugger lying in bed and he's rat-shit. He's covered in bandages from bumhole to breakfast. His arms and legs are raised in traction, and you can just see his eyes and mouth for the bandages around his head.

"My unfortunate fellow, where can I measure you for your compensation?" The little chap thinks hard and finally he says:

"I'd like you to measure from the tip of my penis to my balls."

"What a fine fellow you are," says the assessor, "You're not trying to take advantage of your government like some others present." And he glares daggers at the second bloke.

He moves over to the man's bed and gently pulls back the sheet, his tape measure at the ready.

"My God man, where are your testicles?"

"They're still in fucking Vietnam mate!"

"Bahahahahahahahahahahahahahahahahaha!"

The fellow in the bed opposite me laughed so raucously I thought he might choke, and at his own joke. Neil, a slender, fine haired man of about 35 gave a short laugh as if he'd heard it 100 times, and he probably had – I'd have thought Greg, my new comedian roommate from across the hospital dormitory, had probably tried the joke on every new fellow through Repat. They had both been here a while I surmised. Colin to my left, the guy with the burns, gave a short sharp laugh that turned into a coughing fit. His ruined lungs were not up to the exercise.

"Shit, sorry Colin, I didn't mean to get you coughing."

Colin waved weakly from his cot. Despite the air fresheners the nurses had hung around Colin's bed like Christmas decorations Colin still smelled faintly of burnt flesh and he knew it. It's a smell you never forget. The nose seems to go to it and mark its presence. He'd apologize often, as if it were his fault. Colin was only with our merry band for a couple of weeks. One morning the bed to my left was empty. The whole dorm had slept through his disappearance. As the self-appointed dormitory welcomer, Greg was inconsolable he hadn't said goodbye.

"It's a cracker of a joke Terry, isn't it?"

It struck me that Greg had the decency to ascertain what my ailments were before he told me his joke. He would ask every one that came through the same thing before launching into it during our long stay at the Heidelberg Veterans Repatriation Hospital through all of 1971 and a fair slice of 1972. Even a troglodyte like old Greggy had enough empathy to know that a fellow whose knackers had been blown off might not find a joke about a guy whose knackers had been blown off, funny!

Like my little mate Ricky, Greg was one of those guys who looked for a laugh in any situation. He'd been an engineer in Nam and had most of his fingers blown away attempting to diffuse a mine just outside *Binh Ba*. Probably one of ours repurposed by the nimble fingers of some Viet Cong kid. Fortunately for Greg, when the mine exploded, as they were want to do, it had been poorly constructed and had only taken his fingers, "and not my whole bloody head" he used to say with a grin. Shrapnel had torn through sections of his bowel as well and the constant threat of peritonitis ensured Greg was there for the long haul. Greg was not the sharpest tool in the shed but having a bloke around who could still laugh with seven missing fingers and a thumb was not so bad. Me, I thought I'd probably never find anything else in my life even slightly humorous. When I didn't smile Greg asked.

"Whatdchathink Tez, good one."

I didn't answer but closed my eyes.

"It's all good Greg," said Neil," I think he's heard it."

"No worries!" said Greg.

"It's a cracker Grego," I managed.

"It is a beauty alright." I could hear the smile in his voice. "My mate Homer told it to me over there. I changed it a bit to make it more Aussie, you know. Homer was this big black Seppo and we got on really well. He was just this whippet thin bloke with the darkest skin. I used to say to him…"

Greg's banal banter sent me off into a morphine induced, dreamless sleep. I welcomed the release. Greg was a good one but as my Pop used to say… he could talk the hat off a head.

"Hello Terry, my name is Doctor Keysor and I'm the senior consultant here at the Repat." Dr Keysor spoke with the impatient air doctors can get when they'd much rather be on the golf course. Maybe I'm being harsh. He just seemed a bit of a knob. Some guys are born a knob and some guys are seduced by knobdom. I decided, almost immediately, Dr K was of the former inclination. The orderly who had wheeled me into his small white room, which smelled of ammonia and soap, handed over my chart on a bulldog clipped board and left the room. Dr K stood beside the bed and tapped his foot on the white tiles as he read. He flicked over the next two pages and turned his gaze on me.

"I believe you triaged your wounds yourself, is that right?"

"Well, I was the first one there," I mumbled.

"Right," he said with a sigh.

"I had help. The man who found me."

"All right, I suppose I should have a look at you."

I lay before him wearing only a pair of white, cotton underpants and half a mile of bandages. I was rake thin before I left for Vietnam and since my misfortune, I had lost most of whatever fat I possessed. My hipbones protruded like elbows. If not for the pain killers distending my clogged-up bowels I might have blown under the door and been swept out with the garbage. If you've ever seen that classic silent Vampire film *Nosferatu*, you'd know those long, gnarled hands that floated toward the throat of some heavily made-up, blond. Well, those hands were resting on the hospital sheets looking impossibly pale. One clenched in a fist, the other lay like a dead fish, it's belly pointing to the sky. The puncture wounds at the tops of my thighs were already exposed and the doc had only to peer down to assess the damage the sharpened and shit-covered punji sticks had done at the bottom of the hellish pit I was eventually dragged from. The nurse had removed the bandages that morning, and she had left the wounds uncovered and untreated for the doctor to see. My thighs and my left knee, which came to rest on those terrible sticks, burned and itched; itched, and burned. They had swollen so I could see them without lifting my head. I'd developed quite the nastiest bug in the jungle. The loathsome microorganisms, much like the VC, were small, pernicious, and more than happy to play the long game. They mightn't get you straight away, but they'd get you in the end. The Vietnamese had been fighting guerrilla wars for millennia against all comers. Young nations like Aussies and Yanks may have impetuousness and vigour, but it's the Ancient cultures that beat you with wisdom, patience, and guile. Science could defeat an assailant through exploration and experimentation, but the military found great comfort in a dogged refusal to learn from history. Shock, awe, and stupidity. Their doom. The Vietnamese, like the virus, usually found a way.

The doctor inspected my legs closely, looking over the top of the half-moon spectacles that hung on the end of his nose. A small silver chain ran from each arm and around the back of his head.

"How long were you in the Australian Field Hospital?"

"About a week I think, maybe five days, to get me stable for travel." I didn't have much idea to be honest. I was really out of it after Lax bought me in. I'll tell you all about Lax later. My story is also Lax's story in a lot of ways.

"And then they shipped you out to the US Hospital in Saigon or *Long Bihn*?"

"Saigon, yeah. The Yanks had a look at the infection in my legs. I needed to go on stronger antibiotics than we had available at the time."

"God bless America then I suppose," he offered without looking up. I said nothing. I'd have rolled my eyes if I could have. He poked one wound and I grunted.

"I could have inspected you under sedation if this is too uncomfortable," he said looking at my good eye over my swollen thighs. I said nothing.

"Right then, let's look at the bullet wound." Dr Keysor removed the bandages from around my shoulder and my right arm as I lay shivering in his cold little room. I liked the cold actually. I had been a raging fire of infection for so long I craved even the draft. My legs dangled a full foot over the end of the cot and my uncovered feet appeared to be turning blue. As he removed the last of the gauze it caught a little on the dried ooze and I winced. He asked about my pain medication.

"I wanted to be clear in the head for this examination. I haven't had any meds this morning."

"Keeping an eye on me, are you?" His tone was light, but there was a slight petulance. This was a man not used to being questioned. Doctors back in 1970 walked around the place like they held the mortgage.

"Yeah. I was."

"Oh, right. I suppose you can tell me about the arm then if you feel inclined."

"I was shot with an AK-47 round at very close quarters. The bullet entered my right bicep and travelled up through the axilla, bounced off the edge of scapula and tore through the head of my humerus where it splintered. Here it created a lesion of the brachial plexus, rendering my right arm as useless as tits on a bull. Fragments exited through the supraspinatus at the back of my shoulder in three separate places."

"Right," he said.

"And YES, to your next question."

"And what is my next question?"

"Yes, I am right-handed?" Dr Keysor smiled.

"Well, I was about to ask what your preferred hand was. Nifty party trick," he added dryly. The brachial plexus is a problematic area but there have been some advancements in dedicated surgery. There's one thing for sure about a war, and I apologise if I sound unsympathetic, war advances medicine exponentially. So many injuries in such a short span of time. There may be options for you but we're going to get you stable and infection-free first."

He turned and jotted a few notes into a ledger he had on a small table next to his chair. The ledger rested on a packet of Viscount. All the doctors and nurses smoked. You'd have thought they would have known better. A non-smoker, I found it bemusing.

"Righto – now for the eye. Are you able to sit up?" Dr K. watched me try to raise myself on my one good elbow for an endless time before he decided to help. I'd been trying to inch forward enough so that my shrieking knees could bend over the end of the narrow bed, and I could counter lever my top half into sitting. My pustulating thighs left pink streams on the bedsheet. Without relinquishing the clipboard he held to his chest, the doctor placed his shoulder behind mine and pushed until I was seated. My feet almost brushed the white tiled floor.

"Right," he said rising up on his toes to grab the bandages swathed around my head. "Let's see what's under here." Now he did put my medical files down as he realised this would be a job for two hands. I felt this moment poignantly. My life would forever more be a one-handed wrestle. As he rolled the bandages from around my head, I felt the loss of light on that side stung more than the pain of my torn face. He scooped the bandages and placed them onto the table in a sticky clump. He grasped my head tightly and slowly lowered my head and moved it around looking deeply into the void where a large, green eye once sat snuggly.

"It, the socket I mean, looks nice and clean. At some point, down the track, we should be able to fit you with a glass eye. The wounds around your socket are a still quite infected, they will still take some time." He picked up my file again and pulled the pen from the breast pocket of his white coat. He tapped it twice on his lip and scribbled. He tapped the page with the back of the pen and said, "Right, we're on track with the antibiotics, but the infections aren't clearing as fast as we would like. I want you to get back on the pain medication. No skipping it to give me your medical insights in the future. I don't need the assistance. You're going to need quite a bit of physical therapy on this arm and you're going to need to adjust to the changes to your depth of field. Finally, if we don't put some weight on you, we are not going to be able to increase the methadone. You will have to be with us for a while, I think. My advice is start eating." Dr Keysor walked to the end of the bed and placed the clipboard in the holder. He turned to go then caught himself and turned toward me.

"I see you studied medicine."

"Yeah."

"You did four years at Melbourne Uni?"

"That's right," I said thickly.

"Were you a nasho?"

"Yeah, my number came up."

"Then why the hell did you go?" I ignored the question as he rolled on. "Students didn't have to do service, especially medical students, I'm sure a bright fellow like you was aware of that. Let me get this right. They were willing to wait until you'd finished your course – in those four years you could have easily put in for exemption. The Uni would have written it up for you. You didn't need to heed the call-up. For a start, I would have thought a bloke 12 feet 17 would stand out like a pimple on the Mona Lisa. You had no place being in a warzone – why go?"

I just looked at him. I should have told him to get stuffed. There are probably 25 thousand different ways to tell someone to get stuffed, but I didn't have any of them ready. I just blinked at him which, I'm sure, made me look as stupid as he was trying to make me feel.

"For the last decade I've had to scrape together so many young men like yourself who have been chewed up and spat out in a distant, pointless war. Young men in the prime of their lives. Some had visions of glory. Some wanted to serve. Some just too stupid to say 'no!' Most conscripts didn't have a choice, but you did. Why you'd want to risk it all is beyond me, a medical student like you."

"Maybe I wanted to help," I croaked.

"Noble thoughts son, but now you're of no use to anyone." He waved his hand over me like he was shooing a fly and with that turned and left the room. Dr K was an opinionated prick. I wasn't too stupid to have picked that from the moment he entered the room.

Of course, I'd asked myself "why" a thousand times. A million times. I couldn't give Dr K a definitive answer as I really didn't have one. Initially I had been horrified when my birth date was pulled from the barrel, but there was also a nagging sense of, I don't know, call it obligation, maybe duty. No, duty always seemed more an American concept. The Yanks always went on about their duty to the motherland. I'll go with "responsibility", that might be a better word for it. Maybe it was just the ever-present nag of Catholic guilt that got me moving, Catholic guilt is a pretty powerful force, honestly – anything that can stop a teenage boy playing with his todger is pretty bloody powerful. My motivation was based on a myriad of reasons and stimuli. It was complicated. Complicated for me and far too complicated to sum up neatly for Dr fucking Keysor.

There was a tingling of excitement about Vietnam, I'm not going to lie. I'd never, really been out of Fitzroy except to trek into the city and the MCG for the cricket and footy. My life, until I departed, had been spent in a 15-mile square of Melbourne suburbia. Even the stimulation of Melbourne University with its bars and clubs and campus full of love beads and mini-skirts, flares, and free love; Uni was still a short tram ride from where I'd grown up. In the army I could go and see the world, all expenses paid. Sure, I was naïve, a little incognizant, but which 22 year-old isn't, that's why they recruit us isn't it. We're bullet-proof. Life is there to be savoured; consequences are for your parents. Rosemary, my girlfriend, and I we're getting on well too, so I didn't fall into the jilted lover category. We'd been together for three of the four years I'd been studying, and we'd been a hot item – despite the fact that Rosemary, with her Thai parents' genes, barely scraped 5'2". We must have looked a right pair twirling away on the dance floor. Rosemary used to laugh it off.

"You're all the same size lying down," she used to say.

The student union fees were a factor I suppose, the medical textbooks, the equipment, lab coats, stethoscopes, human skeletons to tinker with – it all adds up. I was working my arse off labouring on building sites to keep up with the fees and Mum's wage wasn't much help, bless her heart. That wasn't really it either. When it's all said and done it was probably

Kevin Beechworth who really got me motivated to do my part. Kevin was a Fitzroy boy like me. He was a National Serviceman like me. He even went to All Saints Primary School as I did, although a few years older and I'd never met him. Private Kevin Beechworth was called up in the first wave of conscripts in 1966 and was placed in the 1st Australian Task Force, based in *Nui Dat* in the *Phuoc Tuy* province. He was in a field operations unit of a rifleman platoon and was moving the inhabitants of *Long Hải* village, outside of *Long Điền*, to be resettled nearby. While spraying defoliant on the jungle to clear the vegetation the *Viet Cong* hide in, he stepped on a mine and didn't even live long enough to fight at *Long Tan*. Mum knew Kevin's parents from church. They were inconsolable and ended up divorced. They both moved away. This young bloke, younger than me when I went, is going about his life, his mum, and dad are happy, church-going people. There was nothing more important in his days than drinking beers with his mates, trying to find a job, watching the footy and chasing girls in the pubs and nightclubs. All of a sudden, his marble is plucked from a barrel, he is bussed to Puckapunyal and called all sorts of names by rusted on Army arseholes who didn't like "nashos". The papers are chock full of stories about the Regulars not wanting the nashos there. He's called lazy, listless, inexperienced, and dangerous by the enlisted troops. As a "nasho" he was going to get good soldiers killed. A "nasho" didn't care about anyone but himself: if he did he would have joined up already. Politicians screamed at him if he refused the call, and celebrities and sport stars screamed at him if he did. He's evil and a puppet. He was taught how to kill, fitted for a green suit, shipped over to a warzone, deployed to kick people out of their homes and spray a deadly poison defoliant with no idea what it could be doing to the food bowl and in turn the starving people of Vietnam, let alone himself. He spent days covered in the stinking, burning shit. He's eating tasteless, crappy food, he's drinking chlorinated water. He's scared. He's hot. He's sleep-deprived and every single person outside his perimeter wants to see his body bloody and maimed. One particularly horrible day beneath a Biblical tempest of blinding rain and booming thunder Kevin steps on a land mine and he is torn into pieces.

Tạm Biệt Kevin.

The anti-war protestors at my Uni say it's his own fault for being there and his government refuses to pay to bring his body home because he wasn't a Victoria Cross winner! His mum and dad can't face looking at each other anymore without crying. They separate. They move on in a stupor of grief. His girlfriend is heartbroken, the life they planned together is now dead and gone. His mates' lives are changed forever. Kev has sliced away some of their hearts and haunts their dreams. Kevin's story, a man I never even met, touched me. I wanted to go over to Vietnam and try and save the next Kevin I met, if I could, and if I couldn't, well at least I fucking tried. I reckon this world could do with more Kevin's and a few less Dr Keysors.

God only knows, I wish I'd had those words when that entitled arsehole asked me why I went to Vietnam.

Ah well. The best comebacks always occur to you much too late don't they? We'll be ready for the prick next time.

Kev, you with me?

LAX

Tall people get used to ducking. Door frames, tram ceilings, hanging pots, tree branches. The very tall are imperilled by things short-arses never even have to consider. This is doubly true in Vietnam. God, Buddha, or Uncle Ho did not have people like me in mind when they drew up plans for Vietnam, the land of the short-arse – nor did the Australian Armed Services for that matter. Aeroplanes are interminable, army jeeps incommodious. The cots are too short, the tents too low and the hanging light fixtures were a constant hazard. When glowing brightly I could avoid them but in a darkened room I'd set them swinging just entering.

I was thinking about my morning encounter with a hanging bulb as I bent low to enter the mess tent. I hadn't broken our bulb with my forehead, but I had sent it swinging so wildly I had to scramble to catch it and set it straight. Golly Hawkins, Jungles and Balls, my three tent mates, never failed to be amused.

"Lofty, leave our bloody light alone," they'd chorus.

I was late for breakfast this particular morning; I was often late for breakfast if the truth be told. I liked to take my first hour of a morning, while it was still cool and the brain hadn't begun to overheat, to check and double-check my medic pack, re-stock, and roll through my book on emergency medicine – especially if we had a patrol in the afternoon, as we did on this sweltering Sunday. I was a conscripted medic in the Australian armed forces, at the Australian base, in the middle of the *Nui Dat* rubber plantation, in the province of *Phước Tuy* – South Vietnam. I think I'd been at the base about a month. I'd been in Nam a little longer though. I was shown the ropes at the Australian Field Hospital in *Vũng Tàu*. I was very green. It was in *Vũng Tàu* the RMO (Regimental Medical Officer), Major Howard 'the Rabbi' Lightfoot, turned me from a private to a Lance Corporal (LCPL) with a flick of his magic promotion pen. Rabbs reasoned the privates were more likely to listen to a medic if he outranked them. He was also the type of man who believed in his heart that doctors were just a little more important, a bit smarter and walked taller than ordinary men. He reasoned that no-one in Nam walked taller than I.

The story as to how Major Lightfoot came to be known as "The Rabbi" is legendary. He was treating a bloke from the 5TH Battalion who had a most debilitating case of gonorrhoea – the STD that rampaged through the ranks of the soldiery in Nam. Apparently, it was this fella's fifth such dose and Rabbs had treated them all with some success. As he lay in his hospital bed, penicillin being fed into his arm yet again, this sexual recidivist suggested to the exasperated doctor that if only his dear old mum had had the foresight to have him circumcised as a baby he may not have had such a terrible run of luck with the pleasure girls and prostitutes of *Vũng Tàu*. Dr Rabbs, who had been having a terrible day during what was a terrible war, is said to have grabbed a large pair of scissors he'd been using to cut bandages, held them under the patients nose and roared,

"The only way to keep YOU from getting the clap is to cut your fucking dick completely off, and even then I'm not so sure it'll do the trick! Next time I see you in my hospital that's exactly what I'm going to do, and I'll feed the 'effing' thing to the hospital cat and hope to God it doesn't kill it!" He then stormed out. They didn't have a hospital cat of course, but our hero didn't know that. The sergeant was said to have gone as white as his bed sheets and the RMO's nickname was born.

I scanned the mess tent for Golly and the others, but they were spread around the open-sided tent either deep in conversations or deeper into their brekky. I grabbed a metal tray and joined the line of men waiting patiently for the cooks, not quite affectionately known as the "baitlayers", to load up the morning fare. Thin porridge, even thinner and blackened bacon. Toast and powdered eggs unevenly scrambled. A tiny pink, and brown spotted sausage and a large metal mug of hot and sweetened tea. I thanked the cook who grunted "Lofty" at me with a nod. He was already ladling steamy goodness onto the proffered tray behind mine. I quickly scanned the room and plonked myself on the hard wooded bench of the only vacant table available. As I sat, I felt, rather than heard, the air being sucked from the room. Fifty or sixty digger's mouths, some half full of their last spoonful gasped in unison. The general hubbub died away to silence. I had, with apparent impertinence, sat myself on someone's table and I wasn't welcome. I felt the withering gaze of the only other occupant through the top of my head. I'd not seen him, but God knows I could smell him, and it was enough to spoil the appetite of even the hungriest man. My nose was assailed by the smell of blood and madness, of shit and sugar. The man smelled like death. I gagged and looked up into the bluest eyes I have ever seen. These weren't the blue of Marylin's eyes or the Nordic goddess blue of Anita Ekberg. Those blue eyes you could dive into and paddle around in for hours. You could lay on your back and watch clouds morph into animal shapes across that blue. You'd happily drown in that blue. Nope, these eyes flashed with a fierce blue flame likely to envelope everything they touched. They were galvanic. These eyes were laser and they bore into the top of my head and out the back, without blinking. These eyes were the blue of unreasoned insanity. God I wish I'd sat somewhere else.

Every digger in the tent gaped at us, even the kitchen staff came out of their burrow to gawk over the counter. The table of meatheads (the military police) appeared to place their hands on their holsters as if they'd spotted light on the wire. I looked up and met the eyes, and immediately regretted it. He was a demon of dirt. His eyes shone from a Dickensian, urchin face thick with filth and gore, sewerage and what appeared to be fresh blood. His smell curdled the milk in my tea.

"Ggg-day…" I stammered struggling to meet the fierce gaze with my own. The guy was hunched over two heaped trays with enough bacon to clog the arteries of most of the soldiers in the tent. His hands had spurned the eating irons and held two pieces of toast upon which he had piled a mountain of egg. They were caked in what may have been mud, blood, tomato sauce or grease. He stared at me above this mess and without a word of response, he started to chew. He wore what appeared to be a clean pressed army shirt which struck me as out of place, before I realised it was a US Army issue shirt, and that of an officer to boot. On closer inspection there appeared to be a spreading cauliflower of red blossoming over his heart. This blood looked fresh. Too fresh.

My training kicked in, despite every fibre of my being telling me not to engage. I'd forgotten the others staring at our duet. We were the only two people in the room.

"Excuse me sir, are you bleeding?"

"I'm-m a m-medic," I stammered. Finally, he turned his gaze from me and back to his meal. It felt like I was being released. I sat staring stupidly as he ate, noticing spots of blood all over the shirt now. The pressed collar of the shirt seemed to blacken with every movement of his head.

After the longest time the man drawled slowly, softly, in a broad strine.

"Yeah."

"Excuse me sir."

"You asked if I was bleedin'."

"Yes sir, are you?"

"Probably, but I think it's someone else's blood." And with that he took another huge bite of his breakfast, dropped the remainder onto his tray and noisily drained a large metal coffee mug. I returned to my own breakfast. I entered the Boozer quite famished. The lumpy, black fingerprints on the table in front of the guy were putting me off my Army issue porridge. They seemed to squirm. I stirred my coffee slowly trying to decide if I should get up and move. Would he be insulted? This was one bloke it didn't seem wise to offend. I glanced up again and he was staring at me. After another interminable pause he said,

"So, what's the story Dig, too shit scared to move to another table or too polite?"

"Pardon sir?"

"You can knock off with the sirs, Doc. No fucking Sirs at this table."

"OK, sorry," I said. The guy spoke without looking up at me now.

"And drop the sorrys too," I said nothing.

"The mad stare is usually enough. I am in a US captain's shirt and covered in crap and corruption, I usually only have to give a fresh, wet behind the ears pup like you the mad as a shithouse rat stare and they usually find somewhere else to plant their bums. Một, Hai, Ba, Dzô, 1, 2, 3, cheers!" he said and tilted the empty pannikin toward me.

"Honestly. I sat down before I even noticed you." His short, syncopated laugh was a raven caw.

"You probably noticed the stench though, I've become good at breathing through my mouth, but I can see their noses twisting." He swept a blackened hand in an arc encompassing the other soldiers. Grease and spots of blood flew from his fingers in a fine spray.

"Oh, yes indeed, I noticed that," I said and nodded slowly. "I'm not a mouth breather."

"You'll learn a lot of new things over here pup," he said, "Although very few learn to mind their own business. Every fucker in here is trying to eavesdrop on our conversation."

There was a general clamour as the nearest tables started back at their breakfasts. Almost every person in the tent was indeed trying to hear our discussion, convinced it was only a matter of time before this spectre of grime flew up from his seat to slice open my jugular vein with a butter knife. He took another large bite of his heavily laden toast.

"Ummm, Are you sure I can't help you, medically wise I

mean. Some of that blood looks dried, some seems to be freshly staining your shirt."

"Well, that might be a problem… if it were my shirt." He grinned and his white teeth lit up his face like someone had turned on a torch.

"Not your blood or your shirt, is anything actually yours?" I asked.

"This brekky is mine."

"And you're welcome to it, you and the other five blokes that are gonna help you eat it all."

"Hahahahahaha." The laugh was pure and natural, and I think it surprised him as much as it did me. He looked me up and down, slowly, like he was reading a notice board.

"You're a tall fella for the army. Where are they gonna hide you on operations."

"I was wondering that myself. I have been out in the jungle, twice now, but I haven't had to hide as yet."

"Be careful what you wish for pup, the green is still alive, and the trees speak Vietnamese." I looked at him quizzically and he smiled that winning grin again and I almost forgot about the arterial spray that cut across his nose and cheek like he'd been slapped with a raw steak.

"I'm in no great hurry to see the action, of course. I don't want anyone getting hurt."

"War is hell, haven't you heard, just try to do your job. They'll be plenty of poor bastards needing your services… too bloody many. "

"I understand."

He got up then, grabbing his coffee mug from the table as

he made his way to the end of the queue to the large coffee urn. I turned to watch him go, as did every other eye in the place – the show was just too bizarre to ignore. Beneath the US Army shirt, he wore a tattered pair of black pyjama pants like the Vietnamese wore, like the Viet Cong wore, like bloody everyone in Vietnam wore. His feet were wrapped in what looked like home-made bandages, frayed, and fraying with lines of cotton trailing behind him. The bandages were so soaked with blood, it looked a little like he was wearing red shoes. He walked across the mess floor as if it were covered in broken glass and needles. As he stepped gingerly he left bloody red footprints in the dust. The back of his shirt was wet with blood and sweat. He reminded me of those paintings of Christ after the flogging, only minus the thorny crown headgear. He returned with his coffee and had another for me.

"Thank you sir… thanks," I said and reached for the mug. The coffee was thick, black, and very sweet. He placed his on the table and lowered himself with a low groan. We sipped our coffee as the other tables started to clear. The kitchen staff were hauling the large, metal trays of dregs out into a back room where the cacophony of trays being washed and stacked could be heard above the general banter of the men. The soldiers were finishing up and scraping their trays into a large metal bin near the entrance. They piled them on a table, the cutlery chimed on the sides of a metal box. As they left. Golly, one of my "house mates", caught my eye and raised his eyebrows at me. I nodded and raised both thumbs from the tabletop. He nodded but looked unconvinced. He turned with his hands in his pockets and quickstepped to catch the others. My breakfast sat untouched, and he nodded at it.

"Not hungry?"

"No."

"The smell?"

"No," I lied. We sat in silence and drank our coffee until suddenly I reached across and proffered my hand.

"I'm Terry Shepherd," I said.

"Shepherd," he said thoughtfully, "Like the dog. I like dogs." He looked down at his black hand as if he was seeing it for the first time and he wiped it on the leg of his pants. I swear it came away just as black if not blacker after the wipe.

I took it in my hand, and we shook. I fought the urge to wipe my now filthy hand on my own pants leg. I thought it would be rude.

"Well Pup, if the offer is still open I might get you to take a look at my feet, I may have done myself a mischief. I need to clean up first. I'm heading to the showers. If you wouldn't mind grabbing your kit and meeting me at my tent in an hour that'd be ripper – if you've got time. I don't want to go to the medical tent – that place is fucking depressing."

"Of course," I said, "which tent is yours?"

"It's the one on the perimeter fence. Out the back of all the others. It's under a large pine. If you can't find it ask someone on their second tour. They'll know."

"Right," I said.

"They call me Lax. Actually, they call me a lot of things, but I only answer to Lax."

"Nice to meet you Lax," I said and I stood up from the bench. His eyes widened as I rose above him. Lax was a little man, probably 5'3" in bare feet and his feet, I found out, were usually bare when not bleeding and wrapped in bandages. I towered a foot and a half over him.

"Look at you. Look at us. Ain't we the pair Pup?" he said as he flashed that dazzling grin at me again. "Roll up, roll up. Barham's circus freaks are touring Vitenam." Lax turned and limped from the tent, leaving blood stains in the mud.

As I neared my tent I could see my fellow campers lying on their 'farters.' That was the name for the inflated mattresses we were issued. They made noises in the night with every roll. Some wizened old vet once described war, all war, as periods of boredom punctuated by moments of sheer terror. So far my war had been all boredom. My conversation with Lax had been about the most interesting thing that had happened to me since I'd arrived. We spent a lot of time lying on our bunks and chatting, especially if we had a late patrol as we did on this day. Camp duties and doing nothing was about the score. Maybe manning the perimeter and gun bunkers. I'd heard in the past the men would often spend the day drinking luke-warm beer, but the CO had put a two-can limit on everyone after a series of legendary incidents including some nong who dropped a purple flare down the ventilator shaft of B Company's command post. I kid you not. Without beer there was even less to do. As I entered our tent the boys all leapt to their feet.

"Hell's bells Shep, that was Lax you were talking to, the fucking Night Crawler. You had a conversation with the Vampire of Vietnam and lived to tell the tale," said Golly Hawkins, who was on his second tour and always the last bastion of camp lore and anecdote. Golly was a large, hairy bunyip of a man from far

North Queensland. His head was covered by a tightly ringed afro and a handlebar moustache that nearly covered his mouth. The hairy monstrosity must have weighed about three pounds. He liked to comb this shaggy mass daily and liked nothing more than drowning it in XXXX beer which he called 'Moustache shampoo' and 'Queensland's greatest export' after himself. We Victorians hated the stuff on principle more than anything else. Golly loved XXXX beer of course, but it was nothing to his unbridled passion for his moustache. In hindsight, I believe he liked the way it took the focus from his wonky teeth which, as "Balls" Lindesay once said, "looked like the tombstones in a long-abandoned cemetery". Balls was also a second-time tourist and slept noisily in the cot nearest mine. Ball's first name was Walter, and he believed his nickname "Billiard Balls" was derived from the champion billiard player, Walter Lindrum – their names being similar. Golly unkindly suggested that Balls received his name because he was forever with his hands in his pockets scratching them. Playing "pocket billiards". Balls refuted this heartily, but if the truth be told, he did spend an inordinate amount of time tending his orchestras. Counting, rearranging, and counting again.

Most of us had "jock itch" in this merciless Petri dish of a country. Vietnam was a holiday resort for the worst microbial life in evolutionary history. Most of the soldiery had long ago dispensed with wearing underwear as it created a warm wet climate for the bugs, biters, and bacteria. Even more disturbingly, undies were also a snug place for the leeches to hide. These buggers could grow to the size of cigars, and they made a bee line for your bum hole if you weren't careful.

The fourth of our Musketeers was a stocky, young Nasho Golly dubbed "Jungles" because he was thick, dense and green. He was around at the time I met Lax. We always seemed to have trouble keeping our newest member when I look back. There always seemed to be a new face in the tent. Jungles, the sweet, stupid and affable Northern Territorian was only with us for two months. He wasn't wounded as such; his story was far worse. One night while Jungles slept, breaking the night's peace with an open mouth snoring that sounded like a razorback pig with a chainsaw, a wasp the size of a Volkswagen found it's way through his battered and torn netting, crawled into his cool, wet mouth, bit the inside of his throat and nearly killed him.

"What are you on about Goll?" I said to the three gawking heads before me. Jungles had less idea of what Golly was talking about than I did, but then, Jungles, God love him, always had a little less idea of what was going on than those around him.

"That was Lax, the Biggy Rat, the *Hô Tinh*!" the last Golly pronounced "Hoating" in his nasal Queenslander orthoepy, as if it was something VC sailors did on the river during Tet.

"Lax is the original bogeyman Shep. I've been here nearly two years and I've only seen him no more than, say, a few times."

"He's the bogeyman Shep, the *Hô Tinh*. The VC scare their kids with stories about Lax. He's the king of the tunnel rats. The man's a ghost. He scares me shitless," Balls piped in.

"Even the Yanks are scared of him, ay. He never sleeps and they say he creeps through your foot lockers at night grabbing stuff he might need on his one-man patrols. They used to set up alarms and warning devices, tin cans that clattered in the night and shit, to keep him out like, but the vampire is too sharp for the lot of them."

"They couldn't keep him out," continued Balls. "In the end they just let him take what he wants."

"If anything goes missing in a US camp they say – 'Oooooh, the Night Crawler got ya!" Goll finished with an American twang that hit the mark pretty sweetly.

"Slow down boys," I said "You've never mentioned this bloke to me before and I've been here over a month. I've never even seen him before."

"Of course, you haven't – the guy is a riddle, wrapped in a mystery inside an enigma as ol' Uncle Winston used to say. Churchill may as well have been talking about Lax."

"They've probably got a photo of him next to bogeyman in the dictionary," Balls said.

"He prowls the jungle at night in his birthday suit carrying only a knife and he slides down the nearest tunnel slicing and dicing any enemy he comes across, ay."

"The Yanks say he drinks their blood if he can't find a decent meal beneath the ground." Balls again. Balls liked to add the macabre accents to Golly's twisted tale.

"He'll spend months underground and live like the VC do. There's tunnel networks all over fucking Vietnam – you know that much ay? From *Nui Dat* all the way to *Long Tân* and on to Cambodia. They reckon *Củ Chi*, over near Siagon, is so riddled with tunnels you have to watch were you step or else you'll fall through to fuckin' Shanghai!

"The Ginger beers (engineers) reckon they even found them leading all the way inside our wire!" said Balls.

"So Lax is a tunnel rat. I heard they only ever go out in teams, or at least pairs. Didn't one guy asphyxiate in a *Củ Chi* tunnel?" I asked.

"Dumb it down Dr Flagpole, we're not at your University now. Here we be simple folk," Balls said. Golly ignored him.

"Plenty have suffocated Shep. They build them so they shrink away to nothing, and you get stuck. Or they booby trap off-shoot tunnels that they are too crafty to go down. They're sneaky bastards all right. Some tunnels just collapse. They are constantly being pounded by the Yanks. They drop everything they might have left over from a mission on *Củ Chi*, just out of spite.

"Just about the whole VC army live in these tunnels. They live, root, shit, shave and squeeze out little VC underground. They even bury their dead in the walls. We can't get to them with bombs and shit, and they sneak up on you and bang, you've got an AK-47 in your swag – and you didn't even see him coming," said Balls. "They reckon some bloke found a small tunnel entrance, no bigger than a letterbox and they dropped a smoke bomb down it and bugger me if all these puffs of smoke started appearing all over the jungle from connecting tunnels and air holes."

"That's why we have guys like Lax to chase them where they live, ay." Goll again. "Lax is the King, the superstar – the nastiest rat of them all!"

"And here's the lanky Shep taking tea and bloody asparagus horse-doevers with him like he's the King of bloody England, with their pinky fingers pointing at the sky: God strike me," added Balls. Golly and Balls laughed heartily.

"What's a How-Ting?" asked Jungles who had been trying to follow the conversation but didn't get much passed Golly's butchering of Vietnamese.

"It's *Hô Tinh*," said Balls. "According to my little mate Truc, the interpreter with the ARVN, the *Hô Tinh* is a sort of monster the Viets scare their kids with. It's some sort of great, sabre-tooth fox with nine tails and it steals and eats kids who don't eat up all their fish heads and rice!"

"It's supposed to live in caves and change shape into a beautiful woman to lure unsuspecting knob jockeys like you, Jungles into girly bars to eat up your John Thomas!

"So, look out when on the town young fella, ay." Golly and Balls both laughed loudly at this. Jungles just looked perturbed.

"Right," I said, "we have a celebrity in our midst I see."

"Mate, you see nothin' – if you haven't guessed it yet this guy is bad news, ay."

"He's bat-shit crazy Shep," added Balls. "I'd be keeping well away from him." Golly went and stretched himself on his bunk, the mattress groaned and blurted as was its nature. He crossed his bare feet and called back:

"Chuck us a fag and a light will ya Ballzo, cheers mate?"

Balls flicked a pack of cigarettes off his cot toward Golly. He took a box of Redheads from his shirt pocket and tossed them to Golly who caught them in his out-stretched hand. As he lit I moved over to my cot where my recently assembled medical kit sat on the thin nylon blanket. Golly yawned, a little drowsy from his large breakfast, "The Yanks say he takes trophies you know."

"No way," said Jungles.

"Ey-yup. So, I hear."

"Bloody hell," said Jungles again in a hushed voice, "what trophies?" He had moved across the room and was sitting across his cot near the tent entrance. Sweat across his naked chest seemed to shimmer in the light. It was going to be a stinker of a day.

Golly continued. "You know how the Yanks are so gung-ho for body counts, as if the only way they can feel like they're winning the war over here is to have a 20 to one kill ratio – grunts to Gooks, you know."

"Ok," said Jungles.

"They make them up too," said Balls, "My mate Douglas reckons they blow some poor bastard into pieces and count the body parts as different KIAs. My mate reckons, by their figures, they'll have a kill count twice the population of Vietnam, Cambodia and half of China."

"And farmers and school kids and…" said Jungles, but Golly cut him off.

"Whether that be the case or not, some of the Aussie brass have these big bloody chips on their shoulders when it comes to the Yanks. They're desperate to prove we're pulling our weight over here and killing as many VC as we can. I heard that an Australian officer wanted to test Lax's credentials and asked him to prove his kill counts. He'd report his count to Lt Col Yolka. Yolka is the only fucker he'll talk to. This bloke put the hard word on Lax. Never a good idea. This was back in '65 or '66, I think."

"How long has the poor bugger been over here?" I asked.

"At least that long, I've heard he started in the 1st Battalion."

"Hells bells," I said.

"Any-waaaay…" said Golly with exasperation.

"They reckon Lax returned with a coffee bag bulging and dripping blood and shit all over the Officer's desk and when he looked in the bag it was full of index fingers, ay."

'Trigger fingers," said Balls.

"There was like a hundred in there, over a hundred."

"Why the trigger fingers?" asked Jungles. "They aren't going to be shooting anyone if they're dead, are they?"

"Fair point young fellow," said Balls. "Call it a metaphor."

"A what."

"A symbol. He was making a point."

"That's right," said Golly. "In the middle ages when the Poms caught French archers. The guys with the long bows, they would cut they're index and middle fingers off. To make a point. The long bow takes a bit of muscle, and you can't pull a long bow without these two beauties, ay?" Golly held up his index and middle fingers. "Hey Pommy bastards – up your clacker, I've still got mine!"

Jungles laughed at this and rolled back on his bed.

"That's rubbish," I said smiling, "about Lax taking fingers I mean."

"I get that from an impeccable source my willowy friend."

"What, the bloke who sent him out told you? I doubt that very much."

"Let's just say a good reporter never reveals his sources, ay," said Golly with a wink.

"You know he's a captain?" said Balls.

"No way," I said as I threw my pack over my shoulder. I was starting to regret chatting to Lax. I was enjoying a quiet war and I didn't need a psychopath, one who possibly collected index fingers; anywhere near it. Especially a psychopath who was an officer.

"He's a captain, I swear to God," said Balls.

"So, this mad bastard who lives underground cutting fingers off was made a Captain? Who would have promoted him?" I asked.

"The story goes, in the early days he was a private, but he was showing exceptional abilities in some areas of soldiering, but let's say he was falling down in some of the others. There was this Staff Sergeant they called "Fritz" McCarthy I think. Apparently the boys called him Fritz because he was such a Nazi with the rules and regs. A proper prick I'm told. Anyway, he was this big fella and he thought he could smack Lax into line a little. He was just a thug; little blokes always have to watch out for those types. Some pricks are born bullies and stay bullies until a bigger fish comes along." I wanted to add that tall, skinny fellas also had to watch out for these types as they get a perverse kick out of taking down the biggest guy in the room. I've met a few in my time. A couple of the sergeants at Puckapunyal fit this mould.

"So, this fella wakes up early one morning with an itchy lip and without opening his eyes he sticks his tongue on it and something little and hard stings it. He flies out of bed to find his cot absolutely crawling with scorpions. Nasty, bitey, and there's literally hundreds of them, all over him. He screamed bloody murder, but his tongue has already swollen to the size of an apple and all he can do is make a sort of a loud grunt. It was enough to wake the other blokes in his tent. They all scramble out into the dirt and the sergeant, his eyes bulging apparently, takes out his Zippo and sets fire to his cot. The other blokes have to grab him and hold him down as it looks as though he's trying to set fire to the whole bloody tent. Turns out they'd gotten into his shirt and shorts, and he was covered in stings, even some of the blokes holding him down got stung. He had to be medivacced out in a Huey and on to Australia, never to grace the drab green again. No-one knows who did it. The fucker must have been collecting scorpions for a month. The CO made Lax a captain the very next day. He'd worked out they had a secret weapon, one who didn't need to be taking orders from anyone but the top brass, and even then, only if very careful."

"Well, thank you for that riveting tale Balls my good friend, right before I have to sew up the bogeyman's feet," I said.

"We're just saying be careful with this one Shep. His cheese might just have slipped off his cracker, ay," said Goll.

"And the three of us are sick of finding decent, God-fearing Christian blokes to fill that fourth bed." added Balls.

"I appreciate the thoughts gentlemen," I said as I swung the medi backpack across my shoulder and rose to leave. Jungles piped up as I was going out the door.

"Where does Lax come from, is it some middle eastern name or something?"

"It's short for Lax-ative. Lax. I hear some of the guys started calling him Lax and he quite liked it. It's better than "The Vampire", ay."

"They call him Laxative because he's the one they go to when there some shit that needs to be cleaned out," said Balls.

"He spends all his time down the 'S' bend, ay," added Golly.

"Well, that's bloody delightful isn't it?" I called as I made my way passed our tent.

"Hey Shep!" Golly yelled.

"What?" I yelled back.

"If you don't come back can I keep the photos of your

Rosemary – just for personal use you understand." I didn't bother replying although I could hear the three of them tittering like schoolboys.

It took me another twenty minutes to find Lax's tent. Most guys I asked had never heard of him, others recalled him with a shudder but didn't know where his tent was. I finally crossed an old hygiene sergeant, he was probably only 30, and when I ask him for directions he asked me in an apprehensive voice.

"What do you want with him?" I said I needed to treat a wound he was known to have, and he looked at me gravely.

"He's down at the end of the perimeter where the fences meet at a large pine. In and out son, you got me? Don't hang around with this one, right? He's not the full complement if you know what I mean," and he tapped his temple twice. I looked at him gravely and said,

"Thank you Staff Sergeant." As I strode away I heard the old guy muttering to himself. Lax's tent was at least 100 feet from everyone else. This was a guy that liked his "me" time.

Once I was set on the trail it wasn't too hard to follow the bloody footprints that led to the open flap of his tent. It sat, as he had said, in the cool shadow, well a slightly cooler shadow, of a large pine tree which seemed to be the only one on the whole base. I peered into the tent, and although filled with all manner of things, it appeared devoid of people, vampires or *Hô Tinhs*. There were back-packs piled high, NVA helmets, weapons of all shapes and sizes, none of which had been turned in to the MPs who usually had to count all weapons seized, especially enemy hardware. On one table was a pile of papers and maps that appeared to reach halfway to the roof. These were weighted down with what looked like an AK-47. Lax was like a bower bird, adorning his home with every shiny thing that took his fancy.

It was then I heard soft retching sounds coming from the back of the tent. I popped my head around through the rear flap to see Lax, most of his back to me, retching over a hole he'd dug between his accommodation and the perimeter fence. He sounded terrible. He was completely naked except for what appeared to be fresh bandages on his feet. His body was skinny and pale, but wiry, the underlying muscles looked hard and sinewy. He'd washed a lot of the crap off his body since I'd last seen him. He was cleaner but not sparkling. I came to understand Lax rarely sparkled, except his eyes. Lax liked the dirt, the earthy smells. He could hide beneath them. They were important in his line of work.

"Excuse me sir," I said, "Are you alright?" I spoke loudly, but Lax didn't flinch. He knew I was behind him before I spoke.

"Yup. I'm good. Nearly there." Lax said hoarsely. He turned. Lax's skinny body was a lattice work of small scars and wounds. Some of which looked to be bleeding still. I wondered how much blood this little man must have left; rivulets of blood ran down the back of his legs. Since we met he had done nothing but leak. I could see his stomach pop and lock as he struggled to keep it under control.

"It's that breakfast I had. This western food, my gut is just not used to it."

"You ate a lot, sir," I said.

"Pup. Forget the sirs will ya, call me Lax."

"But I heard you're a captain."

"Who told you that?"

"They did," I said.

"They talk a lot don't they."

"They do Lax." He looked up at me and I smiled.

"I think I need a few sutures, there's a few spots I just can't seem to get to. You ever tried to sew the bottom of your feet. It's bloody impossible." Lax limped into his tent and he lay down on his cot. He had two deep puncture wounds in each buttock. They had been cleaned but looked red and angry. He also had four or five in his thighs. His feet when I finally got to them were punctured in a dozen places. Some of the wounds were quite deep too, his feet were the worst. They were all starting to show signs of infection. I believe I have mentioned that Vietnam was a great one for infections.

He stretched out on a thick, plastic body bag he had placed on his cot to keep it relatively clean. He rose up on his elbows and nodded at me.

"Do your worst Doc. I'll try not to squeal."

RAT

I found Lax to be delightful company. He didn't feel the need to play the pantomime villain with me and my questioning of his wounds, as I sewed him back together, opened Pandora's box. I was still a little wary. From what the boys had told me this strange little Dr Jekyll, who lay on his stomach on an army cot, barely flinching as I pushed my needle into his skin, might yet discover his Mr Hyde. I never saw the dark, not in the whole time I knew him. What he saw in me and why he decided to let me in though, I'll never know.

Lax had been away for three weeks on his latest mission – most of that time was spent beneath ground in the tunnels around *Xuyên Môc*. He was chasing a large company from D445 Provincial Mobile Battalion, hard-line North Vietnamese army. Lax told me he wouldn't eat for two days before a mission to cleanse his body of Western smells.

"They have dogs under there you know. They sniff you out. I once had a small dog follow me around for a couple of weeks after I fed him. He used to warn me about booby traps. He could smell them. He used to lead me around underground. The dog walking the owner." He laughed at this.

"Never gave it a name but it was a ripper. Took off after a rat one day and I never saw him again. Lot of rats under there. They get into the food stores or gorge themselves on the dead. The Cong often bury their dead in the cave walls."

"I've heard that," I said.

"A Vietnamese soldier can smell an Australian soldier from 100 feet away if the wind is right, just by their meat diet. They tell me they can smell a US grunt up to a mile away with the toothpaste, deodorant, and aftershave. They don't need their noses to know where the Yanks are either because you can hear them from miles off. They make a hell of a lot of noise."

Lax said he would often have to move quickly when he could hear jets above him, it often meant bombs would be a dropping and the bombs didn't discriminate.

"Napalm was the worst; the firestorm would suck all the air from the tunnels and people would just suffocate. I found whole families, once, the best party of a squad. Still, it was a better way to go than being struck by Napalm which melts the bloody skin. I pray there's a hot place in hell for the bastard that invented Napalm." Lax said he hadn't eaten for days when I met him in the mess that morning.

"I usually eat what I find underground, or from friendly farmers. Even the Cong are doing it tough at the moment. There's very little food around. The defoliant spray has destroyed so many crops that people are starving – and not just the enemy. If the farmers do get something to grow it is taxed (stolen) by the NVA and shipped North." Lax said he sometimes led some of the farmers to underground grain stores after he had cleaned out the enemy.

Lax had been on his way back to camp when he came across a tunnel system. "I had this tunnel I often used to sneak into camp."

"There's a what?" I said with honest surprise.

"It beats getting shot at by some green, jumpy nasho kid who thought he'd heard a noise."

"Are you telling me you have a tunnel that comes under the wire."

"I am, but that information stays strictly between us both OK! Remember, I know where you sleep." Lax didn't wink and I didn't smile. He continued, "The VC forces had pulled back quite a way. I thought I'd report back to the boss. I'd been out long enough and felt like I could use a cooked meal. Wasn't that a mistake? It was very quiet out there which often means the enemy are massing and planning. I heard some movement and voices underground," he said.

"You often hear whispers and noises from above, muffled like, through the earth. These whispers were as clear as day. If I'm that close to the Cong I can usually smell the *nước chấm*, you know, that spicy fish sauce they like to mix with their rice." I didn't know of it; I was still new to the country. I had been lucky enough not to meet the enemy. I was in no great hurry too either.

"I could hear a slight scratching and I finally realised they must be in a tunnel running parallel with the one I was in," Lax said, "he must have been very close; I could hear them whisper." Lax said he grabbed the sheathed knife he had taped to the small of his back. He tore the tape off slowly, well aware that if he could hear the Cong, they would be able to hear him. He hoped their whispers would drown any noise he might make. He moved forward, about 20 feet, beyond the two voices and attacked the wall between the two tunnels with long, deep pulls on his knife. Finally, he breached the wall. He made the hole big enough to climb through. He found himself behind two very surprised VC in an adjacent crawlspace. "They were heading toward our perimeter. They took off on their bellies, yelling and carrying on and I went after them only to discover I'd come up between the two at the front and another at his rear." He discovered his mistake when his right foot was speared with a sharpened piece of bamboo.

"I'd missed one little prick in the dark and he came up behind me with a long, sharpened bamboo pole he'd been running up to the forward pair as a digging tool. I'd found myself caught between those escaping in front and this guy with the pole at my rear. Now, you can't turn around in the tunnels and I realised if the bastard behind me was able to yell to the Nogs up front, I could get caught between them. Goodnight Irene! I had to back up quickly and hope to get back to my hole between the tunnels. Then I could turn around. Bamboo boy wasn't too happy about this and started pokey, pokey with the sharp end screaming blue and bloody murder. I had a gun in a small bag tied around my foot, and I was a bit worried he might find this too. I usually had enough line on it so I could back up over her and grab it in a pinch. I still didn't have room to open the gun bag, it was very, very squeezy in this one. I still had my knife, but it was in my hand. No good in the tight space with the enemy behind me. I had to keep backing up and all the while he was poking me with that bloody stick. I was a bit worried he'd hit my tackle or even worse, shove it up my bum and rupture my bowel or something. Wouldn't that be glorious? They were the choices. Finally, we backed up far enough and I was back at the hole I came through. It was pitch black, but I could feel the light change of breeze on my face. I think he'd decided to get the hell out and the poking had finished thank God. I could hear his grunting and shuffling. I was able to squeeze me legs through and turn around.

"Now Pup, I had a choice. I could get away through my tunnel or I could take off after the bastard that had been trying to shove his stick where the sun don't shine. It was still a bit tricky as I knew there were two Nogs behind me and they might have climbed out of the tunnel, armed themselves and could be coming back my way to find their mate. Number three had taken off at pace, but I thought I could catch him before he made his way out. I really didn't have a choice because if the bastard made the light he'd just wait up there until I showed my head and then he'd lop it off. I needed to chase and catch him before he got too far. I kept the knife in my hand and crawled as fast as I could. The tunnel opened up a little the further I went, and I was able to even get onto all fours. I felt like the tunnel was heading slightly upward and I knew we were heading out. I usually move through the tunnels feeling for offshoots and trap doors, but I didn't have time to mess around. If there was a booby trap he knew about and I didn't, I was stuffed." Lax said he turned a slight bend in the tunnel and felt a light breeze on his right ear.

"I sensed movement. I stopped dead and I felt the bastard's arm come straight passed my face. His knuckles brushed my nose. There was a trap door in the wall of the cave, and he was waiting for me. He must have heard me and timed his attack almost perfectly. Almost. I was nearly skewered. He'd found a knife from somewhere, probably hid it for just such an event. Always pays to be prepared as the Boy Scouts say. I was lucky. He wasn't."

"What did you do?" I asked, pausing from the stiches. The

story was riveting, and I was finding it hard to concentrate on my sewing.

"I had his arm and knew his neck would be somewhere in the vicinity. I still had me knife. We grappled and grunted. He was brave." I didn't press him.

"I stuffed him back through the trap door," Lax continued. "Now I had to decide if I crawled back the way I'd come they might be waiting for me in the tunnel, and if I kept going forward I could come out into the light and be shot trying to squeeze through if they had come overland. Did they take the low road or the high road and who would get to Scotland first? I decided it'd be pretty easy for them to just wait for me on the outside with a bead on the tunnel entrance and pick me off from a distance. That's what I'd do. Fighting in a dark tunnel was not for the faint-hearted. I couldn't wait them out of course. I was leaking from a few too many spots and I needed to sew them up, or the ones I could get too anyhow. If I passed out in the tunnel that would be it. I decided to bolt forward and meet them on the outside." Lax said he knew the other two would try to find their mate. Even if he was dead.

"The VC are under orders to recover the dead. They know it pisses off the Yanks. They love the kill count. The VC even go into battle with loops of rope through the legs of their pants. If they get shot the others can just reach down, grab on, and drag them out. It's why you see blood trails and no KIA." Lax said he leapt through a small tunnel opening which had been concealed in the mouth of a small overhang. He almost accepted he'd get pinged.

"I came out in a small, short cave. This was a stroke of luck as it was dark and made it hard for anyone to see into it. I was lucky they weren't there, so I hid nearby and waited, just in case they came back. I watched the trail and tried to tend to myself a little. Much later they came sneaking back along the track. They had the body of their mate with them. I guess they had decided I had taken off.

"The NVA regs crept from cave opening and into a small break in the jungle canopy. The ground was bathed in silvery moonlight shining on the wet mud. The man at the back was lugging the dead guy on his shoulders, the guy at the front was smelling the air. They must have waited down there hoping the night would cover their getaway". Lax was able to get in behind them.

"I got lucky," was all he would say. "I decided to head back to the Dat and get some tucker. I'd had enough." He turned from his cot to look at me.

"At some point after that I bought a cow with magic beans, climbed a bean stalk, stole a magical harp and met a giant in the mess tent who is currently sewing me back together."

"The Brother's Grimm have got nothing on you mate. What a story." I was pulling silk through a wound in his feet and looked up to see Lax up on his elbows staring at me thoughtfully.

"I didn't mean you were making it up mate. Just it was an amazing story." Lax raised his hand.

"It's all good Pup. Not sure why I told you. Maybe you're just a good listener. There's not many left. Most people spend listening time thinking about the next time they get to speak."

"That is very true mate," I said.

"You know the difference between a fairytale and war story

Pup?"

"What's that?"

"A fairytale is a story remembered over many, many lifetimes."

"Yeah," I said as I pulled the thread through his foot, "and a war story?"

"Will take a lifetime to forget." He nodded.

"When all this shit is over PUP a lot of people are going to have to forget a hell of a lot of stuff... or take it to the grave."

Lax spent the next two weeks on his stomach in his cluttered tent trying to heal. He refused to go to the infirmary, and so, I became the nursemaid to the bogeyman. I suppose everybody could sleep more soundly knowing Lax was not going through their stuff in the middle of the night. I took him three square meals a day unless I was out on patrol or dolling out medicines and healthcare in nearby villages, and generally trying to win the hearts and minds of the population. When I wasn't able to get to him I asked the surly hygiene sergeant to drop some food in, a role he accepted with great reluctance. He refused to enter Lax's tent and left plates of food on the ground at the tent flap. He'd announce in a loud voice, "Come and get it!" then march away double time. He wanted to spend as little time as possible near the vampire. Lax said he had to get moving when he'd hear the call if he wanted to get anything to eat. Downpours could explode from even the clearest skies creating rivers that would wash his meal away. Or there were the jungle rats, some as big as bread loaves. They would sneak in through the fence and make off with every last crumb. Lax said he would often leave the rats to the food; he wasn't a big eater and he reckoned, "We rats need to look out for each other."

I spent a lot of time with Lax over those two weeks, and then right up until I was shipped home. This was the cause of quite a bit of consternation with my company I can tell you. Everybody, even the officers, were scared of him – and even some of the guys looked at me with narrowed eyes as the word got around that I was consorting with the vampire. Lax couldn't have given a tinker's cuss of course – this guy didn't go out of his way trying to win any Aussie or US hearts and minds. Any Vietnamese on the base, interpreters, or the occasional South Vietnamese soldier (the Australians had a hard and fast rule about letting non-combatants into camp, it was too hard to know who's side they were on) would turn and practically run from the sight of him. They knew he was a *Hô Tinh*, the nine-tailed fox, with needle like teeth who might pounce on them and tear out their throat

I just liked him. I liked him a lot. He was indeed an enigma. Lax had a savage intellect with a sense of humour much too dry for that soggy country. He had a directness born of not having to deal with societal norms and mores which would have scared most people off even before he became a dreaded myth. He was direct and seemed to have very little time for people. An impenetrable veneer he allowed very, very few to pierce. He dispensed great wisdom without any understanding of its importance. He was untamed and untameable and totally unsuited to Army life and yet he had enlisted as soon as he could and was now deep in his fourth tour. The rumours and sideways glances never seemed to faze him. He spent next to no time with other people yet had an innate understanding of human nature and its motivations. It all made him such a formidable weapon. An assassin. He was the last rays of sun before night and in the next sentence he became the darkness before dawn.

There was a fatalism to him, that I found really disturbing though. I came to understand that Lax had decided he would die in Vietnam. He would continue to do his work until the country was ready to take him.

OFF

She ain't got no money,
Her clothes are kinda funny
Her hair is kinda wild and free,
Oh, but Love grows where my Rosemary goes
And nobody knows like me.

I hated that song. It was performed by an English pop band with the preposterous name of Edison Lighthouse, and it was pumped through the repatriation hospital speakers throughout that 1971 I spent trying to move my right hand and get used to a new depth of field. The former was all frustration. The latter, a constant headache that would have killed a small horse. I think the radio stations played that dreadful song on permanent rotation just to shit me. Love might be growing where my Rosemary was going, but it was a sad fact that she'd left nothing growing in me but resentment.

Nobody knows where MY Rosemary went.

Rosemary and I married in a Sydney registry office, just near Circular Quay. It was barely two hours before I climbed aboard HMAS *Sydney* bound for the mysterious South Eastern Asia. Tying the knot had been my idea. I wanted to make sure, if I were to be killed in Nam, Rosemary would be taken care of. A widow's pension or something. Unfortunately for Rosemary, I survived – goodbye Government handout.

We spent the time calling her mum and dad, and my mum, with the good news. Her parents, Lily and Kulap and her teenage sister Iris, seemed happy enough. My mother – not so much. We drank gin mixed with cans of Tarax lemonade – "Be a Top Man, Drink a bottle or a can" – and eating fish and chips from a newspaper. We also shared a joint she'd kept for the occasion. We even consummated our nuptials in the back seat of my white roofed, green-grey Holden EH that was quite a bit more rooted than I was on that cold Sydney day. The combination of a lack of privacy, the weed and some passing joggers made sure I was in for a good time not a long time on our 'momentous' day. Later we sat looking at the Opera House, me in my army fatigue wedding suit, Rosemary in a white cotton dress and white boots. She was breathtaking. My Aussie/Thai princess.

We sat down near the Rocks, by the water in view of the Bridge. We made all sorts of plans. She would wave me off and take the Holden back to Melbourne the next day.

She determined to get pregnant the day I returned from the war. I wondered aloud if it were a good idea for Rosemary to have a baby.

"ROSEMARY'S BABY!" I needled. "Not the greatest omen. Read the book, see the movie and give birth to the devil's very own bub." She pooched her lips and threw the rolled fish and chip paper at me. Ira Levin's seminal horror novel was all the rage in the late 60s. We'd both read it at university. I read the whole book in two nights when I should have been studying. Rosie got three quarters of the way through and then left it in the sand on St. Kilda beach in the shadow of a quietly whispering palm, one hot summer's day. She finished it sitting on the floor in a bookshop on Acland Street two months later, oblivious to the dirty looks she was getting from the hatchet-faced woman behind the counter. I think a Roman Polanski's movie with Mia Farrow was released when I was in Nam. I've still never seen it. What with my marriage and the Vietnam war, I'd had a little too much horror.

Rosemary had borrowed her wealthy uncle's Polaroid camera to record our day. The grainy, white bordered, instant photos were a miracle of technology. We asked a schoolgirl to take some shots of us in front of the shimmering harbour. All three of us gathered around, shaking the images into life. Rosemary placed two of the photos beneath her glorious left cheek as she told me the heat would speed up the process. We made the schoolgirl's day. The girl and I had never seen a Polaroid photo before. Rosie took the girl's portrait as a thank you, and she was rapt. I took three of our wedding photographs and placed them in my shirt pocket. I told Rosemary I was placing them over my heart. We kissed and hugged, me bending low and Rosie on her tippy toes. We were blissfully oblivious to the smiles, stares, and the occasional wolf-whistle from departing troops. I boarded and stood with a hundred other men on the front of the ship, totally alone. I was homesick and I hadn't even left. I waved and blew kisses from the bow of the ship and was still trying to see my beautiful wife in the white dress as we passed through the heads. I kept those photos pinned to my tent and waited for her letters – she promised to write every day. I didn't even get a "Dear John", or a "Dear Shep" letter in my case. I corresponded nearly every week. I never received one in return. That was tough, I'm not going to lie. Some marriages go the distance, some marriages last seven years before the itching. My marriage lasted exactly four hours and thirty-three minutes, right up until I walked up the gangway to climb aboard the "Saigon Express". As I waved to my Thai Princess from the bow I'd become a wartime cliché. In Vietnam I started to get the picture, but you fight the truth for the longest time. In wartime our delusions are sometimes the only thing left to hold onto.

I was led to believe that marriage was forever – I don't know why. My father didn't share my view, nor did Sister Michael Aloysius Christ. Why did I think Rosie would? At first I blamed myself for going away. I blamed the bloody war for taking me away. Eventually, I lay the blame squarely at Rosie's feet. She was the one who refused to wait. Rosemary took my Holden that day as I sailed away.

I never saw either of them again.

I still miss that car.

MUM

Mum, the President of the Save Our Sons Fitzroy chapter, came to fuss over me in Hospital three times a week. It was about three times too many for me of course. My dorm mates loved her coming as she bought in freshly baked scones or pies and shared them around. My injuries had made Mum a bit of celebrity amongst the Save Our Sons women. I was a National Serviceman who came home maimed in an unjust war. The outraged women at the S.O.S. would bake, knit, and sew with all the indignation they could muster, and all the injured and maimed vets benefitted from their efforts. Sometimes some of the S.O.S. ladies would come in with her and they'd tsk and mutter and move from bed-to-bed clasping hands and occasionally weep. Mum would rail against the war mongers in the Government breaking up families and killing our sons. They would pray for the boys still over in Nam and the Vietnamese people being tortured and killed by the US and their allies. Some of the patients used to get quite upset and tell them to 'piss off', but not the boys in my dorm, they loved the extra food, the scarves, and quilts. They didn't like it when Mum bought the local catholic priest, Father Conlan, though. It wasn't his moralising or his preaching they objected to, but that the fact that, "The fat bastard ate all the bloody lamingtons," said an outraged Greg who remained at the Repat almost as long as me. I suppose the S.O.S. broke up the long and monotonous days of convalescence, but I hated them coming in.

Eventually we found out Colin had died in his sleep. He was the one with the terrible burns. Poor bugger just didn't have enough of his lungs working to get him through. A nurse finally confided to Greg who immediately informed the rest of us. Neil, the lieutenant, was moved on after a couple of months I think. There were plenty of others to come and go over the many long months I spent in that damned hospital. On a positive however, I didn't have to deal with Dr Keysor again after I hit him in the face with a bedpan. I know this made Greg's day.

We had a young fellow in our dorm who had lost both his legs after stepping on a Jumping Jack mine. These were Americans mines, laid by Aussie engineers, and repurposed by the VC. He'd been a bit of a football star apparently. Keysor had said something to him after a consultation, something along the lines of throwing away a possible VFL career by volunteeing to go to war. Dr K, I believe I've illustrated, didn't have the greatest bedside manner. The boy filled me in after I asked why he was so upset. This was a bit of a watershed moment for me I have to admit. Most of my time at the repat was spent so enveloped within my dark tunnel of self-pity I could barely hold a conversation. The young fellow took Dr Keysor's words very hard indeed. One night he tried to hang himself with a bedsheet. He had twisted it tightly and tied it to the thick metal bars of his bedhead. Then he rolled himself off. The sheet was too long though and he landed on the floor with a scream of pain as the stumps, that had once been strong and muscular legs, hit the cold tiles. We never saw that poor kid again. I don't even recall his name. I did however bide my time and when next I saw Dr Keysor I sconed him between the eyes with a bedpan I had requested and not needed. Dr K hit the floor. I believe I swore at him and told him if I ever saw him again the next bedpan would be full. It was an idle threat of course, I'm not a total barbarian. Still, a full bedpan would have been my *coup de grâce*. Greggy laughed so hard I thought he was going to have a coronary. His pure merriment startled everyone else in the room. They stared at the good doctor with mouth agape. A trickle of giggles grew to a torrent of laughter. Even the matron smiled and tried to hide her face behind a clipboard. In the face of this tumult Dr Keysor fled the room, a white knuckled fist to his forehead. Keysor refused to have anything further to do with me and I thought that was just fine. Greg asked if I would like to borrow his piss bottle for round two!

I remember that day clearly as the day I decided I would be able to get out of the Repat. That was the day I discovered there was still a little fight left in me. I also discovered I could hit a target with a left-handed throw! This was no small thing, I can tell you. Who would have thought Dr K would pull me through? God works in mysterious ways all right, That bastard Dr K lit the fire in my engine that pushed me forward with my life. Dr Bloody Keysor. I just wish I'd have had a box of scorpions to thank him properly.

Mum and I caught a train to the small weatherboard house in Fitzroy. My childhood home. At the station we were surrounded by a much smaller crowd on a Saturday morning than the usual peak hour crowd battling the morning commute. Thank heavens. It all seemed so alien. In Vietnam people were being burned, maimed, and killed while back in Melbourne life went on unabated – insular and oblivious. Skinny girls with bee-hive hairdos and Milady heels stepped around teenage boys with shirts untucked on a bird-speckled platform. There were tradesmen wearing soon to be muddied overalls standing beside men in grey suits with thin black ties and thick black glasses. Women wore slacks, young blokes wore flairs. There were Hush Puppies, T-straps and even the odd pair of Go-Go boots. There were sideburns and safari suits. Cardigans, cable knits, cravats, and Brent hats. Every second person pulled on a cigarette. A small circle of private school girls, in knee high socks and straw hats, passed a butt around their group. Practised looks of disdain. I wondered if the smoking was the reason for their Saturday attendance. On the whole, the throng were too busy bustling through their lives to notice the skeletal spectre with the large, black eye patch and useless right arm. Only the occasional commuter glanced my way. Mum buzzed around me like some demented wasp, flitting from my left to right as she shooed people away.

    I preferred the eye-patch to the glass eye as it mostly concealed the puckered scar that ran in a red lightning bolt from my left temple across my eye socket, cut a hard right and came to a stop on the point of my cheekbone. They had found me a glass eye startingly similar to my right eye, but its lifelessness depressed me. In the mirror all I could see was the lolling eye of a dead fish. I'd had a little plastic surgery on my scars and my ruined eyelid, and it had worked well enough, but I still felt a little like Dr Frankenstein's (or was he Mary Shelley's) creature. I was *Ho Chi Minh*'s monster.

"Make way there; you there, make way!" Mum shrilled as I bent to enter the crowded carriage. Mum made a young fellow give up his seat. He was choofing away on a hand rolled smoke and trying to manoeuvre a newspaper without clouting anyone.

Mum said in a sugary voice, "Would you mind if my son took your seat, as you can see, he's incapacitated." The guy was helpless to refuse. He inelegantly folded the paper, elbowed his mate and they both jumped up to let us sit. I was better standing really. My legs had healed well, but they were still long, bony, and hard to arrange in a crowded train carriage. I had to fold them into the aisle and re-arrange them at every stop. Blank-faced people had to climb over them. Sometimes they uttered exasperated *harrumphs*. From the train windows I could see a jellybean assortment of colourful cars pressed up to the boom gates. A sea of metal waiting for us to pass. I looked for my old Holden to pass the time. I carried a red TAA bag full of toiletries, undies, and socks. They were the few items of clothing Mum had bought in during my stay at the Repat. I'd kicked this under the seat and Mum had to get down on all fours to retrieve it. She did it with a lot of grunting, breaking the sullen silence of the commute. At Clifton Hill station she commandeered a conductor to make room for me to alight from the train.

It was about a three kilometre stroll from the station to our house on Little George Street. I caught every eye in Fitzroy. At six feet nine I was familiar with being stared at. I'd suggest very tall people even get used to it. Eventually the looks roll off your back. The dopey comments and puerile jokes take a little longer.

"How's the weather up there?" or "Thank God you're here I need something from the top shelf."

Years ago, I was standing with Rosemary in the Napier Hotel when one drunken dill, with a nose so battered with rosacea it looked to be glowing, asked if Rosemary was my girlfriend. He asked three times before I finally said, "Yes."

"Who put her up to it?" he slurred and his two fat, middle aged mates at the bar roared their approval and slapped each other on the shoulders. They told the same weak joke three times before we decided to find a new pub.

You never quite get used to the stupid questions…

"Do you have to get your shoes specially made?"

"Where do you buy your clothes?" and the ubiquitous "Do you play basketball?" which I started to counter with, "Do you play minigolf?" I also used to go with, "You know, up here I can see your hair is starting to thin a little." That tended to shut most of blokes up pretty quickly. My point is, it's just something you get accustomed to. "It is what it is," Mum used to say. At six feet nine it's your lot in life, you're gonna stand out. It didn't bother me so much. On the day I returned home from the Repat however, the first day of my new myopic life, the looks I was getting that day bit me deeply. I rolled with a staccato gate born of scarred thighs and months and months off my feet, through the streets of Fitzroy. I was self-conscious, of course. It was my first foray into my new world with an arm that hung lifeless from my shoulder. People stared, usually from a distance, or they averted their gaze, which was somehow worse. Old Greeks and Italians stared at me without compunction. It was their nature, and to be fair, they would probably have stared at me anyway without me moving like some re-animated, unwrapped, and elongated Egyptian mummy. The older they are, the more they stare, the entitlement of age. The Aussies sort of put their heads down and try to peek through their eyebrows. Kids looked at me as though the circus was in town, and I was about to start handing out free tickets and fairy floss. One chubby little girl holding her mother's hand even removed her index finger from a snot caked nostril to point up at me and declare, "Look Mummy, a pirate!" The mother almost froze with embarrassment as Mum sniffed loudly and pushed passed them. I wanted to smile at the mother to show I wasn't offended but I decided I'd better check to see what my smile looked like in the mirror before I flashed it at housewives and little round nose-pickers lest I haunt their dreams.

Mum was beset with a maternal zeal that was almost as mortifying as the rubbernecking. With her head held high, and through a pair of austere diamond shaped glasses, Mum tried to catch the eye of every gawker, man, woman, and child. She was coiled like a tomcat and waiting to pounce. On Gertrude Street her head was on a swivel and if looks could kill she would have laid waste to a couple of dozen at least. As we passed the open double doors of the TAB, a couple of young blokes in skin-tight jeans and open shirts, laughing loudly at some private joke, burst through the ticket strewn doorway, and nearly bowled her over.

"Watch how you go there!" Mum spat viciously.

"Sorry honey," he said pulling up so quickly, his friend, who was stuffing his shirt pocket with a recently purchased betting slip, cannoned into his back.

"Jeeyzus mate," he said around a cigarette held loosely between his lips, and shielding his eyes from the late morning sun as he looked up at me,

"What the fuck happened to you?"

"Language!" said Mum in her haughty school mistress voice.

"My son was injured fighting for his country in Vietnam."

"Fuck me," he said, ignoring her admonishment.

"You should see the other bloke," said his mate at the back and the first guy guffawed and nearly lost his cigarette.

"What would a couple of potty mouthed layabouts like you both care about good young men dying on foreign soil?" said Mum, her voice rising to a shrill crescendo that even tore the attention of the crowd in the TAB from their form guides. This was the voice, I came to discover, that was held in rapturous wonder by her small group of Save Our Sons devotees.

"Potty mouth!" said the first indignantly, "Well I never," he elbowed his mate who chuckled.

"You're a layabout Col – she got you in one!" They sauntered off to a 'baby-poo' coloured Valiant parked a little way down the street. They climbed in without another glance. Mum was furious and the rest of our walk home involved her storming forward and then waiting impatiently for me to catch her up. She was spoiling for a fight. I, however, wanted to climb into a bed I hadn't slept in for over three years, pull the covers over my aching head and stay there until Christmas. My first steps into the world as an invalid weren't going very well.

Finally, halfway up Little George Street, Mum held our small, mewling wire gate open for me and I shuffled through into the front yard of our little single-fronted weatherboard which was starting to look its age. Agapanthus strained purple and violet against the wire of the front fence and Mum cleared them back with the sweep of the gate. The wood panels on the porch looked like a mouthful of greying teeth. The veranda was listing ever so slightly to the right. Still, the sweet smell of Mum's magnolia by the front step bought me home as did the liquid amber that was, now, much too big for this small yard. I swung the TAA bag onto my shoulder and reached to steady myself on its sturdy trunk. Ricky and I used to sit in this tree most Saturdays, just for something to do. Ricky used to spit on the ground when someone came along and would apologise to the startled pedestrian and declare he had not seen them coming. I remember he actually spat on our neighbour Mrs Tranquilli's woollen hat and she shuffled down the street unaware. We laughed until we cried at this; God knows why, it wasn't that funny. I don't know why Ricky did half the things he did, he was just a strange kid I suppose. I patted the trunk and felt a lightening of my soul on the memory. It was sort of nice to be home again.

"Oi! Hello there!" A loud Scott's brogue raised me from my woolgathering. Mr Heath from across the road had been concealed on his hands and knees pulling weeds from a manicured lawn. He stood up and yelled over his short front hedge; he must have heard the gate.

"Is that young Terry? Why it is!" he called, "How're you doing lad, so good to see you're back?"

"Mr Heath," I called back, half turning. I meant to wave but my right arm was having none of it.

"He's very tired now Dougal," my mother said loudly, "it's been a big day."

"Of course, it has, of course it has," he yelled with empathetic nods. "You go on and rest son. Just wanted to pass on my best. Some of us are proud of you, young boyos over there. Don't you forget it." Mum waved over her shoulder as she manoeuvred through the gate which caterwauled loudly and clanged closed behind her. She hustled past me grabbing the TAA bag and made her way up the two concrete steps to the front door. I was a little surprised to see her stop and take a front door key from her small handbag. She had started locking the door. Well, I suppose she had been on her own for a while. Still, not sure why she'd have bothered. There had always been very little to steal inside.

The house hadn't changed. The hall rug was a little more threadbare and it may have smelled a bit more perfumed than I remember, a smell of soap and cheap perfume that I always thought of as an old lady smell. The house was dark, cold, and choked with memories.

"Go sit in the lounge Terry," Mum said, leaving the morning's angst on the other side of the door. She was just Mum again, not an avenging angel of death. "I'll go and make you a sandwich. I have some lovely silverside from last night. Unless you'd like something hot, I could do some eggs?"

"I'm right thanks Mum, don't fuss," I said as I made my way into the loungeroom and headed to the couch.

"Terry," she said with a little of that earlier timbre in her voice when setting the young blokes on Gertrude Street straight, "You need to eat. I can guess that hospital food might be hard to stomach, but my boy, you're wasting away to nothing. I'll buy good, healthy food and I'll be cooking it. All you have to do is eat it and get yourself healthy. Now Terry, I don't want you to come home to an argument, but I want no contrariness on this one, do you understand."

I smiled and said, "Well then, I'd say you've talked me into it. A silverside sandwich would be bloody lovely, as long as it comes with pickles."

"Yes, I have sweet mustard pickles, but you can forget the swearing in this house, or it'll be coming with Keen's mustard for your tongue and very little else."

"Righto," I laughed, "silverside and pickles, hold the potty mouth."

"That's right," she said as she flicked the overhead light on. "How's the pain, are you feeling OK after the walk from the train."

"I feel OK Mum. They gave me some meds this morning and they're still good to go." In truth, I hadn't taken anything. I'd been avoiding everything but a couple of aspirin when the pain was really bad. I'd been months and months on all sorts of things, and I wanted to get a break from it all or I might never have had a normal bowel movement again. It's probably why I'd been eating so little, I always felt full. The pain was manageable. The constipation was frustrating.

"Are you cold?"

"Nah, it's not too bad."

"It's a bit chilly. I'll get a fire going after the sandwich. There's a blanket on the couch. Put it over your knees for now. Better still, lie down on the couch and rest. Yesterday's newspaper is on the table – I grabbed it from the milk bar yesterday morning. I haven't been able to get today's. I haven't done the crosswords or found the Hook yet, so get to it if you feel up to it."

"No worries. Want to have a squizz at the Lions team too, so that'll be beaut."

"Good oh, we've got the Bombers at the Junction Oval," she said. "Take it easy and I'll be back in two shakes of a lamb's tail. Would you like a cuppa too, I'll pop the kettle on?"

"A cup of tea would be nice. Thanks Mum."

"Milk and two sugars coming up."

I decided I might handle the fire and I made my way over to the hearth. I grabbed a box of matches from the mantle and came face to face with myself. A fresher, newly married Terry, dressed in jungle greens, a floppy hat on his head, peered out at me with two bright, green eyes. The photograph was in a little silver frame. It had to be one of the shots Rosemary had taken with her uncle's camera in Sydney before I left. Yes it was, I could see the edge of the Harbour Bridge in the background. Mum must have heard from Rosemary. This was an interesting development, I thought. She'd never mentioned Rosemary during my whole stay in the Repat. I decided to ask her "later-Ron". I attempted to get down on my knees and grab some of the smaller sticks from the small pile of wood in the curved metal bowl beside the fireplace and my thighs screamed their dissent. My legs began to shake. I wasn't ready to get down on my knees as yet. Good to know. The fire would have to wait for Mum.

I sat on the couch behind more than one newspaper. They were strewn across the coffee table. Interestingly, Mum had been buying the *Sporting Globe* as well, its pink pages peeped

from beneath the white of the *Sun News-Pictorial*s. I lifted it
and saw one of the *Globes* was open to the horse racing. Mum
had been working the guide, circling horses she liked in Biro.
This was a side to Mum I'd never seen. She never had a punt. I
found this slightly disquieting without any idea why. I suppose
in Vietnam we create a vision of home in our heads and snap
off an internal Polaroid. Our focus is on our job and getting
home in one piece. I spent well over a year in hospitals, a time
dilation where it slows to an excruciating crawl. We forget that
time is still moving forward around us, people are changing.
To prove this point, I turned to the front page of the paper.
The Sun, Friday July 21st, 1972. There was a story about the
Aboriginal Embassy being torn down in Canberra. I didn't even
know we had an Aboriginal Embassy. I'd have thought it was
a good idea to have an Aboriginal Embassy. Others obviously
didn't. I was careful not to read anything about Nam. I really
had lost my appetite for that shit-show. I'd always read the
paper back to front, ever since I was a kid. Frankly, I was just
more interested in the sport than the events of the world. I was
almost pleased that, having spent the last three years swallowed
in world events that I'd still rather see what was happening
in the footy before I was smashed with the world's various
miseries. Citizens crushed in cars, robbed at knifepoint, or
blown to pieces in faraway lands. I flipped to the back of the
paper. The world and Vietnam be damned, I want to see who
was playing for the Roys. I glanced across at the folded blanket
on the couch and decided I'd take her advice. I grabbed it and
spread it across my lap and bony knees, feeling for all the world
like an imposter. A lad of 25 pretending to be a grandma with

a shawl over his legs. I can imagine what Golly Hawkins and Balls Lindesay would say about this. Well, bugger them, they weren't there, and I was bloody freezing. Mum was probably right; I needed some insulation on my bones.

The back page announced in bold, san serif that Fitzroy ruckman Russel Crowe may be dropped for the game against Essendon. I didn't read the article as this was yesterday's news after all and the coach might have changed his mind after a large dinner and good night's tossing, turning, and pondering. I flicked backwards through the pages until I found the Jeff Hook cartoon. Mum and I thought Jeff Hook a pure genius. He was the *Sun* editorial and political cartoonist and he summed up the day's big story in a beautifully rendered cartoon, often with a succinct and biting commentary. Mum thought he was the greatest cartoonist the country had ever had and that included WEG, who drew the VFL Premiership team mascot on a very collectable poster. I dreamed of WEG one day drawing a Lion's poster although, as we were perennial "cellar dwellers" the Fitzroy Premiership poster seemed light years away. Still, a boy could dream and WEG was my man. I did love to find the Hook with Mum though. Jeff used to hide a small fishhook in his daily cartoon and Mum and I used to take a few minutes scouring the cartoon for the squiggle. We weren't on our own either. Sometimes the whole of Melbourne slowed to a crawl until the Hook had been found. God knows what would happen to the state if he ever forgot to squeeze it in. The wheels of industry would grind to a halt. Today's cartoon was about the Aboriginal Embassy being torn asunder. Two Indigenous men were drawn in his loose black line, strolling passed

Government house before which a billowing tumult of flying arms, feet, tents, and police hats erupted in a dust cloud. One protagonist was saying, "They get stranded here by some travel agency in 1770, then act like they own the place." This cartoon was full of squiggly lines and I'm sure Jeff did this to make the pursuit of the 'hook' ever harder. He made you work for your reward. I found his 'hook' amongst the lines of the dust cloud in the melee, behind the two men in conversation.

"I found the hook!' I called out to Mum in a loud voice as the kettle burst into life with an anxious whistle.

"I found it!" was the gauntlet thrown down in the race to find the hook. You didn't point out where it was of course, that would spoil the other's search. You just smugly sat back, folded your arms across your chest and declared your superiority. This would often result in a closer and more feverish search of the panel. Mum often beat me to the punch and I'm a little ashamed to admit I, occasionally, proclaimed I'd found it without any idea where it was. Mum caught me out once or twice and it became a game between us. If I announced I'd found it she'd retort, "Are you fibbing again Terry?" but she'd double her efforts anyway. If she found it first I'd say the same. Sometimes we'd find it at the same time.

"Ahh, you're just pretending to have found it so that I come in and show you where it is." She'd changed the retort. I was going to have to get used to these little changes now I was home. She came into the room with a large sandwich on a plate and hot cup of tea.

"Why are you smiling?"

"Happy to be home I guess."

"It's so good to have you home Terry." Mum placed the sandwich on the coffee table and squeezed my knee.

"Oh Heavens, that didn't hurt did it?" Mum pulled her hand away like I'd tried to bite it.

"No Mum, all good. The knees are fine."

"Thanks goodness." She nodded and then said slowly, "Ahh Terry."

"Yeeees Mum."

"I just wanted to let you know…" She paused and looked to the ceiling as if carefully formulating a sentence.

"Yeah…" I said, a little warily.

"The hook is in the dust cloud, just next to the talking blackfella's right shoe. I found it first; I always find them first," and she spun around and went back into the kitchen.

"I don't think they like being called that Mum," I called.

"Who, what?" As she emerged into the lounge carrying a smaller sandwich and her own cuppa.

"Aboriginals," I said, "I don't think you're supposed to call them blackfellas – they don't like it."

"Oh, stuff and nonsense. Are they black?"

"I guess so."

"And are they fellas?"

"Not all of them. The women aren't," I said.

"Well, the two in the cartoon then. Are they fellas?"

"Yeeeeeah."

"Well then they're blackfellas, stop being silly." And she placed her tea and sandwich on top of the paper.

"Right then," I said, "We're staying in the 50s then I see," and lifted the tea to my lips. It was hot and sweet and warmed my insides.

"Stop your silliness. Righteo, let me see to that fire, it's freezing in here," she said. As she busied herself I took a large bite of my corned beef and pickles. It was delicious. The Repat food hadn't been terrible. It was a damn sight better than the army tucker in *Nui Dat* anyway. This bread was fresh and lightly toasted on the grill. Mum had cut it into thick slices. The meat was even thicker. The pickles were a bright, fluorescent yellow and scrumptious. Mum grabbed up her cup and saucer and sat heavily in her chair as the flames began to take hold in the small pile of sticks and paper she'd arranged in the hearth. She sat back and took bird-sized bites of her sandwich. The firelight illuminated the deepening lines around her mouth and eyes. Mum had aged while I was away. She had worry lines that I'd never seen before. I probably contributed to most of those. We ate in relative silence, she sipped, I slurped, and our sandwiches disappeared. Suddenly, she leapt up from her armchair.

"Oh heavens. What time is it?" Mum strode quickly across the lounge and turned on the radio sitting on the mantlepiece, beside my photograph. She checked her watch.

"I dunno?" I said.

"The girls and I have a quaddie going in the first at Flemington today. I'll just stick the wireless on."

"My mother the mug punter," I said, "This is new!"

"No mugs allowed," she proclaimed. "We have a system and we're doing very well indeed, I thank you very much."

"Oooh, so you're the punter that wins money, I heard there was one out there, but I had no idea my own mother was the tipping genius."

"Some of the girls in the S.O.S. got me involved. They study the form, and we are a little way in front."

"And do you confess this to your priest on a Sunday," I teased.

"I'll have you know that Father Damien gives us the best tips. He loves a punt. His father was a bookie up in Sydney, used to work at Randwick. Father Damien put us onto Silver Knight in last year's Melbourne Cup. We took him at 12 to 1 and cleaned up."

"Gosh and begorrah, I go away to war and my mother is dancing with the devil."

"Shush now, they're about to kick." The radio burst to life with the nasal twang of the race caller describing the scene as mounts were pushed into stalls.

"Who do you have so I can barrack along?"

"We need Short Order, the four horse," she said.

"Come on Short Order," I cried but she ignored me. The horses jumped and the twang raised at a feverish, inaudible garble.

I could hear the name Short Order only fleetingly and it sounded like it was gone for all money. Apparently, it swung wide on the final turn and charged to the line. All of a sudden, Short Order was the only name the caller seemed to know. Mum was staring at the radio with rapt attention as if it the thing was about to start spewing gold nuggets from its oval mouth.

"Come on Short Order. Come on girl. Come on!" she chanted rhythmically as the announcer's voice whined like the kettle.

"Short Order is flying wide down the straight. Summer Rain

and Black Soul are reaching for the line. Short Order may run them down here. It's Summer Rain now. Short Order is reaching. Summer Rain. Short order hits the line and it's Short Order by a nose and the cross."

"You beauty!" squealed Mum as she turned to me, her eyes wide and her fist clenched.

"Well done Mum," I said through a mouthful of sandwich.

"I told you there's no mug punters here, just four canny girls who know how to read the form."

"Don't forget the soon to be defrocked priest who is leading his congregation astray," I said.

"Lead away if he keeps tipping us winners, Short Order was one of his."

"I'm alerting the Pope."

"Oh, stop being jealous." The phone suddenly bawled into life in the kitchen and Mum looked me in the eye.

"That'll be Glenis. I better get it." And with that she grabbed the radio and the *Sporting Globe* from the table and flew into the kitchen where she stayed for the best part of the whole afternoon, and I didn't get to ask about Rosemary's picture of me and how she came by it.

I lay in my too-short bed that night, in my too-short room, and I tossed it all around in my head. It was my first night out of the Repat. I was trying to sleep without pain assistance, and it didn't go well. When I first hit the hospital, upon arriving back in Oz, sleep was a godsend for a body that desperately needed some quiet time to heal itself. All I wanted to do was sleep. For that first five or six months my sleep was more like a coma. Deep, dreamless sleep with moments of cloudy wakefulness. I was battling the infections which resurfaced periodically for the best part of that first year. Finally, the antibiotics began to wrestle the bugs into submission. Later still they wound back the pain meds. I started to sleep unassisted and this opened the door to some horrific nightmares. The nights became long, loaded, and lonely. I'd never had a problem being alone with my thoughts before I went to Nam. As a medical student, I walked backward and forward over text and lecture reinforcing everything I was being taught. The sleeplessness hit me on the back of some of the more harrowing incidents I experienced over there, and they just piled up with everything and anything that happened after. Like dear old Dad, lots of guys self-medicated with grog; the alcohol helped but was not a long-term solution. As a medic, I feared for those I could see using it as a crutch. I cautioned the boys I was closest too. Some took it well. Some told me to go forth and multiply.

   I always felt rushed over there, despite the long moments of boring nothingness. I never seemed to have enough time to compartmentalize everything I was seeing, experiencing and which bits I needed to excise. Cast them off before they embedded themselves. Some of my demons managed to track me down when I slept and I wrestled them in the wee hours. Before long I began to approach sleep with trepidation. Now I'd made it home to Little George I knew it was only a matter of time before they found the address. I spent hours in bed that night with my absent wife, my gone girl, Rosemary. I suppose I finally dropped off to sleep at about 4 am. I was sleeping in a comfortable single bed that had been extended with a wooden frame I slapped together myself almost ten years before. I tired of folding myself in to sleep with my knees bent, my feet pressed hard against the bed frame. I cut and taped up an old mattress and placed it on top of a wooden coffee crate. My longer bed made it hard to open my closet, but I never regretted the decision.

I felt like a time traveller in that room. I'd fallen through the portal and was surrounded by the flotsam and jetsam of adolescence. Pictures carefully clipped from newspapers, a shoebox full of footy cards, my first cricket bat. An old red capped fire hydrant cover stood beside my pillow on which a small radio alarm clock perched. Half of the room had been compulsorily acquired by Mum to store piles of musty, smelly clothing she was keeping for what, heaven only knew. They gave off a nasty camphor smell that I decided not to let bother me. I thought about Rosemary in that makeshift bed in Little George Street Fitzroy. Sleep finally shanghaied me. Trussed me up in ropes. The monsters crawled from the pit and I was back in Vietnam.

RAY

I'm broaching a small mound between two banana trees that bowed like John Wayne's legs above his pigeon toes. I look down the incline across a natural clearing of about 60 metres, just grass. Directly ahead of me I can see three diggers spread in a line, about ten metres apart. They walk slowly toward ugly, tattered rubber trees at the end of the dell. Blood is drumming behind my ears. I am a guitar strung much too tightly. We're all on edge as we've had reports from a US LOACH – light observational helicopter – that they may have spotted an encampment in our area.

"Beyond the rubber there's thick bush. Search under the triple canopy," they said. We've been ordered to check it out.

It's hotter than the devil. I can feel sweat pool on my brow and run down the length of my nose. Fear intensifies the heat. The skies have just bucketed us with heavy rain. It stops as if someone has turned off a tap. The rain offers little respite from the grill, just adds an uncomfortable clamminess you fight for breathable air. The men ahead of me shimmer in the humidity which seems to sit just above the wet grass. Balls is on point, and I can see him raise his forearm, his fist is clenched tightly. The men stop. The digger on the right mimics the gesture. I scan the scene. There are twenty men spread in a long V shape. An unkindness of migrating raven. Throughout the long elephant grass the men stop advancing and crouch. I can just see the tops of their soft hats; the sweat colours their jungle greens dark and sickly. The colour of a stagnant, festering pool. Golly is in this group, as is Lieutenant "Frangers" Condon, our platoon CO. Golly is not more than ten feet to my left. I'm behind the CO and our radio operator in the middle of the phalanx. Rifles front, machinegunners on our wings. I stop moving. Balls raises his M16 rifle and moves forward into the trees. He is swallowed. I can see the two men to either side remain standing. No-one moves. I realise I'm holding my breath. The guy on the left is bent forward. I think it's Dan Collins but it's hard to tell from this distance. He moves like Dan. His head appears to be cocked slightly to the left. He is listening for a signal, a whisper. He moves slowly forward into the trees and he too, is devoured by shadow. The rear men are as still as the white Buddha. I am in a half crouch. I am exposed on the slight crest. I decide to get down with the others in the long green elephant grass. Slowly. One hour to move 100 feet we are often told. The slim guy on the right has to be Ray. He peers into the foreboding dark of a high hedge row with small flowers of blood red just beyond the rubber trees. He has taken root. He is a rubber tree. A hot breeze stirs him gently; it carries him forward. Ray ducks his head imperceptibly and bends into the bushes…

And the tree line explodes.

Ray was 20. A good-looking kid with fine, almost feminine features. He'd been growing a rusty red moustache to look tougher. He complained it was taking an age to come in. He was a nasho. He'd grown up in Kilmore, just outside of Melbourne. He went to Assumption College. He had a loving family and a pretty girlfriend named Lucy. He'd showed us all a photograph.

He shared our tent for just two months after Jungles chomped on the wasp. Balls had taken Ray under his wing and was teaching him soldiering. That's why he was close to Balls in his last moment. Ray was a smart, fit young kid who didn't mind mixing it with Golly and Balls. He copped the shit and was more than happy to give it back. He was quick and as dry as the Nullarbor. He grew on us all really quickly.

There is a blinding flash, and a thundering roar shatters the afternoon silence.

"A mine!" I think to myself, "hanging in the trees" and I drop my head to the glare as I begin to run. I get no more than two or three steps forward when a large black shape comes through the sun, blotting it out. It's heavy, black, and flying at great speed. It's moving impossibly fast and even if I could move I am helplessly in its arc. Just before it smashes into my chin I see a face. It's Ray's face. Rays head is flying at me. His eyes are open and he's screaming.

Ray's screaming head is blotting out the sun.

Ray's screaming head hits me on the chin and knocks me out cold.

Ray's screaming head has been shattering my dreams now for over a year.

Ray's head sometimes has Tim's face.

I suppose I'll need to tell you about Tim.

Tim saved my life, even after I took his.

PIC

I tried to get the kettle off the heat before it squealed but Mum had heard me in the kitchen anyway and got up to chide me for being up so early on a Sunday morning. She said I needed to rest and heal. I told her that I'd just spent over a year in bed. I intended to help out around the place even if it meant only bringing her the odd 'cuppa'.

"Tea in bed, Oooh lad-dee-da, ain't I the Queen," she said in a passable Eliza Doolittle. She was dressed in a heavy, pale blue dressing gown which hovered above bright, pink slippers. Her long, greying hair swept down over her shoulders. I smiled and I grabbed the loaf of bread from the metal bread bin on the bench. It had one of those sliding rounded doors with a little wooden knob. The loaf, hiding inside, had been started and it was sitting cut-face down on the bread board to keep fresh. I reached in and pulled it and the board out. I intended to make some toast for us both. I grabbed the serrated knife from the drawer and turned to the bread… and just looked at it.

"How am I gonna do this?" I thought. I contemplated holding the bread with my chin and sawing into the crust, but that left me in danger of sawing off my nose. I could sit my useless arm on it, but I knew it wouldn't be heavy enough to hold it steady while I cut. As if Mum was reading my thoughts she said, "I think we just get sliced bread from now on Terry.

You can get a toasting loaf where they cut the slices nice and thickly like you like them. Leave the toast to me and get a pot of tea going will you? Remember, a spoonful for you, a spoonful for me and one for the pot."

"I remember", I said. I set the small, green, Formica table then. Teacups and plates. I went to the cupboard and grabbed the butter, honey, and vegemite. It took three trips.

"Terry, there will be a bottle of milk on the doorstep. The 'milky' might have come although we are a little early."

"I'll have a look," I said. I swung the door open and looked down to see the white, wire milk tray sitting empty.

"Morning!" a deep voice said loudly. "You're up early son." I was so startled I stepped back, caught my foot on the edge of the little step and went down on my back the length of the short, tiled landing. My head hit the front door hard, and it swung open and banged loudly on the hallway wall. The large ruddy face of the milkman loomed over the gate. He had a silver topped milk bottle in his hand.

"Oh, sorry son, I didn't mean to scare the horses. I'll leave it here." He leant over our rusty gate and placed the bottle on the ground. He turned, his eyes wide, and hurried back to his cart laden with pallets of milk. The cart was being pulled by a large brown draught horse who was stepping slowly down the middle of the street. It was a dance the two performed every morning. I felt like my heart had burst. I could feel sweat break out on my back and a tender spot on the back of my head began to pulse. My legs barked loudly. My arm, eerily quiet.

Later, on the couch, and sipping my hard-won cup of tea I finally got to ask Mum about the photo of Rosie and me.

It turned out Lily, Rosemary's mum, had sent it to her with a short note in very broken English. No return address. Lily was a beautiful soul. Rosemary's mum and dad owned a small Chinese restaurant in Richmond called Chī, which I was told is Chinese for "eat". I'd only been to Chī a couple of times, Rosemary hated eating there. She resented the fact her parents, who were Thai, cooked Chinese food. She and her dad would have loud arguments about it. She would go on about the wonderful flavours of Thai and her dad, Kulap, would argue that it was hard enough to get Aussies to eat Chinese food let alone try something even more foreign to their tongues. I agreed with Kulap, Aussies had pretty bland tastes. Meat and three veg. Salt, the only spice required. Maybe a little pepper if they were feeling particularly adventurous. Mum came from the English school of beating the cow black and boiling the vegetables until all the fight was gone. Then and only then could they be mashed and presented. Mum's idea of *haute cuisine* was mixing the mashed pumpkin with the mashed potato. If she was feeling particularly adventurous she'd also mash in the Brussels sprouts, but only on really special occasions like weddings or baptisms.

The smells of Thai cooking, which often filled Rosemary's small bedroom above the restaurant, were a new world to my untrained nose. There was a wooden staircase up to the second floor where the family lived. Rosemary had a room at the back, closest to the back door and wooden stairs that sat on the outside of the building. Iris, her younger sister, had a tiny room at the top of the inside stairs. Kulap and Lily slept in the larger bedroom that faced onto Bridge Road. Rosie and I used to sneak to her room, often very late on a Saturday night after hitting the bars and dances in the area. We aimed to get up to no good.

The traditional Thai meals Kulap or Lily would make the family always smelled more delicious, more exotic, than the chicken chow mien and fried rice with frozen peas of the restaurant. They were mouth-watering. Of the times I was asked to join the family for dinner they were, as they say in the TV commercials, "a taste sensation". I didn't get involved in the arguments with Rosie and Kulap. I was smart enough to know that no good would come from stepping into a family disagreement, especially when cyclone Rosemary was in destructo mode.

"I've not heard from Rosemary, Terry, not a peep. Honestly those photos Lily sent me were the only contact I've had from that family."

"So, there was more than one photo Mum?" I asked.

"There were three," she replied.

"Can I see them?" I added when it became obvious that Mum had no intention of getting up to get them.

"If you must," she said caustically and moved over to the mantle. Behind the ornate wooden clock that had last been wound when Adam was a pup, she drew a dust covered envelope and dropped it on the table in front of me. I drew out two Polaroids without lifting the sleeve and shook the dust from them just as we had shaken them to life in the cool breeze blowing off Sydney Harbour. One was a photograph of Rosemary and me – almost a double of the one I'd pinned on the wall of our tent in Nam. The other was of Rosemary alone.

Mum looked away, her nose to the ceiling. She refused to gaze upon my erstwhile wife. Rosie looked radiant in the white dress, and I felt that familiar sting of lust, loss, and regret.

"Can I keep these Mum?"

"Well, they are yours," she snapped. "Although why you'd want to keep a bad memory is beyond me. Best forgotten I say."

I picked up the dusty envelope to replace the pic and noticed a small square of paper which had been overlooked. It sat face down, but I could see black swirls where the handwriting bled through. I pulled it out and turned it over. It was a note, from Rosemary. In tight black Pentel pen she had written:

> Terry.
> I have feelings for you, but I can't just sit here pretending you'll come back. It's too much.
> Goodbye Terry.
>   Rosemary.

I stood motionless for a full minute. I didn't re-read the note, I didn't have to, it was all clear enough. I slid the pics into the envelope and placed them in the pocket of my dressing gown.

"What did it say Terry?" asked Mum.

"Goodbye."

"It was from Rosemary?"

"Yeah."

"You OK son?" Mum asked.

"I'm fine Mum." And I was too. I think I just wanted to hear something, anything. Now I had, I felt OK. I felt a wash of anger and, again, I welcomed the burn. The fact that Rosie had not even wanted to keep a single photo of us was not lost on me. She couldn't wait for me. Apparently it was too much. How would she have coped with my wounds, my convalescence? The new, lesser me. She wouldn't have. I think Rosie probably did me a favour. Having to see her face, her distaste, that may have been a little too much to bear. A little soul destroying. God knows my soul had been destroyed enough. Rosie was there when I needed her, even if she was already gunning my Holden to parts unknown. Rosie lived, rent free, in my head; in Vietnam and in the pit with me and Tim. Her memory helped me through. I had to remember too, she rejected me before I was deformed. That is something at least.

"Good riddance Mum," I said with a little more fervour than I meant to. At the end of the day, I was going to spend a lot of energy repairing my body. I couldn't waste time on "the might-have-beens". Nobody knows where my Rosemary goes and I was happy to admit, as of that morning and that note, I really couldn't give a damn.

S.O.S.

A lot of my time during the first few months back in Fitzroy was spent in my cramped bedroom, trying to escape the well-meaning women of the Save Our Sons brigade. I had a constant, low-level headache which was never debilitating, but always distracting. I was pretty sure it was my brain adjusting to navigating a new and cyclopic world; it would eventually pass, but it was taking its sweet bloody time. I loved to read but I found I could only manage short spurts between the jackets. The legs were feeling good though. They still looked like a pair of stilts of course, but I decided they were getting a little thicker. Maybe I was just kidding myself. It showed a positive frame of mind at the very least. The dead arm was the greatest vexation. The ache in the shoulders, the crushed glass tingle of the severed nerves, the dead weight pulling on my neck. It was ever present and a pain in the arse.

My predominant annoyance, and unwelcome distraction, however, were Mum's acolytes from the S.O.S. They could appear at any time of the day, in singles, pairs or large groups. On the weekends they rarely left. There were six regulars and more than one or two blow-ins every week. They'd listen to the footy and bet on the races and fuss around me until I'd sneak away and leave them to their slow and steady inebriation. They'd arrive with enough food and drink to sink two small barges. Sometimes they bought wine, sometimes sherry. They always had beer. Long-necked brown bottles secreted in the bottom of their string shopping or brown paper supermarket bags. A few of the ladies rolled around their covered shopping trollies and they lined them up at the front door like doctors and lawyers left golf bags around a green.

On one memorable day Mrs Hobson rolled in with a bottle of Glenfiddich she'd pinched from her fella after they had a 'right royal blue' she said. They all ended up pissed as newts. I had to help Mum to bed later that night and I swear I heard her heaving in the bathroom in the wee hours, a charge she vehemently denied the next morning. I don't recall her ever touching the stuff again. She even missed her Sunday morning mass and had to go the 5.30 session she abhorred for some long-forgotten reason. I bet more than one of her friends were at the 5.30, all trying to shake off hangovers.

They could all cook though and our fridge was always full of tasty bits and pieces. Janine Davies liked to bring me up an assorted selection of delicacies on a plate and the other ladies would rib her about being in a man's bedroom. Miss Davies was a spinster who had never even had a boyfriend, according to Mum. She was about 20 years older than me, and Mrs Crawford called her the "cradle snatcher". She would redden and protest, but it never stopped her arriving at my bedroom with plate about an hour after I'd fled the S.O.S. incursions. The food was wonderful and that's big coming from me as I'm such a terrible eater. The food could be as dangerous as Vietnam. Nearly every culinary excursion had a toothpick in it. The number of trees cut down just so the rissoles and asparagus sandwiches could be held together would boggle the mind. There were devils on horseback – prunes wrapped in bacon. A cordillera of skewered cheese squares, a cabal of cabana. Little speared cocktail onions appeared for all the world like a plated echidna. The devilled eggs contained toothpicks for no other reason than they were too slippery to handle. Even plates of olives had toothpicks.

Mum's speciality was a pork and pineapple casserole which she always had pre-prepared and kept in the fridge to just heat and serve upon the pop-in. She was also quite fond of aspic and took great delight in jellying fish or chicken depending on her mood. Vol-au-vents were all the rage. They were considered the height of classy dining, with these girls anyway.

The sweets were a sight to behold. I'm not a big dessert eater as a rule, but some of these creations blew my mind. Apple or rhubarb pies or a sponge cake with passionfruit icing. Lamingtons were a coconut-sprinkled constant and someone always brought a pavlova. Swiss rolls and marble cake – always a chocolate mousse.

Sometimes Father Conlan would drop by, always empty handed. He'd leave with a full belly, a few beers under his belt and a large grin. He drove a noisy, clapped-out FJ Holden from the rectory which couldn't have been more than half a mile away. I swear you could hear him start it up. The car was a symbol of his piety as was the Christophany of the oil stain it left on the Little George Street bitumen.

It wasn't the food or grog that scared me off or even the company, they were nice enough old girls, it was just that I seemed to fuel their fervour. I'd flame the belly fire just by walking into the room. It'd start with a little fawning, flavoured by copious dollops of sympathy. We'd career headlong into the pity. I personified the cause. A brilliant young, soon-to-be doctor, struck down in his prime by evil men forcing our sons into a war we shouldn't be fighting. The son of the very President of the Save Our Sons – North Fitzroy chapter. They practically begged me to join their protests. I, of course, declined. Mrs James and Mrs Canetti were the worst. They just wouldn't let up. Mum knew it made me uncomfortable and finally had a quiet word to the both of them. They backed off a little. I didn't want to be rude to them, especially Mrs James who had lost her son Steven over there a couple of years before.

Most vets I'd met didn't feel comfortable talking about Vietnam when they got back, and I was no different. It was all best forgotten. I knew I'd be back there every night and the longer you could go along disavowing it all the more sleep you might get. The S.O.S. North Fitzroy chapter would never understand. I realised Mrs James wanted to get some sort of feeling for Steven's terrible time over there, but I honestly, selfishly, felt the toll on my own peace of mind was onerous. Sometimes I felt my own grip on my emotions too tenuous for conversation. I didn't want to pull the finger from the dyke in case I couldn't get it back in. Then, to make it all so much worse, I'd feel guilty for not talking about it to her and try to explain myself. It was all too much to be honest and I'd escape to my room, again and again.

Mrs James, maybe as a peace offering, crocheted me a brick red, woollen jumper which I happily wore that winter with the sleeves rolled up as they only reached to about where my watch sat. She was a nice lady, but I always felt pretty shitty around her. Call it survivor's guilt. I always wondered if she looked at me thinking, why did Terry make it back and not Steve? She would have taken a one-armed, one-eyed Steven in a heartbeat.

My active roll with the Save Our Sons – North Fitzroy chapter consisted of doing a final spell check before they painted a placard or poster and driving some of the drunken women home in Mrs James' R series green Chrysler Valiant, when Mum decided they'd had too much and may do themselves a mischief. They were hilarious trips actually and always cold. The women would be singing and laughing, two in the front and sometimes four in the back. All the windows rolled down as Mrs Hobson said their combined 'change of life', hot flushes would fog up the windscreen. This didn't bother me as I was still dealing miserably with close spaces a bit in those early days. They'd be fanning themselves while belting out the songs on the radio. I'd be struggling with the gear stick while holding the steering wheel with my shoulder. None of it good for the headache, nor were the headlights of other cars coming towards us. Depth of field issues didn't help either. Still, I enjoyed the laugh. Janine Davies offered to sit in the middle and gently hold the underside of the wheel while I was shifting gears. This was a great help.

I never attended the protests; these were the S.O.S.'s fights, not mine. I wasn't a performing seal. They could get a bit rowdy too. I'd seen a few donnybrooks on the telly. There's always one or two nuts at every protest who are only there in the hope they get to punch a copper. The S.O.S. ladies preferred the silent protest – God knows what good that would do. Not much point in protesting silently if no-one is watching. I sometimes wished they'd adopt the silent protest with me on the drunken car rides home, but as Pop Dempsey used to say, "If wishes were cars, beggars would drive Ferraris!" Pop also used to say, "If wishes were nuggets, beggars would shit gold ones", but never when Nan was in ear shot.

There was one memorable occasion when I had to collect the ladies from the Melbourne police watch-house in the Valiant after they were rounded up by the boys in blue. The S.O.S. informed me the fiery Mrs Canetti had whacked a copper with her handbag and they were all stuffed into a divvy van. The desk sergeant confided to me the police had decided to move the ladies out of harm's way. There was a bit of a rough element at this particular protest and the cops thought it could get willing. I think a few of them were hoping it would anyway. The police didn't have a high opinion of the S.O.S. as a rule. A lot of the cops thought they were communists. This didn't mean they wanted them getting hurt when the fists and boots started swinging. I thanked him and stuffed them all into Mrs James car, which she'd parked at our place. I dropped them all home. Alas, no silent protest on that ride either. Mrs Canetti promised the desk sergeant a home cooked lasagne for letting them go.

When I really wanted to escape the noise of the S.O.S. I was happy to hit the footpaths and take in the fresh air, as Melbourne struggled from a dour winter into buoyant spring, I welcomed the sun like a long-lost friend. I walked every day, usually with a book. I adjusted to life back in Australia, and reading books, at my own pace. My time at the Repat, and conversations with staff and patients there, had given me an idea of what life after war might consist of. My psychology studies at uni and a couple of the old textbooks were a great help too. I listened, read, and tried to take it all in. Guys talked about the dreams and night sweats. We discussed dealing with crowds and the constant search for escape routes when entering a room. There were the dangers of self-pity, which I knew I was a prime candidate for. I'd always thought I was a bit soft in the centre if the truth be told. Probably a son of a single mum thing. I don't think I had any hard edges before I went away. That was a little bit of a concern. Now I'd made it home I worried the centre would harden too much and I'd lose empathy or become swampy, and I'd drown in it. I came back physically messed up, but I was damned if I was going to be mentally stuffed as well.

The constant surveillance was hard to shake and quite tiring. There was this feeling of being watched or stalked, born of the endless patrols. I found this difficult to deal with, that feeling that someone was behind you. Not right behind you but off in the distance watching and plotting. It's almost funny that when the bastards did come it was from the front, around a blind corner actually, but this is a story for later. We'll get there in time.

I'd walk for hours and sit in the beautiful parks around Melbourne and read a bit, until the headaches began baying. I'd take to the shoes again and head to the Fitzroy gardens or the Exhibition Building. I'd people-watch and people would watch me.

When I walked I'd stick my right hand in my jeans pocket to get it out of the way. After a time, I noticed I would rub all the skin off the back of my hand against the denim, sometimes it even bled. I hated it hanging loose and swinging, so I bought a pair of thin, leather gloves and put the left one in the top drawer of the chest in my room. I wore the other. Now putting a glove on a hand that refuses to help is a kind of murder and rarely did it end up "fitting like a glove" without loose, flappy bits on one or two fingers. Still, the glove did the job and stopped the bleeding.

I always wore a shirt with two breast pockets and always kept my cash and public transport ticket in the right one. Trying to navigate the wrong pocket retrieval at 6' 9" in a packed train carriage or tram was a task only Houdini himself could master.

I found myself walking further and further each day and felt it was doing me the world of good. My legs were getting stronger, but more importantly, I felt it was sorting my head out as well. I still fought Vietnam in the nights, but I was able to evaluate the dreams and night terrors in the daylight. It was better than drowning them in a bar, and cheaper too. I was cautious with the booze. It had taken Dad and it could get its talons into me. I still loved a beer, but it would always be on my terms.

I found myself constantly walking in the direction of the Repat Hospital in Heidelberg. I was drawn to it like a bee to a hive. I started arriving there in September after a long walk. I'd spend an hour or two checking to see if there was anyone I still knew. Shared experience created a camaraderie and let's face it, most of the country in the 1970s couldn't give a rat's arse about returned serviceman from Vietnam, even the RSL (Return Servicemen's League). This I thought was insanity. Without returned servicemen would the RSL even exist. I think not! Apparently they believed some wars were better than others. We'd all heard the tales of how our guys had been told, 'The Vietnam war was a police action, not a real war.' My mates were just as dead from my war as theirs were. My wounds were just as real. We still fought for our country. It felt bloody real to the alma mata of the Repat I can tell you for free.

There were one or two long-timers in the hospital that I spent some time with, and they were very happy to see a friendly face. I was introduced to lots of new guys, and I began rolling in every second day to just chat and listen. We didn't mention the war that much to be honest. We just batted stuff around. It was good and we all got something out of it.

As I became a regular face Sister Melanie, the senior charge nurse, coerced me into giving the Austin hospital nurses a hand with the cystic fibrosis kids only a short walk away. This was really rewarding. We'd cup our hands, or in my case, hand, and pound them on the back as they lay watching telly. It would loosen the phlegm in their lungs and get them coughing. The kids said my big hand was perfect for the task. The CF kids were terrific, and I think they enjoyed the sessions as much as I did. We'd discuss footy, cricket, horses, and animals. I'd think up trivia questions for them to answer. No talk of war, wounds, or politics.

I saw Dr Keysor a few times while in at the hospital, while visiting with the returned soldiers at the Repat. Initially he would see me in my chair at the end of the room and decide there was somewhere else he needed to be. After a while he realised this was ridiculous and he bit the bullet and walked up to shake my hand. He even proffered his left hand which not many people get right!

"Morning Terry," he said "How did you go with those anger issues son? Thrown any bedpans recently?" He looked at me like

I might be an unpinned grenade. It was so unexpected I laughed.

"Not recently Doc and I fear I may be out of practice." He even allowed himself a smile.

"Thank God for that," he added. "Are you here for anything medically?"

"No Doc. I have an assessment in November. I just drop in to chat with the guys that feel like chatting and shut up if they don't."

"Good work," he said and nodded at me. "Feeling fit?"

"I'm getting by Doc. I walked here from Fitzroy."

"Good effort." He nodded again and turned to a young bloke nicknamed Spider, after his red back spider neck tattoo. Spider had been hit in the cheek by some mortar fragments in *Long Khánh*.

His cheekbones had been powdered. Spider's jaw was broken and most of his teeth lay in the mud in Vietnam. Dr K peered under his bandages and checked that Spider could still focus on one long finger held up before his face. Satisfied that Spider's eyesight seemed unimpaired he grunted and prepared to move to the next patient, Sister Melanie shadowing him holding an armful of patient reports.

I asked loudly,

"Doc, is it OK if I bring a radio in for the boys to listen to the Grand Final next week?"

"Go Piesth" spat Spider through his toothless wound of a mouth. Dr Keysor looked at Sister Melanie and they stared at each other for a moment. There was an unspoken concession.

"Be buggered Spider. Go the mighty Navy Blues!" said Dr Keysor loudly. "You go right ahead Terry and I'll even listen to the Blues take apart Richmond with you lot. Your Pies didn't even get past the Saints in the semi."

"BULLSTHIT! Spat Spider and a few of the guys laughed.

"I'll even supply the champagne to celebrate!" said Dr K.

"HOORAY!" shouted the ward.

"Wouldn't you know it; Dr K is a Carlton supporter. I knew he was a bastard," I added and the boys all roared their approval. Nurse Melanie laughed and even Dr K smiled.

A week later, on the 7th of October, a short time after the last anti-war moratorium in the city, faithfully attended by the women of my mother's S.O.S. – North Fitzroy chapter, and just two months before the last of the Australian troops were repatriated from Vietnam, we listened to the highest scoring Grand Final in history. The match between Carlton and Richmond at the mighty MCG was attended by over 112,000 footy-mad supporters. I had bought a radio on my walk over and a spare set of AA batteries. I set it up at the end of the ward on a wheeled meal tray. Carlton Captain/Coach, John Nicholls kicked six goals from the forward pocket and the great Alex "Jezza" Jesaulenko kicked seven. The Blues won 28.9 to 22.19 with hard nut Neale Balme kicking five for the losers. That's 50 goals between them. The constant scoring had the whole ward cheering. Dr K, true to his word, broke open two bottles of champagne when Carlton got up and Spider, despite his antipathy towards the Blues, enjoyed a celebratory toast to a great game.

I had two glasses of champagne and begrudgingly toasted the Blues win. Unfortunately, a few of the boys weren't permitted to ingest alcohol and they looked on with envy. I gulped them down quickly not wanting to rub it in. I decided to leave for the train home soon after. I was feeling a little lightheaded as I suppose I hadn't had a lot of alcohol over the last year or so.

As I sat on the train and cradling the radio in my lap. I decided I couldn't face the house full of excited, probably pissed, S.O.S. women gabbing on about yet another protest. I breezed by North Fitzroy station; I was heading to Jolimont Station near the MCG. I decided I felt like a little Chinese food. It was about time I worked up the courage to visit Lily and Kulap. After all, I'd been back in Australia nearly two years, and I was still married to their daughter. As I left the train at Jolimont I stepped into the largest football crowd footy I had ever seen. I was a bloody Fitzroy man with one of the lowest supporter bases in the league. What did I know about big crowds? I stepped from a practically empty carriage and waded into a sea of "yellow and black" Tiger gear and navy-blue jerseys and scarfs, replete with Carlton's CFC insignia. I thought they'd all be gone; the game had finished almost 45 minutes before. The air was alive with excitement and disappointment. It stunk of sweat, cigarette smoke and beer. The noise of a thousand voices all talking over each other swelled in the ears and filled the head. I could only catch snippets.

"Big Nick got 6!"
"JEEEEZZZZZZAAAAAAAAR!"
"CHOCKERS!"
"Poor T-shirt Tommy Hafey."
"Bloody Carlton."
"Bloody Richmond."

"Bloody crowd!"

I pushed through the flood of humanity spilling in through the yawning doorway of the train. I was holding the radio against my chest and my pointy elbow swung into some poor lady's face as she pushed to get on. The niceties of waiting for passengers to disembark was lost in the panic to get out of the crush. She didn't even flinch such was her eagerness to try and grab one of the fast-filling bench seats. I towered above the multitude and was able to spot my escape up the walkway to Wellington Parade. I didn't even have time to contemplate whether the whole idea had been a monumental mistake. There were thousands more people at street level. They wound around the demolition of the old Clivedon Mansions, where they were building the Hilton Hotel, and they poured from the various pubs and bars, laughing, and shouting. The masses waiting for the trams chilled me to the core. Renditions of *Lily from Laguna*, the tune of Carlton's theme song broke out with ever increasing regularity.

"NUH, NUH, NUH, NUH, NUH… WE ARE THE NAVY BLUES!" I decided to avoid the tram and walk to the restaurant – although, I wasn't totally sure where it was. As I made my way across Punt Road I fell into step with even more people flooding down Bridge Road. Many clutched the WEG Premiership poster they'd purchased after the game. The rolled white tubes of paper stood out like white sails on a yellow, black and blue sea.

Every pub down Bridge Road churned with patrons. The Mountain View Hotel bubbled and spewed out onto the road. I had to leap across the gutter just to get around it. The cars and trams were gridlocked so I had made the right decision to walk. Grim faces pressed against the windows of the stationary 48 and 75 trams. Fathers choked by scarfs held young kids up to small open windows. They breathed in air filled with the exhaust fumes of a barricade of idle and idling cars.

I could feel anxiety writhe its serpentine way along my spine. My neck was slick and becoming icy as the night began to cool. Moving helped. Being able to wind through the people helped keep the panic at bay. I breathed deeply and focussed on my one goal. Find the restaurant. Respite from this heaving mass of humanity. I was headed to Chī. Then I realised I might have made another error. I tried to expel the thought, but it kept trying to claw its way to my consciousness. The closer I got to Chī, the more the beast roared. It hadn't occurred to me at first but now the trepidation became a certainty. It shrieked like a banshee

What if Rosemary was there?

So much for being over her.

CHĪ

Chī – Chinese Restaurant, Eat in or Take-away.
I found it on the corner of Hunter Street and Bridge Road. To be honest I didn't even have to look that hard, muscle memory led me straight there. It was open and serving food and like every other restaurant that night, it was packed. People waiting for take-away flowed out the door and around into Hunter Street. I stood in front of the large window scrawled with yellow and red lettering and couldn't see a single spare seat. As I shifted my radio to the crook of my arm I turned to leave. The whole adventure may have been a bad idea. A tap, tap, tap on the window. I had to refocus to see a small woman in white trying to get my attention. I could see inquisitive faces staring at me from tables piled high with food. She put up a splayed hand in a stop gesture. She ran to the door.

"TERRY!"

"Hello Iris," I smiled down at her. I was a little surprised when she rushed forward and wrapped her arms around me in a warm embrace. There was little I could do but stand and be hugged.

"It's good to see you."

"It's great to see you too – wow busy night!"

"The busiest, we're under the pump tonight. I gotta get back in." She grabbed my arm.

"Hey, you can't go without saying hi to Mum. She talks about you a lot. Just say hi. She's in the kitchen." She looked solemnly at the ground.

"It's just us. We haven't heard from Rosemary since you left. Come in. You've got to come in." Iris started to drag me inside.

"OK, OK," I laughed, "I'm coming in." We were obviously a sight for the patrons, the diminutive waitress wrestling the eye-patched giant through the doorway. Every eye in the place was on us. Iris jumped in behind me and pushed me to the kitchen. I had to step around the knees of the take-away customers lucky enough to get a seat on the pew against the wall.

"Ma!" she yelled over the general hubbub, and she pushed me through the multi-coloured plastic curtain that hung from the doorframe and hurried back to her tables. Lily tossed a large wok full of rice into the air with one hand and pushed around pork spareribs on a flaming grill with the other. She was almost consumed by a cloud of steam. Her long black hair was tied in a bun; long strands fell about her face. She blew them out of her eyes as she worked.

"*Swasdi* Lily." She turned her head, and her harried face broke into a wide smile.

"Terry. I love to see you. We very busy. You put down the radio and put on apron. You can get to work. We speak later. OK, OK?"

"But I…"

"No talk now Terry." Lily nodded to an apron on a hook by the plastic doorway.

"My arm…" I said feebly.

"Oh it's OK. You go fast as you can, that's all." Lily was not taking no for an answer apparently. "Iris help you tie up. If you can clean dishes. We are running out of glass and plate." Lily was talking over her shoulder as she juggled, sizzled, bubbled, and flamed. "Go, go, you sent from heaven Terry!"

And that's how I spent Grand Final evening 1972. Taking take-away orders, handing over plastic bags full of Chinese food, washing and drying dishes. It was fucking brilliant.

I had barely practiced writing since getting out of the Repat and my script was totally illegible, yet Iris had no trouble reading it as she'd yelled the orders to her mum. Lily was a machine. She was bagging up steamed dim sims, frying chop suey rolls and tossing chow mien and foo young and God only knows what else in five different woks she'd shake over gas burners with metronomic regularity. Iris waitressed, cleared tables and did absolutely everything else. How they managed before I walked in is a mystery and quite possibly a miracle.

It was probably the most work I'd done since I got home, not probably, definitely. It was tough mentally too. I had to manoeuvre my way around my various tasks efficiently. It was a steep learning curve. Washing could be done by wedging everything at the bottom of the sink. Cutlery was fiddly but chopsticks a breeze. Grab them with a cloth and bang then against your chest, drawing the cloth along their length. Drying was accomplished on the bench against my belly, one side and then the other. Place the plates on the long shelf above the sink. Cutlery air-dried standing in a tall wire basket. There was another shelf stacked with plastic containers that ran along the right-hand wall. The sink was on the east wall, the stove and cooktop on the west. Lily and I had stood with our backs to each other as we worked.

It would be an understatement to say they threw me into the deep end: we went solidly until around 9.30 when the walk-in customers began to peter away, and the takeaway customers were sated. By 10.30, there were only a couple of tables of stragglers left. It was tough. My apron was a sopping mess. It was smoky, sweaty, and totally exhilarating. I had a left-handed dexterity I had no idea I had. I was packing plastic tubs into bags and slinging them to customers with aplomb. They may have been put off by my scarred face and useless, swinging right arm, but I was much too busy to care. It was a joy to find myself "of use". Glorious!

A little later I found myself sitting with Lily at the now empty tables. We were exhausted. Iris was in the kitchen finishing the last of the drying up. She had shooed me out with the wave of a tea-towel. She said I looked dead on my feet. I felt a little dead on my feet to be honest. We were sipping on a cold lemonade each, all that was left in the fridge. Lily looked at me and smiled.

"Lucky you came Terry, or we might have had the heart attack – too busy. Crazy busy."

"It certainly was," I agreed. "I couldn't believe how fast you cooked everything up. You were like a magician. Where was Kulap to help tonight. Out partying?" Lily sipped her soft drink and looked at me over the can.

"Kulap dead Terry." My smile slid from my face.

"Oh, I'm sorry to hear that Lily. That's terrible."

"He got the lung cancer. Too much smoking. He always smoking. It was very fast. Very sad too. Silly man, smoke too much." We sat for a minute or two, quietly sipping our drinks. Finally, Lily said, "I miss him but he very sick. He cough blood. You know. It's better now he at peace. No more coughing. It just Iris and me now. We work the restaurant," she added brightly.

"We manage but tonight it crazy with the footy." Lily placed the back of her hands on the table and raised her shoulders. She looked at me solemnly.

"Terry, Rosemary gone away. We not hear anything from her for maybe two years. She just disappeared. We are very sorry Terry."

"Right!" I said and nodded. "Did she know about her dad?"

"No. She don't even come to Kulap's funeral. That was sad. No – she just disappear. We get no letter or phone call. She came from Sydney and told us she and you are married. She stay for maybe one month then tell us she doesn't want to be waitress." Lily reached across the table and squeezed my hand on the tabletop, "Or a wife." She carefully watched my reaction. "She say she had bigger plans with her life. Then Rosemary pack the car with her things and drive away. We haven't seen her since."

"My old Holden," I said.

"Yes, your car Terry. I very sorry about that too."

"Don't be sorry Lily, none of this is your fault."

"Maybe yes, maybe no," she said thoughtfully. "Maybe we push too hard with the restaurant. She always say she didn't want to be a waitress. Maybe Kulap push her too hard. She was a girl with a very strong mind. They argue all the time. They are too much the same. I always tell him, Kulap, you can't split hard wood with hard wood."

"She was stubborn," I smiled. "It was one of the things I loved about her. Rosie was nobody's fool." Lily just nodded and drained the last of her lemonade. Iris announced her arrival by pulling the ring pull of her own can, it made a loud *Phiiiizzzzz*!

"Would you guys like another can Terry?"

"I'm fine thanks Iris."

"Mum?" she asked.

"I good too *Luksaw Khn swy*". Lily smiled.

"Now she calls me beautiful daughter," Iris said with a grin as she grabbed a chair at our table and swung it around. She sat resting her arms over its back. She placed her opened lemonade in front of her.

"When we were under pressure she called me names they don't say in the Bible." Lily and I both laughed.

"I think she said I was a buffalo," Iris said and Lily laughed aloud.

"I say *Rīb khun*. It means go faster. Hurry up."

"I was going like a blue-arsed fly Mum." She smiled. "Thank god Terry turned up or we would have been truly stuffed."

"I know," Lily agreed. "He an angel."

"I'm just glad to be able to help," I said. Lily looked at me for a long time as if reading me. She looked through to the back of my head.

"Your poor face Terry. It happen in the war, yes?"

"Shush Mum," Iris cut across my answer. "He probably doesn't want to talk about Vietnam."

"It's OK Iris," I said. "I lost my eye over there."

"Oh no," said Lily. "And you arm not working?"

"Mum…" said Iris but I smiled.

"No, I'm afraid not. I got shot in the shoulder and it severed the nerves in there."

"Oooh shot," Lily gasped.

"Yep, it's just a big piece of dead meat now I'm afraid."

"Is there much pain Terry?" It was Iris asking me questions now.

"I thought it was rude to ask me questions," I teased. She looked at me with surprise. I smiled and she lit up in a wide grin.

"Oh, I'm sorry Terry, but is there?"

"I can't feel anything with the arm so no, no pain. Sometimes some phantom tingling in the fingertips but that is all. That doesn't hurt, just disconcerting if you know what I mean. It's almost like I have feeling coming back. It messes with your head a little I suppose. I get headaches too sometimes; this is a bit of a reaction to suddenly being one-eyed they tell me. I'm not too bad really, pain wise. It's just all bloody annoying at the moment but I reckon I'll get used to it."

"Did you get shot in the eye Terry?"

"No Lily, I fell in a pit onto a sharpened stick. "It's a bit of a long story really. It was like a booby-trap."

"What does bobby-trap mean?" asked Lily.

"It's like an animal trap Mum," said Iris. "Like a trap set for an animal you're trying to catch."

"Or slow down," I added. "They can kill you, but the idea is to hurt you enough, so you become a burden. They sort of try to make you a burden for the rest of the guys. It slows everybody down having to look after you. Do you know what I mean?"

"Yes," said Lily.

"How long have you been back Terry?"

"Nearly two years. As good as two years anyway. I was in hospital here for quite a while. I was in hospital for a bit in Vietnam as well."

"Wow," said Iris. "Have you seen Rosemary, Terry? Did she contact you at all?" Iris asked.

"No. I haven't seen her since I got back."

"So, she didn't even visit you in hospital."

"No," I said.

"Just bloody disappeared. Selfish bitch," Iris said, anger flashed in her dark eyes. "You got married too didn't you?"

"We did. Yep. Look, that was probably a mistake, but I thought if, God forbid, I got killed in Vietnam she'd be able to get a wife's pension or something. She'd be looked after."

"Terry Shepherd, always the angel. You were too bloody good for her," Iris said. I felt blood rise into my cheeks.

"It's not like that Iris. I wasn't trying to be a saint. I just thought if I died over there then somebody would have to pay something for sending me over there. Might as well be Rosie. I loved her after-all."

"You still love her after she steals your car and breaks your heart. Tough one to love our Rosie."

"Well, I loved her. In the past tense. Things change I suppose."

"Shush now Iris. Don't get angry," said Lily. "Friends for a meal are easy to find. Friends for life are not so easy." We sat in silence.

"Where you living Terry?" asked Lily.

"I'm back in Fitzroy, with Mum, where you sent the wedding photos. Thank you for your kindness. Mum loved them." I didn't mention she had hidden the pics of Rosie.

"Ahh, you live with your mother. She look after you?"

"Of course. She's great. It's a bit hard landing on her after so long away I suppose. She has her own life and friends. I get in the way a little. It's fine though. We'll work out a system." We sat in silence then until Iris broke it scraping her chair on the floor and rising from the table.

"Well, I'm putting the kettle on. Anyone like a cuppa, oh shit!

Terry have you eaten anything," she added, and I laughed.

"Actually, I was actually coming in for dinner and to say hello."

"And we make you our slave. Oh my god Terry, we so sorry. I make you special fried rice now. I'm soooo sorry," said Lily.

"Don't be silly, I was happy to help."

"You sit there, and I make now. Oh, we so rude."

"Lily, it's fine."

"You stop, I make now. You want dim sum or egg roll too?" said Lily.

"Special fried rice will be perfect. I'm sorry you've cleaned everything up."

"Too easy Terry, it's no trouble for Mum, she's a whizz," said Iris.

"I've seen," I said.

"I have one important question though."

"What?" asked Lily.

"I've always wanted to know, and it's bugged me for years."

"OK," said Lily, her full attention on my face.

"What's the difference between fried rice and SPECIAL fried rice?"

"It about 50 cents," said Lily and we all laughed loudly as she got up from her chair and went to the kitchen.

Ten minutes later Lily placed a large, steaming plate of special fried rice in front of me with enough prawn crackers to sink the HMAS *Sydney*. I told them it was too much, and Iris grabbed a bowl and helped herself to some. She sprinkled it with soy sauce and handed me a fork. She grabbed a pair of chop sticks. To be fair I'd become quite adept at using the sticks in the East, but I'd never even tried with my left. I was happy to go with the four-pronged attack. The rice was wonderful, and I found myself a lot hungrier than I thought. Iris and I finished the plate and nearly all of the crackers. There was a clock behind the counter and as I stretched and pushed away from the table I was stunned to see it was half past midnight.

"Shit a brick!" I exclaimed "It's half passed bloody 12. I think I've missed my train."

"No, no, no," said Lily. "You must stay here. You have a room upstairs."

"What, Rosie's room?" I asked.

"Yes, yes. It your room now. We have your things."

"Really? What things."

"Mum kept Rosie's room for you Terry in case you came by. It has some clothes, a toiletries bag, even a toothbrush."

"It is your room Terry. We have cricket bag," said Lily.

"My old cricket coffin, you're kidding. I haven't even thought about that in two years."

"You always sneak in here with Rosie. You think you were very quiet up the back stairs. Kulap say Terry sneak around Richmond like Godzilla sneak around Tokyo. You two make so much noise." Lily smiled and Iris caught my eye. She wore a devilish grin.

"Ahhh, a back door man I see." If the truth be told we did sneak up the back stair to Rosie's room, usually a little worse for wear, and yes, we did think we were the models of stealth and discretion. I felt my face begin to warm again.

Lily said, "You sneak out in the morning after Kulap leave for the Dandenong market. Kulap always laugh and say, this way we don't have to make breakfast for you." Lily and Iris both laughed loudly. I joined in with them.

"You stay Terry. You work here. You are too old to live with mother and we can use help."

"Lily, I know you're just being kind. Wouldn't you be better with someone…"? She cut me off.

"We better off with you. No more talk. You family. We love you. Kulap love you. He was very happy you marry Rosemary. He say "Now you can fight with her, and he don't have too."

"Looks like she's not taking NO for an answer brother-in-law."

And that's how I ended up working and living at the Chī – Chinese Restaurant, Eat In or Take-away. I wasn't there for a long time. The restaurant wasn't there for a long time.

It was a SPECIAL time though.

BUB

"Pup, you awake?"

I opened my eyes and found Lax's family jewels biting distance from my face.

"What the fu…" He reaches down and puts a firm hand over my mouth cutting off my protestations.

"Get up mate, I need you and we gotta go now."

"Shit, Right!" I said and shook off the last vestiges of sleep. I jumped out of bed. Lax appeared to be dressing himself in Percy's uniform which had been folded on top of his footlocker. Percy Ellis, dubbed "Mr Percival" by Balls after the clever pelican in Colin Thiele's book *Storm Boy*, was the young fellow that had replaced the unfortunate and greatly missed Ray in our quartet. There was a pungent pile of clothes in the middle of the floor that Lax kicked into a corner. Percy was going to find himself with only the boots he was wearing as morning broke. Percy always slept in his boots; he'd read somewhere it could save your life not messing with boot laces in an attack. We tried to tell him this was for sleeping in the jungle, but he wouldn't have it. You just can't reason with some people. We'd have been better off with the pelican.

"Beauty! I knew he was about my size. Just borrowing these. Square it with the young bloke later will you." I ignored him as I dressed.

"Emergency? Where?"

"Talk moving big fella. Bring all your stuff, everything, OK. Need help carrying it?"

"No mate – it's packed and ready."

"Good!" and with that Lax disappeared into the night. Golly, Balls and Percy had not even stirred. I tied my boots, grabbed my medic pack. I actually paused looking down at my rifle. I hated carrying it. It usually just got in the way. I never had any real intention of using it. It remained in the tent. I leapt through the sandbags piled high at the front of our tent and out into the hot night air.

Lax moved with a sinewy grace that I could never match. I could see his shape in the silvery light of a large full moon. He was heading toward the helipad where a nimble little Hughes OH-6 Cayuse sat, its blades turning slowly. This LOACH was used almost exclusively by the US forces.

Lax is trying to steal a US chopper I thought with trepidation. I bent low beneath the blades and up to the open door to find Lax in an argument with the pilot, a shiny faced African American man with a shaved head, goatee beard and the whitest teeth I have ever seen.

"Shiiiiiit man – you never said nothing about him being a cracker Wilt Chamberlain. He's for basketball not chopper riding. How the fuck am I gonna squeeze this giant pipe cleaner into my little spruce Cayuse! We gotta fly high on this moonlit night or Chuck will be throwing everything but the kitchen sink at us," yelled the pilot as the blades burst into life.

"Bullshit! Pup wouldn't weigh more than 8 stone in two pairs of boots and I'm a piddling jockey," Lax yelled. "Together we wouldn't be even be close to your fat arse general who usually rides for free." The pilot laughed heartily.

"Shit Lax, you're fucking crazy man. Don't let him hear you say that."

"Ahh, what's fat arse gonna do, shoot me – actually I wouldn't put it past him. You Yanks shoot everything."

"That we do my brother," the pilot said with a wide smile flashing those brilliant teeth. "That we do." He moved the throttle and the blades screamed like a Tassie devil.

"Hey, where's your fucking weapons." The pilot looked at us with wonder.

"Pup, doesn't carry and I've got my knife."

"Are you shitting me, you've got no arsenal at all?"

"If I need a gun I'll prise one from your cold, dead fingers. Now, are you gonna fly us or not?" Lax yelled over the whining blades.

"How do you figure you'll both fit?"

"I'm gonna ride this horse side saddle. Climb in Pup."

I climbed aboard and nodded to the pilot who gave me a thumbs up. Talking now would be impossible. Lax climbed in between my two knees which were bent up so far I felt like I could rest my earlobes on them. My head was pushed forward by the Perspex bubble. Lax's matted hair was in my face. It smelled strongly of fresh earth and stale water. Lax patted my right knee with a filthy hand and we rose high above the base and off over the inky black jungle full of terrors. It was my first time in a helicopter, and this thing was like a kid's toy; to say I was scared witless would be understating my terror.

Thank God I hadn't eaten, I thought as my stomach flipped

on its back not for the last time. I'd hate to have messed up the machine, wouldn't that have pissed off our pilot. We flew very high above the low cloud and were unmolested. After 10 or 15 minutes we broke through and the light of a US Fire Support base burned below. A large central howitzer was pounding illumination rounds which lit up the night sky. It was awesome and terrifying. Six smaller big guns then poured fire at everything the big boy had missed. We Aussies called them 9-mile snipers. You could hear the deep *WHUMP, WHUMP* over the chopper's whine. Someone below dropped purple smoke grenades which they lit from underneath with a light. The pilot dropped straight in and landed with a *Thump*! Lax was off almost before we hit. The pilot gave me a whack on the shoulder and a large grin, and I tried to smile back but I couldn't seem to work my jaw. I was bent very low as I ran beneath the blades trying to follow Lax. Finally, I felt safe enough to stand. I found him speaking to an American three-star general who was standing amongst a small group of soldiers. A few were wearing sunglasses despite it being 4 in the morning.

"There you go big fella, back in one piece, she's all yours!"

The general just glared at him. I gave him a nod and a thumbs up. He glowered at me, and he yelled something inaudible as I rushed past. Lax turned and stopped me with a hand on my chest just beyond the lights.

"I guess you've got some questions Pup, but we have very little time."

"I have about a billion."

"OK, I'll tell you what I can. We're on US Fire Base just near the *Boi Loi* woods. We're southwest of *Gò Dầu Hạ*."

"Wherever the fuck that is." I tried for blasé yet sounded a little shrill to my own ears.

"Doesn't really matter anyway."

"Am I AWOL Lax?"

"No mate – it's all squared off with Lt Yolka. You heard of him right? He's got our back. I was doing a bit of stuff with him in the tunnels around here. Anyway, we're heading toward a small village a little way west of here. I'd usually go through the tunnels but we're in a hurry and I'd never take a bloke like you into a tunnel, you'd take all the oxygen with that huge sniffer." Lax didn't laugh. He wasn't joking.

"We have to travel fast, and we have to be quiet. There's NVA buggers all over these woods but I really don't won't to run into a Yank patrol either. They'll let one go at you and call it – 'saying hello to the neighbours'."

"OK, OK," I said breathlessly. "And what's the emergency?"

"There's a family. They're friends. The daughter is dying Pup and you can save her."

"Sure, no worries mate. What's the problem?"

"You ever delivered a baby?"

He pulled me close before we left the US Fire Base and told me to walk in his footsteps, keep up and don't breathe. He had a quick word with the sentry on the western edge of the base who got on his radio while giving Lax a wide berth – everybody gave Lax a wide berth it seemed, even if they'd never met him before. He had an aura. I, however, was incapable of wide berthing him. I ran into his back three times on our midnight run. Lax would stop and sniff the air and I'd barrel into his back. In my defence I was also trying to avoid tree branches that Lax swept under with nary a care. The final time I hit him we both ended up on our faces in the rotting vegetation across the rudimentary track. He held a finger to his lips, then put a hand over my mouth to shut out my panting. We sat like this for a full minute before he allowed me to breathe. I don't know what he heard, and I really didn't want to. We practically ran ten kilometres in the dark that night through the *Boi Loi* woods. Following Lax was trying to follow an eel as it flashed through the murky depths of the Yarra.

A fiery dawn was just beginning to elbow its way through the dark sky as we burst through the thick jungle canopy and onto a wide dirt road heading into what appeared to be a ghost town. The streets were awash with bricks and cinder blocks and the stuff of day-to-day village living in Nam, all reduced to piles of rubbish. Every standing wall was pockmarked from bullets and shrapnel. Blackened and charred patches told of thatched houses no match for soldiers with Zippos. Was it ours or there's who did this? Did it matter? The poor buggers probably didn't live to tell. There was a temple that stood solid along the jungles edge, it seemed to be in better nick than most of the smashed houses around it. Lax turned, waved me on and sprinted to it.

"*Dược rồi. Tôi đây. Mở ra,*" He called in a half whisper and slowly the large door pulled wide and a worried looking Vietnamese man stood and beckoned us in. He looked 40-ish but who could ever tell with the Vietnamese. He may have been 70. Apart from a fleck of grey around the temples his thick head of hair was the colour of boot polish. Viet build, five-foot nothin' and likely to blow away in a stiff breeze. Of course, I was cognizant by now that you underestimated the size of the fight in the Vietnamese at your peril.

"Lax," he said, "*Tôi nghĩ cô ấy sẽ chết.*"

"She won't die now, I've bought Pup. He is Thiên thần."

We leapt the stone steps, through the large doorway and into the belly of the temple. The large room had been converted to a home. There was a rudimentary kitchen along one wall, beds along another. I could see through the temple to a small garden beyond the rear door before the deep green of the jungle swallowed the light. The place had been shelled in the past, and although these people had done their best to repair the larger holes, the morning sun still shone through one or two places. There were four other people in the room beside the man. A small boy in a thin cotton shirt and a white pair of underpants. Another girl in what looked like spotted pyjamas. They saw me enter and stood mouths agape with wonderment and fear. The little boy silently cut and ran, and we didn't see him for ages, which was a good thing as it turned out. There was an old woman who appeared to be about 200. She sat on the floor, in a large pool of dark blood, wiping the brow of a girl of about 17. The girl was impossibly pregnant. She was on all fours in the middle of a blood drenched mat, and she was moaning. It was deep, resonant, and heartbreaking. The room smelled of blood, sweat and panic. Lax turned to me and spoke softly. His face betrayed none of my stress.

"These people are my friends. The girl is Hoa. She is going to die if we don't get the baby out. I don't know much about delivering bubs, but I know they don't come out feet first."

I went to the girl who had begun panting in short, staccato breaths. I gently lifted the white *áo dài* she was wearing and saw the problem. It was a footling breech birth. I had done a bit of obstetrics; pregnancy, birth and the postpartum but I'd never delivered a baby. I'd never even seen a live birth except on an old grainy film in the theatre at Melbourne Uni. There was too much blood here. She was in trouble. I threw off my pack and opened it. I tipped the contents on a clear space of floor.

"OK! Clean up first," I said as I tipped a small bottle of alcohol on my hands and briskly rubbed them together.

"Lax, clean the shit off your hands with this, I'm going to need your help." Lax grabbed the bottle and did as he was ordered.

"Now, you speak Vietnamese. Tell her I'm here to help and she can trust me."

"Hoa, *người đàn ông này là tinh thần của tổ tiên bạn!*" Hoa quietened but still flinched beneath my touch. I pulled her eyelids up to see the colour of her eyes. They were a milky white. I checked her teeth and gums, and they also showed the tell-tale signs of massive blood loss. I knew she'd lost blood: I was kneeling in it and could feel it coating my legs through my pants. This girl was going to go into hypovolaemic shock and if this were to happen we'll probably lose them both. Hoa was fully dilated and one pink foot was already showing. The other foot could be caught on the lip of the cervix, and it may have torn. It could also be an incomplete breech and the leg is pointing straight up, I could clearly recall the black and white pencil sketch from the textbook. This could mean that the blood is coming, not from a cervical tear, but a uterine tear and then we were in big trouble. I didn't know how I could fix that in a bombed temple in the middle of a war.

"Lax, how do I say, it's alright?"

"*Không sao cả,*" he said.

"*Không sao cả,*" I repeated. Tell her I need to check where the other leg is.

"I'm not sure I can say that."

"Well, I said testily. "Work it out, we haven't much time!" Hoa had her eyes shut tightly so I nodded to the old woman who nodded back to me gravely. I pushed my long fingers in and around where I guessed the other foot could be caught. It took some time. I found the leg and it seemed to be bent. I tried to run my fingers down to the foot. Hoa screamed weakly. Every instinct I had was to stop the exploratory. I hesitated. On cue Lax said quietly.

"Don't stop now mate."

"She could die, she's at her end," I said. The look he gave me then said it all. There weren't any choices here. I tried again on a slightly different angle. The old lady mopped Hoa's brow with a bloody rag. She reached out and patted my hand imploringly.

I found the leg again and I traced it down to the foot which was indeed caught on the cervix. I was able to push it back and loose as Hoa screamed and collapsed into the sticky wet of her own blood. The foot arrived with another gush.

"*Thông minh,*" I said which I think meant excellent. "I've got the other foot." Hoa moaned. She was so weak now, from the blood loss and the rigours of the birth. The pain must have been excruciating but I couldn't medicate her, I only had morphine and this would have finished off our bub. Lax was kneeling low next to the old woman and whispering to them both. He was rubbing the old lady's back as she wept. She had raised clasped hands at me, the rag between her fingers almost entirely red.

We weren't out of the woods of course; you never are until the head is clear. My primary concern was the umbilical cord being occluded. Hoa being on all fours might help, but vaginal breech deliveries were notoriously tricky. The cervix isn't filled by the cranium and the cord can slip down and get squashed, cutting off the baby's oxygen. It hadn't prolapsed, (it wasn't poking out) so that was a good thing. That may have happened when her waters broke, how long ago now I was afraid to guess. Breech is birthing in reverse. Usually, the head squeezes through and the body follows with a flick of the wrist. I was drawing the body out slowly trying to avoid pinching the cord. Sure enough, the cord appeared to be around the baby's throat.

Good God, I thought, what else?

"Lax," I barked, "I need you up this end." I told him to try to keep slack around the cord and I'll try to get the head out as quickly as I can. I had the chin now, but I wasn't getting any movement, forward or back.

"Lax, you have to hold the baby. Don't pull on it or you'll damage the back. Cradle it lightly while I manoeuvre Hoa's hips."

"Oh, Pup, bloody hell! I can't do this!" but he did take the baby's body from my hands. I shuffled forward in the ooze that had attracted all sorts of flying creatures looking for a feed. I grabbed her hips with my thumbs and my fingers fell into the greater sciatic notch. I began to swivel Hoa's hips.

Lax was yelling, "*KHông sao cả, Không sao cả*" to reassure himself and maybe even Hoa. Hoa was mewling weakly now.

How she was still conscious was a miracle.

"Any movement mate?"

"I think it's coming Pup. I felt some give."

"Don't pull..." Suddenly the baby came in a rush and Pup caught the baby to his chest. The shock more than the momentum sat him heavily on his bum. He landed with a little splash and slid backwards in the wet and sticky pool staining the floor. Lax held the limp body like a live grenade.

"It's not breathing Pup. Shit. He, she's not breathing." The umbilical was indeed around the baby's throat.

"Is baby dead?" came a voice in my ear which made me start. Apparently the man had been there the whole time trying to help but at a loss to know how.

"OK, carefully hand him to me mate."

"Him Pup. Is it a boy?" Lax said.

"That would be a penis mate, I may not be an obstetrician but..."

I removed the cord and held the baby up by its heels. It was turning blue. I gave it a swift smack on the bottom trying to think of what I should do next. There was a heartbeat, I could feel the pulse in the neck and the cord wasn't bent or squished. I listened to the baby's chest and could hear a small grunting. This bloke was trying to breath. I grabbed the baby and placed him on the floor. I was about to perform CPR when I noticed there was blood coming from his nose. I think he had aspirated his mother's blood. I covered the nose and mouth with mine and, instead of blowing, I sucked, hard. Suddenly my mouth filled with copper, and I spat a dark clot onto the blood-soaked floor. The baby took a long deep breath and started bawling.

I looked at Lax and our eyes met. I wondered if I looked as flummoxed as he was.

"*Quá nhiều máu*," said the old lady and I looked up to see Hoa had collapsed in the gore of the birth. I handed the screaming baby to Lax, this time he held him surely, and I moved over to Hoa and turned her as gently as I could onto her back. She was bathed in blood.

"Lax, she's still in trouble. I have to deliver the placenta but first I need you to cut the umbilical cord about an inch from the belly button." The man, eager to be of assistance, was already handing Lax a knife. I pushed the unconscious Hoa's knees up as the old lady cradled her head in her lap and stroked her forehead. The young girl appeared and began wiping up some of the blood with some old clothing. She was weeping too. The placenta came relatively easily, but bad luck comes in three's as Pop Dempsey used to say, "If Murphy don't get ya, Brophy will." The placenta wasn't whole. There were some small tears in the cervix, but I believed they would heal themselves, but the missing placenta would cause the blood vessels in the uterus to withhold full contraction and continue to bleed. We had to get it all out.

"Lax, what blood type are you?"

"My blood!"

"Yeah. What blood type are you do you know?"

"I'm O, I think. Yep O."

"O what? Are you O positive or O negative?"

"Ummm, O pos, no no, O neg."

"It's on your identity discs!"

"I don't wear identity discs!" he said helplessly.

"WELL, WHAT THE FUCK IS IT, O POS. OR O NEG.?

"I'm 90 percent sure I'm O pos. 95% mate."

"Too risky."

"O," said the man pointing to his chest. He drew an O in the blood besides us. He followed it with a small minus sign.

"He'd know," said Lax. "He was a soldier. The VC knew their blood types to give blood in the field."

The man removed his shirt and lay next to Hoa. He placed his arm against hers.

"Great. Universal donor. You're gonna save a life my friend." I put a hand on his forehead and left a bloody mess behind. He just looked at me with a determined grimace. I moved quickly. I took a needle and piping from the packs contents I'd strewn on the floor. I grabbed a bottle of an intravascular blood expander I kept safely wrapped in an old rag. I hoped with the man's blood and the plasma expander I could create a larger volume going in than what the poor kid had coming out; at least until I could stop the haemorrhage. I beckoned the young girl over and told her to keep the jar up and I fed the tube into the bottle. I sucked the fluid forth and stuck the needle in the mother's skinny vein which was purple against her cyanotic skin. I nodded at the little girl then, who still looked at me like I may grow fangs and tear the collective family throats out and moved my head upward. She lifted the bottle and watched the fluid flow through the plastic tubing. I moved around the man and unwrapped the second tubing. I had it wrapped around my bicep. I'd pre-affixed needles to both ends. The man's arm was thin and sinewy, and I had to struggle to find a vein. I tried quite a few times before the blood rushed forth. I found the girl's vein and I motioned to the man to keep the tube straight and lower than the girl's heart. He nodded.

"Mate", I said to Lax. "We're not finished. The blood coming out is going to be more than the blood going in if we don't get the rest of the placenta out. My hands are too big on such a small girl. I found the foot, but this is worse. Further in. I need you mate. She needs you."

"Pup," Lax said, "What's a pla-centa?"

I pointed to the congealing placenta on the ground.

"What do I, wha… what did you need?"

"You're going to have to reach in and try to clear any gelatinous lumps that have attached themselves to the uterus wall mate. I've got to try to piece it together and make sure you've got it all."

"Pup, I can't do that, I'll, I can't…" and a shroud of emotion hooded his face: an expression so alien. The vampire of Vietnam, the night crawler, the horrible *Hô Tinh* was absolutely petrified.

"I'm not asking Lax," I said with as much iron as I could muster.

"Can the young girl do it? The old lady? They have little hands."

"I can't direct them Lax, and we don't have much time for you to translate."

"I don't know what I'm doing Pup. I can't mate, I told you. What if she dies."

"She's dying now! Man-up bugger ya, I need you mate." The young girl holding the bottle with "Plasma" written in black texta on the side. She caught Lax's eye and said, "*Chị tôi.*" (My sister.) Lax nodded slowly at the girl and moved forward.

Finally, our luck turned. Lax was able to find two small fragments and I was able to piece together the placenta. The old lady gently placed Hoa's head on the ground, got up and wrapped the completed placenta in the wet cloth she had been using on the girl's brow and disappeared out the back door. I checked Hoa's eyelids and the colour was starting to trickle back. I looked down at our man on the floor and said, "Little more, OK?" He blinked once. I noticed the hand holding the tubing into Hoa's arm was missing the first two knuckles of his right index finger. Against a far wall I noticed the little boy had appeared from his hiding place. He had grabbed up the baby and was cradling it in his arms. His skinny, bent legs looked like brown twigs sticking out of thin grey underpants. He was cooing gently to the baby while he stroked its hair. I removed the needles and stuck a band-aid on the man's and Hoa's arms. I then rescued the bottle from the girl who raised her arm up and down and squeezed her elbow. I chuckled and squeezed her shoulder. She flinched but looked up and tried a smile. Then I took Hoa's pulse; weak but getting stronger. I checked Hoa's cervix, barely bleeding now. I decided there was a little vaginal damage that I could probably sew up, but I decided to do it after I fell down. Lax was lying on his back and I lay down next to him.

"Unbefuckinglievable," he said to the pockmarked ceiling.

"You're an angel mate. You're a gift. You did it."

"I'm no angel mate." I reached for his small hand and held it triumphantly in the air as if he'd just kicked the winning goal for the Lions.

"These little hands saved two lives today. Not bad for a vampire." I thought I may have gone too far with that one but Lax just lay in the gore smiling broadly. He didn't reply.

"We were bloody lucky mate. I've never done anything like that before."

"No luck mate," he said to the blue sky peeking through the holes. "You've an angel Pup. You just don't bloody know it."

The old woman returned from the yard and gently picked up the baby from the young girl who had plucked it from the boy. She carried it over to Hoa who lay covered in an army blanket. Her head was now in the man's lap. The old woman gently dabbed the baby's feet on her forehead, her stomach, her arms, and her vagina. She then lightly touched the feet on the man who sat in a sort of stupor on the stained concrete. He lowered his head to accept the blessing. She placed both feet on Lax's forehead and then turned and did the same to me. She stroked them three times across my brow. The baby was sleeping peacefully, I could hear the soft whimper as it breathed. What a wonderful sound.

As I let exhaustion take me I saw people coming into the temple. They just materialized. I was too tired to feel any trepidation. I fought off the lethargy as I still needed to give Hoa a couple of stitches and monitor her vitals. The poor kid had gone through a lot. She was as brave as any soldier I saw on my tour. It was, by far, the most beautiful, wonderful experience I had in that horrible war.

I had the Monster of Vietnam to thank for it.

EGG

What can I tell you about Yolka? There are good leaders in every war if you look hard enough for them. They don't always rise to the very top like the head on a beer. Sometimes they can do better from below. I always thought the Việt Nam War was a quagmire of bad people making bad decisions, inexperienced people out of their depth and ambitious people making decisions to suit themselves. It cost many people, soldier and civilian, their lives. Some of the guys in charge couldn't run a chook raffle. Some of the Aussie officers and a few of the American brass bucked the trend. Lt Col. 'Yolka' was the best. He was so fine an operational officer that he was constantly seconded to the US services to help them out. This was a big deal as the Yank brass rarely rated the Australian way of things. They felt the Aussies were over cautious. There were never enough engagements for their liking. Our body counts were too low. Sometimes we wondered what pissed them off more: the low body count of the enemy or the low body count of us diggers. Finally, however, when the hubbub of discontent at home in the states became a cacophony, political pressure meant gung-ho, politically ambitious US officers needed to change. That's my reading of it all anyway. Add that to the unrest in Nam with troops filling body bags, added to the numbers being killed with friendly fire and, then multiplied by the cases of fragging; soldiers murdering superiors or rivals, often with a grenade dropped into an occupied latrine, became almost commonplace), the Americans started to have a good, close look at the Aussie modus operandi. The kills to loss ratio blew them away; pun intended. The elite SASR (Special Air Services Regiment) sections made up of the best Australian soldiers, which included a New Zealand section in each, were known as the *ma rừng*, Vietnamese for phantoms of the jungle. The VC admitted post war they were the only troops in Vietnam they truly feared. The SASR barely lost a man over there and Yolka was one of the brains behind their success. Yolka made sure the 'wisdom drain' that saw good soldiers sent back home to Australia was crazy. Yolka insisted the best of the best be given commissions and asked to hang around.

Yolka's MO was shoot and scoot. He liked a meticulous grid-square by grid-square overview of the land. He didn't like surprises. He loved Lax who epitomised stealth and silence. Yolka used to bring him in on as many operations as he could, always on Lax's terms though. Lax was determined to fight his war his way, as we've established.

The origins of Yolka's name is a beauty. He was a short, squat, and hairy man with a huge head and a bullock's neck to support it. He was also formidably strong. A career soldier, he had been a decorated hero in WWII fighting in Africa and New Guinea, (still in his African uniform) and had again proved himself in the theatre of Korea where he was decorated yet again. Yolka received the Korea Medal after single-handedly attacking a Chinese machinegun nest with a can of petrol and a cigarette lighter. The ensuing conflagration resulted in Yolka setting his hands, head, and hair alight. The burns healed but the hair never grew back. Soon after his brief hospital stay Yolka was in the

Officer's bar complaining that his head now looked like a boiled egg. One of his mates piped up with, "God help the chicken that gave birth to that monster egg. It'd be a double yolker at least!" And with that the name Yolka was hatched.

    I found out later that Lt Col Yolka had politely asked the US 3-Star if Lax could retrieve a doctor from Nui Dat in his private helicopter. The General replied with an unequivocable, "No fucking way. What, and leave me here in this shithole!" Yolka calmly explained it would take no more than half an hour.

    "Use one of our doctors."

    "No," said Yolka. "We need our own guy."

    "What's the fucking emergency."

    "We have a Vietnamese civilian and a very tricky birth. The baby is that of a US soldier; it may have been non-consensual. She will die if she doesn't get assistance and the Aussie press have already got wind of her predicament." Yolka knew this was a lie, but he also knew that the American hierarchy had nothing but antipathy for the Aussie journos who were flaming the flames of anti-war sentiment back in Australia and then the US in turn. The general finally acquiesced and that's how Lax and I ended up making our midnight dash to a small dot on the Vietnamese map to try and save his friend. He also radioed forward and explained where I was so I wouldn't be shot for going AWOL if I were to make it back. I never met Lt Col Yolka. I only really knew what Lax told me about him. He seemed like a fine officer. He had the right priorities. I believe he would have been a fine man to shake hands with.

RIC

Stepping into Rosie's room for the first time after it had become my room was tough. It was full of Rosie's stuff, well the stuff she didn't want I guess. An appropriate place for me. I sat on the edge of the bed and took it all in. It was bigger than my room in Little George Street. Lily had cleared the walls of the hippie posters Rosie had plastered everywhere. A spirited flower child whose free love came at quite a cost. Lily had tried her best to make it less Rosie and more me. The scent of Rosie still transuded from the walls. Every cupboard or drawer I opened abounding with the mould of memory, the mildew of loss.

Iris came to the door after a time.

"Is this too hard? We could swap rooms Terry if this one contains too many memories." She sat heavily on the bed next to me, the bedsprings whinged and whined. I had a distant memory of antipathy to those springs. It made me wince.

"I'm a big boy. Every day I'm further from Vietnam and that bit further from Rosie. You know what they say, time wounds all heels." She reached across and touched the hand that lay lifeless on the burgundy bedspread. I could see her hand, yet I felt nothing.

"Time won't heal that." She looked up at me peering just beneath a black fringe of shining hair. Her dark eyes large and serious.

"Life tests us all. It's how we respond to the tests that defines us."

"Confucius also say, he who paint toilet not necessarily shithouse painter."

"Smartarse," said Iris punching my leg.

"I'm just lightening the mood here; I do appreciate the advice." I smiled at her, and she blushed. She changed the subject.

"This will cheer you up anyway. We girls know how much you boys love playing with balls." With a cheeky giggle she reached down over the base of the bed and struggled up with my old cricket kit. Finally, she dropped it on the bed and we both bounced. The springs groaned. It was heavy.

"My old kit. Good Lord!" I stared at it as my emotions broiled. The old cricket kit was a memory of days when all that mattered was how many wickets I might take, runs I might make and beers I might celebrate with.

"Thanks for the help there Tezz," she said.

"Invalid, remember. War casualty!" She laughed as I twisted my body around to reach for the zipper with my left hand. I felt an electric jolt of change as I touched it.

"My old cricket coffin, I can't believe I left it here."

"Mum kept it for you. She always said you'd be coming back you know?"

"I don't know how she knew; I didn't know I would be back."

"Mum just knows stuff. She's a bit witchy."

"She is indeed," I said as I ran my hand along the bag.

"Terry," Iris asked with those same serious eyes, "Is it true they call it a coffin because cricket will bore you to death?"

"Cheeky bugger!" I swore with feigned indignation. "The

gentleman's game, you ignoramus!" I pushed her shoulder and she rolled onto her back with a snort of derision. Lily appeared in the doorway.

"The room OK Terry?"

"It's perfect Lily. You're very kind." Lily smiled.

"I go to bed now. I got market in the morn."

"Come and get me and I'll come and give you a hand. I work here now."

"Are you crazy!" Iris looked at me as if I'd lost my marbles. I knew the look from the Repat.

"It very, very early Terry," Lily said.

"Lily, I'm happy to help and I don't sleep much anyway. You'll be doing me a favour."

"OK. I leave in three more hour. You must try and get some sleep, or you will be no good to help. Iris – let him sleep now."

"OK Mum, Jeez!" Iris said with a smile. "Night Mum, night Terry. Happy to have you here brother-in-law." She then leapt off the bed and flounced from the room.

I turned back to the bed and the bag. I must have had a few drinks after my last game which was probably true. I used to have a few after most games if the truth be told. Rosie and I must have made plans to head out post-match and I'd not headed home. I closed the door so as not to disturb my new housemates and unzipped the coffin. I was assailed by the smell of rubber, and linseed; old grass and new leather. It was divine! It couldn't help myself and I shook it all out onto the bed. A couple of old cork net balls rolled across the bed and onto the floor where they bounced loudly across the room.

"Sorry!" I said softly to the quiet house. There was no reply.

There were gloves and my old plastic box. There were two new cricket balls, still wrapped in tissue paper. Wonder how I scored those unsullied crimson orbs. Must have been wash-outs and being the opening bowler, I might have snaffled them and tossed them into the kit for a less rainy day. The heady thrill of a brand-new Kookaburra never really leaves you. I reached beyond the zipper and I felt the hard willow; it was my bat. My beloved cricket bat. The Ian Chappell signed Gray-Nicholls – cost me an arm and a leg but I somehow felt the great man was with me for the very few balls I ever lasted. As a batsman I was a ferret, the guy that came in after the bunnies. I did love that bat though. I grabbed it in my left and swung it through the air, feeling the balance and weight, noting the lack of meaningfully placed cherries on its face. There was at least one beauty in its middle; I was happy with that.

I was able to use the trusty blade to shift a large bird's nest that had filled up the flue in the kitchen and contributed, in no small way, to the smokiness every time Lily cooked. Ian Chappell comes to the rescue again. I wouldn't be using the bat for cricket anymore, so I took immense pleasure finding various uses for Ian now we were both post-cricket. It was an added bonus that my Ian was much more competent as a jack-of-all-trades than it'd ever been as a bat! We had a plastic lined umbrella stand just beside the doorway to the kitchen, for when the Melbourne weather became inclement; Sydney people might haughtily suggest that could be an hourly proposition. Four seasons in one day, that was Melbourne. I placed Ian Chappell in the stand and that's where he would stay until required. Until he could be of use.

I dropped back into Fitzroy a couple of days later and explained my new accommodation to Mum. She complained that she'd only got me back and I was off again. I told her I was only a suburb away and I'd be back all the time for the S.O.S. meetings and to spend some quality time with Janine Davies. Mum spat her cup of tea across the room, then scolded me for making her laugh and burning her lip. I laughed for ten minutes while she held an ice cube to it. I promised to buy her dinner at Chī every week to apologise for my rudeness. It was more like every fortnight, but Mum made the trek over every second Thursday afternoon. Lily and Iris were so happy to see her and Lily refused to let her pay for her meal. I made them promise to take it out of my wage. She was my problem after all, not theirs.

I'd been working at the Chī, and living above it, for just under three months before Ricky Pepi walked into the restaurant with a leggy date who tottered above him on skinny ankles and skinnier heels. She had closely cropped hair, her racoon eyes bore mascara which appeared to be an inch thick. She had long eyelashes, and a face so pale under the thick make-up she looked anaemic. It was just before Christmas. Ricky had changed a lot in the years since we'd grown apart. He'd grown older but not up. Ricky was never one to grow wiser, it wasn't in his make-up. He liked to be known as Ric now, but I was helpless to call him anything but Ricky, except occasionally "fuck-knuckle". Our lives diverged after school, I got involved with uni, Ricky chose petty crime. Well, that's probably a little unfair. He'd been selling a little weed after school. He had some family in Mildura who used to supply him with it. He used to manage a couple of clubs in Collingwood and a bar down the beach in Seaford. They gave him the perfect cover to shop the family merch.

Ricky wore gold jewellery over a thick black, turtleneck skivvy beneath a thin black moustache that Ian Chappell would have been embarrassed by - the batsman not the bat! He was still a laugh a minute though. It was his laugh I noticed first. I was scrubbing pans and plates and passing them to Iris to dry. It was a quiet Wednesday, our first night on for the week. We always had Monday and Tuesday off and I'd try to get to the Repat or the CF kids as often as I could on these days. Lily welcomed Ricky and his lady in and sat them near the counter. I heard the cheeky laugh and I stopped dead. Iris looked at me quizzically as I straightened and cocked my head. I grabbed the tea-towel and dried my hands as I stood in the doorway.

"JAYZUS CHYSSST!" yelled Ricky, scaring the enamel off his date who was mid-story. She swivelled around expecting to see Elvis or Jesus or both.

"Terry Shepherd, you skinny macaroni! I heard you were fucking dead!" He jumped up and grabbed me around the waist in a mighty hug. I wrapped the good arm around his shoulders laughing.

"Well, if it's not Ricky Pepi beneath that sweet and sour stained moustache. I can get you a wet cloth if you'd like to wipe that off." Ricky held me at arm's length for appraisal. Never one for delicacy he blurted out,

"Where the fuck's your eye?"

"In a tree in Vietnam mate. Where's your bottom two feet?" I asked with mock astonishment looking him up and down.

"That is the million dollar question my friend. I think the old man left half of me in his pyjamas." He laughed again. It was a loud, easy, machinegun laugh if that's possible. It was a laugh often accompanied by tears, and usually ended with him repeating the final line of the joke.

"In his fucking pyjamas." Like all great wags Ricky laughed even harder at his own jokes than yours and usually harder on the second telling. You never minded though as his cachinnation fed your soul. God, I loved that laugh.

"Come and meet Candice. I keep calling her Candy, but she assures me it's Candice." Ricky grabbed my apron and pulled me over to the table. We were the only people in the place.

"Candy, sorry I mean Candice, meet Terry, my tallest friend and the best ruckman Sacred Heart Primary ever had. He's a nun kisser of great renown – I swear to God – a fucking nun kisser!" Candy smiled weakly and proffered her hand as I approached. I could see the smile fade and the eyes widen as she appraised my height, my impossibly long hand, the scar on my check beneath the shiny black eye-patch. She left me hanging completely flummoxed as to how she could shake my left hand with her right. I grabbed the back of her hand and shook it firmly saying,

"Candy, nice to meet you. Any friend of Ricky's… needs to get psychiatric help." Candice looked unsure while Ricky laughed like he was going to choke.

"Psychiatric help!" he guffawed. After introducing us Ricky then proceeded to completely ignore his date for the next two hours while we ate and laughed, drank, and laughed, reminisced, and laughed, and laughed. When Candy stood to leave about 10.30 Ricky said, "Lovely to see you again Candy. I'll give you a call, OK, Lovely."

With a stunned look turning from Ricky to me, Candice stuck

out her right hand, pulled it back, tried again, looked down at it, turned and left.

"Not sure Candy is gonna take that call," I said with a smile.

"I'm thinking not. I don't think Candy is very happy with me. It's probably for the best. The lights are on, but the place is empty. I need someone to a least try to get my jokes." I nodded in sombre agreement.

"Candy is a singer; well Candy thinks she can sing. I think she wanted to jump my bones so I'd get her band a gig at the club. Oh well, *A caval donato non si guarda in bocca.*" At that he took a long drink of his wine and pulled a cigarette from a pack sitting on the table.

"I take it you are still a non-smoker."

"You take it correctly."

"Candy isn't for me. She is a bit scary if I'm being honest. She used to go out with some Sharps. I'd rather keep my distance from those fucking psychos I tell you. Fucking psychos!"

"A what?" I said.

"A Sharp, a Sharpie. You've never heard of a Sharpie?"

"I can honestly say I haven't." Ricky's eyes darkened as he played with the chopsticks in front of him, bouncing their ends on the tablecloth.

"Sharpies, per se, aren't so bad. They like funny clothes and crap haircuts. They dress nice enough, that's why they call themselves Sharpies, they think they look sharp. They like very loud rock music. They like a drink. They love a fight most of all. They're just wild kids really. Probably on their way out now as the punks and mods are taking over. They never hang around our place because our bands play more refined types of music.

Soul, rhythm, and blues. Good vibes. This disco stuff starting up in the US is gonna be huge. Good thing too. The Sharps can be a pain in the arse."

"Right," I said, a little unsurely.

"There's some particularly nasty fuckers just near here actually. I've had some dealings with them but no more. They are freaking insane. The North Richmond Sharps are clinging on to their rebellious youth with white knuckles. They are evil fuckers and they're best left well alone."

"Do they hang around here?"

"Yes mate. Nearby. They're the lords of the pill and needle in these parts. Weapons. Porn. Girls. You name it, these guys have their skanky hands all over it. They are the bearers of bad news. The cops hate their guts, especially Sid the Scorpion – he's a nasty prick that one."

"Sid the Scorpion," I laughed, "Sounds like a character in a kid's cartoon."

"Sid's like the head honcho. He's the biggest prick of the lot. He's not a cartoon my skinny friend. He's more like a malignant tumour, a bloody cancer."

"Sounds like a very pleasant fellow," I said. "They ever give you trouble?"

"Yes indeedy. We're not meeting Saturdays for English Breakfast and cucumber sandwiches."

"What happened?" I asked. Ricky looked at me and pursed his lips.

"As we pass through the S-bend of life Macaroni we can sometimes find ourselves swimming in a bit of shit. I was a customer and then a salesman. I decided I needed to keep my head above their sewage and the North Richmond Sharps don't like hearing the word 'no'."

"O-K," I said slowly. "They sound like fine fellows." Ricky stopped playing with the chopsticks and pointed one at me.

"They're a little wary of my out-of-town *famiglia*, but not Sid. He doesn't give a shit. Mad as a cut snake that one!" Ricky looked up at me and narrowed his eyes.

"Shep, cross the street if you see these pricks mate. They're bad news, especially for a clean-living, non-smoking, nun rooter like you. You've got enough on your plate." He waved the chopstick in an arc taking in my eye patch and my arm. "Those pricks have nothing you want."

"Alright, alright. You don't have to paint me a picture. Keep away from the Sharps," I said, writing in the air with an imaginary pencil. I ticked it with a flourish. "Coz Ricky Pepi is shit-scarred of them." Ricky reached across to tick the air three times with the chopstick.

"You better fucking believe it ol' buddy," he said with a large grin, "I hate fucking Sharpies."

Later that night, as Iris passed my bedroom door on the way to clean her teeth, I asked her about the North Richmond Sharpies.

"Yeah. Not good Tezz. They're pretty horrible."

"Right, that's what Ricky said."

"Originally they were just scallywags but as they got older they got into more heavy shit. Now I swear they just push the Sharpie bit so they can get close to punters in pubs and clubs and sell their drugs. Why do you ask?"

"Ricky mentioned them, he got all serious too."

"Yeah, they're pretty crazy. They have a compound just off

Palmer Street. Not far from here. Where the old factories are. It's all barbed wire and big pig-dogs. The cops are always there. You often see some of them in Bridge Road when they're not in gaol. They have to report to the police station most days as part of their parole.

"Do you and Lily have any problems with them?"

"Ahh, sometimes. They eat here sometimes and scare our customers away."

"Right," I said.

"I think their main guy, Sid, had the hots for me," Iris visibly shuddered. "He beat up my first boyfriend. Poor Pete. They just started laying into him in the street. No guy will come near me now. Those arseholes think they run everything around here." As Iris skipped to the bathroom she called back, "Why the hell did you want to talk about him for? Now I'll have bloody nightmares."

"Sorry about that," I called after her, but she was off.

I got to see the North Richmond Sharps for myself the very next day. Maybe I was looking for them. If not for the conversation with Ricky I probably wouldn't have even noticed. I was making my way to the milk bar on Bridge Road for the morning paper. As I turned to step into the doorway, my head down, I almost walked into a thick set bloke about my age standing with his arms folded across his chest. His square jaw jutted truculently as he gave me the hairy eyeball. He wore a tight-fitting jumper and even tighter pants that left nothing to the imagination. His testicles were sharply delineated through the fabric. It looked painful. I hoped he didn't see my glance down there.

How does he walk? I thought to myself.

"Where you are going champ," he spat caustically.

"Ah, just getting a paper mate." My response sounded a little pastel to my ears, so I added as an afterthought.

"If it's any of your business," adding a soft-hued undertone and wishing I'd just shut up. I looked past him to where another short-haired guy stood at the counter. He appeared to be in deep discussion with Mr Dwyer, the owner.

"You can just fucking wait 'till we're finished in here; right!" He had his head tilted up at me; his brow furrowed beneath a spiky hedge row of reddish hair. It burst the banks on his skull to cascade down the back of his neck and splashed onto his shoulders. He cracked his clenched knuckles that bore skinny, ragged tattoos that looked like they'd be drawn on with a blue Biro. They were pathetic. I nodded at his knuckles.

"You draw those yourself?" I asked. I was happier with this one. A dash of crimson.

"What the fuck?" he asked as his face started to redden. Suddenly he was joined by his mate who barged passed him into the doorway. He was bigger than the first. He was a brute. He had jet-black hair, a thick fringe across the top of his skull that looked like it had been cut with a Stanley knife and a metal ruler. He sported a long handled, thin moustache that ran down passed his mouth and ended in a puddle around his stubbled chin. His dark eyes were predatory, soulless, like a shark. They crinkled in a smile. They became malefic; and somehow even worse. He wore a heavy black duffle coat, skinny jeans, and a twisted smile. A cigarette hung slackly from thin lips barely concealing chipped and yellowing teeth.

"Fuck me drunk Slug," he said, his cigarette danced up and down in a brume of blue smoke."If it isn't Lurch from the *Addam's Family*." Slug, the spikey redhead, chortled and patted Duffle coat's shoulder obsequiously.

"Our Lurch seems to have been in the wars." Upon the hand pointing at my missing eye danced a drawing of a scorpion in the same thin bluey, grey line as his mate's tattoos. Its head pointed toward his elbows, its long, scaly tail ran down his index finger and hooked into a vicious spike above the nail.

"Yooouuu rang!" drawled Slug in the catchcry of the TV character and the scorpion tattoo tittered in an effeminate laugh, incongruous with his hefty build. He returned the shoulder slap. They stepped around me and bounced along the footpath. I turned and watched them saunter away.

I'd reckon I just met Sid the Scorpion, I thought to myself. Ricky was right, he wasn't like any cartoon character I'd ever seen before. He looked like just what he was. A bad, and possibly mad bastard who was best left alone. That turned out to be easier said than done.

About a month later four of the gang came for dinner. They walked in with an Esky full of beer and commandeered a table. I was in the kitchen when Iris poked her head through the colourific plastic streamers dividing the kitchen from the restaurant to inform me.

"Remember you asked me about the Sharpies?"

"Yes," I said.

"Well, a bunch of them just rolled in for a meal."

"Terrific," I said. "They're money is as good as anyone else's I suppose."

"It is if they bloody pay," she added dryly and disappeared from the doorway.

Lily placed the pan she was shaking over a large flame down and turned off the heat.

"I go help Iris," she said as she undid the greying apron she wore from around her waist.

"I can go Lily," I said. "You stay. I can't cook, remember."

"OK," she said. "Thank you Terry." As I entered the restaurant it was apparent that the recently loud and bubbling room had become quieter. Two of the four tables eating and talking happily had hurriedly decided to leave. Catching the waitress's eye, hands scribbling phantom cheques in the air.

The North Richmond Sharpies aren't great for business, I thought to myself. Iris was at the table asking if they would like glasses for their beer.

"Glasses," one of the men scoffed. "Why dirty glasses?" he laughed and proceeded to raise the long-necked bottle and swallowed as much as he could. His Adam's apple danced up and down as he pulled the beer down. The other three Sharps whooped and cheered. The man banged the bottle on the table making it spit a white froth down the side and onto the tablecloth. He breathed heavily, wiped the back of his hand across his mouth and let go a long, loud belch. The others cheered.

"Better out than in I always say." He laughed and sat down heavily in his chair.

"How about some fucking food Iris," said the man at the head of the table. I remembered him from the milk bar, Sid the Scorpion had called him Slug. I assumed it was his Sharpie name unless he was baptised Slug. A fine name all the same. One to be proud of. Iris walked towards him, her pad and pencil at the ready when Slug noticed my arrival.

"Well, if it isn't Lurch. Who raaaaaaang for you?"

The others at the table all swirled around in my direction. The guy with his back to me scraped his chair loudly as he spun. It was Sid.

"Ahhh. So, it is," he cried. "Don't tell me you work in this Chinky chonky. I hope you're not the fucking chef, you'd probably burn everything." The other three men laughed heartily.

"The ladies cook, I clean," I said with as much frost as I could muster.

"A one-eyed, one-armed dishwasher. I've seen it all. Is he the only bastard to answer the Help Wanted ad?" said yet another.

"Of course you're all free to dine somewhere else if it bothers you. Can I show you the door?"

"No Lurch old buddy, I think we'll stay right here. Iris here always looks after us. Don't you gorgeous?" Sid reached across and tried to grab Iris on the bottom, but she skilfully dodged his big hand and he grabbed only air. Sid laughed the same stupid high-pitched titter I'd heard in the milk bar "This guy is a moron," I thought.

"What can I get you?" Iris said without inflection.

"We want fried rice, egg rolls, dim sims and some stews, meat and stuff to mix into it. Just keep bringing shit and we'll tell you when to stop," Sid said amiably.

"And we want cuttle-ry, I'm not eating with no bloody chopsticks!" said another Sharpie with a very round and fuzz-covered head.

"And what the fuck are you gonna do Lurch, feed it all to us?" said the redheaded Slug, his belligerent chin poked toward me again, his eyes, grey slits.

"I just clean up," I said.

"Then we'll be sure to make a huge mess, so you earn your money," said the guy that belched. "We'll look after you and your mum Iris," he said and they all laughed. I could see another of the tables trying to catch my eye to get their bill. I walked over and told them it'd be coming right up. I walked back to the counter and added up their total. The redhead followed me with his eyes as I went. I'm not sure Slug liked me very much.

The four men ate plenty, drank more and made a huge mess, as they had promised. They stayed very late, probably to taunt us. Lily, her kitchen closed for the night, leant on the counter, and watched them closely like a mother hawk watching over her eyas now predators were nearby. Iris sat with me in the kitchen. We chatted softly. I'd washed and packed away the Sharps' dishes ages ago. For two hours they had just been emptying their Esky. They were determined not to leave until every last drop had been swallowed. As if on cue Sid tipped the last bottle down his throat and banged it down on the table. It toppled as he let it go and the four men watched it roll and smash onto the floor. I walked back in from the kitchen at the noise, ducking through the streamers and stood up next to the counter.

"YOU RAAAANG!" said Sid and the four thugs laughed as if they were going to burst. They were all quite drunk. Sid rose quickly from the table and stretched his thick arms into a yawn. The back of his knees hit his chair and the heavy coat he had over its back saw it topple. As the coat landed a heavy black shape skittered from a pocket and across the tiled floor of the room.

"Ooops!" said Sid with a giggle and chased it bent low. He actually swung his arm at it twice before he was able to pick it up. He tucked it into the back of his ridiculously tight jeans.

"Better not lose that Lurchy boy," he said to me as he turned and winked. "I might need that for all my enemies."

"I'd be guessing you'd have more than a few."

"I used to Lurchy-boy although their numbers are getting fewer and fewer by the day." Three of the men laughed sardonically. Slug just glared. The fourth guy, a wiry looking fellow with blond hair cut so close to his scalp he looked bald, eyed me suspiciously. He had a pinched face with a fleshy top lip atop an insipid chin. His ears were a bright crimson as was a thin puckered scar beneath one eye that ran across the bridge of his nose and stopped just before the crook of his right eye. He raised his head and slurred.

"I hear Ricky Pepi is a mate of yours." He cocked his head and appraised me, one eyebrow raised.

They already know we're mates, I thought, there would be no benefit in lying.

"He is. One of the best," I said.

"Fucking greasy wop slime bucket more like it," said Slug with venom.

"Just tell Ric we need to chat with him can you Lurch," said the guy.

"My name is Terry and I'm not an errand boy. Tell him yourself."

"No, you're a dishwasher," said the scar-faced one.

"Fucking dishwasher and a smartarse," said Slug. Sid raised his hands.

"All good boys. Just need to chat to him," he said. Sid had begun to noticeably sway. He grabbed the back of a chair to steady himself.

"Just let him know when you next see him." I motioned to speak; Sid held up a hand.

"Next time you see him, ahh Terry isn't it? That OK with you." He reached his hand around behind him and he noticed me move towards him. He pulled a large roll of notes from his back pocket and waved them at me with a wide grin.

"Relax Pop-eye. Just settling up the bill," he said and Slug snorted. "What's the damage Iris?" he said and grinned lecherously. As Iris handed him the bill she'd had at the ready for the last hour Sid reached for it and swiftly grabbed her by the hand. He pulled her close.

"Why don't I just let you suck my cock, and we call it evens!" he said softly. Lily roared.

"Let her go!"

I started towards him.

"Relax guys," he said and waved his hands in the air. "I was just joking with her. Apologies Lurch my boy, I didn't know she was your little mole." With a stagger toward the table, he peeled a fifty dollar note from the fat roll and let it flutter to the floor.

"I reckon this'll cover it," he said and tottered sideways a couple of steps.

"And here's your tip!" said Slug who proceeded to sniff, snort and spit on the floor. One of them cackled as they grabbed their jackets from the chair backs and made for the door. Scarface stooped and swept up the Esky as he passed over it. It banged the doorframe as he walked through hard enough to make the large plate glass window with the words Chī – Chinese Restaurant, Eat in or Take-away, rattle in its frame. And the they were gone. Iris and I looked at each other with a wide-eyed grimace.

"I don't like those boys. *Heīy mæng sạndān phx mụng mæ mụng*!" said Lily bitterly.

"Mum, language please. How can such a sweet lady have such a nasty mouth," she teased. "I'm sorry you had to hear that Terry." Lily turned to me.

"What did she say?" I asked.

"It's Thai. It sort of means, motherfucker I suppose."

"What do you think Terry?" Lily asked.

"I'd say they are motherfuckers Lily." Lily raised her shoulders and eyebrows in vindication at Iris who smiled at her mum. A pretty smile that danced in her eyes and lit up her face.

"Well, they pay well but I don't like the bloody tip," Iris said and bent low to pick up the $50. She handed it to Lily who squeezed it in her fist.

"They no come in here again," said Lily, "They banned."

"We might have trouble stopping them Lily," I said.

She sighed deeply and moved to the table where she began scooping up the empty beer bottles. As she made her way toward the bins in the kitchen she said without turning, "you tell Ricky to be careful Terry OK. I like him. He very funny. I don't want him to get hurt."

"Neither do I Lill."

BOY

I awoke with a start to find a small crowd of small people had gathered around me. It took me a few seconds to realise I was still in the little temple/birthing suite, in a bullet-riddled village in a bullet-riddled country. I couldn't have been asleep longer than ten minutes but already Hoa was awake, sitting up and taking small sips from a cup the old woman was holding beneath her lips. They breed them tough in Vietnam I thought, not for the first time. A tiny woman in a faded pink shirt was trying to get the newborn to attach to her breast. I didn't notice any small children amongst the small group. She must have a young'un somewhere to be able to wetnurse. Where? Maybe it died. These emaciated people, I thought. How are they surviving? I hoped Hoa had milk. She looked completely exhausted. They all did. The village people, who appeared as if by magic, stood silently around me two-deep. No-one stood around Lax as his invisible force-field kept them at bay. He was a walking, occasionally talking, electric fence.

I raised up onto my elbows, then sat up. I was sore and stiff. Lax sat beside me with his arms encircling his knees. His naked back was slick with sweat and Hoa's blood. The Vietnamese man, the soldier, sat heavily facing us and nodded with an exhausted sigh.

"Lax, tell him I say thanks for his blood, his help. He saved Hoa's life."

"I understand," he said in English. "Very kind."

The young girl came across and gave the three of us a hug – even Lax. Lax hugged her warmly. I was happy to note that there were some people immune to the Lax electricity. Not many but one or two.

Sometime later Lax and I sat in a small side room, on a dirt floor, in blood-stained shorts. We waited for our clothes to be cleaned with rock and puddle by the appreciative village people. It was fortuitous Lax wore my tent mate Percy's shorts beneath Percy's uniform. He was a big one for dressing down commando-style as we've established. Lax decided we would wait out the day and head back to *Nui Dat* at night.

"I'd rather not to be around here in the daylight, the place is crawling with North Viet Army. I can't take you through the caves to avoid them." He also said he had no intention of going anywhere near the US Fire Base because, "They will probably shoot us."

We noticed the big guns had gone silent and that meant foot patrols. Theirs, ours, and everybody's. The idea was to head a little further west and see if we could catch a ride with some APC's, (Armoured Personnel Carriers) if we could find any. If not we'd just hoof it back.

The small room was divided by a tattered wicker screen to give us a bit of privacy but mainly, I believed, to get us out of the way while the little band of people cleaned up. Through the open doorway I could see the jungle, unmoved by any breeze in the thick, steamy air. I was happy to wait out the heat of the day. I was buggered, physically and mentally. It also gave me a few more hours to monitor Hoa and the baby. They were both being well cared for by the village women. Hoa did need to be stitched up a little as the baby's traumatic birth had taken quite a toll on his mum. She could ill afford to lose any more blood and I'd nearly exsanguinated the VC guy. The baby appeared to be pretty bruised but healthy enough despite his ordeal. His chest sounded clear, his cheeks were pink, he was even feeding. His legs and hips seemed to be working fine.

"Where did the people come from?" I asked Lax as we sat with our backs against a cool concrete wall that looked as if it may take our weight.

"There's a bit of a cave and tunnel network out in the jungle beyond the temple. They're like field mice running for cover at the first sign of danger. I don't blame them though; this is a bad spot. Arseholes on all sides."

"Nowhere to go I suppose."

"Nowhere is safe in a war. These people have been here, working these fields for generation on generation, what's left of them. It'd be pretty hard to leave, especially when there's nowhere to go."

"How did you guys get to know each other?"

"That's a story."

"We've got all day," I said. Lax never told stories. No-one dared get close enough to ask. I felt a prick of pride that he felt comfortable enough to tell me anything. I just may be the only person alive Lax confided in. Maybe he spoke to Lt Col Yolka. How that relationship worked was beyond my understanding. How do you tether a whirlwind?

Lax had tracked down a VC patrol that had ambushed an Aussie section back in '67. They had shot a couple of Aussie guys, one died, and they disappeared. Lax found the tunnels and followed the patrol into the jungle. They split and he found the two that went north. The next night he tracked those that headed east. The two remaining men were resting in a dry riverbed. One slept while the other was on look-out. He watched and waited until the man on watch fell asleep. He moved in. The man from the temple, whose name was Gai, had fought Lax very bravely and when Lax finally had him down the man had said, in English, "I am a farmer, not a killer. I would like to go home to my family."

Lax said they ended up speaking together most of the night. By the morning Lax had decided to help him. Gai had a wife, Mei, and two daughters, Hoa and Huong. They had been forcibly removed from the village we were now sitting in and resettled by the South Vietnamese Government into one of those soulless hamlets they built under the pretence of getting the population out of harm's way. That was only part of the story. The Allies didn't want the villagers' tending crops which might feed the VC and NVA. The problem with the hamlets was that the South Vietnamese, whose job it was to protect them, didn't. The VC came in, murdered all the chiefs and anyone thought to be a collaborator. Gai's wife stood up to them. They cut off both her hands. She died from blood loss. They took the food, abused the women, forcibly recruited any boy, and many girls, that could hold a rifle and left. Not all the recruits were reluctant either. Forcing people from home created a resentment which was easily flamed into hostility and enlistment. Gai and Lax made their way to the hamlet where Gai reunited with his daughters. They left and returned to their village.

"So, you're about to shoot this bloke and then end up shooting the breeze until morning?" I asked.

"Yep."

"And then you decide to rescue the man's family?"

"I didn't have much on at the time. He was very persuasive," I laughed incredulously. "He's a very brave man. A warrior. I just liked him."

Their village was shelled by the US Forces after the people left. The South Korean Tigers came through later and burned all the crops and shot anyone they could find. I'd heard about the Tigers. There were stories about these madmen, so eager to get amongst it, they'd jump to their deaths from helicopters before they'd landed. God only knows what battle drugs they were filling these boys with.

When they arrived home, Gai and the girls set about burying any bodies they found. The little boy from the night before had been the son of a neighbour who had been killed. The girls took him in. Two or three of the people we saw today had been hiding in the tunnels and avoided the Yanks and the Tigers. Others found their way back over time; like the sparrows of Capistrano, they felt a magnetic connection to home. They started coming in ones and twos and over the last few months the little family had grown to just under 15.

"I get back when I can and bring some food and seeds. Whatever I think they can use," Lax said. Earlier, I watched Lax work the room like a grubby Santa Claus handing packets of seed and bread to the people in the room from an army backpack I hadn't even noticed him carrying; and he sat on my knee in a helicopter! Lax had bought a little meat in his pack, in the form of short offcuts and leftover sausages. The bit of iron in the meat would be a godsend for a new mum.

We sat in silence for a while before I worked up the courage to ask Lax the question that had been buzzing around in my head like a bee in a jar.

"The baby is pretty dark for a Vietnamese kid, even with its face all back and blue from the delivery."

"Yep," he said without commitment.

"His father was black wouldn't you guess?"

"That'd be a good guess I'd reckon."

"Is he yours mate?"

"How do you know I'm black?" he shot back.

"Oh," I said honestly. "I just assumed mate." I then wondered if I should change the subject. Lax didn't answer for a long moment. He just stared into the distance. Just as I thought I'd really overstepped. Lax cleared his throat.

"I've never talked about this, to anyone, mate, ever. Not much to say anyway. I haven't the foggiest. I grew up in an orphanage in Broken Hill. Never did get adopted. I was an unlikable mongrel even as a kid." He laughed bitterly. I said nothing. "Hit the road when I was a whippersnapper so I couldn't even tell you how old I am – not that it matters I 'spose. I could be one of the originals. I could be a Punchbowl Kalathumpian. I could be Skippy the Bush Kangaroo, mate. Your guess is as good as mine. I've got a touch of the tan all right, but how do we account for the blue eyes? I used to get asked what mob I came from all the time. He looked at me and shrugged. "Spose, I'll never know Pup." Lax sat in thought. He had a long, thin tree branch which he was using to make swirls in the dust.

Eventually he said, "The dad was a skinny, silly black kid with a head of wild curls. He and Hoa were really tight. Not sure how they met but he was stationed at the fire base. He kept sneaking out to see her, had a mate on the watch. According to Gai, one day he ran into a VC patrol. They found him all sliced up, tied to a tree. Hoa was devastated and then pregnant. They were going to marry. Poor kid. Just another horror story in a world full of them."

We sat in silence for a time. Lax worked the dust into patterns. He spat between his feet.

"It'll be a shit life for that little bugger you know. The bub. The Vietnamese call them 'bụi đời,' the dust of life. They're the dust children these kids from soldiers."

"Right," I said. "I wasn't aware."

"Gai will be cool and some of the others from the villages but the older people. He'll do it tough. They can be pretty hard the Viets."

"I've noticed," I said and rolled my eyes. Lax laughed. "It's not like he can hide either. He'll stand out like a sore thumb."

"Poor little bugger," he said again, "The dust of life mate. Just like me I suppose."

It was late afternoon. Lax and I had been in no rush to grab our clothes from a small clothesline an elderly man had strung between two thin trees, just to the left of our little room. Our shirts, pants and socks were tied loosely around the line and were now cooling as the large yellow sun began to descend behind the crowded expanse of jungle not thirty feet from the doorway. Even our boots were cleaned. Mine sat against the temple wall,

Lax's in the sun beneath the rudimentry clothes line. The temple stood at a tangent, about a thirty-degree angle to the jungle's gaping mouth made black now as the sun died. I'd arranged my pack in readiness for our trip back to camp. Hoa was starting to regain some colour and I put a few stitches in and made sure all bleeding had stopped. She didn't have her milk as yet, and she was much too weak to feed but the old woman was making do with a young wetnurse and some powered milk Lax had packed. The man himself was leaning back against the stone wall, lost in his thoughts. Suddenly he sat forward to attention. His nose in the air as if he were searching for a scent. He reminded me of my Pop's old cattle dog Mate, who was forever hearing things beyond our capacity. Lax extended his arm, his hand splayed to get my attention. He put a finger to his lips. Rising, he crept from the room. His face told the story, something wicked this way comes. I couldn't hear a thing. He was back in a heartbeat, filling the doorway. He was breathless.

"Soldiers. NVA. They look like deserters. All beat up and shit. They'll be trouble," he whispered. I nodded without a word.

"Head straight to the jungle, the people will show you where to go. Keep low and try to keep out of sight. Grab the pack and go now. No time. I'll roll around behind them and make sure there aren't any more, then meet you. We better sit this one out mate." He took off without a sound. As I got through the door, in nothing but bloody undershorts, two men were already carrying Hoa between them on my army blanket. The old lady was following with the baby. The young girl, Huong, beckoned me to follow. It was tight. I ran in a low crouch, my boots, and my pack in alternate hands. I still felt horribly exposed as I crossed the short grass and sparsely treed clearing around the building. The dirt track into the village wound around to my right and if the soldiers were coming up the middle they would be able to see a six foot nine Aussie trying to be invisible and doing a very poor job of it. I felt much safer as I moved into the cool darkness beneath the trees. About five metres ahead of me the woman in pink lowered the baby toward, what appeared to be, a small hole about the size of a letterbox beneath a large fern. Two arms protruded from the ground to take him down and out of harm's way. It was surreal. Hoa was carried deeper into the jungle. Many hands grabbed me and dragged me behind a low mound on the jungle's edge. They pushed me down. Huong put her face near to mine and with a finger to her mouth she whispered.

"Shhhh. Don't move. OK?"

From my vantage peering over my little mound of wet earth I could just see the track into the village and the path to the front door of the temple. I could even see into the building through a couple of larger shell holes blown into the concrete wall. One, on the floor line and a larger hole a little higher. It appeared that Gai had gone out to meet the men as they came up the path. The lush growth blocked the view, and the men hadn't come into sight as yet. I could hear Gai's voice quite clearly in the silence. He sounded like he was welcoming the soldiers in. They appeared. There were five of them. They were National Liberation Front soldiers. These VC were dressed in tattered black outfits. One of them had a bloodied bandage around his head. Two were bootless, one limped badly. Even at a distance I could tell they were in a bad state. They were dirty and bedraggled. They were also clearly agitated. They came into view with their ugly black rifles high and aimed at Gai's chest. The one at the front with the bandage barked orders and waved the barrel of his weapon in an arc toward the door of the temple. Gai raised his hands in submission and shook his head. The soldier moved slowly. When he was level he viciously swung the butt of the rifle into Gai's jaw who dropped to the dust. Two men then charged forward, into the temple and out of sight. The bandaged head guy appeared to be calling the shots. He moved forward cautiously and also disappeared into the building. The last two men held their AK-47s on Gai who sat on the ground rubbing his jaw.

I craned forward and felt many hands reach and grip me tightly, they held me in place. Their tension was palpable. The villages had made an art of making themselves invisible. My presence created a variable. An unpredictability. They were frightened. They didn't want me involved.

"They want food and money," Huong whispered.

One of the shoeless VC soldiers came out of the temple. He approached the two standing over Gai and gestured to one of the others to move around the far side of the building. Shoeless and the one with the limp proceeded to move around the side towards us, across the front of the temple, the front left corner of which pointed towards where we hid in the shadows.

They moved ponderously, rifles high. They looked like hell. Smeared with mud and blood. Neither wore anything on their head.

"Keep down!" a voice said in my ear, and I was so startled I nearly gasped. I didn't even know Lax was with us.

"There's two inside and these two and the one coming around the other side. Gai will try to move them on. You stay

Pup. No heroics. These guys are desperate." And with that Lax moved away. He was a small man, by the average Aussie soldier standard, but even so, his ability to move without sound was sort of eerie. He was an owl, silent, cognizant, pernicious.

An old whiskered man on my right started gesticulating wildly. He pointed to the building. I followed the finger but saw nothing.

"Dồng phục!" he whispered. "Dồng phục, dồng phục!!"

"The uniforms drying!" said Huong quietly. "The soldiers will find them."

"Shit!" Lax and my uniforms were knotted over a thin line between thin trees. The soldiers couldn't miss them. It was only a matter of time before they noticed enemy clothing and they would know Gai wasn't alone. It just got extremely dangerous for us all. Suddenly the young boy broke from the jungle cover and sprinted off towards the line. There was a slight slope to the ground before the jungles edge and he bent low almost beneath the grass. He was just small enough to avoid being seen by the two soldiers at the front of the building. God only knew how far the third soldier on the far side had moved. As the clothesline was roughly 15 feet from the temple I could just see the top half of the boy as he leapt up to grab our clothes.

"I can help," I whispered to Huong.

"No. You stay here."

"He'll be killed," I whispered.

"If they find you we all killed."

The boy had most of the washing bundled in his arms. They all pulled away easily. He then turned to grab Lax's boots sitting in one of the last sunny patches afforded by a gap in the thick wall of green behind us. With arms overflowing he leapt up to grab the last shirt. It wouldn't give. Private Percy Ellis's stolen shirt refused to budge. The men on the left still moved towards us. In a few moments they would be at the corner of the building and then they'd surely see the boy. Huong leapt up and moved away through the shadows. I grabbed at her, but she was off before I could pull her back down. She emerged from the jungle in a low crouch behind the boy and just out of sight of the first two soldiers who were hugging the temple wall. I watched as they grabbed at the shirt together. Finally, it came free. They turned and ran for the trees.

"TẠM DỪNG LẠI!" screamed a voice from behind them. The third deserter must have spotted the movement.

"TẠM DỪNG LẠI!" he screamed again, and Huong stopped dead and stood up straight, her hands in the air. The boy ran hard for the safety of the trees. An explosion of machinegun fire rent the air. The little boy's body was lifted into the air flung forward. His arms clawed at the sky as his little body pitched into the long grass, his skinny, brown legs bounced once and disappeared from sight. The gunfire broke the peace of the afternoon and set a small flock of birds to flight from the upmost branches of the forest. The birds shrieked and cried. The villagers did not make a sound.

Many hands held me in place then. Two or three of the villagers actually lay across my legs. It was very clear; they didn't want me involved. It was my only time in Vietnam that I wished I had a gun. I'd have been killed but at that moment I'd have been happy to go if I could have taken that murdering prick with me.

Huong stood motionless in the little clearing at the back of the temple, her arms high and head bowed. She appeared to be sobbing, her shoulders heaved. The two VC moved quickly around the corner now and also pointed their rifles at the small girl. A man appeared from behind Huong then. He grabbed a handful of her thick black hair and drew her in to his chest. He turned and waved the other men into the shadows, towards our position; to where the boy had been heading. The soldiers raised their rifles higher and took slow deliberate steps forward. They had only to come about ten feet into the shadows to see the mound of earth we hid behind. If they got that far we were dead. I thought about moving back away from the men and as if they had read my thoughts another villager lay across me, pinning me down. The soldiers would find a large, Australian soldier suffocated by well-meaning locals.

The soldiers split up then. One moved a little to our left, the other went right. They moved slowly; the only sound was the grass beneath their feet. One of the men crept towards us along the edge of the growing shadows. I felt helpless in my undershorts. I'd determined to rush the closest one and try and get his gun. These bastards had just killed a little boy and would have no qualms killing us all. As they moved from the light to the shadow under the canopy the closest man turned his AK-47. A dark third eye, peered out; we shied from its gaze. He passed a large palm tree. With a speed I could barely comprehend, a knife flicked out from behind it. It flashed in the dying, and dappled light beneath the canopy. It was impossibly fast. It opened the man's throat. The soldier fell forward with a heavy thump and landed not two feet from me. He dropped his rifle and tried to hold his torn throat together as his life's blood drained through his clawed hands. One of the villagers scrabbled forward and grabbed the gun, another fell upon the stricken soldier's back. Lax materialised. Without a sound he leapt from the shadows before the soldier could die. The second soldier turned at the throaty groan of his comrade. He saw the small nearly-naked man running directly at him. He fired a burst from his hip before he had completely turned. The bullets flew wide as Lax vaulted into the air over the fallen branches this soldier had been picking his way through. Lax's knife now clenched in two hands. He bought it down into the side of the soldier's head. They rolled together into the undergrowth. The man holding Huong had his hand around her throat now. He had heard the commotion but didn't seem to be able to see the plight of his comrades.

"BẠN THẤY GÌ?" (What do you see?) "BẠN THẤY GÌ?" He screamed. Surely the other two inside the temple would be on their way out, alerted by the rifle fire. I fought the villagers off then and climbed to my feet as they grappled with me. I stood tall while the soldier who held Huong searched the shadows to my right where the soldier had fired. He must have sensed movement and as I motioned forward he turned. He was looking straight at me. He roared and swung his rifle in my direction. At that moment Lax leapt from the trees. As he ran he moved the blade to his left hand and swept up something from the ground without breaking stride. His feet seemed to run above the ground barely disturbing the leaf litter. I know this is impossible but that's how it appeared. The man's attention was on me.

"BITE HIM HUONG!" screamed Lax. The little girl grabbed the hand on her throat and bit hard into the webbing between his thumb and finger. The man grunted and tried to pull the offended hand away. Lax threw a rock the size of an orange with an almighty force. It hit the soldier in the face, between two furrowed brows. He went to his knees. Lax dived on the man like a raptor. He landed with both knees on his chest. I could clearly hear the *WHUMP* of expelled air as Lax fell upon him. It would be his last breath. With two hands Lax buried the knife into the soldier's heart. He sprang away, landed and rolled into a ball before springing once again to his feet already running. Huong had been thrown clear and sat off to the side. She too leapt up and raced after Lax who had rounded the far side of the temple and out of my line of sight.

Another soldier came out of the front door now. He came towards me in a limping run. Behind him I could clearly see the last deserter, the leader with his head swathed in bandages, inside the temple. He had positioned himself at a large crater in the shattered temple wall. His upper half and his AK-47 protruded from the hole as he steadied the rifle.

KAKAKAKAKAKAKAKAKAK!

A loud burst of gunfire went high and smashed into the leaves and branches above our heads. He steadied himself and lifted his gun to fire again. Lax came into sight at the top of the building, he was sprinting. The limping man was oblivious. Then Lax was on him. He slashed low at the man's kidneys. As the deserter pitched forward Lax swung under the falling body in a frenzy of cutting and slashing. It was efficient, lethal, and horrifying. Lax rolled from under the man even before he hit the ground.

The soldier looking through the wall fired towards us again. Bullets splintered trees around the villagers. I dropped low as they whipped up the dirt around me. The lengthening shadows were making it hard for him to see us, but he knew we were there. It was only a matter of time before his bullets found their targets. Then there was a commotion inside, choking concrete dust and a blue grey gun smoke poured from its doors and craters. I saw Lax turn and leap up the stairs and into the billowing dust. There was another short burst from within the temple then the gun fell silent.

Gai had jumped on the bandaged leader of the gang armed with a rock. It had once been part of the door lintel and a was nice fit for his hand. Gai had taken a bullet to the upper thigh and another to his lower right arm. They both passed through. I patched him up and told him he would survive. The villagers buried the deserters deep in the jungle near their vegetable garden. The old woman told me their bodies would now help to keep the rest of their small community alive.

The little boy was buried under the clothesline where his bravery had saved us all.

We all cried over his grave.

IAN

The North Richmond Sharpies did come to the restaurant again and as expected, we were helpless to stop them. It was a Sunday night in early March. They came en-mass, they came drunk, they came stoned. They were over-wound like a cymbal-banging monkey. Their eyes spinning, teeth clenched, manic, noisy, deranged. It was Ricky who alerted me. He'd just finished his chicken chow mien, our number 37, and was chatting to Lily over a shared bottle of Victorian Bitter. There were only two other tables in the place, and they were finishing up as it was almost 9 o'clock. Ricky stuck his head in the kitchen door looking two shades paler than white.

"The Sharpies have just rolled in, all of them. They've got Eskies. They look shit-faced. The Scorpion is with them; I think he's tripping. Sorry, but I'm going to POQ brother," and without another word he opened the side door, the one to the bathrooms, and "pissed off quickly". He must have climbed over the fence, which is a fair feat for a short-arse. The Sharpies must really put the wind up him.

"You will be honoured for your bravery *señor* Pepi," I called after him. I doubt he heard me; such was his hurry to be gone.

It didn't take long. It was an animal roar of pain and anger above a crescendo of breaking glass that roused me from my thoughts as I stood above the white bubbles cresting the lip of my sink. My hand was in the warm water, and I was many miles away. A chair scraped across the floor. There was a heavy thump amongst the shrill crash of restaurant-ware shattering. Much later Iris filled me in on the details. The Sharpies were already buzzed when they arrived and proceeded to crash through their laden Eskies at breakneck speed. There was nine of them in all, six blokes and three Sharpettes, if that is what they are called. Ricky's one-time date Candy was with them. I noticed her later when the shit was hitting the fan. They ordered a truckload of food which kept Lily working the wok and fryer like she was two people. Iris was holding the fort, running food, opening bottles, clearing up mess and dancing around groping hands and cutting tongues.

"Sid was high on speed or something," she said. "His eyes were spinning, and he was really aggressive. He kept trying to grab me, couldn't keep his hands off me. You know, asking for a kiss and stuff." Sid was telling the others that Iris wanted him badly. As the table ate up his little show, Sid became more and more brazen. He made Iris reach across him to pick up the empty plates. He kept moving them further and further out of her reach. Finally, Iris reached across the table with both hands to lift a heavy pile of plates and cutlery. Sid, moving quickly, ran his hand under her skirt and grabbed her hard on the fanny.

"And here's desert…" he sniggered as Iris bought her elbow back with great force and connected with the Scorpion's nose as he leered forward. Iris said it was an instinctive reaction. There was a loud crunching sound and Sid's head rocked backward. The chair, which balanced on two legs beneath him, skidded away toward the wall. He went down on his back. He hit the floor hard.

"YOU SLANTY-EYED CUNT!" he roared from the worn vinyl tiles. I heard the angry bellow clearly and it roused me from my woolgathering. There was a short, pained scream.

"Iris!" Lily flew through the door before I could turn. Raised voices, running feet, scraping chairs. Another short and truncated scream. A low grunt. The bell on the front door jangled my nerves like fingernails on a blackboard.

I have a mental photograph of the scene before me as I stood beneath the colourful plastic doorway, the threshold between my kitchen and the dining room. It is vivid, the colours an acid glow in my mind's eye. It is hot and intense and tinged red; a mist of red, filling my eyes and brain. As I stood in the doorway, with Ian Chappell lifted from the umbrella stand and gripped tightly in my left hand, I saw Iris being hauled by the hair, backwards across the table. Sid was getting up from the floor. The chair he had been sitting on with his dark, heavy coat draped on the back, rested overturned on the floor. A short-bladed flick knife held in his hand. His crimson face a mask of malignant rage. Two streams of blood ran from his nostrils and stained his long thin moustache. Iris was being pulled backwards across the table by a large, brutish thug with a very round head covered in a thick, coconut fuzz. Iris's own dark hair was laced through his clenched fists as he held her down cruelly. The two couples on the far table, brave enough not to hit the footpath as soon as the North Richmond Sharpies came in with their laden Eskies and barren souls, were bustling each other out of the front door. The bells above the door shrieked again and again as they disappeared into the night. Three Sharpie girls stood clutching each other, possum eyes swimming in a sea of mascara. Two blonds and a brunette. A spikey helmet of shaved hair sat above long feathery locks which brushed their shoulders. The painted eyes were head lights, their scarlet mouths, tight little bullet holes of tension and bewilderment. They'd backed away from the table, beyond the ring of fallen glasses and plates. Beer-bottle-brown teeth smiled cruelly from the floor where they'd rolled off and smashed.

"Make every swing count Shep," I thought as I ducked beneath the streamers and entered the room. It was the mantra I rehearsed as I carried Ian out for my turn to bat. I might not last long, but I was always determined to go downplaying my shots. One Sharpie, a skinny rat-faced creep in a ridiculously tight, grey, and burgundy striped Coney top, had run around the counter and was at the cash register. He clutched a handful of notes in greedy fists. He noticed me enter and the stupid smile became a frozen rictus as he saw the bat in my hand.

"Watch the ball!" I spat through gritted teeth and raised Ian high, bringing it down on the grasping fingers. I obliterated the hand and the plastic-lined drawer beneath it. Coins of all sizes, silver, and copper, flew in every direction. They bounced off the counter or clattered to the floor. He crumpled as he coddled his smashed fingers and howled. His partner in crime was leaning forward over the counter expectantly. He was pressed forward over his hands, craning at the register, cooing at the spoils therein. With a roll of my shoulders, I arced the face of the bat, backhanded, through the air and connected with the side of his head. He hadn't even looked up. He fell back off the counter and beneath the feet of a third Sharpie who had raised a heavy metal chair above his head and was running toward me. His face unhinged, crimson with anger. I recognized the red brush-bristle hair. It was Slug.

"FOUR!" I bellowed as he stumbled forward. I held Ian Chappell up and in a fencing balestra, lunged the blade into his exposed Adam's apple. He dropped the chair on himself as he wrapped hands around his throat. He genuflected as I leaped over him. My hard and pointy knee connected his head with a dull and gratifying *THUD*, and he toppled to his back. A bright pink welt already erupted across a shiny forehead, just above a dark red monobrow. Ah well, Slug never liked me anyway, I thought. Momentum and anger carried me on toward the coconut headed thug holding Iris by the hair. He looked dumbfounded by the tall, skinny, daemon springing toward him over his stricken mates. I swung the bat hard at his vacant gaze, but he managed to sway back and out of the way as if avoiding a bouncer bowled at his head by the menacing Englishman John Snow. I continued with the swing however, hoping to collect Sid in its curving trajectory. I was almost as pleased to see the bat catch the hand gripping his knife and hear the crack of his metacarpals. The blade flew. It turned over languidly in the air and clattered to the floor beyond his reach. Sid bawled in fury and pain. The bat came loose then, flew, and struck the plaster wall just beside the head of the sixth guy who was wrestling with Lily. He was the wiry blond with the long thin scar. I remembered him from our first encounter. They appeared to be dancing until I noticed she was trying to claw at his face with fingers clenched into talons.

A few more scars for this one, I thought stupidly.

As Ian flew from my slick hand and into the wall with a puff of plaster not far from the goon's head his attention was diverted from the hellion he was grappling with. He let out a high-pitched squeal as Lily sank her teeth into the purlicue of his hand and he slapped at her with the free one trying to fend her off. He wrapped his left arm around her waist, arched his back and lifted her off the ground. Lily raised two legs and kicked off the wall. They hurtled backwards into a table. As it squalled across the floor they tangled in the cloth and collapsed in a heap beneath the flotsam and jetsam of the meal.

Sid was getting up off the floor again. A raging beast. Now Ian-less I lurched forward and landed heavily on Sid-the-Scorpion's broad chest with both of my knees. He pitched backward as my weight forced the breath out of him, WHOOOOP!

Sid's bloodied face was a paroxysm of rancour. He gasped for air as I swung my fist into his jaw. Once, twice, three times. He screamed up at me then, raging at his helplessness in disbelief. His dark eyes were on fire. The man under me screamed and the walls of the little restaurant became hedge rows, the table legs rubber trees. Sid howled again and I was no longer in Richmond. I was disconnected. Untethered. Transported. Somebody was screaming. His pale green uniform cauliflowered blood from the countless holes as the punji sticks punctured his body and my own. He screamed soundlessly now. I was in the *Hoa Long* hills. I was wounded, bleeding, dying. The man trapped and squirming beneath me, his mouth opening and closing like a gutted fish in its death throes. Sharpened, shit-covered sticks slowly ate through his body and then into mine. The man, Sid-the-Scorpion, NVA soldier, beat at my chest with his fists. I felt nothing. I closed my hand over that screaming mouth.

To stop the screaming.

End the screaming.

The screaming would drive me mad.

Then the North Vietnamese soldier was no longer screaming. He was dead.

Two men grabbed me from behind and forcefully pulled me backwards off the Scorpion and out of Vietnam. They each had an arm and we all lay on our backs amongst the rice, glass, and mess.

"He was trying to fucking kill him!" screamed the Coconut who had held Iris by the hair. The other guy was Slug. I'd hit him in the throat. He was saying nothing.

Sid rose onto his elbows and shook his head. He sniffed deeply and spat a large cot of blood onto the floor. It begat a harsh rasping cough. I struggled against their grip, but they held me fast. Sid looked at me from the corner of his eye and pulled his hand across his battered nose. Traversing the hand, a bright and bloody trail.

"Looks like old Lurch here didn't lose his balls in Vietnam," he sneered as he slowly wiped his palm across the breast pocket of his checked shirt. Front, back, front again.

"You think you can touch me? FUCKING TOUCH ME!" He bellowed. "I think I'll hang those balls from the rear-view mirror of my car. You bastards hold him tight. Where's my fucking knife?"

Suddenly Iris's foot connected with the cheekbone of the man who had, moments before, held her hair. He'd released her to try to stop me killing his illustrious leader.

"Leave him alone!" she yelled as she swung her foot at his head again. The Sharpettes, raised from their stupor, grabbed at her, and pulled her away before she could connect again

"Bitch!" cried the thug. I could see his eyes fill with water. He wanted to go after Iris then, but he had his hands full holding me. The girls rolled on the floor. It was Iris against three and I'm proud to say, she was more than holding her own. This little hellion takes after her mother I thought stupidly. It was then that Sid slashed me above my good right eye. He must have retrieved the knife while I struggled with the Coconut and the Slug. The blade was sharp, very sharp, and my dander was up. I barely felt the knife slice across my brow. My vision turned red as the blood poured over my eye and down my cheek. Sid held the knife in front of my face and said in a voice choked with venom and menace.

"What say we finish the job the gooks started and take your other eye. We'll see how you swing a bat when you're a blind man!"

"Do it!" said Slug as Lily screamed,

"LEAVE HIM ALONE." Suddenly the doorbells chimed, and Sid turned. He left me then and lunged for his coat which was still sitting under his upturned chair. Through the blood I could see a flurry of activity. Sid stopped dead. A voice rang out. Almost shrill. Whoever it was, he was battling with his panic.

"LET HIM GO NOW OR I WILL PUT A BULLET RIGHT BETWEEN THIS FUCKWIT'S EYES!"

It was Ricky.

"WHO WANTS TO SEE IF I'M BLUFFING?" He was standing by the door and next to the humped and furry beast that was

Sid's jacket. He had raced Sid to the gun, and won. He held the squat, ugly, black weapon at arm's length, his finger on the trigger. He had it pointed at Sid's head.

"You, junky cu…"

"Chose your next word very carefully *paisan*, I'll get the fucking key to the city for ridding the world of a cancer like you."

"Bullshit!" spat Sid. "You're just a chicken shit…"

BANG!

Ricky had pointed the gun at the roof and fired a shot. The noise in the small room was deafening. The bullet passed through the roof and probably into Lily's bed. All of the Sharpies stopped their battles. Every eye was on the little moustached man in the black skivvy. The Sharpettes ceased fighting Iris. The Sharp fighting Lily sat on the floor holding his bloodied face.

"ARE YOUR FUCKING EARS PAINTED ON?" Ricky boomed at the two holding me down. "LET HIM GO… NOW!" Ricky stepped forward and touched the end of the smoking gun between Sid's eyes and pressed firmly. I thought I could hear the hot muzzle sizzle as it touched the sweat-slick forehead.

"LET ALL OF THEM GO!" Coconut shuffled away from me on his knees, his palms held empty in front of him, a "what me?" look of pathetic innocence on his face. Slug, as ever, reluctant and scowling. Finally, he backed away. Lily and Iris ran to me and helped me up. I don't know why but I went over and picked up Ian off the floor and brushed the plaster dust off its face almost lovingly. Slug looked up at me with saucer eyes. He thought I was going to club him with it. He tried to regain his surly composure when he realised I wasn't going to cave in his head. Instead, I pointed Ian Chappell at him and said, "You all leave now. Any of you ever come back in here we call the police."

"The Cops. Hahahahaha, I own the fucking cops!" scoffed Sid and Ricky pushed forward with the pistol. Sid's head rolled back slowly under the force of the gun. Sid raised his hands and stood up. He stood motionless as he regained himself. He wiped bloodied hands on his trousers, and methodically tucked his shirt beneath his heavy silver belt buckle. He reached down and brushed off his knees. Ever so slowly he walked to where his crumpled coat lay after Ricky had retrieved the gun from the pocket. Ricky followed every movement with the gun trained on Sid's head. He shook the coat, punched an arm into it, then the other. He pulled the collar up with a slow, arrogant defiance as if he and his gang hadn't just been bested by a rag-tag group of pissed off café owners and a skinny little Italian with a ludicrous moustache. He turned toward me, ignoring Ricky who still held his gun.

"Oh, we'll be back Popeye, that is a fucking promise." He turned and spread his arms wide, his palms flat. Beatific; a fallen angel. He waved them expansively taking us all in the sweep. "And when we do, you're all... dead."

"You," he said pointing a pistol finger at Lily.

"You." He pointed at Iris.

"You, you junky cocksucker and especially the fucking circus freak. I'm going to gut you like a fish Lurch. I'm going to feed you to my fucking dogs. Look at my face big fella and tell me if I'm lying." I said nothing. What could I say? To be honest, his steely resolve after being so soundly beaten scared the crap out of me. It confirmed what I had suspected all along; Sid the Scorpion was as mad as a cut snake. Sid walked toward the door and as he passed

Ricky he held his hand out. Without looking at him he beckoned for the gun. It was such an audacious move, for a horrible second, I actually thought Ricky was going to hand it to him.

"Nice try shithead. You must be certifiable if you think you're getting this back. You can have the bullets though, wanna catch them?" said Ricky as he pointed it towards him.

"You're dead!" said Sid calmly and he drew an imaginary weapon in the air with a thumb and forefinger. He pointed it at Ricky.

"PEW PEW!" he said. Ricky, despite holding a real gun, flinched backwards. Sid wiped the blood from his leaking nose before studiously spreading it across the cloth on the table beside him. He rounded quickly on his charges.

"GET UP NOW AND GET THOSE TWO… FUCKING… WASTES… OF… SPACE… SORTED!" he boomed and pointed at the Sharpie Ian had hit in the head. He was still out cold. The other was on the floor behind the counter and we could still hear him whimper over his battered fingers. Slug got up slowly and joined Scarface whose cheeks Lily had torn with her nails. Three angry stripes from brow to chin. She got him a beauty. They moved over to the counter and got beneath the arms of the sleeping Sharp. They raised him slowly and sat him in a chair. He stirred awake and moaned softly. The side of his face was scarlet and shiny.

"We're out of here. Can you walk?" said Slug

"Yeah," he croaked. "Wha… what, where?" he moaned.

"Later! We're leaving." Slug pulled him to his feet. The little man with the battered fingers, rose, spied me, standing holding Ian and shuddered.

Sid moved to the door and swung it wide. The chimes squealed. The blood beneath his nose coated the top of his moustache with a crimson crust. His eyes red and lined like streets in a road map. He waited as his horde made their way onto the Richmond footpath, determined to have the last word. The Sharpettes filed through first, eager to get away from Iris who stood breathing heavily, tufts of blond and brown rat tails curled through her clenched fists. One by one they filed through, casting sullen glares at Ricky, who had lowered the gun to his side, and at me who had done the same with Ian. Coconut, who was a big man, hefted the concussed one. He was tucked under his arm. Feet shuffled; legs threatened to buckle. He looked green. Slug sneered and looked ready to spit on the floor again; his signature move on exiting a room. I pointed Ian at him and moved forward. I smiled grimly daring him to go ahead. He swallowed, turned, and left. Sid was last to go. He spun in the doorway and pointed a finger across the threshold.

"You're all fucking dead. This place," he said waving his finger in a circle in the air. "This place, I'm going to burn to the ground!" He turned and started to leave, as an afterthought he turned back and kicked the glass door hard. The bottom panel shattered as it swung in and banged loudly against the wall, the bells shrieked. We all jumped. With that the Sharpies were gone.

We stood like survivors after the blitz. Incapable of movement. Ricky spoke first.

"Well, that was fucking insane!" the tremor still in his voice. "I think we made some enemies tonight."

"They're pigs!" said Iris. She was wiping Sharpette hair from her hands against her apron and onto the floor which was littered with broken plates and food scraps.

"Are you OK Lily?" I asked.

"I not hurt Terry, a little sore. I thought Iris was hurt."

"I'm OK Mum," Iris said, a flintiness in her voice. This girl was no shrinking violet. "I hope I broke that bastard's nose. What a creep."

"You take this mate," said Ricky as he held the gun to me.

"Why?"

"Take it! I can't get caught with a gun."

"Whatever the fuck that means."

"Just take the bloody gun Shep."

"What do I know about guns?" I raised the bottom of the apron and wiped my brow with its tail. The sliced skin there had stopped bleeding. I still had blood in my eye which stung like hell.

"Says the war hero," said Iris as she reached across and plucked the pistol from Ricky's hand. "I'll take the bloody gun." She slid it into the pocket of her apron, a look of such definitiveness we were powerless to argue.

"Thank Christ, you got to the gun first. Thank God you knew where he kept it," I said to Ric.

"He always carries that gun. I JUST beat him to it. Hell's Bells if I hadn't! He probably would have used it; he was pretty shit-faced." Ricky paused and shook his head.

"Thanks goodness," said Lily.

"I'm out of here guys," Ricky said. "I might disappear for a bit. These boys will be looking for me I reckon." Iris stepped forward and cupped his skinny face in both hands. She kissed him gently on the lips.

"Thank you Ricky," she said. Ricky smiled, a little embarrassed, Lily walked over and kissed Ricky on the cheek.

She then reached up and grabbed the straps of my apron to pull me down to her level. She kissed my cheek as well.

"You two boys very brave."

"Now I REALLY have to go before Shep decides he wants to kiss me as well."

"Only in your dreams *paisan*," I laughed. Ricky winked.

"I'd be happy to kiss you little fella. Who knew you had balls like pineapples? Thanks for coming back."

"I had to come back," he smiled, "It's my favourite restaurant." He gave us two thumbs. Though the subtle tremor that shook his hands belied his braggadocio. He turned to pull the door. He took a moment to scan the street for disgruntled Sharpies then walked quickly up Bridge Road. He gave a short wave as he passed by the restaurant window.

Of course, we should have known Sid the Scorpion was not the type to make idle threats. That very night, before we'd properly cleaned the restaurant or made a police report, someone scaled the side fence and lobbed a brick through the small kitchen window. This they followed with a tin of petrol, a lit rag stuffed in its round mouth.

Chī never stood a chance.

COP

He was a solid, thickset fellow, late 50s at a guess. He wore a brown tailored suit with a stiff, brown hat pulled down to his eyebrows. It cast his face in shadow. He held a small pencil between squat, meaty fingers and jotted into a notebook as he spoke to the coppers. They all stood on the footpath in front of the blackened shell that was once our home. Firemen busied themselves as firemen do once the flames have been extinguished and there's clean-up to be done. The charred mess was lit by the headlights of two trucks with two fat tyres on the roadway, two fat tyres on the footpath. Hoses ran like arteries from large, blocky, ladder-laden hearts. Two police cars had been left at right angles to block all coming and going traffic. The cold Monday morning was lit by slowly revolving red and blue lights, incongruous without the sirens. The shadows they cast were eerie, ominous. They bounced off the silent buildings and made masks of the faces of the gawkers who always appeared when given the opportunity to stare at other people's misfortune. Some wore dressing gowns; slippered feet. They were so keen to rubberneck it took priority over dressing. The onerous silence now belied the frantic activity and raucous din of the last hour. The soggy, swish of firm bristled brooms shifting tinkling glass played a mesmeric rhythm. I sat on the gutter across Bridge Road and absorbed it all with my left arm around Iris's shoulders as she shivered beneath the light blanket the paramedic had placed around us. My other arm lay in my lap. Lily on my right; her torn and bloodied feet were swathed in the bandages a nurse had wrapped around them. She sobbed quietly. They had wanted to take her to St Vincent's hospital to do a thorough check. She had cut them on shattered glass when the front window exploded. Lily refused to leave. She needed to say goodbye to everything she owned. I wanted to hug her as well but, my arm betrayed me. Instead, I watched her squeeze my hand, I felt nothing. She said nothing. There was nothing to say.

They cleaned my sliced brow too. The paramedic suggested I could get a stich or two. I declined. So, they suggested the tape they applied would probably do the trick.

"It may scar," she said.

"I'll add it to the collection," I replied. She smiled warmly and placed a hand on my shoulder and pushed herself up to her feet.

We all made it out, thank God. I suppose we could thank Ray's screaming head for getting us out. He had shattered my sleep moments before I heard the brick shatter the kitchen window. I leapt from bed and ran to the stairs in time to see the petrol can explode in a ball of flame that chased me back up. I ran to Lily's bedroom and burst through the door. I dragged her by the arm, out of bed, onto the floor. There was no time for subtlety.

"FIRE!" I roared. She grabbed her handbag off the bedpost as I yelled for her to leave it.

"NO TIME. GO!" I pushed her before me from the room.
I screamed Iris's name as we ran down the hallway. Her door opened, then her head poked through, wild, slept on hair, wilder

face full of alarm. I grabbed a handful of Iris's pyjama top and pushed the two women before me as we made for the wooden staircase that ran down the back of the building.

"If they are alight too, we are in deep shit," I thought. As we passed the inside stairs the fire had already swallowed the restaurant. Upstairs would be the second course. Fingers of flame roared toward us. It spewed golden light. The heat was painful. I could feel it grab at my ears and lick the back of my neck. Smoke choked the landing as we bent low and pushed through it. The back stairs were unassailed. We careered down them and hit the ground running. We bolted to the front of the shop to watch it die. We turned onto Bridge Road as the front window exploded.

The tidy, brown man marched across the road and made a bee line for the three of us sitting in the only clothing we now owned. I hadn't even been able to grab my eye patch or my green and glassy eye. I couldn't shake the thought that it would have watched the on-rushing flames helpless and unblinking. I felt a little self-conscious without it. Iris and Lily couldn't have cared a jot. He stood before us with an empathetic sigh and gave two sharp shakes of his head with a detective's no-nonsense curtness. He looked as though he'd just stepped from the set of the TV show *Homicide*. The brown suited man pushed the hat back from a wide face with bright, intelligent eyes. A grey flecked moustache sat heavily on thin lips. His jaw might have been forged. It was a steely, square head that age was just starting to knock some of the corners off.

"Really sorry for your loss people," he said with a voice so full of gravel it must have been painful to talk. "My name is Gordon. I've had a quick word to the uniformed police, and they gave me the gist of your night. I'd just like to confirm with you all, is that alright?" He pulled the pencil and pad from his pocket and looked at us earnestly. "I believe you are Iris Chakan, you are Iris's mother, Lily Chakan." He licked the end of the small pencil and noted in his book. "Your name is Terry Shepherd. Am I right?"

"Yes mister," said Lily. Iris and I nodded. He gave a short nod in return.

"The firemen here said you were very lucky to get out of the building in time."

"Terry woke us," said Iris.

"He save us… again," said Lily.

"I'm a light sleeper that's all. I heard the kitchen window break and went to investigate," I said.

"Did you see anyone Son?"

"No mate. As I got about halfway down the stairs, I smelt petrol, I saw the explosion. I bolted to wake up the girls."

"Good thing you did Terry. Did you hear anything, voices maybe?"

"No, just the window breaking."

"Right," he said and jotted into his pad. "The arsonists used an accelerant, petrol. Do you know of anyone that would want to hurt you three or the restaurant?"

"We had some trouble here tonight," said Iris.

"What kind of trouble Iris?" Gordon asked.

"Bastard trouble," said Lily.

"And who are these bastards, ah, Lily?" Gordon asked checking his note pad. Iris looked at me and I nodded for her to continue.

"We've had a little bit of trouble with these Sharpies. They are a gang that live near here. They were drunk and eating in our place, and it got pretty crazy. Terry had to kick them out."

"Right," Gordon said. "How many were there?"

"There were six men and three women," said Iris. He wrote in the pad again.

"Did they go quietly."

"Not so much," I said with a wry grin. "They were pretty pissed or stoned. Pretty boisterous."

"Right," He said. "Was there a fight?"

"Bit of a skirmish," I said.

"A skirmish?" he repeated. "You three on nine, was it," he said without looking up from the pad.

"They weren't all fighting," I said. The girls lowered their eyes.

"You took on six drunk, or stoned, blokes and three girls with one arm Terry?" He pointed the pencil at the hand in my lap.

"Ian and I asked them to leave, and they eventually left." He looked up then.

"Ian is my cricket bat. I waved the bat at them. There was a little scuffle and they left."

"Right. A scuffle. Ok." Gordon looked at me thoughtfully. Eventually, he said, "Mr Shepherd, can I just have a quick word in private please."

"Call me Terry."

"Terry then." I crawled from under my blanket and Iris moved across and cuddled her mum. Lily had tears in her eyes. I draped my blanket over their shoulders. I walked up the street a little with Gordon. It was cold and I shivered. I wore a t-shirt and a pair of white boxers. I was shoeless, sockless, eyeless. "Bloody hopeless," my Pop would have said. The man noticed I was uncomfortable. The crowd had thinned out now. People realised they needed to rise for a working Monday in a few hours and left to grab some more sleep. He pointed to a shiny, burgundy, HG Holden parked the wrong way just beyond the police tape.

"This is me here, mate. Jump in the shotgun seat out of the cold." The car was spotless. There was a slight smell of cigarettes despite the air freshener hanging from the rear-view mirror. A non-smoker can always tell.

"Right," he said, "I'd offer you a cigarette…"

"All good. I don't smoke."

"Anyone else in the restaurant when these troublemakers came in?"

"There were three or four tables when they arrived. Some left immediately, all took off pretty quickly when the Sharps started to get rowdy."

"Anyone else?" I thought of Ricky but for some indeterminate reason I wanted to keep him out of this. He didn't deserve it. God knows what would have happened if Ricky hadn't ridden in like Alan Ladd, an even smaller Alan Ladd, and saved the day.

"No," I lied.

"Right," He said again. "What can you tell me about these blokes causing the trouble?"

"Not much really. They call themselves the North Richmond Sharpies. They have a place on Palmer Street I'm told, a few streets over."

"Do you think they may have started the fire Terry?"

"Dunno."

"What does your gut say?"

"Bloody oath."

"Do you have any names?"

"I believe there's one named Sid. He has a naïve scorpion tattooed on the back of his right hand."

"A scorpion you say. Very tasteful," Gordon said.

"I reckon there's one they call Slug but that's really all we know. They seem to be the leaders but how would I know. Sid is the main man."

"Sid and Slug," he said.

"Not the Flower-pot men," I said. Gordon pursed his lips and ignored my comment.

"Did you mention these fellows to the uniforms Terry?"

"No."

"Any reason why not?"

"They didn't ask."

"Right."

"The arm, the eye. The scars on the legs. You were hurt in Vietnam Terry?"

"I was," I said. I turned into his gaze. His face, inscrutable.

"Trouble sleeping? Is that why you were awake?"

"Sometimes, yeah, maybe. I don't sleep much." This guy was even sharper than he looked.

"Have you left Vietnam behind Terry?"

"Does anyone?"

"Can I be blunt Terry?"

"You mean can you be even more blunt?" He smiled wryly.

"Fair call Son. I just want to be clear. The police don't want any heroes Terry."

"We didn't start this crap Gordon."

"Just hear me out Terry. Can you do that son?"

"Fine," I said testily.

"No-one needs the lawlessness of Nam on the streets of Richmond. That's what I'm getting at here mate." Gordon said as he pointed the end of the short pencil toward me.

"You are obviously no push over, but you are going to have to let us handle this from here son. We don't want you seeking out a little payback on these, what did you call them. Sharpers."

"Sharpies," I corrected a little peevishly. "What the hell do you think I'm gonna do. You noticed my arm, right?"

"You tell me son."

"No. It's your job. You tell me. We're the victims here."

"You are. Of course, you are. It's just I've seen ex-soldiers on the streets here in Melbourne. Some of them are still fighting the wars in their heads. You're no dill son but you've also been through a lot by the look of you. Seen a lot. I just want to impress upon you that the police can handle a situation like this. Leave it to them. Keep well away from Sid, Snot, and the rest of those bastards. Do we understand each other."

"I'd be happy to never see those bastards again mate." He looked at me and pulled a plastic bag full of tobacco from the inside pocket of his coat and tossed it onto the dashboard. He didn't make any motion to roll it into a cigarette.

"Righteo," he said. "This is what happens now. The uniform guys will be paying these boys of, errr… Palmer Street a little visit soon enough and we'll see where that takes them. We need to get the two ladies out of the cold. Have you three anywhere to go or do you need a hotel? We can't have you roaming the streets of Richmond in your jim-jams. You walk around in those shorts son, and someone is apt to arrest you for indecency."

"We could go to my mum's I suppose," I said. "For tonight anyway."

"And where is she?" Gordon asked.

"She's in Little George Street, Fitzroy," I replied.

"On my way home," he said. "I'll drop you all there. Room for all three?"

"We'll make it work."

"Excellent," Gordon said. "Right then. Well, there's nothing you guys can do here now. We'll keep the site safe in case there's anything you might want to salvage but between you and me, there doesn't look like much has survived the flames." I nodded slowly.

"I agree."

"Help the ladies into the car while I have another quick word with the blue boys then we're off."

"That'd be great."

"All part of the service, Terry," he said and he pulled the brim of the brown trilby. "Bear with me son and I'll be back as quick as a wink," and with that he headed back toward the uniforms.

I rounded up the girls and about twenty minutes later I was knocking my mother awake in Little George Street.

Knock-knock-knock.

N.V.A.

Lax was at the rolled flap of our tent. He sat on the sandbags just beyond the entrance, his crossed feet dangled in the air above the shallow trench we used if a mortar round managed to find its way in from the jungle. Lax wore boots which made me nervous. Even more unsettlingly, Lax carried an AK-47. The last light of a dying moon made silver the crossed munition belts he wore over his, or someone else's, green shirt. It was already patched and camouflaged with darkening pools of sweat. He looked like a Mexican bandit in a Spaghetti Western. Lax rarely carried a gun and when he did it was never the Belgian FN FAL self-loading rifle which was our Aussie issue. It was always more exotic.

"The SLR has too much shit going on, too hard to control. Blokes end up shooting clouds and the bloody worms when they have a head full of steam." Lax was even less complimentary of the US M-16. He called them the "limp noodle".

"An M-16 is like erectile dysfunction," he once told me. "You want to shoot but your weapon keeps letting you down. They seize up. You might as well be carrying a cricket bat, at least that's got a comfortable grip. Give me a knife," he said as he twirled one between his fingers. "Get close. Push in, pull out. Never lets you down. Keep it sharp and clean and it'll take care of you. Much more intimate you might say." Today Lax carried an AK-47, the Russian made *Avtomat Kalashnikov*, the weapon of choice for the NVA. Whatever the next couple of weeks held for us, one thing was sure, it was going to be feisty.

The early morning humidity hit you in the face like a wet towel. Lax smiled broadly when he saw me. His eyes flashed metallic blue; his teeth illuminated his tanned face. It was still at least half an hour before our daily double: the pill parade and breakfast briefing. Lax may well have been there all night waiting for me to wake. I wouldn't have put it past him. Vampires are not great sleepers – or so it says in the classics.

"Pup," he said brightly. "Dreaming of sugar plumb fairies again? Do you know you sing in your sleep?"

"At least I bloody sleep. You should try it some time."

"What, and miss the best part of the day? The peace and quiet. No-one whinging. People are at their best when sleeping." Balls and Dave poked their heads through the tent flap. They seemed a little alarmed with Lax beyond our door. Balls was always a little alarmed when Lax was at our door.

Golly, the big Queenslander was home by then. He had been returned to Oz almost a month before. His second 12-month stint had come to an end, and he'd had enough. No third term for Goll. The whingeing Lax spoke of was probably Golly. Toward the end of his days, he'd become a whinger of Olympic potential. Definitely a medalist, probably gold. Everything got on his goat. I'd come to see it a bit with blokes whose days were short. The leap for the line became all-consuming and the ever-present threats in a war zone became personal. It turned fearless, devil-may-care soldiers into nervous wrecks. They saw doom and devastation behind every tree, under every bush and lurking maliciously in every meal. Being a short-timer eats away the nerve they were renowned for. It did with Golly. The bitching and moaning became such a constant that I had a quiet word with him before he drove us all insane. It didn't help much.

Golly's biggest gripe was the "insanity of the 12-month soldier" as he called it. Golly could never understand spending 12 months teaching green recruits how to be useful only for them to be sent home as soon as they could work out their arse from their elbows. The ones that didn't end up in body bags anyway. Golly said he had seen enough guys get killed and jumped on the RTA plane with no regrets. We rejoiced in the blessed release from his constant carping. Golly's "wakey", his last night before departure, was an all-nighter that took me three days to get over. The worst hangover of my life. Bloody XXXX beer. I think the Xs are for the brain cells you cross out when drinking it. Probably unfair to blame the beer as Golly didn't even appear to be tipsy.

To be honest, Balls and I were gutted to see Golly go. He was our mate and a terrific soldier before he wasn't. He hadn't been replaced as yet; you can't really replace the irreplaceable. Golly's leaving left us all diminished.

Dave, who replaced the ill-fated Ray, had been with us for about two months and just caught the end of Golly. He missed the best of him.

"Was Golly always such a punch to the goolies?" he asked me once.

Some of the nastier types in camp suggested our fourth

member was beyond cursed. It was written in the stars that he would have a shortened lifespan. They would razz him unmercifully.

"Hey Dave, can I get a photo to remember you by? And the even less subtle, "Hey Dave, can I have your boots when your legs are blown off?" He took the jibes and warnings from the other men in his stride. Dave was a young tough from Sydney's northern beaches. The jokes didn't faze him at all. Golly hadn't had much time for him but then Golly's head was in Queensland for that two months. Dave smiled along but confided in me later that with Golly gone we were but three. The curse of the fourth man was his worry no longer!

Now, standing just inside the tent, Dave made to light a breakfast cigarette which dangled precariously on his lip. It shook as he grunted and nodded a greeting toward Lax. Lax shook his head almost imperceptibly. Lax hated smoking and hated anyone smoking around him. He said he could often smell the cheap and nasty Vietnamese cigarettes in the tunnels well before he heard a sound. It gave him an edge. Dave took the fag from his mouth and nestled it behind his ear. He disappeared into the dark of the tent to dress. Balls pushed on through. He stood with arms folded across a sparsely haired chest and the mild swelling of what would one day, I foresaw, be a generous beer belly. Green undershorts and identity tags. Balls pointed languidly at the rifle resting on Lax's lap.

"What have you heard?"

"We're all heading north around *Bô Dúc*. We'll be about 40 clicks north of the *Boi-Loi* woods. Whole company. The Seppo's are breaking up the FZ down there and have been copping some shit. We're going to push south through the woods and try and bottle up Charlie between us and them." We no longer marvelled at what Lax knew or how he knew it. He fought a war within the war we knew nothing about. He turned to me and said cryptically, "We'll be near that village. Thought they could do with a home visit. You up for that Pup?"

"Yep," I said and Lax grinned.

"How long do they reckon we'll be at it," said Balls.

"Long as it takes I reckon."

"Right, better put on the bag of fruit then." He ducked inside. I turned to Lax,

"A rifle mate, that's unlike you," I said.

"Wouldn't hurt you to grab one too. It could be willing. It's a Charlie barbie from what I hear. That's sort of why I want to check on the kids."

"No rifle for me thanks. I patch up holes not make them."

"Thought you'd say that. How they let you get away with not carrying is beyond me."

"Got my hands full of medical equipment." Lax reached around and pulled a small Browning 9mm pistol from the back of his waistband. It looked like a toy.

"This is for you then. Right! 14 rounds, one's in the nose. It's semi-auto, so it'll keep firing as long as you pull on it."

"I did basic mate. I've fired a Browning." He pursed his lips and with an eye roll proffered the fat, squat gun. I hesitated and he waved it impatiently.

"Fine." I sighed and grabbed it. It was heavier than it looked.

"Not in your pack either. Carry it on you, right! Breast pocket, shoulder holster be better."

"Oh, right. My mum gave me one of those for Christmas."

"Smart arse." He smiled. "I might have one in the tent."

"Breast pocket is fine." I grabbed the gun.

"How hot?" I asked.

"It'll be OK. I have it on good authority that if we lose anyone, it won't be anyone I like."

"That doesn't narrow it down much, you don't like anyone."

"I like you Pup," he said grinning broadly. "That's why I gave you my gun. Now go and get dressed or you'll be late for work."

I had an odd sense of déjà vu as I approached the huge US Fire Support Patrol Base in our Bell UH-1 Iroquois Helicopter. I'd made this trip before. Last time I had Lax sitting on me, this time I had the whole section. The air inside the helicopter was so thick with sweat and tension it was like trying to breath through custard. Rifles and elbows made it uncomfortable until bullets fired from the sea of trees below us rang off the tail. Uncomfortable became unbearable. Men squirmed against each other in the belief that moving, even slightly, would make them harder to hit. I had my wings up and over their heads. I tried to keep my long arms out of the way. I still managed to give as good as I got as the Huey pitched and shook.

We were dropping into a hot zone. The US forces had been carrying their big guns out, and tractors in, slung beneath behemoth Chinhook helicopters for a couple of days and this had alerted all of the Northern Forces that numbers would be low, and some of those devilish big guns would be gone. The NVA saw an opportunity. The brass had organised two New Zealand Artillery support bases to the east and west of the US

LZ to pound the jungle as we moved in.

The Free Fire Zone was an ugly, razed, and smoking scar as we approached from the south. The jungle above appeared to be swallowing the bare land below like the tide subsuming the sandcastles I left on the beach in more carefree days. The sun was high, bright, and hot but it's light failed to penetrate. This green tide was dark, abundant, and teeming with enemy. An RPG-7 shoulder fired from below as we passed over the FSPB. They were usually kept for tanks. The rocket emitted an ear-piercing scream as it passed beneath us riding a tail of white, broiling exhaust. Almost directly under the two leading helicopters it clipped the much smaller and immeasurably unluckier fix-wing Cessna spotter plane which was flying a little too low. Our phalanx of Australian and US helicopters which carried a large chunk of the battalion, rolled along at 1500 feet to avoid ground fire. The light plane disintegrated. The flaming ball spun in a shower of twisted metal and sparks and disappeared into the depths. Soldiers turned and craned to see the carnage, making it so much more cramped and claustrophobic. This was not a good start to our trip.

The rotor blades whined and the droning unintelligible crackle from the cockpit dialled up to an unintelligible scream. Large eyes swivelled on craning necks to see the next rocket, possibly carrying our names. I'd been scared to meet the NVA in the *Boi Loi* woods but now I prayed to be anywhere but up in this raucous and unwieldy coffin. Lax sat quietly to my right. He had commandeered the twin mounted machineguns. Even in this heaving mass of humanity Lax had managed to find space. His force-field. The gunner had offered his weapon wordlessly when Lax moved over and door gunners never, ever did that. Lax scanned the trees and never fired a shot.

"Door gunners fire at ghosts. Should make them pay for the bullets. That'd teach them a little restraint," he used to say.

We pushed on over the woods. Every now and then I could see the sun flash white off water below us. Streams and marshes I knew we would have to ford on our way back to the US Fire Base. Finally, a wide plain of grassland broke through the endless green and snaked yellow toward the horizon. Our Huey leaned over and headed toward it. Someone below had tossed red and purple smoke into the grass and the pilot hovered into position. The vapour was no match for our downdraft. It cavorted briefly, then dissipated. We dropped like a stone. Stomachs, already churning, missed the cue and pinballed off our internal organs. Men had climbed out of the doors and prepared to leap from the skids as the ground rushed toward us. They were desperate to get some air. I could hear the *PLINK, PLINK* of bullets hitting the outside of the Huey. She groaned and fell. White knuckles grasped frame, leather strap or each other's arms. Lax leapt into the tall grass from a great height. He hit the ground and sprinted for the trees. He broke through the wall of vegetation as bullets traced his path, every fifth shot a tracer that flared colour. They smashed leaves and branches where he had entered. The welcome was very warm indeed. Men leapt and ran; most followed the path Lax blazed. I wondered if the other Hueys were taking fire.

"GO! GO! GO!" Someone was bellowing. I jumped from the skids into thigh-high grass and ankle-deep sludge. Smoke grenades were thrown before us to cover our dash from the enemy. Coloured smoke was whipped into curlicues by shuddering blades. The roaring beasts rose again to reload, some never even touched the ground. As one left another took its place, then another. I sprinted for the trees. I felt a thump on my back and thought I'd been hit. As I sprinted through the grass I felt acutely aware of my height. Long legs were great for running through grass but not when people were shooting at you. As I made the relative safety of the trees I could see our guys charging forward toward the enemy. Machinegun fire, ours, rang out through the canopy. I looked back and watched the other helicopters disgorge. Sappers charged through churning smoke with guns raised all along the length of grassland. A great flock of Huey. I turned back the way I had come. Did we all make it? Was there blood? Did I see a hand? I stood up tall and tried to peer over the grass. Definitely movement. I had to check. As young guy ran past me, SLR high, eyes wide. I grabbed him by the bicep.

"I think there may be blokes down out there. I'm might need another pair of arms."

"Yes sir," he replied without hesitation and threw his rifle over his shoulder. We ran bent almost double, trying to be inconspicuous. Charlie had, most likely, been seen off by our numbers, but the thought didn't make me any less perturbed. The thick slop beneath our feet grabbed at out boots as we made our way back. It let go reluctantly, an audible squelch of discontent. I almost ran over him. He was on his elbows trying to push through the wet earth. He looked up and actually smiled.

"Thank God it's you Doc. Caught one in the upper leg. Hurts like a bastard." Lucesi was a member of my platoon. An old timer, might even have been over 29. Positively ancient. Without a word the young bloke and I grabbed him beneath the armpits and dragged him into the shadows. He grunted but didn't cry out. We lay him down under a tree on some dry ground. There was no blood on the back of his trousers, there was no exit wound.

The young fellow and I carefully rolled him over.

"I'll be right here mate. Better get moving and catch up with your unit," I said.

"Right," said the boy and he turned and hurried off.

Lucesi had been hit in the middle of his right thigh. The bullet must have lodged in the bone, or completely shattered upon hitting it.

"Righteo," I said. "I'll clean you up and give you a shot of morphine. Then we'll get one of those choppers back to take you to *Vũng Tàu*. OK."

"Thanks mate," he said through gritted teeth. I threw off my pack and removed everything I thought I may need. I gave him a shot. I cut the leg of his pants off, just above the wound and cleaned and dressed it. He told me he had tried to shadow me off the chopper, figuring I made a bigger target, and he might be able to hide behind me.

"I was tugging your belt. Feel kinda bad now with you being so nice to me and all," he said as he fished for a cigarette in his top pocket.

"Missed you and got me. Hit my noggin on your pack as I fell." Lucesi, or Lucky as the boys had named him, had been luckier than two others that shared the return chopper. One hit in the lungs. One hit in the head. One probably wouldn't see Australia again, the other wouldn't see the hospital. Ricky's mum Giuseppina used to say, "God he is makin' you a book. Whenna come to you page – You dead. Doesnmadder – You dead!" God had put away the novels and opted for the novella. Some of these kids in Nam died with nothing but a short story.

Our men chased off the enemy, described by Lax as "A small troop of NVA regulars who decided to shoot up the choppers. It started as a recce (reconnaissance) that became a shoot and scoot. NVA helmets, on the move, and fast. They know we're here and they're trying to draw us in. Better be on the ball." The battalion broke up into companies, then designated sections.

Our rifle company pushed off across the vast grasslands before heading into the forest. Our platoon made our way east to the Ho Chi Minh trail. It ran inside Cambodia, just past the Vietnam border and had been a freeway for the VC and NVA to move everything. Soldiers, civilians, supplies, drugs, weapons, and women. It was always spicy. The VC were known to amass and even train in the relative safety of Cambodia.

The Australian battalion had spread itself for a couple of miles around, to the far east of the *Boi Loi* woods. They were far enough apart, they hoped, that they could corral the enemy without happening on, and shooting the hell out of each other. They all inched forward attempting to squeeze the VC between us and the Yanks (or the spetic tanks in the rhyming verncular) on the other end. We were on the extreme eastern wing, further east than the Aussies had fought before. Smack bang in the middle of *Boi Loi*, and that suited Lax just fine. Our determined route would take us right though Hoa's village. Hell, he probably chose the route, maybe the whole bloody operation.

Who knew? The border was also a labyrinth of tunnels, so it was going to be tricky stopping our quarry hiding as we passed over him only to emerge in behind us. We felt like we were exposed on the edge, so far from the rest of the company. We were all relieved we had the king of the tunnel rats with our merry band, that was for sure.

Initially, it was all fairly uneventful out on the extreme flank. It was very slow going through high grass and near-impenetrable brush. The woods were dark even on the brightest day and you had to work hard to maintain contact with the rest of the section. Lax had been on point for the first five days. Lax was always on point, as if he didn't trust anyone else to do it properly. He was that bloke that always had to walk in front. You know the type, the ones who find it impossible to walk beside you. You'd start out shoulder to shoulder and in the blink of an eye you'd be appraising the back of their head. My Pop was one. We'd meander through the bush out the back of the couple of acres he owned near Yarck. It was between Yea and Merton on the way to Bonnie Doon about two hours from Melbourne. We'd push through a noisily protesting fly screen door, hit the overgrown yard and in two steps you'd be swimming in his wake while he stopped and stooped, picking up bones or stones, snake skins or old bottles. He'd show them to me and Mum, then he'd be off again. I used to mess with him sometimes and push to the front, just to see how long it would take him the wrest back control. He'd just choose another route and leave you high and dry. Mum, Nan, and I would laugh later. When his knees started playing up and he couldn't take the lead he just gave up walking. Lax was a trailblazer like Pop. In Nam of course, no one tried to best him.

Lax had a sixth sense for danger and we all trusted him to sniff it out. Of course, no one really wanted to be near him anyway and were happy for him to lead us from way up front. Blokes would fall over themselves to avoid brushing against him. They loved the safety he afforded them but found him much too disconcerting to chat to. He didn't help himself of course. He gave them nothing but the 'crazy eyes' while sullenly, endlessly, sharpening his blade with a whet stone he kept in his pocket. If he did speak, everyone, and I mean everyone, shut up and listened, usually while shitting bricks as Lax's presence meant things would never be routine.

He wouldn't let anyone smoke. No deodorant. No cooking smells. Sleeves down. Shirts buttoned. Both hands on the weapon. You had to tape your identity-tags, the Yanks called them dog-tags, together in case they clinked. If you brushed your teeth, you did so quietly and dry. No-one spoke above a whisper, ever. Lax's rule was absolute and delivered only once. He admonished with a sideways glance or a shake of his head. A grimace meant you had overstepped. Each gesture was always met with total compliance. No one questioned his despotic regime. Sure, we were always alert and ready, but the tension was ramped up to maximum whenever he led us out.

I always bought up the rear of the patrol and I had no say in it. Far back and out of the way, but never too far to be cut off. You didn't want the enemy getting between you and your section.

"If we lose you then we really are in a world of hurt out there Shep," the Lieutenant would say.

"We'd be fucked!" Balls would add with his colourful turn of phrase. "Who's gonna piece us up if you get that trunk of yours shot off. Stay at the back and pretend you're a rubber tree. We'll call you up when we need you."

The officers loved having Lax with us. When Lax joined our patrol they were happy to have him do the heavy lifting, walking point, tunnel clean out, prisoner interrogation. Lax had a good handle on Vietnamese and a malevolent intensity that got lips moving. This also meant we didn't need any South Vietnamese interrogators when he was along. These guys could be either, over-zealous and brutal, or lazy and hard to control. A couple of times we had ex-VC interrogators who had been turned. These guys could be undercover VC, full of duplicity and deceit. The brass would send them down the line and we'd send them back the next day. Most of the officers I knew, deferred to Lax, while trying to maintain the guise of authority, even if they outranked him. We all knew who was running the show. Lax sometimes only spoke through me, refusing to give officers he didn't rate even the slightest regard. The really incompetent brass didn't last long with Lax around. Yolka would eventually move them sideways if Lax didn't approve. He didn't have any friends except me. Lax almost liked Balls, probably because he was my mate. Balls, as I've mentioned, respected Lax as a soldier but thought he was totally unhinged. He was petrified of him. This thwarted any long-term camaraderie. Let's just say Balls would never be sending Lax Christmas cards if any of us made it back to Oz.

After a job, all the boys would get around me to ask incessant questions about Lax. Questions born of myth and gossip.

"Does have a cot in a tunnel and prefers to sleep

underground?"

"Is it true he once shot a man for smoking near him?"

"Does he collect the trigger fingers from his victims?"

"They say he once ate a man's heart!"

"They say he's killed entire families while they slept underground."

"Is it true the CIA were trying to get him to assassinate Ho Chi Minh?" Let's just say I never let the truth get in the way of a good story. The myth kept the soldiery at arm's length and that suited Lax just fine. Some of the men thought the most unnerving thing about Lax was his penchant for the hated ham and lima beans in our ration kits. No-one enjoyed the ham and lima beans except, apparently, Lax. Some of the more impressionable sappers would leave their ham and lima beans cans near Lax's hooch as if making an offering to some beatific, benevolent deity. I don't know if Lax ate them or tossed them away. We never discussed it. I choose to think he tossed them instead of eating them. He was mad but he wasn't that crazy.

We pushed through the bush, grid by grid. By day five we'd found no-one. We moved methodically from long razor-sharp elephant grass, then low-lying, murky, leech filled, marshland. Finally, we started the climb into the hills which lay under a thick blanket of leaves. It was a respite from the harsh sun but not the insects that hounded us night and day. Cuts and scrapes became septic in the tepid warmth of the jungle. Forward movement became a crawl over fallen logs or stagnant pools of slimy water that had been collecting in shell craters. Smashed trees were reduced to ugly, jagged spikes. We saw no-one. We weren't taking chances all the same. Each evening at about 1600 we laid a perimeter of Claymore mines to warn us and maim anyone trying to come in the night. We'd try and find a dry spot to sleep, inevitably give up, and throw up our sleeping mat anywhere we thought might get us through a cold, wet night of misery. None of us slept for more than 10 minutes at a stretch. At night we could hear sporadic shots and mortar fire over on our far-left, way in the distance. This kept us on our toes. Our rations were getting low, and we were a little too close to Cambodia to be re-stocked. We never flew into Cambodia. Despite harbouring our enemy, we didn't want the Cambodians to join the war, boots and all. We cut back and tried to resist drinking all of our water. We were like sailors adrift. Water, water everywhere but none of it fit to drink.

By day I was kept pretty busy treating bites, sores and puncture wounds from sharp sticks that could penetrate our boots. Branches would tear ears, cheeks. One guy was a mere bee's willy from losing an eye. A sharp branch he'd not seen. Everyone had a case of dysentery. There were the colds and influenza, though no-one dared cough when Lax was about. Skin problems were common as the guys were soaking wet for days at a time. Tinea was ever present. Everyone had hookworm. You name the bug, worm or parasite and someone in Nam was dealing with it. We would swallow or be bitten by a every bug known to man. Vietnam is a parasitologist's nirvana. I also spent a stupid amount of time removing leeches. I never understood the whole leech imbroglio. I swear some soldiers would rather get shot than have a leech on them. Total knuckleheadery I always thought. The much-maligned leech only took a little of our blood and heaven knows we had enough to spare. I remember as a kid waiting in shorts and thongs in waist deep water by the open drain at Pop's farm. I was trying to catch frogs. Leeches fascinated me. I thought finding a little, plump bloodsucker a bit of a thrill. You just pulled them off or waited until they'd had their fill and dropped off. The leeches in Vietnam loved us Aussies and were almost universally reviled in return. The boys almost told more horror stories about them than they told stories about Lax. Almost.

"The jaws break off inside you and keep eating!"

"They crawl into your eyes and get under your eyelids. They can suck your eyes dry."

"They get in your ears and chew on your brain."

"They try to crawl up your arsehole and have been found inside a man's penis!!!" Our army issue insect juice did nothing to stop the insects, but the leeches hated it. I spent a large part of my day dabbing it on and de-leeching soldiers. Much ado about nothing I always thought. Still, it kept their minds off mines, bullets, and bombs if even for a little while.

HIT

We walked into an ambush on day six. Lax wasn't on point. He was underground and had told us to keep moving forward. Dave stumbled on a cave entrance while hammering in a piss tube beneath some bushes, just before dawn. We peed into tubes knocked into the ground to cover our ablutions in enemy territory. Dave knocked a small wooden panel in the ground askew and even Lax was impressed by his willingness to head in and investigate.

"I've got it dig," he said laconically then added. "Good find." Dave swelled like a toad, big grin on his face. Later we lowered Lax into the tunnel by his feet, his arms stretched before him. His favourite knife, a long thin Gerber combat dagger with the cantered blade and a cat's tongue grip, taped to his bare back; a small miners light was strapped to the middle of his forehead. He carried a pistol in his left hand and a bayonet, for any booby traps, in his right. He was completely naked but for the dried dark mud, charcoal, and grease he had covered himself in and two lengths of calico he had tied around his elbows which were his principal mode of locomotion underground. He had a small calico bag tied to his ankle which contained a gas mask, a pair of shorts and three grenades. He would drag this along as he moved forward. The uniform he'd been wearing was neatly tucked into my pack. The mud was making his ankles hard to hold. Lax squeezed in and disappeared into the dark. Some of the others shook their heads in disbelief.

Lieutenant Frangers Condon moved us forward. Dave, buzzing at being acknowledged by the formidable Biggy Rat volunteered to go on point. What we didn't know then was that a large company of heavily armed N.V.A had moved in on us during the night. These were well trained, well-armed fighters. An assault force, heavily camouflaged with branches and covered in charcoal and grease. They were as game as fighting cocks too. It was said they reported directly to High Command in *Hanoi*. They were commandoes, assassins, raiders. They are hitting large installations and bases like the American Fire base. They knew we were coming. They'd been watching just a step ahead. They avoided our Claymores at night and had been waiting for the right moment to pounce. They set up two machineguns and a mortar at the foot of a natural clearing. It was about 200 meters long and 150 metres wide. It consisted of sticky mud and elephant grass, between the walls of trees. The rest had spread wide to the right and left. When we moved into the long, skinny patch of grassland they would try to flank us and chop us to pieces in the crossfire. They waited silently for our approach.

The sun refused to come up on day six. Wringing, tormented hands of black cloud strangled the light from the day, then ruptured. Rain so heavy it pushed you into the sodden ground. You had to hold your hand over your mouth and nose for the space to breathe. The darkness gave the sappers an advantage. The deafening rain was ours. They couldn't hear our approach and our sector were loathe to leave the cover of the bigger trees if only to avoid the rain. Our forward movement had been tortuous, and it was almost 1500 when we came upon the long, skinny patch of grassland. Dave and a young conscript named Cornelius, who had been at the head of our arrow-shaped formation, left the jungle cautiously to scout the grass. Lt Frangers was wary of the open ground and decided not to over commit our numbers. Dave and Cornelius crept forward, beaten low under the deluge. The machineguns waited patiently for us all to follow them in. Our two scouts inched forward, a blur of fetid green through the torrent that seemed to be coming from above and below us at the same time. Only as our forward scouts neared the very tip of the clearing did Frangers urge us forward. Dave was almost on the machinegunners when they opened up. An eruption of noise and light. Pte Cornelius was cut in half, a burst of red on the tumult. Dave disappeared. Rocket propelled grenades hit the tree line. Trees exploded. Jagged branches speared downward as leaves burned, fluttered, and sizzled out in the spreading mud. The men in the clearing dived onto their faces. Most of the men were still within the trees, some of which were burning in their upper most branches. A bugle rang out somewhere. Cries of, "LEFT FLANK. ENEMY ON THE LEFT," above the din. I turned to see black phantoms flit from tree to tree. They were coming. Our boys pushed forward bravely and opened up. The intense fire under the canopy was deafening. We needed to get away from the machineguns in the clearing. The men there would have to crawl out. If we couldn't push back the N.V.A, trying to flank us, they might surround us.

Lt Condon urged us to our right to meet the incoming enemy

before they could dig in. He called the base but gave up under the racket of rain and fire. An explosion behind us. Big. A mine? I turned to see flame lick the air as huge piles of earth thumped down with a splash into fetid water. Black smoke billowed and dispersed. Two men broke from the grass. One had been hit in the arm. Slash of crimson within the black mud that covered him. I couldn't recognize either under the filth.

"Our guys in there Shep. Mines too. Head in where we came out and you'll be right." He pointed back the way he had come. They both lifted weapons and headed back into the fray at a run. I didn't even get to check their wounds.

A machinegun opened up again as if to remind me why I shouldn't go in. He must have seen the movement. I dived into the mud as bullets rent the air around me. A furious rain doubled its efforts. I thought I was going to be shot, blown up or actually drown in the squelchy bog. I crawled forward on my hands and knees, praying my large pack wasn't showing above the grass. Bullets flew over me. The gunner had seen me go in and was trying to guess where I was moving to. Then, like God bending a kink in the hose, the rain stopped. The very jungle was alert to our presence. Every movement a grimace. Soggy leaf litter squelched under my body. I was a floundering ship as waves of panic and nausea crashed against me. The machinegun ceased. Its echo all around us as it bounced off the trees. Rifles barked somewhere. Everywhere. My friend on the machinegun was listening, watching, waiting for me. My heart beat a harsh rhythm. A rocket flew straight over my head and burst on a tree behind me. I decided to make a run forward toward the wounded man and had just started to climb to my feet when Balls landed on me with all his weight.

"Down mate. They're firing grenades in here."

"You don't say."

"Need your expertise Shep."

"Who's down Balls?"

"Four down in this shithole. Two dead. Two gunna be if you don't hurry."

"Let's go then."

"Keep that skinny arse down mate 'cause this bloke on the automatic is desperate to give you a new hole or two." I pushed passed him and crawled through thick mud in the direction he'd come. The sharp grass tore at your skin and the mud tried to grab and hold you. I broke through into a small open area and came face to face with Dave. He was on the edge of a large, rapidly filling crater. The grass all around had been scythed by shrapnel. He was bent over a motionless man lying on his face. Blood had pooled in the dirt beside the guy's head. I fell in besides him. The man on his face was unconscious.

"God, Dave," I said. "I thought you were gone."

"Just got lucky. Missed me. Cornelius is gone Doc."

"This guy's not. Not yet anyway," I said this as I felt for and found a light pulse in the man's throat.

"Now listen. We need to roll him over, real slow OK?" As we lifted him slightly I could hear loud, snoring breaths.

"A sucking chest wound!" I whispered to myself. He had taken the blast on his right side. He had his arm forward, crawling probably, and had caught most of the blast in his shoulder and right breast. The right side of his face. We were in trouble here. The mine had been placed in the very centre of the small clearing. By the blast radius I guessed it was a Jumping Jack. Brigadier Stuart Graham had laid 11 kilometres of these nasty bloody things around *Phuoc Tuy* in '67 - US Jumping Jacks. Also called Bouncing Bettys. The Vietnamese had been digging them up and blowing us up with them practically from the moment they were planted. The field could be full of them. The Jumping Jack would leap into the air when triggered and cut a man in half. The poor bugger that tripped this one would be gone. This kid had been on his left. Probably 19, looked 12. His arm was hanging by a twist of skin. I was worried his intestines could slide through the hole in his side. The breathing had become shallow, the snoring through his chest cavity weaker. I lay in the water beside his body, stretching my arms across him and tried to hold him together. Dave rolled him gently onto his back, with my hands on his guts. He was full of holes. I just looked at him. Where could I start? What could I do?

"Oh fuck!" said Balls who had crawled up beside me.

"He's full of holes. Can you do anything?"

"I'll try. Do my best." In war you would have to reverse triage. You'd fix up those with a chance. I'd do my best, but this guy was already gone. You couldn't waste time that might be needed to save another. War is just that bloody awful. I reached into the meat that had been a bicep and finally found the brachial artery and clamped it. Wouldn't help, couldn't hurt, maybe buy him time. Balls was whispering harshly, as we kept as low in the mud as we could. The machinegun sprayed the occasional burst our way but seemed to have developed an interest in the goings on under the trees.

"Cornelius is gone. Tully. Tully kicked the mine. Desmond has been hit in the leg. Maybe the artery. Follow me." Balls turned to Dave.

"Dave. No point staying here, you should get out."

"I'm here until he's not."

"OK. Don't get yourself killed. If it gets too hot, go. That's an order." I believe that was my first. I pulled bandages and equipment from my pack. Everything I thought I would need. I didn't use morphine on the kid. Wouldn't have helped.

"Try to wrap him up if you can. Doesn't have to be perfect, just hold him together. I'll be back as quickly as I can. Keep down. and be careful of the mines."

"OK Boss," he said.

We could hear all hell breaking loose in the trees around us. The crack of gunfire. The deep throaty *whump* of mortar. Trees screamed in flame and groaned as they collapsed.

"If they've whacked mines in here, I don't reckon they'll follow us in," said Balls trying to cheer me up.

"Thanks mate. Made my day. Now, where's my leg?" I followed Balls to Pte Desmond. He had been hit by some of the shrapnel from the mortar meant for me. He'd been opened from knee to knackers by a jagged piece of metal. He lay flat on his back, panting. The rapid rise of his chest. I placed my hand on his stomach and he started to get up.

"Lay down. I need to clean you up. You'll be fine." The ugly wound had gaped wide. Balls was the first one there and had used his belt to pull it together. I delivered a shot of morphine; his breathing slowed a little.

"Am I gonna lose the leg Doc?" he whispered through clench

teeth. Flecks of spittle on his lips. White fear in pale eyes.

"No. Just a scar. Not too deep mate." I cleaned and dressed the wound, as well as I could in the mud, and wound it tightly in bandages.

"It's too hot to land a Huey in a mine field. We'll have to winch him out when we can cool this off. Come back for the others late..."

Two 105 shells screamed overhead cutting Balls off. The jungle in front of us exploded, turning the angry clouds a furious red. The lieutenant had called in the artillery. Things were dire in the trees. We dragged Pte Desmond out of the mire as gently as we could. Taking care to use a path through the mud and grass that someone else had forged. Trying to walk quickly through a minefield is an exquisite form of hell.

"Drag him out of the wet, up on that little rise." I pointed to a small, raised corner of the dark jungle. If you find a couple of stretcher bearers you might be able to get him somewhere safer." The area around us had become a little quieter. The artillery had moved everyone away.

"Grab someone to look after him."

Balls nodded and said, "Be safe mate." He grabbed Pte Desmond by the straps of his pack and dragged him slowly through the slosh and slime. He dug a furrow in the mud which filled with water as he went. Desmond gritted his teeth and didn't make a sound. Dave was still with the kid when I got back.

"Cheers mate. Balls is up that little rise. I want us to slowly drag this fellow up to meet him." Dave nodded and tucked one hand under the kid's armpit, the other hand he put protectively over his balls. I thought about telling Dave that the mine that might take off his wedding tackle would probably take off his hand and both his legs but decided not to make it worse for him. We dragged the kid, in a half crouch, through the slush and up the little rise and lay him beside Des.

"Hey buddy, we'll get you into Vunggers," Dave said although the kid was beyond hearing. Dave placed his hand on the kid's head. I searched for more bandages. We also needed to replace some blood. I worked quickly, really just plugging holes and wrapping him. I strapped his arm to his body, but I knew he'd lose it – I thought the arm the least of his worries. I said a little prayer for him as I wrapped him up like a gory present for the Huey. I checked for a pulse in his neck. There was nothing. I tried CPR. I beat a rhythm on his already battered chest. Blood oozed from everywhere and covered my hands and cuffs. Pulse? No.

I pushed down harder. Rapid compressions. Blood splashed and spread in the water around us. Ground too soft beneath us. I could move him, but I'd lose him.

Pulse? No.

"Come on kid," I whispered.

CPR. Pulse? Nothing.

CPR. Pulse? No.

CPR. Pulse? Nup.

CPR. Pulse? Bugger.

CPR. Pulse? Fuck.

Gone.

FFC

Mum and Lily got on like a house on fire. Pun intended. She was a little coy at first, not quite sure about the homeless people that landed in her lap. She struggled to adjust to me changing her routine after returning from Nam and now she had two others for good measure. I think it was the punt that bought them together, that and the cooking. After the fire, I once again found myself out of work with not a lot to do. Iris got work pulling beers at the Builders Arms, a short walk from the house. Unfortunately, not many establishments were looking for a one-armed barman. In truth, the sort of pubs that would employ me were the sorts of pubs I wouldn't be caught dead in.

I talked Iris into coming to a Fitzroy footy match with me. She'd always had an interest in the game. Occasionally, in the restaurant, you'd hear the nasality of the commentators, more nose than mouth, drift tinnily from the food splattered radio which sat on the shelf above the oven. She liked Harry Bietzel's pantomime whine. Iris was partial to a Tigers game as she lived in Richmond, and the great Freddy Swift had once eaten at Chī. I saw that the radio had melted into a gloop of plastic amongst the blackened mess that had been our livelihood. The fire brigade fellows had eventually allowed us to sift through the scene and attempt to salvage a memento or two. Not a lot to report. Ian Chappell would never hit another four or Sharpie chin. I found the charred handle amongst melted umbrellas near the kitchen door where I'd left it. My beloved bat had gone to that cloud in heaven where grandparents, pets, and favourite toys go. Everything that made the trek from Fitzroy to Richmond was but a memory. My glass eye, my books, my wallet, my watch. My season ticket! There was a lot of Rosemary in that room. Her stuff, her smell, her memory. Gone too.

"Nothing cleanses like a fire," my old Pop used to say.

The Fitzroy Lions had recently moved to the Junction Oval in St Kilda from our forever home just up the road on Brunswick Street. We'd left our heartland, our gluepot, and our passionate supporters, in a search for a home of our own. St Kilda was far from the restrictions and rapidly raising rates of the local Fitzroy council. It was seen as a move of desperation for a team with a perilously small, though passionate, supporter base. We had the nest egg of a fairy wren.

For Iris and me, it meant a tram ride to St Kilda and not a Maytime stroll passed the terrace houses, blue-stone lanes, and smelly petrol stations of Fitzroy. As we travelled along St Kilda road from the city the arteries began to clog with cars and people. Men, heads lowered with a straight-legged stride, pulling basket-and-thermos-laden women and scarfed kids in their wake. The crowd was large for a Lions match as the Magpies had a huge following and it looked like nearly all of their black-and-white clad mass had turned up to see their mob roll their neighbouring team in an unfamiliar neighbourhood. They weren't disappointed. I was. We battled it out though. We went down by 25 points. Our young rover, Garry Wilson, was a star getting touches at will. Wayne Richardson was the difference though. He knocked up getting kicks and finished the day with leather poisoning, my diagnosis as a physician, I declared to Iris post-match. Wayne was a ripper, and his brother Max was almost his equal. I'd have loved them at the Lions.

Iris was entranced by the whole day. I bought her a *Footy Record* from a kid in a red cap standing beside a plastic wrapped pile that reached to his waist. People dropped coins into one hand and grabbed the proffered books from his other. A slight of hand accompanied by the croak, "*Record*, get your *Record* here," in a voice aged by repetition. We bought our tickets at the gate, walked around to queue at the turnstile and handed it to the blue-coated guy with grey baggy eyes and a silver Errol Flynn moustache. He had a large white numbered badge pinned to his lapel. We'd not walked three steps into the ground before two middle aged women, one pinched and one paunched, accosted us. They held thick raffle books in hand. They wore wood-buttoned duffle coats festooned with large yellow numbers and printed fabric images of Fitzroy players. They were hand-sewn onto wherever there was a space. A large pink badge with Fitzroy Football Club Official printed on the front was pinned to their lapels. Iris reached for her purse as I said, "No thanks!"

The two moved quickly to the next possible sale. I answered Iris's quizzical gaze with, "It is widely known in football circles that Fitzroy have been auctioning the same small, portable television for the last ten years."

"How does that work?" she asked.

"They pull a ticket that they never sell," I said.

"What made you so cynical?" she said and bumped me gently.

"Not cynical, wise. With age comes wisdom," I said.

"You must be very, very, VERY wise then," she said solemnly with a slow nod of her head.

"And don't you forget it," I laughed.

Iris loved the unbridled emotion of her first match. She thrilled at the guttural roar that followed a goal and the hound-dog baying, one team and then the other, after an umpire's decision. At quarter time she sat on the uncomfortable, asphalt step, in the shadows of the Blackie Ironmonger stand. She was perched amongst the legs, empty beer cans and discarded hot dog wrappers of the masses. She read the *Footy Record* from cover to cover. She recited, with posh, English sobriety, the names from the middle pages with a mock awe as if presenting listed luminaries to Queen Elizabeth.

"Number 10, his excellency Renato Serifini is in attendance."

"No. 6, The honourable Sir Peter McKenna and the lady McKenna, looking resplendent in a black and white safari suit." There was a photo of our wizened captain, Kevin Bulldog Murray, in our souvenir book as well. Slitted eyes, set jaw and ropey muscles covered in sailor tattoos.

"He looks like Popeye," she said.

"He plays like Popeye. They give him spinach at half time." I pointed him out as he loped on after half time, sandy hair and long arms, fingertips that seemed to brush his boot tops.

"Looks like someone's grandad has climbed over the fence," Iris laughed.

"He really does," I said. "He has false teeth you know, and he hands them to the time-keeper before the game who then slips them into his back pocket for safe keeping."

"What's a time-keeper?"

"There's one appointed from each team. They set a little alarm clock for the length of the quarter and make sure the game goes for the correct time. There's one from each team to ensure there's no hanky-panky. There's time-on and time-off they have to factor in."

"What's that?"

"Doesnmadder!!! Annnnnnyway, the story goes, one day the bloke charged with guarding said chompers only realised, as he sat on the train on his way home that night. That he'd forgotten to give the dentures back to poor Muzza."

"No way!" said Iris incredulously. "Something bit his arse, that's hysterical."

"And to make it worse, Muzza had to go on the telly that night to be interviewed. The Penthouse Club with Bill Collins and Mary Hardy, I think."

"That's brilliant. Who's Muzza!"

"Kevin Murray. The bloke I was pointing to. The old bloke in the photo. Are you following any of this?"

A tubby fellow in a Golden Breed windcheater worn beneath an unbuttoned, thin, blue cotton coat appeared. He supported a rectangular tray of goodies, leather strapped over his shoulders. On his head sat a jauntily placed paper hat. He parted the crowd before him with a loud, raven call,

"Drinks, lollies, chocolates and potato chips!" The cry of the footy interval. I leapt up and bought us two cans of Fanta and two Cherry Ripes. The cash was in my left pocket where I could access it of course. Iris beamed.

"Dinner and a show. This day gets better and better."

At three-quarter time a girl with a blackboard on a pole

walked the boundary. The winning raffle number was chalked on the front. Iris elbowed me in the ribs.

"No-one just won a non-existent telly."

"Now she's up to speed," I teased and Iris laughed. The blackboard girl was followed by a small group of people holding the edges of a blanket. It appeared full of coins. A fellow at the back held yet another chalkboard which read, "For the Royal Children's Hospital. Give that they might grow." People were tossing coins from the crowd and some smaller kids were running around and picking up whatever missed the blanket. The people holding the blanket's corners were ducking and weaving the odd coin that some of the wags in the crowd were piffing at their heads. Iris and I emptied our pockets. She cheered, arms raised, as she landed a 20-cent piece into the blanket.

The absolute highlight of Iris's day, she told me later that evening, was the crowd banter. Some of it banal, some truculent: sometimes petulant and often, very, very funny. She particularly loved the jibes aimed at me.

"Down in front big fella."

"How's a bloke supposed to see past Tiny Tim here?" The catcalls followed me to nearly every football match. They were usually good natured.

"Just my luck I have to stand behind the reserve ruckman." "What's the goal post doing standing in the outer?" and "Two bob to sit on your shoulders Stretch."

Her personal favourite was, "Hey, big fella. Can you see any smoke from my place? I think I left the kettle on!" The whole crowd chuckled at this one. Iris laughed and spat a stream of her Coke on the knitted cardigan of the women in front. She dabbed at it with her serviette, ever so gently, so the woman wouldn't know. Iris was still snickering about that one after the final siren, and again a long time later on the tram ride home.

"I think I left the bloody kettle on!"

I warned Iris the trip home would not be for the faint hearted as we joined the crush of bodies at the tram stop. The carriage was already half full as it slowly approached us, trying to avoid the horde that surged onto the tracks. I stood head and shoulders above most, and I grabbed Iris's hand and pulled her with me up the step and into the bulging belly of the beast. We stood in the footwell of the adjacent door where I could stand without having to crane my neck. A Melbourne tram, much like Vietnam, was not built for anyone 6 feet 9. I spied the conductor. His cod mouthed bag strapped before him. He stood at the end of the aisle leaning against the driver's other door. He'd given up the ticket selling until the throng had thinned.

We changed to a number 11 at Flinders Street Station which was much less crowded. We even got to sit down. Iris had the window, her black purse on her lap. I was on the left, my bad hand in my lap, my good hand wrapped around my knees in a futile effort to keep them clear of the aisle. We'd stepped around a bloke in his late 40s who had obviously had a big day on the booze. Thin strands that had once been combed over his orbicular head now stood straight up in a cockatoo crest. He had a curved beak of a nose that completed the avian picture. He was hatless in a three-piece suit that looked just a little less frayed than he did. A large red and scuffed Qantas bag emblazoned with flying kangaroo was wedged firmly between his feet. In each hand he held a leather strap which was attached to the tram ceiling. He was having a hell of a time trying to balance his hips as the tram rattled and lurched on its journey. One knee would fall, and his hip would swing around. He'd get steady then the other knee would give and swing him counterclockwise. The leather straps groaned under his weight. A sheen of sweat had broken across his brow and the furrow of his top lip. Each stop and start would begin the gyrations over and over again.

"It's a dance we refer to as the tram Elvis," I said to Iris, and she giggled. She was still giggling when the conductor, a beige man in a brown suit, found us.

"Tickets!" he grunted.

"Two please mate."

"I have money you know," Iris whispered.

"My date, my treat," I answered.

"Oh. We're on a date." She smiled winningly up at me. Beige guy ignored the byplay and dropped my coins into his bag. He tore two small yellow tickets off a thick pad and clicked a small hole in each with a small silver device he had concealed in his sweaty hand. He hitched the leather bag like a pregnant belly and shuffled towards the dancing drunk.

"Tickets." The guy raised his hand in a wait gesture and tried to steady himself again. "Tickets," Beige man repeated. The tram stopped with a jerk, sending the drunks hips gyrating so much he almost fell into an old woman's lap. She rose and moved to another seat. He followed her with a smile and a nod that she missed completely. He rummaged quickly in deep pockets and produced a handful of coins, a betting slip which fluttered to the ground, and a handkerchief. He proffered the bundle, and the conductor distastefully removed a few coins as if picking lint from the man's belly button. He punched a ticket and handed it over. They both watched it flutter to the ground. Beige man shuffled away, and the guy could only stare at it forlornly.

"I bought you a little thank-you gift," Iris said as she opened her purse. "I found it when on the way back from the ladies and immediately thought of you." She pulled out a small flap of cardboard which had a rubber strap stapled to it. She handed it to me smiling. I took it and turned the cardboard over. It was a maroon and blue coloured eye-patch, the words, "I'm a one-eyed Lion", were printed in large white Garamond.

"An eye patch," I gushed. "How did you know?" She looked at me a little unsure but smiled widely as I placed it around my head and over the top of the black patch I wore every day.

"I'll never take it off!" I said and Iris giggled again. I was starting to find that giggle irresistible. A young couple struggled with a pink faced baby in a pram up the tram steps. Mr Beige just watched them without offering to lend a hand. The drunk grinned and tried to kick his bag out of the way. The guy smiled back; the girl averted her gaze. They moved to the end of the aisle as far from his bucking and weaving as they could get. The drunk was now almost bent in half, hands wound through the straps head craned upward.

"Maybe I should tell him to sit down before he falls down?" Iris said.

"What… and spoil the show." Just then the man, trying to focus on the street signs to get his bearings reached up and pulled the rubber-coated stop cable running the length of the tram. A loud buzz reverberated up near the driver and we pulled up at the next stop. He grabbed the straps again and wildly lurched forward, pulled back and balanced until he was sure the tram had indeed stopped. Then in a swift motion he swooped down, grabbed the bag by its strap and let the momentum carry him forward and out the tram door which he took in a run, landing on the road in a half crouch.

"Ladies and Gentlemen," I said a little too loudly. "Elvis has left the building!" Every now and then you shoot off a zinger that entertains the whole. Everybody had been fixated on, and amused by, the antics of the drunk and my comment lit a flame. The old woman laughed aloud, tried to catch herself and laughed again. An elderly, square man went into a wheezy, emphysemic chortle which ended in a coughing fit under a handkerchief the size of a bedsheet. Young couple with pram laughed, even the baby gurgled pinkly. Two young office girl types rolled against each other. I saw a couple of young teenagers with long hair and runners punch each other's shoulders. Only Mr Beige refused to get the joke. He turned and shuffled to the other end of the tram. Iris cried with laughter until tears burst from her eyes. She fell helplessly against my shirt, and I could feel the tears against my chest. As the laughter petered out the tram rolled away again. The wheezy man, three rows across croaked,

"Elvis has left the building!" and it set us all off again. Iris looked up at me, grabbed my unresponsive hand in both of hers and raised it. She leant forward and kissed it lightly.

I could tell you I didn't feel anything… but I'd be lying.

I.O.U.

Arriving at Little George Street we walked into a Save Our Sons Fitzroy chapter punting party in full swing. I'd noticed Mrs James' green Chrysler in the street and thought it might be on the cards. The ladies had had a big day on the horses apparently. I opened the front door to an electric mix of tipsy excitement and Thai cooking. The kitchen table was covered in beer and lemonade bottles for the ladies' shandies. 50% beer, 50% lemonade, 0% chance of a hangover; that was the theory anyway. Mrs James, the lady who lost her boy, was there. Mrs Hobson, Mrs Crawford, the fiery Mrs Canetti and even Father Damien, who looked a little redder in the cheeks than usual. Janine Davies was there too, choofing through a pack of Craven A with Mrs Hobson. There was an overflowing ashtray before them. Lily and mum were well into a bottle of gin and bent over a large steaming pot of soup. I don't mind telling you, it made our mouths water.

"I believe that's a Tom Kha Goong on the stove. I'd know that delicious smell anywhere. Yes please," said Iris.

"Afternoon ladies, Father Damien," I said as I shook his hand. "I'm getting the vibe you've all had a good day."

"A very good day young Shepherd," he said. "The Lions?"

"Went down by 25. Played OK."

"Nice eye patch," he said. "And in club colours." I touched the cardboard patch and smiled.

"A gift," I said. The ladies all looked at me. Their gaze was disconcerting. I changed the subject.

"Why is the backdoor open, it's as cold as a…" I quickly catalogued all my cold idiom's, a witch's tit, a digger's arse, a nun's nasty, finding them all inappropriate and aborting the take-off, wisely if not a little spinelessly. "It's really cold in here."

"You don't ask a group of middle-aged ladies what's going through the 'change of life' why the door is open Terry. We're cooking in our own bloody juices over here. Pardon my French of course Father." Glenis Hobson was lighting her next cigarette from her last as she spoke. Golly Hawkins used to call this donkey-rooting. The memory made me smile.

"Feeling a bit warm myself," said Father Damien. "Is menopause contagious?" The women all took a double beat. Had Father D used the M word. Then they all brayed loudly. Mrs Crawford snorted which always drew more laughter.

"This must be Iris," said the spinster Janine Davies as she held out her hand. "I'm Janine, lovely to meet you."

"Nice to meet you too," Iris said and did the rounds of the kitchen. Janine caught my eye and nodded her approval. I must have blushed a little because Janine smiled broadly and winked.

"Iris, you work tonight?" said Lily, her voice a little thick.

"Yes Mum. I have to get a move on too or I'm going to be pretty late," she said and added, "You have a little bit of a buzz on Mum?"

"No, no, don't be silly. I give you soup before you go."

About an hour later, full of soup and my mum's Thai style sausage rolls, hot from the oven, (a new and improved recipe I'm

I.O.U.

happy to say) I walked Iris to the Builders Arms. She held my hand the whole way. At the door she thanked me for a lovely day. I offered to come back and walk her home and she smiled.

"Can hardly wait," she said, her words full of unspoken promise that both confounded and excited. Much later we had a quick beer on closing. Later still we had a cocktail and a dance in Smith Street, Collingwood. At some point in the wee hours, we became a couple. By morning we were lovers, and I can't remember ever being so happy… and not just because I was able to join her in my old bedroom and off the bloody couch.

I went back to long daily walks to the Repat and back-slapping the Cystic Fibrosis kids at the Austin. I was overjoyed to see so many recognizable faces still there. I was happy to see them, but not happy they were still there of course. I was really chuffed they were happy to see me as well. I spent a lot of time at the Repat, helping in any way I could. The Vietnam war was finished for the Aussies but the maimed and broken needed help sorting their bits and pieces. Their war wasn't over. Some of these guys would be fighting Vietnam for the rest of their lives. I hoped to take their minds from their problems, even for a little while.

I could barely face reading about the hell the Americans were still dealing with over there. Throwing the countries' youth away when you could just admit defeat. I felt for the kids on both sides still caught up in the mess. So many lives ruined. There are no winners in a civil war. There are no winners in a political war.

I'd saved a little cash from my time at Chī, and I was getting a disability pension from services. It would have been heaps more if I'd lost the arm and not just totalled it but the payout for an eye was a little higher. All in all, I had money to keep me going. Medicine was going to be my life and that was off the table now. Those cards had been dealt and I refused to be bitter. A positive outlook, I found, was a constant battle but a battle I found so much easier with the beautiful Iris by my side. She was a delight, truly wonderful. Our mums seemed very happy with the arrangement. I would never feel whole again, but Iris made me feel closer to it than at any time since I'd arrived home.

The days rolled by as I tried to settle on where my future lay. I'd walk a bit. Walk and think. I used to head up to Carlton and walk around the tracks near Princes Park. You'd have to keep one eye out for cyclists and the joggers and the other out for dog turds and people's expectorations; problematic for me of course with one eye, and the paths were usually covered in both. You could almost pick the changes in the season by the colours of the phlegm beneath your feet. All the walking was doing me good too. Lily's cooking had put a little meat on my skinny bones and the walking was giving me a little muscle in my battle-scarred legs. My left arm was less like a twig and a little more like a branch. My right arm would always be emaciated. Sometimes Iris joined me on the walks when she wasn't working or studying. She'd just started a law degree at Melbourne Uni. Brains and beauty. God knows what she saw in me.

I tried a moustache around this time. I thought it might cover a little of my facial scarring. Shaving with my left hand was a pain in the arse too. My Gillette razor always made me "look sharp, feel sharp". In my left hand the razor was like shaving with a bayonet. Iris liked the mo, but with the round John Lennon glasses I had started wearing over my patch, and my great height,

I.O.U.

I thought I was the spitting image of Ed Kemper "the Co-ed killer". This horrible fellow had been murdering college girls in California. He was caught around that time, in 1972, after killing his abusive mother and her best friend and the papers were full of his photo. Moustaches were not for me I decided. Ricky, always straight to the point, would have said, "With a nose like that Shep, why would you want to underline it?"

It'd been months since we'd seen neither hide nor hair of Ric. Either the Sharps had scared him so much he'd left town, or he'd forgotten where I used to live. Probably more likely he was laying low as Little George Street had been his second home. I used to say, he put the little in Little George. He'd always follow with "Hey Shep, you put the giant in: what a giant dickhead." I was sure I'd see him soon enough. Ricky was like the prodigal son at the reading of the will. He was always gonna turn up and he'd be looking for his fatted calf. Bad pennies are hard to lose. I'd started to miss him a little all the same. The best friendships never skip a beat. The conversations are always open ended. No-one gets to have the last word.

All of the piss and vinegar had gone out of the S.O.S. Fitzroy Chapter now our troops were out of the East. It seemed to me a lot of beer and lemonade was going in to replace it. Lily was teaching Mum to cook, and my tastebuds worshipped her for it. Mum was teaching Lily how to box up a trifecta and to shop around for the best SP odds; and where the bookies liked to hide. Lily was determined to get another restaurant up and going and had even earmarked a little old house in Johnston Street she thought would be a great spot for her business. The main hold-up was getting a payout from her insurance company.

They were making Lily jump through all sorts of hoops, but Mum had made it her new crusade to hurry them along. The two ladies were on the case and woe betide the insurance agent that crossed their path. Still, she was bound to come up well short. Pop Dempsey, the man with a saying for every occasion, always said insurance was like a hospital gown.

"You're never covered as much as you think you are, and you're usually left with your arse swinging in the breeze."

The highlight of my days were walking Iris to and from the Builders Arms for work or Melbourne Uni for classes. It was only about a 15-minute stroll from Little George. She had uni Monday through Friday and worked shifts to pay for it from Thursday to Saturday. I liked the uni. I had fond memories of my days there. Best of all, it got me out of the house and away from Mum, Lily, and the other ladies; give them their space and maintain my sanity.

Sometimes, when it's all going well, fate can rise up and hit you like a shovel in the face. And that's how it happened with me. Iris and I were too predictable I suppose. Who knows? It turned out that the North Richmond Sharps took their show on the road. One dark night off a short, bluestone lane between Little George and the Builders Arms, Sid, Slug and the skinny, scarred, rat-faced Sharp who, we'd found out later, was known as Ratso swung a long-handled shovel from the late afternoon shadows and knocked me, literally, into next week.

PIT

It was as black as a coal miner's hanky beneath the canopy. We should have had another hour of light, but the rain had hastened the night. We'd decided to bunker down. The monsoon had prevented our air strikes, but the barrage of New Zealand artillery had quietened the enemy. Lt Condon had called three RAAF Hueys and the strafing of the jungle by the door gunners also played a part. Our flyers had enough guts to take to the air in the pelting rain and savage gusting winds that smacked the choppers about with giant fists. The pilots had heard about the mines and couldn't land in the clearing. N.V.A. soldiers released their own smoke cannisters hoping to lure our choppers into an ambush. Lt Condon had to be very cryptic about what colour smoke we were using.

"The colour of our biggest kangaroo," he'd yell into the radio for red and "the colour of Menzies' blood," for blue. The "Vegemite label" for yellow. We had to winch our dead and wounded up in a small square area our guys had cleared in the dense trees. Pte Des gave us the thumbs up as he was loaded inside, a chewed cigarette clamped firmly between his teeth. It was soggy from the unrelenting rain.

We lost four men in the fighting, five more, including Pte Des, were wounded. The worst had been winched up. We decided to keep the bodies of our mates with us until we could clear enough land for the Huey to land for a proper dust-off. The jungle was always going to be too thick to bring the APCs (tracked vehicles) in. Two body bags sat in the middle of our hastily erected fortifications. We were profoundly aware there were two other Aussie soldiers in that thick, oozy quagmire. They would be recovered as soon as we could.

The enemy were also sorting their casualties. We found many blood trails, even body parts, when setting up our perimeter. There were a few weapons recovered. Two small guns, two handmade, long-handled machetes and an AK-47. We found a recoilless rifle that had been destroyed. We also located the base plates of two mortars. These were the only evidence that such a large enemy force even existed. These guys were well trained and extremely disciplined. They were formidable.

The rain refused to surrender. We dug shallow defensive bunkers which quickly filled with water. We ate cold, wet rations, and sat in wet clothes, under wet hooches, and waited out the long night hours. We listened for any sign the N.V.A. were back for a night assault. We heard a few gunshots in the distance. Balls assured me they were the enemy signalling directions to disoriented soldiers.

I removed three fragments of steel from Balls' chest. He'd been quite a distance from the S-mine, the Bouncing Betty, when it exploded, and he was extremely fortunate the damage was not worse. It hadn't even slowed him down. Dave assured me Balls was a "bezerker", one of Odin's bear skin clad shock troops. Dave said it must be so because Balls was such a hairy bastard. Dave had studied Norse mythology. Some things you never saw coming!

I intended to check on the whole patrol through the night to make sure there weren't any other wounds or injuries that needed to be cleaned and treated but Dave and Balls demanded I rest. Balls said I would be needed during the night. You tend to listen to the old guys.

The second attack came just before dawn. Mortar rounds passed over us and lit up the jungle with a wall of flame behind our camp. Lieutenant Condon rallied us as Balls, in the hooch next to mine, tried to triangulate the mortars position for our artillery. An eerie bugle whined like a lonely dog in the distance. They were preparing to charge. Our front line had been digging most of the night and were well in and ready. Condon warned against firing until sure of a target. We'd been resupplied individual rounds, not magazines. A small group had been trying to dry the bullets and share out to every digger. They hadn't got to them all. Our guys were going to have to make our shots count.

The Vietnamese company came through the dark in waves of about twenty men. They tried to hurdle our perimeter Claymores. The mines evaporated the first surge. Those that made it through hurtled straight at our guns. Still, they kept coming. Tracers lit up the sky above our heads as the enemy shot high as they ran. Our guys shot low and straight, and you could hear men scream. Artillery landed behind the attackers then, illuminating leaping men who then disappeared into the inky darkness. One would fall and two more would take his place. Like cutting the heads from the Hydra. The ground shook as our bombs rained down. RPGs flew all around us, obliterating trees, showering the Aussies with flaming detritus. I'd been running ammo to the men until our lieutenant ordered me to the back of the camp and out of harm's way.

"You're too bloody big Shep. I can't see what the fuck's going on."

Then the gods threw buckets of water over the lot of us. Rain came down so hard it hurt. It slapped with hands and kicked at you with feet. Lightning flashed within purple cloud. It was the colour of mourning. The air was charged. It seemed to crackle; it tormented the hair on your face. Thunder rolled across us as another wave of artillery blew men to pieces. It was hard to see anything through the tempest. The first our guys knew N.V.A. soldiers had made our bunker line was when they landed on them. Hand-to-hand fighting saw them off. Barrel, boots, and bayonet. The Aussie soldiers returned to their shooting. I moved to the rear of the perimeter as ordered. I was bent low under the weight of the cascade. I climbed in under a tree and tried to keep my pack, and the bandages within dry with my body. I listened intently for the cry of "medic", but the noise of the rain filled your head. You could barely hear the battle.

A mortar blew up my tree. The shockwave blew me down a short, steep embankment of slippery mud. I awoke at some point later, dazed, and discombobulated. The concussion of the explosion, and a piece of burning wood the size of a cat's head had knocked me senseless.

I'd been concussed before; I fell out of a tree as a kid. I landed on my head and woke up with a huge lump and no idea why I'd been up the tree in the first place. There was a peace as I lay on my back. I couldn't see or feel anything: just that spacey, vacuum sound – the sound you get in your head when you're 9 years old and fall out of a tree your mum told you repeatedly not to climb. An echoey, hollow sound. It always reminded me of the Dr Who theme song. Ricky and I loved watching that show on our little telly. *Hoowooo-ooo, oowooooooo.*

I was on my back, on my pack. The burning tree gave me a little light, but this was almost extinguished by the heavy rain. I realised I wasn't breathing. Was I breathing? Just winded. Should I panic? Something had knocked the wind out of me. The fall. The air would come. I'd been winded before. It was a spasm that would pass. As a kid I'd start breathing again as soon as I convinced myself that I was actually going to die. A fight was still ranging somewhere above me. I had a bluntness of brain which was disconcerting when I knew it was imperative I stay sharp. I was in long grass. I crawled forward on my hands and knees. There was a slope. Streams of mud made it slick and impossible to climb. I crawled away from the rise and found a sapling I was able to drag myself upright against. I stood tall but couldn't see anything. The firefight roared above the rain as I rose, the sound seemed to waver in the moist air. I was all arse about. I knew I was needed where the men were, but I was having a hell of a time getting to them. I decided to wait the rain out. It couldn't beat down like this forever, surely.

The *Boi Loi* Woods were dark and noisy. The only light was of tracers, artillery, and the burning trees. No-one, friend or enemy, fired flares lest they give away their position. I couldn't find my torch and was reticent to open my bag to search for it and get everything else wet. I waded through black ink, trying to skirt the rise and find the fight. The roar of battle was everywhere and nowhere in particular. The sound swirled. It bounced off the gnarled and impenetrable woods. I made my way towards a smaller copse of shattered trunks that smouldered weakly in the driving wet. A loud *BOOM* to my left. Rifle *CRACK* to my right. It seemed counter intuitive to move toward explosions, but I was starting to feel a little lost and a little desperate. If I went too far in the wrong direction I might happen upon or own defensive wire. I saw light then. A weak moonlight traced silver on a saturated path between the trees. Droplets seemed paralysed in its glare. Instinctively I moved toward it. I was a moth about to dance into the flame. I hoped it might give me direction. I sidled between two trees, manoeuvring the pack on my back, and stepped over tall and tangled grass. I stepped into the path of a NVA soldier coming the other way not more than three yards in front of me. He wore the green pith helmet, the bright, yellow star of Vietnam on the front. He was wounded. Blood had turned his saturated grey uniform a deep red from his left knee down. He appeared to carry a Type-56 Assault rifle. The Chinese copy of the Kalashnikov. Light winked on the barrel. Even in the darkness I believed I could see terror on his face. We stood and stared in disbelief. I was an impossibly long and skinny apparition, a phantom appearing between the trees. He looked like a boy playing at war. He regained his senses first but not his composure. He lifted his automatic and fired three quick shots. The first two went wide, the third hit me in the right bicep and spun me around. I pinballed off the small trees I had just stepped between. Pain subsumed my whole body. The soldier was lifting his rifle slowly now, carefully. I saw him breathe deeply and steady his shaking hands. He drew a bead at my heaving chest. Weaponless, I let go an animal scream, a release of pain and panic, and charged at him. In two or three long strides I was on him. His face went white. He hesitated for a micro-second which gave me time to grab the barrel of his gun and wrench it upward. A second volley of shots exploded past my face. The bullets tore holes of weak light in the leaves. My momentum drove us backwards off the slippery track and we crashed through a curtain of brush. I was still roaring, a low guttural noise I'd never replicate. There was a sensation of falling through the air. We landed with a splash. Pain, white, hot, and overwhelming. Something had stung my eye, pierced it. Skewered it. I yanked my head back and I'll never forget the feeling of the stake pulling free or the grinding, squelching noise that echoed around my skull. Blood and ooze ran freely down my face. The pain, indescribable. I needed to get the hell out, live another day. The soldier was screaming now. Bloodcurdling, horrible. I lay atop him in some sort of hole. Pain flared through my upper thighs. My knees were bent. My thighs were impaled and on fire. And still he screamed. The sound filled the pit. Blood filled his mouth. He gargled and choked on it. He was drowning in his own blood. He screamed. Eyes and mouth open, soundlessly. My face inches from his, I could feel his breath. I was helpless to move. The agony, the horror. Panic, pain, and confusion. He squirmed beneath me and the knives in my legs reached deeper. My right arm didn't respond. My left still held the barrel of his gun. I never felt the burn of the barrel. If I could reach the pistol in my breast pocket I'd could have helped him, helped myself; Lax's gun may as well have been sitting on the dark side of the moon. It was impossible to retrieve.

The young soldier died then. He just stopped. Blood spilled from his open mouth and ran down his throat, over his jaws, pooled in his ears. His eyes open and sightless, lit by feeble rays of moonlight that flittered like bats over our pit. Dead eyes. Muscles, bladder, and bowels released. And still, I couldn't move, I couldn't help. He was just a young fella, a kid pulled into a horrific war. No-one should die like he did. No one should die in this pointless war, but still they died gruesomely every day. I knew then with a perfect clarity that I too would die. I was going to die in this rancid, rapidly filling hole. I welcomed death to ease the pain. It was too much. My medical training tried to make sense of what was happening to me. I was going into shock and would probably lose consciousness. Then I was out. I'd come back, and the pain would be there again feasting on my nerve endings, my body, my brain.

This kid's pain was over.

Lucky bastard.

K.I.A.

I awoke in a hospital ward, 12 hours later, in a world of hurt. No concussive peace this time. My cheek was shattered, my head ached, my nose was blocked and throbbing. I needed water. I licked my dry lips; something was wrong with my teeth. Sharpened stubs met my probing tongue painfully. Front teeth snapped, big gap on the right. God I was thirsty. I tried to open my eye; it didn't comply. Finally, after what seemed like an age, I could see. The ward was bright and cool. It looked like the Repat Hospital I was so familiar with. Same tiled floor, same tiled ceiling. Big windows and blue painted door.

"He's awake. Thank god. Terry!" It was Iris. I heard a chair squeak, then felt Iris grasp my cold hand in her warm, soft ones. She leant across and kissed my forehead gently. I raised my arm to touch her and grunted; a sharp pain in my side. My chest felt tight, constricted. Bandaged.

"Lay still now. You've cracked a few ribs son." There was another voice in the room. A male voice. Gravel. A big, bald head loomed in my vision. A square, wizened, kindly face. Grey moustache. Intelligent blue eyes. It was the copper, the detective, the one at the fire.

"Gordon is here, Shep. You've met him before," Iris said as if talking to someone old and infirm.

"Gordon," I said, my voice, weak, my throat parched. I wanted to nod but I was a little afraid to move.

"Should I get the nurse?" Iris asked.

"Wouldn't hurt Iris," said Gordon. "I can look after Terry until you're back." Iris breezed from the room with a grace I would never have managed.

"How you feeling son?"

"Like a bus ran over me, and then backed over me to make sure. I feel like roadkill."

"Yup, I guess you do. Stupid question," he nodded.

"What's happened and why are you here, if that's not a rude question?"

"It's not son. It would be the smart question and I'd expect nothing less." Gordon paused then as if deciding how he should start.

"It would appear son, that the smallest brains have the longest memories." Gordon took a seat at the end of my bed. We were separated from my neighbours by a large blue-green curtain hanging from metal rings.

"It seems that three nasty fellows crept out of the dark and hit a one-armed, one-eyed, ex-serviceman with a shovel, then proceeded to give you a bit of a kicking when you were out to it."

"Sid! After all this time?" I said in wonderment. "Iris, Iris was there. Is she OK? Did they hurt her?"

"Iris is fine Terry. She's too clever for them," he said reaching forward to tap a large, callused hand on my foot; a small hill under the heavy, woollen hospital blanket.

"She's an Amazon that one, Terry. She managed to scare them off. These guys meant business." Iris came back into the room then, a nurse in brilliant white followed closely behind. Iris held a glass of orange juice she'd managed to scare up and she came over to the bed.

"I have orange juice. Are you able to handle it or should I put it to your lips?"

"I'll be fine. Thankyou," I said croakily. "I reached for the glass, the ribs bit like an angry dog. I ignored it; I was pretty keen on the juice. My throat felt like I'd been gargling road screenings. The juice was cool, wet, and welcome. Suddenly, there was an electric shock as the cold liquid hit my battered teeth. Pain flashed in my head but subsided quickly. I made a mental note. My next mouthful would need to avoid my front teeth and what must be an exposed root on the right.

The nurse was busying herself with the chart that hung by a large metal bulldog clip at the end of the cot. She jotted in it with a blue pen attached to a chain around her neck. It was a dance I'd seen played out in another ward at another hospital.

"Welcome back Mr Shepherd. How are you feeling?" she asked pointedly.

"I'm not too bad. Bit fuzzy in the head."

"You've had a nasty concussion. You'll probably have a headache. I can talk you through your injuries when you're feeling a little better. I'd like you to take these for the pain now and I'll bring you a meal presently if you are feeling hungry."

"Not sure I could eat."

"You'll feel better after the meds." She stepped toward a small rectangular table on long, metal legs against the wall and poured me a glass of water from a plastic jug. We exchanged glasses. My empty one for the full one. I swallowed and drank, careful to avoid the nervy tooth on the right. I covered it with my battered tongue.

"Back shortly with a small meal and we'll see how you go. Maybe some sandwiches. Nice and soft." She smiled, spun on her heel.

According to Iris I had a broken nose, and a fractured cheekbone. I had two broken fingers on my bad hand, which were heavily bandaged and didn't hurt at all. I also had two cracked ribs, they hurt a lot. I had quite a few bruises on my jaw, chest, and belly. Gordon sat quietly on his chair to my right. He held his hat between his hands. His face, inscrutable.

"You're OK then Iris? They didn't hurt you?'

"I'm fine Terry."

"Was it Sid?"

"Yeah. There were three of them. Sid hit you with the shovel and then they started kicking you," Iris spoke softly. "I screamed and one of them came to grab me. I swung my handbag and got him in the face. He went down hard. The other two just kept kicking, stomping."

"I screamed at them to leave you alone. There were some people across the road. They ran over and started yelling and the three ran off."

"Did they say anything to you?" Iris looked furtively at Gordon.

"No, they just ran off. Iris stepped forward and grabbed my hand in both of hers, as her eyes welled up. The square, brown suited man got up then and pulled the curtain between my bed, completely circling us in teal. He stood close to me and spoke in a hushed voice.

"I have some bad news to tell you son. I apologise to hit you with this after you've just come back to us."

"Lily. Mum?" I gasped.

"No Terry," said Iris. Gordon continued.

"Ricco Pepi was found floating in the Yarra a couple of days ago, near Dight's Falls in Collingwood. He had been badly beaten and appears to have drowned. He'd been in the water for some time. The coroner is not sure how long. He might have been beaten somewhere else and dumped. I know he was a friend of yours. Iris informs me he was with you both the night the Chinese restaurant burned down."

The numbness of my arm crept through my body. My thoughts clouded.

"I'm so sorry Terry," Iris said. She had tears in her eyes. Iris liked Ricky very much. So did Lily. So did everyone.

"Christ," I whispered. The news hit me as hard as the shovel.

"Bastards," Iris seethed through gritted teeth. "Those fucking bastards."

"We can't be 100% sure it was Sid and his gang."

"Who the fuck else would it have been?" she said. "Sorry Gordon." He just nodded soberly. I tried to sit up and the pain in my ribs felt like I'd been stabbed. Gordon put a big hard hand softly on my chest. He didn't push me back down, but I got the message.

"Don't scare the horses son," he said firmly.

"It was Sid," I said. "Sid and his loyal band of psychopaths."

"I'm not disagreeing with you two. As you may be aware though, Ric sometimes walked with a tough crowd. Family connections. The police need to be sure."

"Gordon," I said flatly with a resigned calm I didn't know I possessed. "They threatened Ricky, they threatened me, they threatened to kill all of us." Gordon nodded.

"God only knows why they waited this long. It's been over a year," I said.

"Maybe they couldn't find us?" Iris asked. Gordon turned and pulled the chair across the floor and bought it up to my bed. He turned it around and rested his big head across arms folded on the back. He leant forward and spoke quietly.

"OK. This is how it is. After the fire the police didn't have anything concrete on the North Richmond Sharps, couldn't charge them with arson, anything. So, they expanded the search. Decided to look into them a little more closely if you get me. They raided their place a couple of times, gave them the occasional tune up. One of them punched an officer and he did two months. Not sure which one. Sid was too smart to take the bait. The Sharps had been running a few girls. Selling the odd weapon. They had dope growing in a little hydroponic set up at the back of the clubhouse. None of this big-time stuff you understand. A few fines here and there. Kept the plain-clothes sniffing around though, making a general nuisance of themselves you see. Eventually they found out they'd also been pushing heroin through underage kids around North Richmond. Bit hard to tie it back to them but uniformed squads started grabbing the youngsters and locking them away. Finally, a young fella did roll on the gang, and they were able to put two of Sid's crew away for a short while. They couldn't get Sid though. Slippery fellow. Well, they all appointed good lawyers. It would seem Sid has plenty of cash." Gordon trained a steely gaze on me now. He moved slightly closer over the back of the chair.

"So, now they're out and the gang is back together. Maybe they've decided to settle old scores. I have no doubt you may have finished up like your friend Ricky but for Iris and some bystanders managing to scare them off."

"Too many witnesses?" said Iris.

"Yeah. I'd say so."

"These three that assaulted you. They will be picked up shortly and Iris will have to pick them out of a line up."

"And make them more pissed off," I said.

"Maybe."

"She'll be an even bigger target."

"You need them off the streets."

"There's others."

"These three seem to be the ringleaders," Gordon said thoughtfully.

"Will they make bail?"

"There should be enough to hold them. For a little while. Assault with a weapon. Affray. Suspected murder. Maybe attempted murder. Again, they have good lawyers and the money to pay them."

"Then they'll be back after us. They obviously know we're in Fitzroy."

"Maybe."

"Gordon. They blow up our home, and nearly us with it and the police can't do anything. They beat Ricky to death for standing up to them. They put me in here and still the police can't guarantee these arseholes are out of our lives. Look at me Gordon, what the hell are we supposed to do?" Gordon regarded me quietly with penetrating blue eyes.

"So, now we just wait until they kick in our door and murder us all in our sleep?"

"The police will do what they can son."

"It's not enough Gordon," said Iris.

He didn't speak for the longest time. He just looked at me, into me. He stood slowly and picked up his hat from the bed.

"I want you to listen to me carefully now, Terry!" His voice barley above a whisper.

"I don't want you doing anything stupid. They are dangerous. Do I make myself clear son?" My anger wilted a little under his blazing gaze.

"I've had this little speech before Gordon," I said coolly. "What choice are you giving me? No-one can guarantee our safety?" Iris squeezed my hand tightly.

"I want you to trust me on this son. I'll do everything I can. However. Do not take matters into your own hands. They will kill you. Am I clear on that Terry?"

"What could I do, mate. It's not like I'm at the peak of my physical powers." The hot magma of anger had become solid in my chest. A weight on my heart. A burden to off-load.

"Get well now son and again, I am very sorry about your friend." I nodded but found myself unable to respond.

"Look after him Iris."

"I will Gordon," she said. "Thank you, for coming."

"Iris", he said. "There is a police car waiting out the front to take you back home. No hurry, take your time here. They have been told to wait for you. They will be in and around Little George Street tonight. The assailants will be keeping their heads low now. They know there were witnesses. You will be fine young lady. I want you to know I'll do everything within my power for you both." Gordon nodded soberly and walked to the door.

"Get well soon."

"Thank you again Gordon," Iris said. He was getting on in years, but he still had a formidable rigidity to him. His blocky frame practically filled the doorway. He placed his hat on his head and was gone.

Iris turned the chair around and sat heavily. She exhaled long and loud. We sat in silence. I rolled it all over in my aching head. My nose throbbed and pounded. I'd already sliced my tongue on the new topography of my teeth. My body hurt in a thousand different places. Whatever the nurse had given me I'm not sure it was enough. I moved and winced.

"Do you need any more pain relief."

"I can wait," I said.

"You don't need to wait if you're sore Terry."

"I want to think, that's all."

"I'm so sorry Terry."

"Yeah," I said. "He didn't deserve that. For helping me, for helping us."

"He loved you Terry. He told me he'd have done anything for you, given everything."

"And he did Iris."

"Yes he did," she said looking at the hands clasped in her lap. The nurse arrived then with a plate of sandwiches and a pot of tea for each of us on a large, rectangular plastic tray.

"Just finish what you can," she said. "How's the pain?"

"I'm OK for now."

"Right. Then I'll be back in a couple of hours with a top up. The head, your eyesight. Any double vision? Having any trouble focussing?"

"Getting there," I said.

"She smiled, jotted in my chart and left the room.

In fact, everything was taking on a sharp focus, but I didn't bother sharing that with the nurse.

It was only later that Iris confided in me there were no passer-by good Samaritans when we were attacked. Sid had hit me with the shovel and Iris said I was out before I hit the footpath. She thought I was dead. The guy named Ratso came at her through the dark of the alley and she swung her handbag at his face catching him just under the jaw.

"I dropped him like a bag of shit." Iris reached under my bed and bought the handbag into her lap. I noticed the strap at one end had come away. It looked scuffed and scratched. She opened it, reached in, and removed the gun. It was Sid's gun. The one Ricky had held at Sid's face in the restaurant. Iris had been carrying the gun all this time. She said she stepped forward and told Sid and the Slug to leave me alone. They turned and Iris said she stepped forward and held the gun against Sid's groin. He was the closest.

"I said I would make him a eunuch. He didn't know what a eunuch was of course, but he gathered from my tone of voice I meant to blow his fucking balls off."

"Hell," I said.

"Slug tried to run at me, but I knew he would, and I was ready. I swung the gun into his face. A John Newcombe backhand. I hit him so hard I thought I would drop it. Mashed my fingers." I turned her hand over in mine. The knuckles scuffed and puffy.

"They hurt like anything," she smiled, then paused to regain her composure and finish her story.

"I stood over you Shep. God, I thought you were dead. The others started to leave but not Sid. He got up and pointed that stupid scorpion finger at me and said, 'This isn't over,' then he called me names. I said, 'Well, I can end it right here you fucking bastard,' and I pointed the gun at his face. The other two, they tried to drag him away. Sid's eyes were spinning. Veins popping. He's not right in the head Terry.

"Ratso said they'd better leave because they might have killed you and then Sid finally turned to go. I nearly shot him then Shep." Iris had begun to cry.

"I wish I had. Fucking arsehole. When they said you were dead I wanted to kill them all, but you moaned, and I bent down to touch your poor face. When I looked up they had gone."

"You didn't tell Gordon any of this did you."

"Not about the gun. I didn't want to lose it. I thought he would take it away." I reached out and held her hand then and pulled her over to me. She pushed her face into the crook of my neck, and I kissed her gently on the forehead.

"A guy came out of his house then and I asked him to call an ambulance." Her voice muffled against me. I could feel the vibration, smell her sweet breath. Her tears wet on my neck.

"Poor Ricky. He saved us Terry. He might have saved our lives," she said.

"I know honey. I know."

"I could have finished it. Finished Sid anyway."

"You're not a killer Iris," I said quietly and stroked her hair. "I

R.I.P.

wouldn't go around with a killer. What would people think?"

It was a massive funeral. Ricky was loved by everybody. Everyone I suppose, except the evil bastards that beat him senseless and left him to drown in the Yarra. Our upside-down river. Nan and Pop even drove down from Yarck for it. They loved Ricky too. Ricky was always around at Little George when we were young and when Nan and Pop were in town they got to know him really well. Pop used to call him Senior Mussolini. Ricky would then point at Pop's denuded head and ask, "And how is Grandpa Billiard Ball?" They would banter for hours. Back and forth all night. Pop loved it.

They stayed with us for a few days. Iris and I were relegated to the mattresses. Pop asked if it was going to be one of those "Eye-tie" full nuptial funerals that go for ever. Nan said it probably would be, and so he stood at the back and spent most of the service out the front with a few of Ricky's cousins and uncles. They smoked cheap cigarettes and took furtive swigs from a large wicker covered bottle of Chianti. They talked footy. Pop said it was pretty boring as they were all Carlton supporters and only wanted to talk about the Sergio Silvagni, even though he'd retired, twice, almost two years before. He was the Blue's Italian bull with pool table legs his socks could never master.

Mum, Nan, Lily, and Iris joined me in the front pew.

Giuseppina Pepi, Ricky's mum, had asked me to make a speech as I was his dearest friend. His father had passed, and she said her English wasn't "too goodenuff". She was also inconsolable; Ricky was an only child. She was surrounded by short, squat bollards. Black clad women under black, lace veils, who rubbed her back, muttered Italian solicitudes and generally fussed around her throughout the service.

The memorial booklet had a grainy photo of Ricky on the cover. He must have been about five. Probably just before school age, before we met I suppose. He wore a dark suit and a big lighter shaded bowtie. You could tell it was red even though the picture was in black and white. He held an ice cream which had smeared his chin. He had a huge grin, what Ricky would call his big, shit-eating grin. Bad haircut, big round ears. He looked like a very cute chimp. He'd have hated it and I loved that he would have hated it. On the back was a more recent pic of Ric. Black skivvy, gold chain over the top. Pencil-thin moustache that looked like it had been draw on. A milk moustache of Indian ink. He held a glass of champagne in the photo. He looked down the lens with a smirk that said, "Hey Shep, I know you've got a thing for habits. Just keep your hands off my Zia, Sister Benedetti or my Uncle Vito will cut off your balls." I rolled and twisted the book tightly on my thigh. I couldn't look at that face. It hurt my heart to look at that face.

Most of Ricky's family gasped when they saw my own battered and bruised face as if I was wearing the stigmata of Ricky's own trials and tribulations. One of his uncles from Mildura, a small balding man with a Trilby hat patted my hand and nodded knowingly. I had no idea what he thought he knew. It was infuriating.

I was very self-conscious of my broken teeth and either talked behind my hand or without opening my mouth. I'd begun to mumble. Mum and Nan kept asking me to repeat myself. Pop told me to, "Speak up for Gorr's sake! One day you might say something worth hearing and I'd hate to miss it!"

"Shoosh now!" Nan scolded him. "Leave the boy alone." Pop asked if I thought the same fellas that hit me with the shovel had bashed my young friend Ricky. I told him I didn't know. He said in his day they would bull-whip cowards like that. Nan said there were dinosaurs and dodos in his days and to leave me be.

Dr Keysor had pulled some strings and kept me in the hospital for an extra day to observe my concussion and treat my various wounds. It was a bit tough as I'd had my fill of hospitals of course. He was terrific all the same and went above and beyond. For all his bluster and bulldust Dr K did look after the servicemen that had become his charges. He'd organised an appointment with his college mate, a dentist. Dr Wittman came into my ward and told me he could make a plate for my missing chompers; my serviceman's pension would pay for it, and I'd be as good as new. I told him I'd think about it.

There was a whole row of very pretty girls who cried and wailed and egged each other on to greater displays of misery. It was as if Ricky had organised the whole thing prior to his passing. His younger male cousins, in the pews near me, were elbowing each other and practically breaking their necks trying to get a good look at Ricky's old girlfriends. He would have loved it.

The priest, a silver-haired, weather-bitten Father Buongiorno, conducted the memorial in two languages which doubled the time and the lamentation. We double mourned. Uncle Vito spoke on behalf of the family. Nieces and nephews read the prayers of the faithful and then Father Buongiorno introduced me as Ricky's oldest and dearest friend. He called me to the altar. All the air was sucked from the room then. It got very real. For the longest moment, I wasn't sure I'd be able to stand. The gathering waited patiently except for one crying baby in the back who refused to adhere to social convention.

Since I'd returned from Vietnam I'd never been asked to stand in front of a room full of people let alone talk to them. Physically, I looked like I should pull up a box and have a long lie down. Smashed cheek. One eye patched, the other almost closed. Useless left arm, swollen beak. What a sight I must have made. I steeled myself then when it seemed as though I'd refused the hurdle. Iris gave me a gentle nudge which said everything really. She thought I could do it. Then I decided, if Ricky could stand up, I could. I owed it to Ricky and, if I made a goose of myself; that would have made him the happiest. How could I lose.

I was a little angry too if the truth be told. I think the anger was the reason the speech went off the rails. As Iris, Nan, Pop, Mum, Lily, and I approached the All-Saints Parish on King William's Street, passing the weatherboard cottages and leafy plain trees, a large group of Ricky's relatives waved me over. Dark men and adolescents, dark suit and dark ties. Large labourers' hands buried in pockets. The women had their own rookery nearby. The ones I knew well greeted us warmly as we approached. I met proffered handshakes with my outstretched left hand, to make them comfortable. I was getting good at this.

One of the guys, Uncle Carlo I think, I didn't know him that well, suggested that they weren't surprised at Ricky's demise. He said Ricky was always a cheeky little smart-arse with a smart mouth who was always going to rub the wrong person the wrong way.

"I'm not saying he deserved to be 'massacred', I'm just saying he could be a *boccolone*." I think it means big mouth. Some of the older guys nodded at the ground. A couple crossed themselves as if it warded off hellfire for speaking ill of the dead. They were so conceited in their belief that Ricky may have bought this on himself; so dismissive. I couldn't answer him then. I turned away. Iris, who held my hand felt me clench. These arseholes knew nothing. I think anger finally got me to stand up for my friend.

I hadn't written anything down as I was still having trouble reading back my own crappy, left-handed writing. I had thought about what I was going to share of our time together. His laugh. His wit. His gregarious nature. His impetuosity. As I shuffled to the pulpit and stood before an expectant congregation my mind went completely blank. I cleared my throat.

"Ahh hmmm." The acoustics in the church were terrific and even the whinging baby shut up. The silence hung heavy above the expectant crowd. I placed the booklet on the pulpit and spread it out flat as if I had written a speech. In my mind's eye I could see Ricky, with the silly moustache, daring me to say something, anything. Willing me, goading me to mess it all up.

"Hello everybody," I said in a fingernails-on-blackboard screech. "Ahh hmmm. I found out something over the last few days, something I'll bet none of you have ever even considered. You can cry real tears even when your eye is missing." Don't ask me why I started with a joke. A pretty unfunny joke at that.

I didn't even know I was going to say it. I heard my Pop caw loudly from the back of the church. He'd left the group out the front to come in and listen to me speak. Just so he could tell me how wonderful it was later over a beer at home. With Pop I had a rusted-on fan. No-one else in the room made a noise. I shuffled the blank sheet in front of me. A large magpie landed on the other side of a stained-glass window to my right. It was a pitch-black silhouette as it walked past the prismatic coloured glass which depicted Jesus being taken down from the cross. Roman spears creating a pointed fence around the scene. The bird shimmered through colours until it came to a clear triangle of glass in the corner and looked in quizzically at me. There was some polite coughing. A murmur. Father Buongiorno smiled and nodded for me to continue. And at last, just as I'd decided I wouldn't be able to say anything, I did.

"I'd like to tell you all a little about courage. I'd like to talk about valour. For those that don't know I just got back from Vietnam. Sure, I got smashed over there. This isn't about me. I'm not a brave man. I met some brave men. I fought with some of the bravest men to pull on an Australian uniform. An American uniform. I patched up some courageous men. I even zipped some of these brave men into body bags. I'd like to think I know a little bit about the bravery of men." The church was silent.

"Brave people can rise above their fears. The truly brave will charge in knowing they are out of their depth. They go anyway. They know there may be no coming back. They know that it may very well mean their end. They stand up. They wade in. They roll up their sleeves and go. Few men or women can walk into a room full of evil men. Truly evil men. Men you are petrified of. These rare people have the courage to walk into that room and put bastards in their place. Great men stand up for their friends, and they pay alright. They pay with their life. That's what real courage is. That's what real love is." I hit the podium with the mass book that my hand found. It was my book I'd rolled into a tight cylinder, and I almost forgot I had it. *WHACK*! The congregation looked at me with shock now. There was absolute silence.

"How do you know when you are truly loved by someone? Well, ahhhh, It's when they give you everything. Some people give you everything, their everything, without wanting anything back."

"That's what selflessness is!" *WHACK*!

"That's what real courage is!" *WHACK*!

"That's what… love is!" *WHACK*!

"That's who Ricky Pepi was."

"Sure, I could tell you Ricky was the funniest and craziest nutbag I've ever met. Sure, he was a bochulony or, bigmouth or whatever. Maybe he was going to rub the wrong people the wrong way at some point like Uncle Carlo said. What I didn't know about Ricky, what Uncle Carlo didn't know and what most of you in this room didn't know about Ricky is that he had real courage. Ricky was as brave as any man I've ever met; and Ricky loved us. The night he walked into a room full of evil men." I lost it then. The words struggled to come.

"He sssstood up and he died. Ricky was a bloody hero." The tears were flowing now. From the good eye and the bad one. They ran down my nose, inside and out. I knew I was pissing this all up, but I couldn't seem to stop. I found Iris, Lily and my family in the crowd and I pointed the Mass book at them.

"Ricky saved me that night. He saved Iris and he saved Lily. He loved us all. That night Ricky showed me he was the bravest of us all. He showed me he loved us, but not half as much as I fucking loved him."

And with that I turned, left the altar, and walked straight out the side door.

How embarrassing is all that? It was pretty horrifying. To think I even said fuck in a church. Father Buongiorno wouldn't have liked that. Mum would be apoplectic. Nan would probably blame Pop for his bad influence. Pop would have freaking loved it. I'm not sure how it all went down with Ricky's family and friends, because I left. I missed the wake and the burial. I went for a stroll around Fitzroy and sat in a park under a palm where a large raven laughed at me. I felt like a twit to be honest. I took a little solace from the thought that Ricky, if he was indeed sitting on a cloud and looking down on me, and not trying to look down the tops of all the girls in the second pew; Ricky, if he was indeed listening, would have been pissing his pants.

"Is this how you turned out," he'd have said in the asthmatic Brando rasp, "Like a Hollywood *finocchio* that cries like a woman?"

M.I.A.

I couldn't even close his eyes. They stared at me, through me. One part recrimination. One part empathy. I looked back at him with envy. He saw the sky. I saw only the abyss of the punji pit that had become our tomb. Our mausoleum. He was dead and I was in torment. Every twitch, every flinch, every blink forced sharpened, shit smeared stakes into my thighs. Somehow night had become day. Cruel sunlight stole in, illuminating the horror of our situation. I could do nothing to help either of us. Where were the others? Where was Balls, Dave? Lieutenant Condon? If we left no-one behind why I was still in the stinking pit?

I doubt he spoke English, but he understood my dilemma. Probably the only one that could. He had a unique perspective you might say. We were in this together. Blood loss had made me weak, and I fell in and out of consciousness. The pain dragged me back to find gravity had pushed us a little further on to the sharpened stakes. I had it worse than Tim of course. Tim was the name I gave my cohabitor, my roommate. I hope he didn't mind. I suppose I should have given him a Vietnamese name, but I couldn't think of a single one. Tim was a good name for a close friend though. You didn't get much closer than we two. Tim had caught the lion's share of the stakes. His body must be riddled with them. He had saved me from many of them, quite decent of him too when you think I pushed him in here in the first place. One stake had run up the side of his neck, just above his shoulder. This is the stake that took out my eye. My whole face on that side was a dull throb. There was a stake that had pushed through the back of Tim's head, most likely just below his skull, and I could see its evil tip swimming in the pool of congealing blood at the back of his throat. A few stakes had missed us both, but not many. I was taller than Tim, but of course I was taller than everyone in Vietnam. The stakes that poked between his legs were deeply buried in my thighs and they hadn't finished with me just yet. They gnawed on me with every shallow breath. They would gnaw through both our bodies until we were swallowed by the fetid ooze the rain, our blood, and God only knew what else, had congealed at the bottom. I prayed I would be dead before I touched that stinking, demon bile. My knees were bent, shins were against the pit wall. I couldn't know if they were below the lip of the pit or sticking rigidly in the air. If my mates looked for me would they see them?

The woods were silent. Not a bird sang, not an insect buzzed. After a firefight every living thing runs as far away as possible. Thankfully the rain had stopped. Rain falling in Tim's open eyes might drive me right off the deep end. Further off the deep end. My left hand still held the barrel of Tim's rifle pointing it at the sky. It's one black eye could see the clouds. I'd have liked to have seen the clouds one last time. I think this was day two, but I had no way of knowing. I may have been out for many days. All I could do was lay there leaking. Soon I would relinquish the last of my lifeblood to the miasma at the bottom and I would join Tim for eternity pinned to Vietnam like two butterflies in a lepidopterist's drawer.

    I woke sometime later screaming in my dreams. I was screamed out. My throat threatened to close once and for all. Pain seared. Must have moved in my sleep. Or Tim did. Night again. Weaker now. Resting my head on Tim's forehead. I'm sure he didn't mind. Soon I'd be getting on terms with the worms as Pop used to say.

"PUP"

A single whispered word at the end of a long tunnel.
"Pup?"
Very close now. A ghostly whisper in the ear of a dead man.
"Pup. Are you dead mate?"
Am I dead? What a stupid question. I think it was the sheer incongruity of the question that got me ticking. I didn't want to come back you understand. A part of me, my subconscious, knew I'd be returning to pain. Why didn't God just let me drift away? And what sort of stupid question is "are you dead?" I awoke with Tim, or so I thought, whispering stupid questions. Another hallucination, I thought, borne of blood loss and fever. I had raging infections that threatened to consume me. I had been experiencing some pretty weird stuff in our pit. Tim and I had a long conversation about Australian music. He was a huge Lobby Loyde fan. Tim knew some of the girls I went to school with. Girls I hadn't seen in years. He told me which ones had got married and if they'd had kids. We debated the intricacies of Socialism, Capitalism, Catholicism and Buddhism, and the importance of Uncle Ho to the campaign. I think Ho even participated in this chat. Tim and I had a heated argument about Rosemary. He said she was a tramp and I threatened to punch him if only I could move my right hand. Tim said he wasn't afraid and that he had it on good authority I was a lover

not a fighter. Tim could see right through me. Those saucer-like fisheyes saw everything. It wouldn't be long before I could see through him.

I felt cool fingers on my throat, scrabbling for a pulse. I couldn't even groan. I felt a little annoyed that Tim had survived while I was still pinned here. How had he crawled from under me? Tim had been kindly holding back the stakes with his body. Would I now be faced with more pain? Still, I was happy to see him up and about. I thought he was dead, but I wouldn't be stupid enough to ask if he was dead. Dead men tell no tales. It's in all the papers. I'd be sorry to be alone in our pit but with a little luck I'd die soon. Bon Voyage Tim.

"Getting you out mate. Stay with me." Tim was moving through the horrible filth at the bottom of the pit. He was moving around me snapping the honed pieces of wood that had been holding us in place. I felt my legs lifted, the searing agony of the stakes leaving my upper thighs was replaced with a dull ache. Still, quite gentlemanly of him really, especially after I'd killed him.

I felt myself being pulled by my feet. Up and away. I opened my right eye, just a fraction. Tim was still there. The stake pushing up from the black maw; it must have been growing. Blood and bone made great fertilizer. I tried to push the thought away. If not Tim, then who had my feet?

I was now under a tree. I was out of that bloody pit. Water was being poured slowly into my mouth. My throat constricted, refused. It was a fight to take anything in. I was so hot I thought the water would evaporate before it even reached my throat. I though it would sizzle as it wet my tongue like water being thrown on the hot coals of a sauna. I became aware someone was talking to me in a low voice. Fussing around me. I was unable to hear him. Someone had removed my pack and spread most of the contents on the mud. I was then swathed in bandages, over my useless left eye and around my head. He then cleaned my legs and my arm with alcohol. I felt nothing. A pulling, tugging, but miles away, countries away. Galaxies away. So weak. Laying, leaking, lost.

It was Lax who'd found me. He'd refused to stop looking. After three days my platoon believed I was dead, but of course, Lax was never one to be told. You could never tell him anything. So, Lt Condon left him to search. The company had decided to regroup and chase the North Vietnamese army regulars that had ambushed us. They would return later, clear the mines and booby traps - do a thorough search for my body. Tim and I spent three days in that stinking pit. There was a very real chance Tim might never leave it.

"Are you with me mate?" Lax said but I couldn't answer.

"I can't believe you're alive Pup."

Alive. I thought. Surely not.

"You're a bit of a mess mate. You've lost a lot of blood. We need to get you out of here but we're just going to have to wait for the platoon to return. Don't want to move you too much." I didn't much care either way. Lax had plugged up most of my holes but I well knew blood loss was a chief factor in soldiers not making it home. A 15% loss of blood and fluids would herald hypovolemic shock, a breakdown of the organs, and usually an unconsciousness I wouldn't wake up from.

Not yet though, I thought. There was a nagging urgency

before I died. I had to hang on long enough to make Lax understand. My body refused to cooperate. Pain crashed waves against me, eroding my time, forcing its way into my consciousness and obliterating thought. Lax noticed panic in my good eye.

"What mate? They're coming. I'll get you out." Could he follow my eyeline? I glanced at the pit. Again, and again. Lax turned and followed my line of sight.

"What mate? What do you see?" he whispered. I tried to project my thoughts into his head.

"In the pit? What is it Pup?" He scooted over without standing and looked in.

"Aarrrrr," I croaked.

"What is it Pup?" he said with a hushed voice. I tried to speak through razor blades.

"Laaaaxxxx!" I managed.

"Yes mate.," he said. "It's OK. What do you need?" I pointed at the pit. Too weak to lift my arm I managed to stretch a long, white, emaciated finger. A gnarled and desiccated twig. I caught it in my periphery and shocked myself. It was the finger of a corpse, a ghoul. Dracula's finger.

"Lax," I tried again. He bought his face close to mine. "Tim in there."

"Where?" He said.

"In pit." I swallowed and tried to nod.

"Bury Tim," I whispered.

"Bury my friend."

BAG

I woke up in a body bag.

Lax had fashioned a sled from a US body bag he'd found somewhere. Hope it had been empty. Heavy duty, black rubberised fabric. Hardy and light. He placed a thick length of bamboo through the handles and tied a length of rope he'd scrounged from somewhere around his chest to pull me along, through the mud. When I woke I was in the bag up to my arms, my feet strained at its end. Lax had tied my damaged arm across my body, my other arm was free. He'd bandaged the handgun to my good hand. I understood it was for anyone that happened upon us from the rear. Lax had treated all my wounds, to the best of his ability, and then mummified me. I was swaddled like a Russian baby, a Christmas ham in a string bag. I noticed two small puncture wounds in my left arm near my elbow joint. Were they made by the stakes in the pit? Too small I thought. Had Lax tried to give me his blood? The thought dissipated beneath a shroud of hurt.

The wet, slippery ground made the going somewhat smoother but, every bump on the track was accompanied with a crashing crescendo of agony. It was unbearable. I squirmed and Lax sensed the movement. He pulled me off the track under a low branch of a tree, out of sight.

"How are you doing Pup?" I could only look up at him,

helpless to respond. He pulled at the canteen on his hip and put it to my lips. The tepid water made me retch, but I took in as much as I was able.

"I decided we needed to move mate." He crouched low next to my head and spoke in an urgent whisper. "The Nogs had doubled back and were making themselves a nuisance. Our boys would follow them and find us, but they mightn't have much of us to find if we didn't get a move on." He placed a firm hand on my shoulder, the good one. "I couldn't take you underground mate, so I waited for the dark and we shot through before it got too hot." He moved closer. "You need help big fella, more than I can give you. With Charlie behind every tree, I can't get you to the section to order a dust off. We're about 12 miles from Hoa's village and I'm going to pull you. I'll be making more noise than I'd like, that's why you're the tail gunner Pup. I figure we better give it a burl and make the village or you're not gonna get through this. At the very least I can leave you in good hands while I piss off and get help," he whispered. I lifted the gun.

"That's the spirit Cocko. Don't shoot 'til you see the whites of their beady little eyes."

Progress was slow and painful, though I kept passing out which helped. Like falling asleep on a long trip, time leapt forward. I felt as helpless as a kitten. Pain in my head mewed, my shoulder snarled, and my thighs roared. They were on fire and the heat within the bag was unbearable. I'd stepped into an oven. I was basting in sweat and blood, stewing in my juices!

In my lucid moments, which weren't many, I thought the whole trip was not only futile but had a very real chance of ending in Lax being killed. He wouldn't be deterred of course, and I was beyond arguing. The heavens opened again, and the rain was a Godsend. It slicked the track which made pulling me easier, although Lax had remarked I weighed so little he kept forgetting I was following him. It cooled my fever-ravaged body too. It evaporated into a cloud of steam as it met my skin. The heavy fall masked the sounds of our progress. We came to a wide and swiftly flowing stream at one point and Lax just waded on in, pulling me quickly through the tepid water despite it being over his head in the middle. Lax didn't want to be in the open. He swam with an AK-47 he'd picked up somewhere, held aloft in his left hand and me in his right, tucked in under his arm. His strong kick had us wallowing in the mud on the other side in no time. The man was a machine. There was a rapid burst of automatic rifle fire which crackled and whistled above our heads just as we made the tree line. It was high and wide. A feeble sun struggled through resentful clouds and lit us up momentarily. We had caught someone's attention. We had no way of knowing if they were friends or foe and Lax wasn't gonna hang around to find out. We hit the tree line at pace. I groaned and waved the pistol in the air and fired in the direction of the muzzle flash. Multiple rifles opened up tearing the canopy above our heads into confetti. The firing was wild and prolonged.

"Young blokes," yelled Lax over the racket. "They're all over the shop." Most men would stop, and keep low to avoid the withering fire, but Lax powered on through the trees and through the wet and rotting leaf litter without pause. I tried to focus on the path behind, but the feeble light was shattered by branches and leaves. My depth of field was destroyed along with the right eye. I'd just be firing blind if anyone followed us in. I decided to save my bullets until I might be of use. I was so weak I could barely keep my head up. The enemy would pick us off before I could fire a shot.

The jungle grew so dark then that Lax must have been travelling by instinct. He managed to find paths that were little more than animal tracks, but the dark meant he was unable to avoid the rocks and tree roots which would shudder through my battered body.

The bag tore at some point and Lax tried dragging me along by my shirt, hands beneath my armpits. Finally, mercifully, he decided he would make better progress without me and resolved to forge ahead to the village and return with some sort of help. He placed me in a relatively dry hollow beneath a large tree and covered me with some large fronds and branches.

"Back soon," was all he said, and he disappeared. Even in the dark Lax could leap from tree root to grassy patch and glide without a sound.

I lay as quietly as I could and listened to the jungle breathe in and out under the night sky. I could hear bowl shaped leaves filling with moisture until they tipped and spilled their contents to the ground. Small things burrowed and scurried in the litter; larger things hovered beyond my hideout with hard wings that churned the air like an electric fan. Still larger things gawped or yowled in a night thick with malice. I busied myself with a stocktake of my wounds and quickly determined I was properly rooted. My greatest fear then was endangering Lax who was putting himself in great peril for me. He was above ground for a start. Uncontrollable tremors from the infections raked my frail and pathetic body with fever. If I began to hallucinate I might give myself away. My head throbbed so it was hard to align two coherent thoughts with each other. I still held the gun in my hand. Pop used to call it "the miracle cure-all. You place a little metal behind the ear, add velocity and all the pain will go away." Usually, he was talking about the rabbits or foxes he'd trapped, occasionally, one of his arthritic old cattle dogs got the "kindest bullet". Even this was not an option for me. A shot might be heard and Lax might return to find others waiting for him. I had to stick it out, after all, he'd gone to so much trouble.

"Pup. Pup you still with me mate," I opened my eye and Lax sighed. "Jeeezus Pup, this time I was sure you were gone." He began to remove the branches from around me. I had no way of knowing how long he had been away.

"They're all gone mate," he whispered into my ear. "The village is empty. Hoa, the baby, everyone. Gone." He placed a hand on my clammy brow.

"Still too hot," he said, almost to himself. "I checked all the usual hides and caves and found no-one. Looks like they were run off by the VC. Place has changed. The vege garden is gone. Still, there's some cover and I know where some supplies are buried. A bit of food, some fresh bandages. So, it's just you and me big fella. We can do this. I have some morph I can dope you up with and I'm going to carry you the rest of the way." I raised my head to protest but he brushed it off. "You don't weigh much more than a duffle bag of firewood so I can do it without breaking a sweat. We'll hit the village and reassess our chances." He stood above me with hands on hips.

"OK then, you good to go?" Without waiting for an answer, he jabbed me with the morphine, and it swallowed me.

ROT

I woke lying on the dirt floor of a small hut. I was once again in Hoa's village, although where Hoa, Huong, their father, the baby and all the others were, was anyone's guess. Lax had apparently carried me on his back. I was alone in the dark. The moon spotlighted through holes in the roof and walls. Dust swam in the weak light. I was alone and once again sentinel to the sounds of the Vietnamese night. The rain had stopped but a light wind had blown up. It threatened to lift the thatched, and patched, grass roof above me. Were they footsteps? Nimble, intermittent footsteps, almost imperceptible. Could they be human? Too small, too tentative. Even too soft to be Lax. A knot of fear twisted in my stomach, I forced it back down before it claimed my throat.

Shhhrunch. Louder now. Closer. The sounds stopped just beyond the door. Was someone stealing themselves to rush me. I raised my left arm and held the pistol up before me. I aimed at the doorway that had once been covered by a sheet. It was now torn and shredded and beyond the job. I steadied my hand and my breathing. Light fell across the threshold which may give me a small advantage. I could barely raise the gun. Advantage receiver. A very small head peered in furtively. It was so tiny I almost missed it. It was there and gone in a flash. Was it a child? I put the gun away. I couldn't shoot anyway, and

I wouldn't be shooting a kid even if it carried a bazooka. Ever so slowly someone entered my hut. A tiny silhouette against the moonlight. It wasn't animal, and it didn't seem to be holding a rifle. Now it moved swiftly toward me and wrapped cold, tiny hands around my face, cooing in a gentle Vietnamese. I recognised my tiny assailant. It was the old woman. The midwife. The healer. The one who helped with Hoa's traumatic delivery. The old woman sang softly when she recognised me. Her kindly white face hovered above me in the half light. I grabbed one of her hands and enveloped it in mine. She patted my face lightly with the other. She seemed as happy to see me alive as I was her. I tried to ask of the other villagers and how she had come to be here still, but we were at an impasse. I knew very little Viet and she had even less English.

    She regarded me gravely then, touched my bandaged head, my shoulder, my legs. The blood had started to show through the bandages on my thighs. It looked black in the moonlight. She sniffed the air above the bandages on my legs and wrinkled her nose. My shoulder bandages were soaked through. She set about unwrapping me. She unwound the wet strapping that enclosed my head. She rolled it carefully as she went. She inspected my wound, so close now I could feel her breath on me. She mewed and tutted. She lay hands on my cheeks and dabbed away dirt and filth from my face with the roll. She then went to work on my shoulder. My legs. She tore my pants away and used them the clean my legs of goo and gore. She washed my wounds with some collected rainwater. I did a stocktake as she worked. The bullet in my arm had hit bone and probably shattered it. I was going to need all those bits out, and any damaged tissue. I'm not a pessimist per se. Sure, medical knowledge affords you a tendency toward pessimism. I considered myself more of a realist. I was realistic enough to know my right arm was stuffed. The wound in my head, even though it took my eye, was the least of my worries. It was relatively superficial. The wounds in my thighs were deep, badly infected and starting to smell. They were open and pustulating and I wouldn't be able to sew the wounds with one hand even if I'd wanted too. The antibiotics were gone now and the infections, jungle ulcers and, most probably gangrene, would kill me.

The old woman held her little hands up, fingers splayed, palms flat, and hurried from the hut with a lightness and natural stealth that might even be the envy of Lax. She was gone for some time and when she returned I never heard a sound. She just appeared in the doorway carrying a gourd of liquid and two small parcels wrapped in a light coloured and fraying cloth. She also held handfuls of grasses and herbs. Some still bore the ball root covered it earth as if she'd hurriedly gathered them up from where they were growing. The liquid turned out to be a weak soup. One package contained a greyish, gelatinous meat and some of the greens that she broke into little pieces and added to the gourd. As she poured the soup down my throat I could smell lemon grass and Vietnamese coriander. There were other smells, other tastes I couldn't place. The soup was tepid and tasteless and exactly what I needed. I hadn't eaten in days. I hadn't been able to stomach the dry army rations Lax had tried to feed me. I felt guilty that this meagre offering might be all the food the old lady might have had for heaven knows how long. She waved away my protestations. I didn't even know if it was soup. Maybe it was some natural medicine.

At the Australian Hospital Hospital at *Vũng Tàu* we'd discussed the medicinal properties of Vietnamese herbs. As she gently poured the liquid into my mouth she deftly unwrapped the second parcel. The old woman scooped live maggots from the second package and packed them into the wounds. The bullet hole below my shoulder and the gaping, putrescence holes in my thighs. She packed them in with a sort of thin paste which looked like it'd been chewed. I felt nothing in my arm. My thighs burned as if they were being slowly roasted. I felt no revulsion, but only marvelled that she, a woman that had seen and experienced so much horror could still find so much compassion for another. An enemy too if you read the papers!

Lax appeared in the hut a little before dawn. He only wore a pair of army pants, and he was filthy, caked in mud from head to toe. He smelled like earth and rotting vegetation. In short, he smelled like the whole of Nam. The old lady acknowledged him with a warm smile. He walked over to her and hugged her to his chest. She hugged him tightly around his waist, her head resting on his sternum. It was clear he was not surprised to see her. On his back Lax carried my pack which he swung heavily to the floor. He and the old lady spoke in Vietnamese as Lax crouched and emptied the contents onto the packed and swept mud. He had what appeared to be parachute fabric which he had torn into clean bandages. Ever the scrounger, he had managed to find some rations, Australian, US army and even what appeared to be VC. He'd filled my canteen with water and managed to track down some antibiotics from somewhere. He'd already exhausted what was left of my medical supplies on me.

It turned out the old lady had been hiding underground when a squad of N.V.A. regulars had cleared out the village of its recalcitrant inhabitants. They had methodically searched tunnel after tunnel, hide after hide. They swept the area clean. Some of the villagers took off into the jungle. Some were discovered. They dragged the people into the light with threats of grenade and gas. People were beaten. Two were shot. The woman changed her position constantly. She crept to holes already searched. She'd told Lax she moved like "the spirits" and managed to evade the soldiers. She cried bitter tears as she described how she buried the bodies where they fell. She had no idea if Hoa, Gai, or the baby were taken or if they escaped into the forest.

"I've had word there is a small Aussie section just south of the old US free fire zone. They're on the move so I need to get after them if I'm gonna get you a chopper." I nodded – still struggling to speak.

"Mai Lin says she will look after you while I'm gone. Keep quiet. The woods are full of Nogs." He lowered onto one knee and gently placed his hand on my head. The hand was cool, almost cold on feverish skin.

"I'm gonna get you home Pup." He rose, grabbed the old lady's hands in his, and nodded warmly. He turned and left us to the evening. The sun was just beginning to set. Mai Lin stayed with me all night. I must have been hard for her above ground, away from her burrow but she fussed around me, checking on the maggots, sharing her meagre meal. Occasionally she nodded forward as she sat with her back against the wall beside me. Soft rhythmic breathing of sleep. I could hear bats rend the air with leathery wings beyond the hut's thin grass walls. The high pitched chitter came from everywhere and nowhere as they cavorted with prey at breakneck speed. I could hear the winds gently play amongst our thatched roof. Frogs coughed. Insects whined. The odd bird called. All night I listened for footsteps.

It was almost a full day before the chopper arrived. God only knew how he found one out here. Lax said he'd called in a favour and got a Huey with a young, shaky Aussie pilot with a large crimson birthmark that traversed his chin and left cheek. He wore aviator sunglasses, much too wide for his hatchet face. Mai Lin heard it before I did. She stood stock still, her little head cocked to one side. I could tell it took all her resolve to stop from bolting to the safety of her den. I could see the moist dust swept up in heavy spirals as it neared a cleared patch beyond the open mouth of our shelter. Lax leapt from the Huey before it settled. He carried a stretcher. A large, bald man followed him out. He held his green, army issued soft hat in his hand. He spied me through the doorway and pointed at me as he ran. It was Balls. The engine roar overwhelmed the senses.

"Shep! Goddamn! It's you. Bugger me dead. I can't believe it." Balls filled the doorway, one hand on his bald melon. He was a bear emerging from the cloud of dust.

"No time for beers and reminiscing Balls. This place is really hot, and the chopper won't have been missed." Lax had already laid the stretcher beside me. "Pup is going to need some fluid or he's not gonna make it."

"Right mate," Balls said as he moved quickly across the small room. He swung the Owen machinegun over his shoulder, out of the way. He called it his Digger's Darling and it just may have been the last one seen in action at that time. He'd refused to relinquish it and in the end the brass stopped trying to take it from him. God knows how he managed to find rounds for it. Balls loved that gun. He crouched low to take hold of my feet. It was only then he got a good look at me, and I could tell as the blood ran from his face, that I was a sight to behold. He caught himself and managed a crooked grin.

"Let's get you back to the boys. It'll make everyone's year you're still with us big fella." The two men effortlessly, efficiently lifted me onto the stretcher and in a blink we were beneath the chopper blades.

"Come on, come on," yelled the pilot. "Even Ho knows we're here by now and he's dead!" As they loaded me on to the scrubbed metal floor of the helicopter I was dismayed to see Lax leap out of the Huey and stand beside Mai Lin in the swirling clouds of moonlit mist. I raised my hand weakly and waved them both on board.

"She won't leave mate. She says this is her home." I took the pistol from my pocket. I grabbed it by the barrel and pointed it towards Mai Lin. Lax grabbed it and handed it to the old woman. She wouldn't handle it. She looked at the gun like it might bite her. Lax waved it in the air and placed it in his pocket. I pointed at him then.

"I can't come Pup." He screamed above the noise. "I have to track Hoa and the baby down. I have to know." I pointed again, more insistently.

"Can't mate. I have to know." Balls was kneeling beside my stretcher, and he gently lowered my hand and placed it on my chest as the screaming Huey rose into the darkening Vietnamese night. Lax waved and became small, smaller, and disappeared from my life.

I never even thanked him.

We made our way to a surgical hospital over a jungle as black as man's hate. I had a slim chance of surviving my injuries if the doctors could halt the infections and the maggots performed the miracles Mai Lin believed they might. If they filled me up with blood, someone else's blood, I might yet survive my tour in the pointless Vietnam war. I might even R.T.A. I'd be changed of course, lesser, halved. My country might be changed too. Less innocent. Less carefree. Sending young men to die can do that to a country. Vietnam had pierced and chewed on my heart as surely as the punji stick had pierced and swallowed my eye. I would never see anything the same again. I looked at Balls who was on one knee besides my stretcher. He peered into the darkness, scanning for light. I reflected on the people I'd met and the people I'd lost. As a medic I had purpose, a role to play in helping people through the fire. Would I ever have purpose again? Would I ever matter? Could I ever be of use? Would my life now be one of helplessness and need? My life had lost certainty, balance: a pirate without a ship, a clock with one hand.

Eventually I was pulled from the roaring machine and rushed toward the milky light of a medical tent. My immediate future unsure. My long-term future unforeseeable. Lax had saved my life, again and again and I'd never even said goodbye. The only certainty I had left in my life was that I would never, ever, get over losing my friend.

EYE

It would be dark for some hours yet. The Melbourne winter nights could be relentless. Wisps-of steam rose listlessly from stinking drains beneath urine yellow streetlights. Grass, weighed down by frost, bowed low. The gun was a solid block of ice in my hand, despite the thin, leather glove I'd finally liberated from my top drawer at Little George. My coat pocket kept the gun hidden but it afforded no warmth. I'd walked over from Fitzroy with it concealed in the back of my pants until the cold chill ran the length of my spine. Firm resolve, cold intention. High time it was returned it to its owner anyway.

In the other pocket my hand rested amongst four large sausages. Unlike my hand, this dead meat would be useful. They give returned servicemen with debilitating injuries powerful sleeping tablets. I'd stuffed the snags with enough to put the whole Lost Dogs' home and most of the staff to sleep. Hopefully it would be enough to knock-out the half rottweiler, half grizzly bear Sid and his mates kept cruelly tethered, with a long chain, to a metal pole in the front yard of their compound. I didn't want its bark/roar waking the North Richmond Sharps until I was at least inside the front door.

I lurked in the shadows across the street. The gate appeared to be chained and locked but as I drew near I could see the heavy chain was simply coiled between the heavily rusted gates. The large padlock I'd spied the day before on my reconnaissance tourl, was nowhere to be seen. Nor was the dog. Two small kids, one walking and one pushed in a pram by a large-eyed, exhausted looking mother, had passed by the compound on the day I drove Mrs James' green Chrysler slowly passed the razor wired fence. I'd offered to do a beer and lemonade run. The bottles of both lay in the passenger seat footwell. This monstrous Cerberus released a deep guttural, coughing bark as it charged the length of its chain with a mindless fury. Spittle flew from its blood red mouth. Dumb, selachian eyes rolled in their sockets. Despite the fence, the mother, now wide awake, quickstepped, dragging the hand of the now wailing toddler as she went. This early morning the dog was nowhere to be seen.

I unwound the heavy chain from around the gates, half expecting the murderous charge, sure that he was stalking me beyond the street light glow and ready to rip me apart as soon as I strayed within its deadly arc. I held the sausages ready and the gun in case he preferred human meat. I'd been back at Mum's for three days after the funeral. Just long enough to discover where Iris had hidden the gun. I'd slipped from the house when she was in a deep sleep, the one where the nose whistles while the eyes roll across the dream landscape under the lids. The gates groaned a little as I squeezed through the gap I made. The very old and recently sharpened wire cutters I'd lifted from Mum's shed were not going to be required. I crossed the cracked concrete path, covered in dry and ice-covered dog turds. I'd intended to find a back door, but I wasn't sure they didn't have another beast patrolling around there as well. This is where I would try my luck. A nagging sliver of doubt gnawed on me then; it all seemed little too easy. Surely they couldn't be expecting me, could they? I pushed the thought away. To be honest, I didn't care. Bravery is going into the breach despite being petrified. Ricky Pepi brave. I wasn't Ricky brave. At that moment I felt nothing but a calm rationality, a clarity of purpose. A Damoclean certainty. These bastards had to go. How many were to go permanently was up to them.

I ached all over. My nose and cheek complained noisily. Hollering from my ribs sent shudders through my body when I twisted in a way they didn't appreciate. My head, however, was never clearer, silent, and focused. The only fear I felt that chilly Melbourne morning was that I probably couldn't get them all. I would kill Sid tonight though, even if I had to tear his throat open with my teeth. I was a realist. I knew the odds were not in my favour. I was still a one-eyed, one-armed man. You didn't have to be a member of Mum and Lily's punters club to work those odds out. There was a very real chance I would be taken down before I could deal with them all. I hoped, with Sid dead, the rest of the North Richmond Sharps, rudderless and abandoned, would dry up and blow away just like the grizzly turds that covered the courtyard. One thing was unequivocable though. If Lily and Iris were to have any sort of life, Sid had to go.

There were three short steps between two wide, white, and flaking pillars which lead up a short, tiled landing before the front door. I leapt up the steps and stood in the dark contemplating my next move. I hoped the front door would be unlocked. Behind chained, padlocked gates and unsocialised hellhounds I hoped the North Richmond Sharps might not bother to lock the front door. What I never anticipated though, not even in all my perfect world scenarios, was that the door would be open. It stood on a slight angle as if someone had just left and didn't intend to be gone for long. I pushed the door open with the barrel of the gun I had taken from my pocket. It swung silently over a threadbare carpet. I didn't hesitate. I stepped beyond the threshold and welcomed my fate.

The large room was bathed in a sickly green glow from a large, black, and white television in one corner of the room. A boxy sentinel on four splayed tubular feet. In shades of grey a test pattern would have announced the end of programming with a ghoulish, hollow howl. At this hour the screen was full of the frenetic clash and jostle of static. Its urgent hiss sounded like Vietnam rain on corrugated iron. The restless light was unnerving. Movement and shadow where there should be dark. It dimly danced on the face on a man who lay with his back against the wall. The pulsing electric flicker, this Frankenstein spark, would never reanimate this one. The head was lowered as if contemplating the black mess that pooled in his lap. His hands appeared to be enveloped by the gore. It had run like treacle and splashed on naked legs which were splayed out at a perfect right angle. His once white Y-fronts now a horror. It was Slug. Slug had hated my guts. I took no comfort in the fact I could see his now, coiled and gripped in cold dead fingers.

The large room smelled of blood. The thick coppery smell you could almost taste. Like licking an old penny. It assailed all the senses. The room was divided by a long couch that ran through the middle facing the TV. Chairs were arranged in an arc around it, a variety of styles and shapes. I pushed the front door wider, and it hit something heavy. Resistance. Someone was behind the door. I froze. The weight remained constant, so I pushed further into the room. My ribs growled and whined. A pair of feet, clad in socks appeared then. Someone was lying face down behind it. I stepped clear and moved the door. A man lay in the dark. I kicked at the legs which didn't kick back. He was dead. What the fuck had happened here? I thought wildly.

I fought the urge to turn and bolt from the compound. I found the light switch by the front door which I meant to swing closed then didn't. I now left it slightly ajar. I couldn't bring myself to be locked in this mausoleum. This tomb of horrible men. I hesitated before I switched the light on. Two darkened doorways led off from the front living area and the killer might be standing in either one. Even worse, I had to flick the light switch with the hand that held the gun. I had to be quick. The first switch turned on an outside light above the small landing. Light filled the two tall, slim windows on either side of the door. I swore under my breath, flicked it off and prayed no one had been watching. I tried to pull myself together and flicked the second switch. A large, plastic green, central light fixture illuminated the living area. I stared into the dark of the doorways. I almost expected some knife wielding maniac to rush out at me. Eventually, I turned to the man on the floor. He wore a tattered grey jumper and cut off jeans. The woollen socks were a vibrant red.

He looks anything but sharp. I thought stupidly. A lake of

blood stained the greying carpet around his throat. His arms lay straight along his sides. I knelt down, ignoring the constant chatter from the rib cage and careful not to place my knee in the thick, slick that had dried into a viscous soup. Even face down I could see the man's throat had been cut. A red line ran around almost to his spine. The knife had been sharp and had almost taken his head off. It lay twisted at an unnatural angle. I felt no desire to check for a pulse. I recognised his pinched face and closely cropped blond hair. Ratso was clearly dead. Where the hell was Sid?

I found him on the couch. He looked asleep, almost peaceful. He lay on his back, a needle and syringe stuck out from his left arm. His right arm fell from the couch, reaching to the floor. I could see the stupid scorpion tattoo on the back of his slack hand. Beneath his fingers lay a large, ornately handled Bowie knife. Its blade-stained red. A low, rectangular coffee table stood between the couch and the TV with its erratic flicker. It was covered in an aluminium sheet. Small, twisted bundles of aluminium foil sat in a pile at one end. White powder sat at the other. I guessed it was smack. A line of telltale purple bruises ran the length of Sid's arms beneath the rolled sleeves of his Connie jumper. It appeared Sid had been getting high on his own supply. A low saucer of water sat beside a Zippo lighter, the kind Jungles used to nervously click open and closed. A memory from another lifetime. Two ashtrays were filled to overflow. More butts on the floor where they'd burned crop circles into the yellowing shag rug. Empty steel beer cans littered the floor around the chairs. Empty bottles of Bourbon and Coca-Cola stood in a row at the table front. I did feel for Sid's pulse. I remember thinking what strange creatures we humans were, as I knelt beside the man I had come to kill, feeling for a pulse to see if he was alive. Was I confirming his demise or trying to see if I could help him live? I wasn't sure. Sid was indeed dead. His body was as cold as the crypt. This hated man who had burned our home, murdered my friend, hit me in the face with a shovel and had sworn to kill us all, was dead. He didn't appear to have stab wounds. He looked asleep. Was it an accidental overdose? Had he killed himself? Had someone killed him? I didn't know what to feel.

I did a quick search of the rest of the house and found it empty. It appeared the rest of the North Richmond Sharpies had fled in a hurry and took the dogs with them. Upstairs bedrooms were strewn with clothing and rubbish. Cupboard doors swung wide revealing empty hangers and piles of unwanted clothes on the floor. The kitchen was the same. Open pantry and ransacked shelves. Empty tins of dog food collected around an overflowing rubbish bin. A fridge that held nothing but rancid milk in a glass bottle and unopened bottles and cans of beer. A half-filled bottle of lemonade. The only food consisted of half a sandwich sitting inside a brown paper bag. It smelled like tuna. Old tuna. It had been there a while. My memory lurched. My stomach leapt into my throat. I swallowed my revulsion. Blood, stale cigarettes, and a rancid tuna sandwich. It smelt like the pit.

I fled that house of horrors without looking back. I fought the urge to run. I fought the urge of the adrenalin now flooding my veins. I needed to get home. I needed to absorb and puzzle out everything I had seen. What the hell was going on?

I made the long walk back to Fitzroy, dumping the sausages in a bin on the way. There's a deep place in hell for those that bait pets, and I didn't want to inadvertently kill someone's Pomeranian by throwing them into a bush. I arrived at Little George Street just as the sun was coming up on a new day. I returned the gun to Iris's hiding place, beneath the loose floorboard inside the bedroom cupboard. I slipped into bed beside her. Iris stirred.

"Roll over Shep and I'll give you a cuddle. You're like a block of ice."

I lay beside Iris playing over the events of the night. It appeared Sid had killed the other two men. Slug he slashed and disembowelled as he entered the room. Ratso appeared to be trying to get out the front door. I envisioned the assailant kneeling on his back as he pulled the man's head back by the forehead and opened his throat from ear to ear. The rest of the cast and crew saw fit to bolt taking cars, dogs, and the truth with them. In a fit of remorse Sid overdoses and passes away. It was a believable pantomime, and the police would probably buy it. Whenever they happened on the bodies; when the stench became so great the neighbours would call someone to investigate. Not that any neighbours were close. It was an industrial area, and the other factories and sheds had their own distinctive odours. There was a lot of gear on that coffee table and the junkies would be around in short order to score. The first one through the door would get a nasty surprise; and enough free smack to last him a junkie's lifetime.

They would get no assistance from me. I had no intention of drawing any attention to myself. I had motive, most of the police force were aware of that. I thought about an anonymous call to the police, or at least Gordon, but what would I say. If Sid had indeed gone berserk and sliced up his second and third in command it would be better for all if the meter reader or the postman, or some druggie customer made the discovery. I owed them nothing.

The whole "crazed Sid goes berserk" story didn't wash with me though. He was a bully and bullies understand the importance of numbers. A true bully would never eliminate his toadies. Having underlings, a gang, gave him power and he would never give that away. I wondered if the three were murdered. It was made to look like a murder/suicide. Maybe by rivals. If it was a rival gang in the drug trade why would they leave a table full of neatly wrapped heroin behind to become police evidence. The whole thing didn't make sense.

Why did I care? It was over. Over for Sid, Ratso and Slug and over for me and those I loved. The North Richmond Sharpies could rot in peace. As horrible as it sounds I felt a little reborn. I'd been gifted a new life free of real monsters.

Just when I thought the adrenaline rush of the night would never allow me sleep, I slept. I was back in Vietnam in moments. Back in my pit. Back in the grave Tim and I shared for a few days. Tim and I chatted about life and the war. I told him about Iris for the 40th time and Sid for the 50th, and I told him the about the demise of the subculture known as the Sharpie.

"You must be happy now," he said. "They are gone, and you are here. You are safe and you didn't have to kill, well, kill again – like you killed me I mean." Tim laughed and clotted blood poured from his gaping mouth and ran like spoiled custard over his blacken lips and green mottled chin. Down into the pit. It bubbled in the corners of his dead eyes and blackened his ears.

"I'm glad they're dead," said Tim. "They were very bad men."

"They were indeed Tim," I concurred. "Very bad."

"You would have died my friend."

"I was prepared to die."

"And now?"

"I have been re-born Tim," I said and Tim smiled.

"Sid has lost his sting. He will be in hell tonight," he said and I nodded. We lay in the pit then, just looking at each other. Tim's corpse slowly putrefying. An ugly thought clawed its way into my head and Tim saw the confusion on my face.

"I have a question my friend," Tim said and looked up at me from black sockets where eyes had shone brightly before they dulled forever.

"Yes mate."

"Sid killed Slug beside the kitchen door, probably as he came through it."

"Right."

"Did Slug have a weapon?"

"I didn't see one near his body."

"Right." He nodded his head thoughtfully. A fat, centipede with crimson legs, waving serrated pincers threateningly at my face, climbed from Tim's mouth where it had been feeding. It left small red footprints as if slithered across the hollow of his cheek.

"Ratso had been trying to crawl to the front door when his throat was cut."

"That's how it looked," I agreed.

"There was not a knife in his hand?"

"I don't believe so."

"So, Ratso also was without a weapon."

"Yes," I agreed.

"Then Pup, my friend, answer me this."

"I'll try mate."

"Who cut off Sid's index finger?"

POP

Life had leapt and bounded in the three years since I discovered the slashed and butchered bodies in the squalid, double story squat in Richmond. Sid, Slug and Ratso were eventually found. A young mother with straw coloured hair pushing a pram had dropped into the police station to report a "terrible smell" coming from the abandoned bottle factory near her home in North Richmond. She held the hand of a screaming toddler as she told her story on air to the Channel 9 crime reporter the next day. Her fifteen minutes had given a rosiness to cheek that had been missing while she balanced life as a single mother and two under two. The police constable interviewed later in the bulletin described the whole gory scene as a double murder and a death by misadventure!

"Three bodies had been discovered in what appeared, at first glance, to be murder/suicide." He batted away questions about drugs and guns with a steely-eyed defiance. He was a tall, silver-haired copper, with an air of general mistrust, spiced with open distain. He was the type of copper who believed a good kick up the crim's clacker got the message across and saved on a lot of paperwork.

"We are chasing up some of the former residents known to frequent the property."

"Yes. The men were well known to us."

"No, We don't believe anyone else was involved."

"To repeat myself. We are not looking for anyone else in relation to this crime."

"Yes. I believe it is a safe area for the residents. Just got a bit safer as a matter of fact."

Pop was watching the news with me as we sat on the old floral-patterned couch in Mum's living room. Pop had felt he might have found a kindred spirit in the big copper.

"You've got to belt some bastards whenever you see them. If they're not coming from trouble they're heading into it."

Pop passed away a year ago now. His heart popped after drinking three VB cans, choofing three Craven A's and starting up the tractor to mow his back paddock. He'd mowed a straight line through Nan's agapanthus, across the wide lawn and into the dam at the bottom of the hill. Nan said it was the only straight line he'd ever cut with that smelly old machine.

Pop's funeral was off the hook. We all travelled up from Melbourne for it, Mum, Lily, Iris, and me. We arrived at a huge scene. It looked like the whole of Yarck and the neighbouring towns like Yea, Molesworth, Trawool and Ghin Ghin, had turned out to pay their respects and sample the free grog. Nan opted for the "full nuptial" funeral, mainly because Pop wasn't there to stop her. A hessian bag to be dropped in the Murray River was all he ever wanted. He would have hated the whole production. His mates were well and truly primed for the wake thanks to the keg in the tray of Bernie Saunder's ute. It sat under a large tarpaulin so as not to offend the ladies. He parked at the back of Our Lady of Dolors church. I remember I imagined her to be the patron saint of money. As the service went on and on the men kept sneaking out the back to imbibe. Half the crowd lined up for Holy Communion while the other half lined up for tepid beer in coffee and teacups.

At the wake Nan made the mistake of passing the lectern to anyone who would like to relate a fond recollection of Pop. His three best mates then took the floor, Bernie, Barrie, and Bob, who were often referred to as the Killer Bees by the country folk. They proceeded to turn the air blue with stories, tall, true and technicolour. Barrie spoke of Pop's wish to be buried on top of a saddleback ridge on his property as it afforded the only view in Yarck of both the milk bar, where he bought his smokes, and the pub, where he filled his afternoons. Toward the end of a long day reminiscing the Killer Bees decided to honour Pop's wish, climbed into Bernie's steam shovel and made their way up to the ridge to dig his grave under a large ghost gum. All three fell into the hole at some point and they returned the next morning, sore, sorry, and nearly sober.

Nan moved in with Mum after her first fall.

"Too many steps in the old place!" she said. I think she was just lonely. There was plenty of room at Mum's anyway as Iris and I had moved out. Mum, forever the Catholic, only approved of our moving out together if we were engaged, completely overlooking the fact that we had been a sharing a room for two years. Of course, as I explained to her at least three times, I couldn't get engaged to Iris as I was still married to her sister.

"Marry in haste, repent at leisure," Mum said still annoyed she didn't get an invite to my first wedding, almost as much as she was annoyed it wasn't in a church.

We took a small apartment above a shopfront on Johnston Street Collingwood on which we got to work refurbishing into a restaurant. It was our dream to open a Thai restaurant. After a year of trying, we finally convinced Lily that Australians would love the exotic tastes and fragrant aromas of Thai food. To be fair, she had spent years in a Chinese restaurant watching Aussie's struggle to cope with chop sticks and fried rice. She had a firm view that Thai would be all too much for them. I argued young Australia was breaking free of the meat and two vegetable colonial palate. I think what finally convinced her was my argument that Thai was the perfect meal for a one-armed man. Scoop and eat. I'd avoided steaks and roast dinners. It was emasculating having to get my mum or girlfriend to cut up my meal. I was the king of Thai food, fully independent. Finally, Lily acquiesced. We called the restaurant Flowers of Thailand.

Mum, Lily, and I went into the venture as equal partners even though Mum had the most money stashed away. She'd been getting a war widow's pension for years it turned out but refused to touch it, even to help my uni bills as if it was tainted by my dad. Flowers of Thailand finally forced her hand.

The restaurant was an instant success. Young people flocked in. They'd even wait in queues for a table which was unheard of. We had a second menu, vegetarian. The college hippies just ate it up, pun intended.

Lily cooked, I cleaned, and Iris worked the tables. Mum did the books and held court on her own table at the back near the cash register. She organised bookings, organised extra staff when necessary, organised sly grog for functions, and was forever entertaining her friends. Lily and Mum would walk home together at the end of a shift. Sometimes, if it was a particularly late night, or if Mum and Lily had had a few too many after work beers, we would set them up on couches upstairs. Best of all, we never had a single Sharpie, or Skinhead for that matter, darken our doorstep. They just mustn't like Thai food. Who knew?

One bright summer's morning Iris told me she was "up the duff" as she like to call it. Lily was over the moon with her impending grand-motherhood and Mum, Nan and Lily spent many a night after that sipping gin and knitting baby clothes in front of *The Graham Kennedy Show* on the nights Flowers was closed, or *Hey, Hey It's Saturday* in the morning before a day of punting. Lily only had a couple of drinks if she was manning the kitchens Saturday night.

Iris and I were thrilled. She was more than I could ever have wished for. I put the cart before the horse, although it had already bolted, and proposed. Iris accepted on condition I get my marriage to Rosie annulled. I told her if I didn't get an annulment it would be bigamy and I could be jailed. Pop would have said the punishment for a bigamist is having two bloody wives! I missed him all over again.

Iris asked if it felt weird having a baby with my sister-in-law. I argued no weirder than marrying one's brother-in-law I'd suspect. In the end I got the marriage to Rosemary annulled as a deserted husband. It turned out to be easy. I turned up at the Town Hall and got the sympathy service. I suppose they thought a guy that looked like me had to grab anyone willing to marry him in a headlock to make sure they didn't get away. How could they stand in my way? I then had to have the marriage annulled by the Church to appease Mum which turned out to be anything but easy. We had to suffer the stupidity of our local priest, Father Damien, who was afforded no first-hand knowledge of marriage, lecturing us about the sacrament, and then parenthood. I asked him as many awkward questions as I could think of. In the end, his face quite crimson, he got up and came back with two bottles of beer. We spent the rest of the night discussing horses and the Australian cricket team.

LSM Nhân-Dũng Böi-Tinh

In the April of 1976 I finally made my way down St Kilda Road to the Shrine of Remembrance to see the dawn service. It took five years, after returning from Vietnam, before I understood Anzac Day as a celebration of life, a time of mourning, and not a glorification of war. My personal war secreted itself in my brain, leaping out at me in a horror mask whenever my guard was down. It curled itself into a corner and like some large-eyed, nocturnal predator, woke in the small hours to prowl my dreams. The physical scars settled. The pain I learned to live with. The mental war lies in wait though; longing to lunge, primed to pounce. To ambush. Maybe the dawn service would be another step to healing. Maybe misery seeks company.

Iris pushed me into going really. She even got up before the sparrows had had their morning ablutions and ventured along. It was a big effort as she was three months pregnant and had spent the best part of the first two throwing up. She was insistent. I believed she wanted to try and understand how the war shaped and disfigured us all.

I sat in The Builder's Arms on ANZAC April 25th, 1976, trying to decide between the bacon, eggs and toast or would I try a bowl of Coco Pops. I was still skinny enough to have no qualms about loading up on the "crunchy chocolate milkshake" and Coco Pops were always a favourite as a kid. Holiday fare. The pub had opened for the ANZAC day crowd. They were allowed to do breakfasts for the marchers and their supporters. The beer was not allowed to start flowing until 1200 hours though. There was word about there might be a small upstairs room that may or may not have jumped the gun with the alcohol. I let this information go through to the keeper. I wasn't that desperate for a beer at 8.00 in the morning. There were probably 15 people in the place including the staff. A small crowd. Maybe there were more upstairs getting pissed. Who knew?

Iris had asked me to order her the bacon and eggs, and an English breakfast tea. She was a coffee girl, but the baby liked tea better. The morning nausea had been replaced by a constant need to pee and attending the march had been logistically tricky. I had to do some reconnaissance to find out where the easiest, cleanest, and most accessible public toilets were. We had to plonk ourselves within easy reach. I didn't march down St Kilda road. This trip was all about getting the feel, and feel I did. It got me, I'm not ashamed to say. I found it all incredibly moving. The last post, the oath, the eternal flame. I'd never even been to the Shrine before, even as a kid. Maybe it was what WW2 had done to Dad. It was just something I never did. We didn't go and watch the soldiers parading, from old wars and new. That would have been too much of an ask of Iris and her bladder. I was interested though, and I determined to check it out next year. See if I knew any faces from Repat. Maybe even from my old battalion. There weren't any trams down St Kilda road with the ANZAC Day march on. Instead, we made the walk from the Shrine to Flinders

Street Station and jumped on a train to Fitzroy.

The door to the pub opened and a smartly dressed soldier in a beautifully pressed officers uniform stepped inside. Brown jacket and tie, ox-blood belt, and sash. He wore a slouch hat pulled low over his eyes. It with pinned with the golden, rising sun badge. He had enough medals on to choke a camel. He was silhouetted in the bright morning light of the doorway, and I turned back to the menu that had been hastily typed on an A4 sheet. It read:

Builders Arms Anzac Day Breafkast.

Fried Bacon and eggs on Toast.

Tost and Vegemite.

Cereal. Rice Bubbels, Corn Flakes. Cocopops.

Tea and Coffee upon request.

Quite an extensive spread. The chef would have his work cut out.

"Hello son. It's been a long time. You look terrific."

I recognized the gravel. If a Harley Davidson could speak.

"My God, Gordon," I said with surprise. I placed my glasses on the table and leapt up to do the awkward left-handed shake. He pumped my hand twice. A cold, hard hand. It felt like shaking hands with a truck's towbar. "How are you mate. What a wonderful blast from the past. I didn't even know you served." Gordon laughed. Something had ruptured the Harley's muffler.

"I'm very well son. All things considered."

"Great to see you," I said with an affection that even surprised me. "Please sit. Iris is here. She's just in the bathroom. Have you got the time?"

"I have a little bit of time Terry. I'm meeting someone but my official duties are done for the day."

"Right, right. Please sit down. Am I supposed to call you Sir or something? Apologies if I am? Iris would love to catch up with you."

"Love to." He smiled. "You can drop the Sir bit, son. I'm fully retired. Just an honorary soldier now." Gordon removed the slouch hat from his large bald head and placed it gingerly on the table. He sat in the chair opposite and clasped his hands together, rubbing them slowly.

"What did you have to do this morning Gordon. What duties did you have?"

"I recited the oath at the Shrine this morning."

"My God, That was you?"

"Were you there, son?"

"You were brilliant. I was really moved. Really moved." There was quite a bit to sort out here I could see.

"Didn't catch your introduction or recognize your voice. I should have really. You have a very distinctive voice." Gordon smiled.

"That's what I'm told." He laughed dryly with a sound you could hear in your fillings.

"Is this your first dawn service son?"

"Yes, yes, mate. My first."

"No uniform?"

"No. Nothing. Didn't have a lot that wasn't cut off me in various hospitals here and in the East. Nothing ever sent back from Vietnam after I was shipped out. Really didn't have much there anyway. Nothing I'd want to keep anyway." I smiled up at him. "Anything I did have went in the fire at the restaurant. On the day we met." I pointed to his chest. "You've got enough for both of us though. I know where to come if I want a couple."

"Yes. That was where we actually met." Gordon looked down at his fingers and left the weight of his words in the air between us. His chair groaned as he leant back to remove a packet of tobacco from his breast pocket. A rectangle of papers poked out from within the leaves. He proceeded to roll himself a cigarette. The squat, stumpy fingers moved effortlessly and efficiently. He saw me admiring the show.

"Just got used to rolling my own, I 'spose."

"Ahhh, can I get you a cup of tea Gordon? Coffee? Actually, I'm told there's a secret room here somewhere they're serving beers if you want one. They won't be able to keep you out, you being an officer and all." He laughed again.

"Too early for me son. I think I'll get a coffee instead."

"I'm about to order breakfast for myself and Iris. I wonder where she got to?" I said scanning the room. "It doesn't look like we'll have table service this morning. Can I get you breakfast? Gordon… can I buy you breakfast?" The big square head began shake and he started to raise his bear paw.

"Please mate. You were very kind to us all at a very hard time. I'd really love to buy you a meal. A very small gesture I know, but it's ANZAC day and you diggers have to let people buy you things on ANZAC day. I believe its even written in the constitution somewhere."

"OK, OK," he smiled. "The bacon and eggs would be lovely." He smiled broadly as smoke wafted through his fingers.

"And a coffee?"

"Hot and black please."

"Righto," I said standing up. I paused for a moment above my chair.

"So good to see you mate," I said and I walked over to the bar where a young bloke with long sea-bleached hair, wearing a tight necklace of puka-seashells stood looking at me expectantly. A pad and pencil in his hands.

"I'll have three of the bacon and egg breakfasts please mate."

"No worries. Fried eggs on toast. That OK?"

"That'd be great."

"They come with baked beans too. All good?"

"Ripper," I said. "Oh, and two English breakfast teas, and a cup of coffee. Hot and black."

"Coming right up. I see you're on the middle table," the young guy said. "Extra cuttle-ry to your right on the sideboard. Tomato sauce, salt, pepper, sugar. Help yourself."

The boy said cuttle-ry. A jolt of memory from a distant past. Where had I heard that before: in Nam? Lost in thought a voice behind me said, "Make that five of the bacon and eggs mate if you don't mind. Oh, and a bowl of rice bubbles please." The voice was like a shot to my heart. I turned so quickly I became lightheaded. A small man in a uniform stood behind me. His hair was neatly combed. He had a beret tied to his shoulder. He carried a parcel wrapped in brown paper. It was tied with a white and red striped string. He had the bluest eyes I had ever seen, and he smiled at me then. A huge smile. It was a big, wide shit-eating grin, Ricky would have said! It was Lax.

"Pup," he said smiling.

"My God. Lax," I breathed. I stepped over quickly, bent low, and wrapped my arm around him. "Lax. I can't believe it." The tears came then. I was a bloody mess, could barely breathe.

"Good to see you Pup," he said as he let me spill tears down the back of his uniform. I stood up then and looked at him. He hadn't changed. He made it back. This man had been all over and under Vietnam. How the hell had he managed to survive. I should have known if anyone was going to survive it would be this miracle man.

"I didn't think you'd recognize me, not all covered in crap."

"Or with a uniform on and not stark naked." I laughed, my good hand on his shoulder. "Who's is it anyway?" I said rubbing tears from my face.

"I have no idea mate. I stole it from someone's bag at the bloody airport." We both laughed loudly; I wasn't sure if he was serious. All eyes in the pub were on us now as we stood appraising each other.

"I never thought I'd see you again mate."

"Or you Pup." He shook his head from side to side.

"When Yolka told me you made it… I dunno. I'd thought I was too late mate. Back in the jungle. I remember I looked for three days. I thought you were gone. Even when I found you I thought you were gone. When I saw you off in the Huey I thought I was saying goodbye."

"So did I Lax. So did I."

"I thought I was too late. I thought I found you too late. You're a tougher bastard than you look big fella." He smiled broadly. The door to the pub opened again and I saw Iris enter. The light was too bright in the dingy room, but I knew her outline. She'd been outside? I thought she was in the bathroom. She walked towards me leading a smaller lady by the hand. She in turn held the hand of a young kid.

"I found them Pup," said Lax. I looked at him trying to comprehend his words.

"I found Hoa and her baby." Suddenly, I did feel faint, and I turned and held onto the bar. Iris came over and held me.

"I don't know if my heart can take this, honey," I whispered.

"You're OK Shep. Come and say hello to Hoa and Cây."

I turned toward Hoa to find her in full gallop. She'd released the hand of the young boy and launched with arms stretched. She wrapped them around my waist. Hoa was sobbing loudly. Her young son looked up at us with panicked bewilderment. He was a handsome boy. He must have been about four, but he looked much older. He was tall for his age. He had the delicate, facial bone structure of the Vietnamese people with a beautiful caramel coloured skin. He also had a head of thick and tight curls. Lax stepped over and behind Hoa. I thought he was going to pull her off me. Instead, he bent down and picked up the boy. He swung him to a hip and said,

"Pup, this is Cây. This is the boy you delivered. I told you were an angel Pup. This is our boy. The boy you saved."

"He's beautiful Hoa." Hoa turned and reached for the boy's hand. His worried frown became a beaming smile. Hoa still had one arm wrapped around my waist.

"*Cây cao* mean tree tall, Pup," Hoa said. "He named Cây. It mean tree in English. The village name him for you Pup because you are so *Cây cao*, so tall like tree. He is alive because of you. I am alive because of you. I so very happy to see you Pup."

"I'm happy to see you both." Hoa hugged me again.

"Your lady is very beautiful too Pup."

"Oh hell. I'm sorry honey," I said. "Lax, can I introduce you to

Iris."

"Oh, we've met mate," he said and he gave Iris a wink.

"What? How… What is going on?"

"Come over to the table Terry," Iris said. "Gordon will explain everything."

"What are you guys talking about?" I asked but they were already heading over to the table where the granite man sat smiling at us over interlocked fingers. The cigarette clasped between two meat slabs. Lax approached the man, still holding Cây. He leant down and kissed the older man on his big, round head.

"Yolka," he said.

"Good to see you again my friend," said Gordon.

"Hang on, hang on. You're Lt Colonel 'Yolka.'"

"Well, actually no," he smiled. "I'm Major-General Gordon 'Yolka' Molloy. I've got pushed up the pole a little." He smiled and tapped the pip on his epaulette which sat above the crossed Mameluke sword and baton.

"Major-General," I said, honestly impressed. "You're the famous Yolka. I've heard so much about you. This bloke here was always going on about you and he never said more than two words about anyone. Are you still a policeman, Gordon?" He winked at me then over his fingers. His eyes twinkled.

"I've never been a policeman, Terry."

"Oh, what the fuck is going on here. It's the bloody Twilight Zone or something? What do you mean you're not a copper? I've got to sit down." I sat heavily in the chair.

"Apologies for the language Hoa, Cây," I said and Hoa laughed. Iris walked over and kissed Major-General Yolka on his cheek.

At that moment the young surfer and one of the kitchen staff – white apron, white hat – appeared with our breakfasts. They filled the table. Pots of tea, steaming cups of coffee. Lax grabbed up and tore open a small blue cereal box. He tipped the Rice Bubbles into a bowl and placed it in front of Cây. He poured milk from a carafe over them. Snap, crackle, and pop. Domestic Lax. I WAS in the Twilight Zone. Everyone sat and dived into their breakfast. This day was not turning out as I'd expected.

The eggs were good. I didn't realize just how hungry I was. No one spoke. Lax sat across from me and shovelled it all into his mouth, all the while smiling a big dopey grin. Actually, they were all smiling at me. I felt like the butt of some great cosmic joke.

"Pup, in the flesh," Lax said through a mouthful of egg. As the staff began to clean our table, I sat turning from Iris, to Hoa, to Lax, to Major-General Gordon. I was confused; I even began to worry if, just maybe, I'd had just one too many concussions.

"I have about a billion questions Lax, Gordon."

"All in good time son. All in good time."

"First things first though Terry. I believe our good friend has a package for you."

"I do mate. Here you go." Lax lifted the wrapped package off the chair he'd sat it on. He passed it across the table to me. I looked quizzically at Iris who smiled.

"Open it," she said nodding her head. Before I placed the package down in front of me I turned it over with my hand. No postage markings. No stamps. I picked up the knife I had eaten with – my plate was the last to be collected as usual. One handed people are the slowest eaters. I placed the package between my legs and, with the blunt knife and a bit of effort, cut through the string. I tore open the package. It was a uniform. A new, clean Australian army uniform.

"For next year's march," said Gordon solemnly.

"There's more," said Lax. I lifted the uniform and underneath there were three flat, black medal cases. I looked up at Lax who was smiling expectantly. I opened one of the boxes which was lined with crimson felt. Inside sat the Vietnam medal. Queen's head one side, muscular figure on the back. It hung from a navy, yellow and blue ribbon, thin red stripes. I placed it atop my new uniform and opened the second box. It contained white six-pointed star with a map of Vietnam at it's center. It had a white and green ribbon.

"That is the Vietnamese Campaign medal," said Gordon. I'd pin them on you mate but you really should be in that new uniform in front of you. He butted his smoke into his ashtray.

"This medal is awarded by the South Vietnamese Government for six months service." He sat looking over his fingers at me. All eyes at the table were on me as I opened the last box. The boxes were stiff and solid, beautifully put together. I found the tight fit of the wooden lid to the base quite satisfying. This one contained a medal I'd never seen before. A small red cross on a sea of white all within a gold border. It had a red and white ribbon. It was beautiful and I held it up where the light caught the gold. It shone.

"Oooh," gasped the table.

"This is a very special award Terry," said Gordon. "It's the Life Saving Medal. The Vietnamese Government awards it to those who show extreme bravery in rescuing the lives of Vietnamese people." I looked up to see Hoa crying again. Crying and nodding. Iris had a tear in her eye as well.

"You boys should be very proud of yourselves. Australia is very proud of you both." Lax removed a twin of the medal from his pocket. He smiled a little awkwardly and tucked it away again.

"They don't give these to everyone Terry," said Gordon. The table rose then, and they all clapped. The small crowd in the pub had grown a little by then and they all turned to watch the ovation. Some even joined in the applause. It was just that type of day.

I was lost for words.

FIN

Later, Gordon, Lax and I jumped on a tram to the city. Gordon said he had to make an appearance at the Returned Services League, on Collins Street. He promised he would explain everything there.

"I'd like to buy you both a beer. It'll almost be a dignified beer-drinking hour by the time we get there." I asked, cheekily to be sure, if we were welcome as I'd heard some Vietnam veterans were made to feel alienated by older members of the RSL Veterans of more "popular" wars.

"That is something I will being addressing son; you mark my words," he said firmly.

Hoa and Iris walked back to Little George to let young Cây have a nap. They carried my uniform and medals home for me. My head was swimming with the events of my morning. Our tram was quite crowded, except around Lax of course. A young guy in jungle greens offered his seat to Yolka who nodded in appreciation. There were a few people in uniform on the tram and most of them saluted the Major-General. As he sat below me, his slouch hat on his lap, I could see the network of scarring across the top of his substantial and completely bald head. We rode silently. I spent the time formulating questions and trying to nut out how we all fitted together.

It was a short ride to Anzac House. Yolka led the way into the building. Every person we met on our way inside stopped and saluted him. We found a quiet table and three beers appeared; I didn't even see him order.

"So, Terry, you have some questions I'd be guessing? The floor is yours young fella." Yolka said leaning forward to grab a glass of beer with a perfect head.

"Questions!" I said. "Where do I bloody start? Why didn't you tell me you were Yolka, my commander in Vietnam? Why didn't you tell me you weren't a policeman? You acted like one. Why the secrecy Major-General. It's all quite weird."

"I suppose it is son. Let me try and piece it together for you. I have a very specific portfolio within the armed services now," he began. "It is true, I am retired, but I offered to keep an eye on our returned men and women, the young people from Vietnam especially."

"Keep an eye?" I asked.

"Yes son. Help where I can. Offer assistance in any capacity I see fit. In this capacity I have a close relationship with the police force. They will often give me a call if one of ours is causing problems, or the victim of any trouble." He took a sip from his beer. "In some ways, it's not unlike the work you do at the Repat Terry. Buoy spirits, a helping hand where you can. We are well aware of the great work you do there, son." He sipped his beer again.

"We try to do what we can off the record. It's not an official role you understand, more like an honorary one. I have some resources. I have access to some amounts of money. In a lot of ways, I help people transition back into the real world. You know better than most there are a lot of fellows back from Vietnam with all sorts of physical and mental problems.

Sometimes arriving from a war zone, back into civilian life can be onerous. Most times I'd suggest. There are a few of us who find ourselves in this role. I prefer to assist the boys from my brigade. I help the best ones."

"The best ones?"

"Yes mate. It's a case-by-case sort of thing. I get involved when my guys and girls run into a bit of bother. I was particularly keen to try and sort the trials and tribulations that beset you, Terry." He sipped his beer again. He placed it down with some deliberation into the exact centre of the beer coaster on the wooden table. He took the tobacco from his breast pocket.

"The work you did in Vietnam Terry, the lives you saved. The work you do back here at the Repat. They way you've dealt with your adversity. You're a very, very special man Terry." I felt the heat in my face.

"I'll drink to that. *thiên thần*," said Lax softly.

"Lax here demanded we help you too, all the way from Vietnam." Yolka tipped his big head towards Lax. "He can be very persuasive son."

"Don't I know that Gordon." The men both laughed. I turned to the small man sitting quietly to my right. "Then how long have you been back Lax? I asked. The little man was sitting with his left arm over the back of his chair. He rubbed the light stubble on his chin.

"I've been back and forth a bit."

"What do you mean. Are you not based in Australia? Where are you living?"

"There's still a lot of work to do back in Vietnam Pup and I like it there. I like the people. I might move back to Australia now that I'm married. One more job to do though."

"You're married!" I said. "That's wonderful." He looked at me with his crooked grin and nodded. Waiting for me to draw the conclusion without him saying it.

"You married Hoa! You two are a couple! That's amazing, wonderful." Lax raised his glass in mock celebration of my working it all out.

"I only found her about a year ago Pup. She and Cây had been moving around quite a bit. The child of dust blown by the winds of his circumstance. I finally found them in a refugee camp in Cambodia."

"With Gai?"

"No Pup. Sadly, Gai was killed. The North dragged him back into the fighting."

"To Gai!" said Yolka and he lifted his beer. We all drained them. A waiter appeared with another three glasses on a tray almost before we set our empty ones down. The bar staff must have been watching us. They were extremely efficient.

"You gave me the idea Pup. In the jungle. You asked if the baby was mine. I decided he was. I convinced the Aussie politicians, and I was able to marry and bring my wife and son to Australia. It was easy with Yolka's help. I have been back here two months now. Cây is an Australian now mate and soon, Hoa will be as well. One day I will even tell him about his other dad. The dopey US kid with the big smile and curly hair."

"Wow," I said. "That's an amazing story. So how long are you here in Melbourne?"

"Until you get sick of us Pup. Iris and I have been chatting on the phone. She even met our train yesterday while you were at the hospital. Your Mum and Lily demanded we stay a few days with you guys."

"You've even met Mum?"

"We wanted to surprise you."

"Surprise me! You've nearly given me a bloody heart attack."

"I'm only in Australia for a couple of weeks or so. I have to go back to Vietnam. One more person to find!"

"Huong?" I said. The image of the brave little Vietnamese girl, Hoa's sister, biting the NVA deserter's hand flooded my memory. It was so vivid I could hear his grunt, smell the moist soil where I lay watching. Lax nodded.

"I'm getting close Pup. I have a few good people on the ground over there. It's even harder now that Saigon has fallen but I'm determined to find her mate. I'll try and bring her here if I can... and if she wants to come."

Yolka trained his steely gaze on me now. All the light that had danced in his eyes gone now. This was a man of hard resolve. Commanding, someone not afraid to make the hard call.

"I'd like to address the elephant in the room if I may," he said, his tone flat and business like. "Lax made his first trip back from Vietnam three years ago. He came to help out a friend." I sat up straight then. Placed my beer on the table.

"This friend had found himself in a bit of a pickle and I believed he was going to do something stupid. Even the best of us can be pushed too far. Even the best of us will push back to save the people they love." felt a chill along my spine, a prickling at the back of my head.

"I still seek Lax's help from time to time, when he's not off doing his thing and trying to win wars on his own." He placed his glass down again, thoughtfully. He waved a flat, slab of hand toward Lax.

"Our mutual friend here was very keen to help."

Lax took a deep breath then. He took his cue to continue the story. "Those guys were going to kill you Pup. I spent two days in the ceiling space in that shitty place of theirs in Richmond."

"What? The Sharps. You were in there? My God: two days! How did you avoid the dogs?" I asked.

"Dogs like me," was all he said.

"It was easy getting in. They were always stoned or pissed. I could have taken a brass band with me." Lax's eyes were blue flame. "They killed your mate Ricky. They bragged about beating him and leaving him in the water. They would get on speed to wind themselves up and just head out to do terrible things. They were disappointed they didn't finish you all off with the fire. Then they were angry they didn't kill you the with the shovel. They blamed Iris. The big one named Sid, the one with the stupid hand tattoo. He boasted about what he would do to her before she died. Terrible things mate."

"I see," I said, my voice a whisper.

"I'd heard enough Pup. One night I quietly suggested to all the people living in the house it would be in their best interests to leave the next morning." He radiated malevolence. His eyes so fierce it hurt to look at them.

"Three of them refused to be persuaded."

"My God mate."

"I was back in Vietnam two days later." The three of us sat in silence then. My body tingled. My heart beat a pounding rhythm in my chest. I could almost see Lax in that filthy house. Naked.

A spectre with a long-bladed knife, razor sharp. Blue torchlight eyes shining from the black mud. I saw him climb down quietly from the manhole in the night. I saw him go from room to room to deliver his edict. They would have been petrified. Lax, removing the obstructions, cleaning out the shit. I could see the battle with Slug, he disembowelled him. With Ratso who tried to escape out the front door. At what point did they realise they had bitten off more than they could chew. What struggle? These three could never imagine a foe like Lax, a single, bloody-minded purpose; of stealth, the skill the violence. They would have been as out of their depth as everyone else that draws breath. Lax was an artist. A machine. The revenant. I could see Lax sit quietly and watch Sid inject himself with the overdose that would end his poisonous time on the planet. What ultimatum had he given. Sid was as mad as the Hatter. What madness had he seen in Lax? I shuddered involuntarily.

Finally, I looked up and said, "You saved my life again mate. How many times? How many times. You searched and found me in the pit. You carried me on your back through the jungle. You get me onto a Huey in the middle of nowhere and get me out of Vietnam. Then you fly in from a war zone to save me from myself. Words just can't express what I owe you Lax."

"I saved…?" Lax said with incredulity. He pointed a finger at me. "I saved you?" He laughed dryly, Lax shook his head slowly from side to side. He took a deep breath, seemingly struggling for words. After the longest time he spoke again, his voice full of emotion.

"You're the bloody life-saver here. I told you in the jungle. You are an angel Pup!" Lax seemed to examine the crimson and gold rug beneath his chair for a moment. He was composing himself, then the words burst from him in a rush.

"I was a dead man in Vietnam. A zombie. I was a night-crawler with a death wish. A ghoul. I had no interest in digging myself out of the *Nui Dat* mud. I'd found my grave. I was the vampire prowling the night, so I didn't have to see people, deal with people. I was the fucking *Hô Tinh*… too far gone, burned all my bridges." I looked at the Major-General who was looking at us thoughtfully. Lax saw my glance. He guessed my thoughts. "Yolka had the guts to try and point a very unstable missile in the right direction. At the enemy. I was a hand grenade Pup, with the bloody ring pulled. It was only a matter of time before I exploded. I was soooo lost. Yolka gave me a purpose… but you saved my soul Pup. Your friendship saved my life. The day you spoke to me in the mess tent was the first time anybody in that camp had spoken to me, directly, in almost a year. I'd never done anything worthy in my life until I met you. You found good in me mate and dragged it out of those black tunnels kicking and screaming. You made me a human again. Saved my bloody life. You saved my wife; you saved our son…"

Lax jumped up from his chair then and grabbed my face. He kissed me on the forehead.

"Saved you?" Lax held my ears in his small hands and looked into my eye. He had my full attention.

"A man doesn't need a lot of friends if he has one, just ONE that is golden." Lax went back to his chair and threw himself down into it. He sat there for a time then roared with laughter.

"Jesus Christ!" he bellowed. "Wasn't that intense?"

Yolka and I looked at each other, eye's wide. A smirk, which set his salt-and-pepper moustache on an uneven inclination, softened the stone wall of his features. We all sat in silence then: lost for words. It was almost a full ten minutes before Yolka said, cryptically, "You know boys. Every day is one day further away from *Nui Dat*."

"To friendship. Old friends, new friends and forever friends," I said raising my glass. Yolka picked up his beer and we clinked the glasses together. Lax clinked his glass against the side of each of ours in turn. He sat heavily in his chair again, drained the glass and placed it down on the table.

"Oh, I almost forgot." Lax was unbuttoning the breast pocket on his army shirt. "There's something I've been meaning to give you Pup. I've been carrying it a while." Lax moved unhurriedly, like a high priest revealing an ancient, fragile relic. A magician sleight of hand. Lax slowly drew something from the depths of his pocket. It was a long white bone. He placed it gingerly in front of me. I stared at Yolka, I stared back at the bone. What else was this crazy day going to serve up?

"My God Lax. Is that Sid's?" My tremulous voice but a squeak. "Is that Sid's finger."

Lax rubbed at his chin, looking at the bone like he had never seen it before. Was he trying to decide who's finger it actually was that he now placed before me? Finally, he looked up he nodded his head slowly with recognition.

"You know Pup. I believe this bone is actually Colonel Sanders. Hoa and I had Kentucky Fried Chicken last night." He looked at me, his eyes twinkled like sapphires.

"Pup, my dear friend, don't believe everything you hear. I never collected people's fingers. That was all part of the myth." He smiled broadly.

"What do you think I am? A fucking monster?"